ZERO TO THE BONE

A NINA ZERO NOVEL

Robert Eversz

SIMON & SCHUSTER

New York   London   Toronto   Sydney

SIMON & SCHUSTER
Rockefeller Center
1230 Avenue of the Americas
New York, NY 10020

SIMON & SCHUSTER and colophon are registered
trademarks of Simon & Schuster, Inc.

For information about special discounts for bulk purchases,
please contact Simon & Schuster Special Sales at
1-800-456-6798 or business@simonandschuster.com

DESIGNED BY LAUREN SIMONETTI

Manufactured in the United States of America

1   3   5   7   9   10   8   6   4   2

Library of Congress Cataloging-in-Publication Data

Eversz, Robert.
Zero to the bone : a Nina Zero novel / Robert Eversz.
p.   cm.
1. Zero, Nina (Fictitious character)—Fiction. 2. Los Angeles (Calif.)—Fiction.
3. Women photographers—Fiction. 4. Tabloid newspapers—Fiction. 5. Ex-con-
victs—Fiction. 6. Paparazzi—Fiction. I. Title.

PS3555.V39Z34 2006
813'.54
2005054467

ISBN-13:   978-1-4165-8522-0
ISBN-10:   1-4165-8522-2

To Nina Zero's readers:
thanks for sharing the wild, bumpy ride.

The strong men, the masters, regain the pure conscience of a beast of prey; monsters filled with joy, they can return from a fearful succession of murder, arson, rape, and torture with the same joy in their hearts, the same contentment in their souls as if they had indulged in some student's rag.

—Friedrich Nietzsche

ZERO
TO
THE BONE

1

A DAY HIKER found her body beneath the thorny skirts of a manzanita bush in the Santa Monica Mountains just north of Malibu, her skin white as sun-bleached bone against the baked earth. She did not look dead to him at first glance and he thought she might be taking sun, but where she lay was not a spot for sunbathing and her clothes lay twisted in the brush rather than folded within reach.

From a distance her body still retained some of the beauty it had possessed in life and so the hiker expected her to stir at his approach but she didn't move, not at all. When he dropped down from the trail and into the brush he saw the bruise circling her neck and death's terrible vacancy in her face.

He grasped her wrist between his thumb and forefinger, hoping to track a faint pulse of blood. Her skin felt less alive than stone. He called 911 and hiked back to the trailhead to wait for the responding officers, out of sight of the body, because the woman was so young and beautiful, even in death, that the only way he could prevent himself from crying was not to look at her.

Later, when questioned by a reporter from a supermarket tabloid, he described in photographic detail the body's pose on the ground and the ruin strangulation had visited upon her face, sordid details expected by the readers of tabloids but ones I'll omit in this telling because I knew the woman, and the brutal manner of her death will haunt me for the rest of my days.

The last time I saw Christine she wore a glittering silver strap-dress to the hanging of my show of photographs at Santa Monica's Leonora Price Gallery, the Betty Boop tattoo on her bared shoulder winking suggestively at the muscular boy in cutoffs who mounted photographs on the near wall. She planned to wear the dress to the opening party two nights later and claimed to want to know whether I liked the style. The photographs were staged tableaux carefully composed to look culled from the pages of the *National Enquirer,* the *Star,* or the paper I freelanced for, *Scandal Times.* Several of the images depicted a blonde bombshell caught by a tabloid-style camera in scandalous scenes involving cars, sex, drugs, and guns. Christine played the role of the blonde bombshell, her wholesome looks shaded at twenty-one with a complicated sexual awareness, the lens capturing little-girl innocence and anything-goes depravity in a single, flashing glance. The depravity made her visually compelling, but in many ways she was far more innocent than depraved. She didn't want my opinion about the dress—I realized that the moment I saw how assertively she wore it. The dress clung to her with the fierce grace of a tango dancer. She knew she looked stunning. She simply couldn't wait for the show to open. She wanted to see what she looked like as a troubled movie starlet, unaware that I cast her in a role she played well enough in real life.

The evening the show opened I was working late in the offices of *Scandal Times,* trying to suppress my anxiety about exhibiting my so-called serious work, when Frank pitched a padded manila envelope onto the desk. Frank was the tabloid's crack investigative reporter, author of such seminal stories as "The Truth about Two-Headed Sheep" and "James Dean's Body Stolen by Space Aliens, Worshipped as God," practically required reading for every budding tabloid reporter and true aficionado of the form. He'd been in the parking lot, having a smoke, and the scent of cigarettes wafted from his hair like a stale aura.

"Since when did you start getting mail here?" he asked.

I glanced at the envelope, addressed to me care of the tabloid, with no return address and twenty Walt Disney commemorative Mickey Mouse stamps pasted down the right side, as though the sender had neither a clue how much postage the envelope required nor the time to get it metered.

"I get mail here all the time." I dipped into the side pocket of my camera bag for a Swiss army knife and slit open the envelope's top flap. "Most of it's from people peddling information, you know, the four Ws of tabloid journalism: who's doing what to whom, and where." I shook something that looked like a CD loose from the envelope.

"I get mail too," Frank said.

"What kind?" I asked.

"Death threats mostly. Last week, Steven Seagal's PR girl threatened not only to kill me but to make sure I was reincarnated as a leech." He fingered the edges of a candid I'd taken of Ben Affleck walking out the door of the Brentwood Starbucks, fingers wrapped around his morning latte. The image was set to run with a story about celebrity caffeine addicts. It had been a slow news week, Hollywood scandal-wise.

"Affleck's easy," he said. "Can't pay more than two hundred for him, plus a hundred bonus points for the coffee. You got anybody else?"

I showed him Owen Wilson in a geeky bucket hat and dark sunglasses, shot through the window of Kings Road Café as he inhaled the fumes wafting from a large porcelain cup. The disguise was effective enough that we argued back and forth about whether Owen Wilson sat beneath the hat or some look-alike, until I settled the argument by tracing the baby-arm-on-steroids contours of his nose, which even the modern miracle of plastic surgery can't duplicate, should it want to try. I walked the CD to the boom box on the shelf behind Frank's desk and pressed play. Nothing happened. Frank pulled open his petty-cash drawer. I forgot about the CD, thinking someone had sent me a blank disk by mistake. He paid five large in advance for the Wilson, plus three for Affleck.

It had been a tough couple of months, financially. I needed the cash to bail my car out of the garage and to finance the black cocktail sheath of a dress I planned to wear to the gallery that night, when friends, models, and art collectors would gather to drink wine and gossip while pretending to look at the so-called art. High art is a low-pay occupation, and I'd pretty much invested—or sunk without trace—the last of my money in producing and then printing the photographs to be exhibited. Then, two weeks before the show was to open, an idiot in a BMW rear-ended me in traffic, sending my beloved 1976 Cadillac Eldorado into the shop for bodywork and a two-hundred-thousand-mile makeover. His insurance was covering the bodywork but not the makeover. The mechanic had offered me a loaner while my car was in the shop. I couldn't afford to say no.

This explains why I pulled into the gallery's parking lot on the biggest night of my life in a six-year-old Chevy Metro with a four-cylinder, 1.3-liter hamster cage for an engine, my toothless Rottweiler riding shotgun, resplendent in a red bow tie and his usual goofy grin. Unlike me, he didn't feel humiliated to be seen in such a car. My Goth-girl niece waited out front, leaning with calculated teenage sullenness against the passenger-side suicide door of a 1967 Lincoln Continental. Cassie had flown in the night before from Phoenix, where she lived with her foster parents, and spent the day shopping for vintage clothing on Melrose Avenue, accompanied by the owner of the Continental, Nephthys, a woman who looked like a punk Barbara Stanwyck. Cassie had met Nephthys and Christine six months before, when they modeled together for several photographs in the show, and since then she clung to them as her new role models. Her lips scrunched as though she bit into something sour when I stepped from the car and she said, "Since when do you wear miniskirts?"

It was the first time she'd seen me in a dress, even if I'd accessorized it with a pair of Doc Martens, a rhinestone nose stud, and a black leather motorcycle jacket. Cassie had just turned fifteen. I was twice her age. To her eye, I was a dinosaur. I gave her a friendly shove and asked where Nephthys was. She shrugged and pointed her chin toward the gallery, its brightly lit picture window framing an exhibition hall more packed than I had a right to expect. When I asked her why she remained outside she sidled up and bumped against my arm, her wary interpretation of a hug. "You're late," she said. "I was afraid you weren't going to show."

I kissed the side of her head. Cassie didn't show sentiment often. I wanted to reward it. Something shoved me from behind—the Rott, eager to bull his way into the party. Cassie broke away from me to kneel and give the dog a bigger hug than I'd ever seen her give a human being. I tossed her the leash and a moment later we swung open the gallery door to a D-list Hollywood arts crowd, not a single true celebrity among the young and trendy who dressed, talked, and gestured like movie stars in training, as though fame awaited them as certainly as age. A half dozen in the crowd had modeled for the faux-tabloid photographs that lined the walls, and all had invited their equally young and beautiful friends. Leonora Price—the sixty-something doyenne of L.A. arts photography—called my name when I pressed through the door and glared at me from behind rhinestone-flecked cat's-eye glasses. She cleaved the crowd, big red-bead necklace swaying above the bodice of her lime green dress, to wrap a withered arm over my shoulder, scold me for being late, and swing me face-to-face with two of the few people in the crowd not wearing black, a doctor and her doctor husband, who announced that they'd just purchased two of my photographs.

"Hold on to them," Leonora advised. "My girl is queen of the tabloids, the first serious photographer to cross over since Weegee." I shook their hands solemnly, embarrassed by such high praise. Leonora promptly slung me toward two men in gray Italian suits, maneuvering me with a hand on the nape of my neck as deftly as a puppeteer. The two men wore black shoes that gleamed with the high shine only the professional classes can achieve, their smiles polished to match. Personal injury lawyers, Leonora whispered, who had just purchased three images for their Century City offices. The lawyer on the left said how much they loved the photos, their jaundiced take on celebrity, and we talked a minute about what it's like to work as a tabloid photographer. "If Leonardo DiCaprio ever breaks your nose while you're snapping his candid," one said, "give us a call, we'd love to represent you." They cawed with laughter and I barked back, two personal injury lawyers and a tabloid photographer, fellow scavengers recognizing each other across the species barrier.

Leonora steered me close to the wall, the long, bony forefinger of her right hand curling toward a red dot beneath the nearest photograph, signifying the work had been sold. She painted her fingernails red to match the sales dots; red and green were her good-luck colors. "The photographs, they look wonderful up, don't you think?" She flicked the nail toward the next photo, and the one framed beyond that, all three marked with red dots. Still gripping the nape of my neck, she turned my head to plant a loud kiss on my brow, her milky blue eyes fierce and gleeful. "Be proud," she said.

The emotion vented through me like scalding water seeking a fissure, and I turned away because I didn't want to burden her with a sudden burst of tears. Two weeks earlier I'd gone alone to see the comic-book flick *Spiderman*, where the sight of Kirsten Dunst lifting enough of Spidey's mask to plant a wet one on Tobey Maguire's lips provoked such a surge of Eros and sorrow that I'd bolted for the bathroom, locked myself in a stall, and sobbed through a half pack of tissues. Since the deaths of my sister and mother I'd been increasingly unable to control my emotions, prone to jagged crying fits at moments that once would have provoked no more than a smirk of irritation. I'm not a photogenic crier, and the only thing that prevented tears from sizzling down my cheeks and snot dripping from my nose was the sight of the Rottweiler towing Cassie through the crowd, Nephthys one step behind.

"Have you seen Christine?" Anxiety thinned Cassie's voice to a whine. "We've been calling her, like, all day. We even stopped at her apartment."

"She'll show." I deflected the Rott with my knee and told him to sit. "She's already seen the photographs, so she's probably planning a big, fashionably late entrance."

"Christine, she's late to everything," Nephthys said, then wrapped me in a congratulatory hug, not oblivious to the fascinated stares of both men and women in the crowd. She wore a thin black halter and stretch shorts, showing as much of her tattooed body as possible in public without getting arrested. She was insanely proud of her tattoos, precise re-creations of the hieroglyphics and pictographs depicting her namesake, the Goddess of the House and Friend of the Dead in Egyptian mythology. She gave the hug full body contact, then pulled her head back to drop a lip kiss on me, unexpected at that moment but not so bad really, in a nonlesbian girlfriend kind of way. "You rock, girl," she said. "The photographs are killer."

"Cindy Sherman meets Weegee," someone said behind me and I turned to see who, because those were exactly the two traditions I intended to cross when I began composing the photographs in my head. The man who had spoken turned to look at me over his shoulder and then this really weird thing happened to time, the glittering hum of voices ground down and vectored out to silence, the crowd at the peripheral fringe of my vision spun into a centrifugal blur, and if I knew I had a soul, I'd say it broke its moorings and lurched momentarily free of my body.

I'd never seen the man before, but still, his face looked strangely familiar, and I would have sworn I knew him in a previous life if I believed in such things, which I don't. Yes, he was handsome in a black-haired, blue-eyed, and black-leather-jacketed way, but I wasn't that conscious of his face; I felt as though I'd found something I wasn't particularly looking for and never thought I needed until that moment, and now that I saw it, I didn't know whether to grab it or run headlong in the opposite direction. I floated toward him, not consciously moving my feet at all, and then the sensation of timelessness wavered and broke, because I'd walked right up to a strange man without an idea in my head about what to say, and that made me feel uncomfortably self-conscious.

"You're the photographer, aren't you?" He turned to a photograph of Christine on the nearest wall. "I can't tell you how many times I stepped into the grubbier version of this scene."

I'd taken the photograph at night off the Pacific Coast Highway a few miles south of Malibu, a white-gowned Christine hitchhiking in the headlight glow of a Mercedes convertible stopped on the shoulder, a little chrome automatic pistol dangling from the forefinger of her opposite hand. The driver's door to the Mercedes wings open into the center of the image and the body of an elegant young man in a white dinner jacket sprawls toward the pavement, his legs and hips still inside the car, the back of his jacket stained with vivid blossoms of light gray, the color of blood in black-and-white photography.

Frank stuck his shaggy head between us and introduced the man I'd been speaking to as Sean Tyler. We shook hands, his palm leathery smooth, like a good work glove. "Let's go out to the car for a sec," Frank said, and hoisted toward Sean the laptop bag slung over his shoulder. "I got something I want to show you." And then they were gone, just like that, Sean's big shoulders gracefully creasing the mob, leaving me face-to-face with Terry Graves, my parole officer, who pinched the muscle between my neck and shoulder and said photographs weren't her thing but these wouldn't be so bad if she could drop a neutron bomb in the middle of the room to eliminate the poseurs. I told her I needed a glass of wine and pressed toward the door, curious about Sean and what kind of business he had with

Frank. He didn't look like the kind of scamming tipster Frank usually met in alleyways and other dark places.

Out in the parking lot they stood hunched over the open trunk to Frank's Honda, a silvery light illuminating their faces from beneath, the blue-black of Los Angeles night blanketed around their shoulders. Frank had parked at the far end of the lot, near the street and away from the casual glance of passing eyes. When he heard my footsteps, and glanced to see me walking toward them he reached down into the trunk and shut off the light.

"There's really nothing you want to see here," he said, and I realized then that the source of light had been his laptop.

"Maybe I should be the one to decide that," I said.

In the washed-out streetlight his face looked flush and his eyes glazed. "The disk somebody mailed you?" He cleared his throat. "It wasn't music."

"If it was sent to me, then I should see it," I said. "In fact, if it was sent to me, you shouldn't even be looking at it."

Frank stared at me like I really didn't get it.

"No, it's all right, she probably needs to see this," Sean said. "I mean, you're not sure, right? She'll know better than you."

Frank reached into the trunk, pressed something, and moved aside. "This was supposed to be a good night for you," he said.

I stepped up to the rear bumper and looked into the mouth of the trunk, where Frank's laptop played a high-resolution amateur bondage video already well in progress. The scene depicted what I imagined to be a routine S&M scenario: a young woman, semiclad in red latex and bound at her wrists to a metal rack, was mounted from behind by a man in a black latex suit and ski mask–style hood. A similar hood covered the woman's head, slits cut for her eyes. A rubber ball was wedged into her mouth, held in place by a strap. With strips of latex disconnecting her features, the woman's face could have been any young woman's face. The eyes were listless. She didn't seem to mind being tied to a rack.

"Ruffies," Sean said.

"Rohypnol," Frank added. "The date rape drug of choice."

I wanted to ask Sean how he knew she was drugged, but before I could speak the man slung a rubber strap around the woman's neck and jerked it taut. Her head snapped back and she twisted her shoulders, trying to pull away. The man strangling her stood over six feet tall and pinned the woman to the rack like a butterfly. I looked away because I didn't want to watch, but then I felt Sean's hand gently supporting my back. The light from the screen illuminated his face from beneath, as though by theatrical stage light, the lupine curve of his lips and miss-nothing intensity of his eyes sadly predatory. I knew then what he was doing there, what he did for a living, and what was happening in the video. When I glanced back at the screen, the latex suit had been unzipped at the back and my eye met the mischievous wink of Betty Boop, tattooed along the upper curve of the woman's right shoulder.

2

I DROVE BACK to Venice Beach trying to convince myself the woman in the video didn't have to be Christine. An early summer inversion had settled over the city, smog condensing with beach fog to form a swirling yellow mist in the spears of light thrown by the Metro's headlights. In the passenger seat, Cassie vied with the Rott to see who could lean their head the farthest out the window. Cassie knew nothing about what might have happened to Christine. When I'd returned to the gallery after answering Sean's questions the crowd had thinned to a few friends, my models, and their hangers-on. I pretended nothing had happened and proposed a toast first to Leonora Price for taking the risk of exhibiting my work, and then to my models for being so photogenic. When I started to cry, everyone thought the emotions of the moment overwhelmed me in a good way. They all seemed happy, both for me and for themselves, like fireflies burning bright for one brief night against the greater darkness that awaits us all.

I'd shot Christine's first set of photographs just before Thanksgiving, and we'd gotten along so well she'd accompanied me to the airport to pick up Cassie, who was flying in from Phoenix, released to my care for the holiday by her foster parents. The idea to stage a photographic scene that involved them both had sprung from Cassie's insistent complaints that I didn't appreciate her talents as an actress or model, begun no more than a minute after she wheeled her suitcase from baggage claim. We talked about it over dinner that night—pasta and pizza at Angeli Caffé on Melrose—and the next day I rented a bungalow at the Beverly Hills Hotel for the shoot, Nephthys pitching in to help with set design and makeup. We'd scoured Cassie's face of Goth-girl makeup, secured a curly blonde wig over her purple hair, slipped her into a white dress, and pho-tographed her as a contemporary adolescent Shirley Temple shooting junk amid a zoo of stuffed animals, Christine as her movie-star mom talking on the phone in the background, back turned, clueless.

Film and photo shoots promote a quick and easy camaraderie among participants, and during ours Cassie bonded instantly with Nephthys and Christine. We drove to Chinatown for Thanksgiving dinner that night, substituting Peking duck for turkey, and then over the weekend rode the bike paths of Venice Beach and watched films together. The experience seemed formative to Cassie, who was short on noncriminal role models just then, and she studied both Christine and Nephthys with the voracious curiosity of a young girl watching those a few years older to figure out the woman she might become. Christine and Nephthys may not have been the most wholesome role models, but by the age of thirteen my niece had already involved her-self in criminal enterprises that would have sentenced her to a juve-nile detention facility for the remainder of her youth had she been caught; any corrupting influences were likely to pass both ways. That Christmas we met again, and though I kept in touch with Nephthys after that, calling her every couple of weeks and meeting occasionally for coffee, Christine and I drifted apart, not from any conflict or lack of interest, but because we had little to talk about ex-cept what each of us was doing at the moment. We rarely talked about our pasts or personal issues. She was always a cipher to me, though a lovely one, a woman whose chatter captivated me even if, after a moment of reflection, I didn't find much meaning in it.

I didn't really know much about Christine's sex life, what turned her on. Some people found strangulation erotic, their partner throt-tling them a few seconds shy of brain damage and death, making the orgasms that much more intense. The video had ended violently but not conclusively, the woman unconscious but not necessarily dead. Maybe the sex had been consensual but had gone a little further than either partner intended. Christine could have been hiding some-where, her silver dress hanging in the closet while she recovered from a bruised throat. The woman didn't even have to be Christine. More than one woman bore a tattoo of Betty Boop on her right shoulder.

I glanced over at Cassie. The Rott stretched across her small body, his head out the window, snapping at the wind as though one night he might catch it. I worried what the polluted air was doing to her young lungs but knew she'd scream if I insisted on raising the window.

"Why did you start crying tonight?" Cassie asked, aware I watched her.

"I just felt like it," I said. I didn't want to tell her, not then, not until I knew something more definitive.

"I hope it wasn't from happiness," she said. "I hate it when people cry from happiness. It's so *Miss America*."

"Maybe you'll grow a heart some day, find out what it's like." It does little good to remind teenagers they're cruel, but Cassie didn't seem to mind. She peered at me from the far side of the passenger seat, her face a shining darkness in the night.

"If I had a heart, I'd just suffer," she said.

Cassie voiced few complaints about going to bed that night, tired enough by the show and her day of shopping to curl under the covers in my bedroom soon after we returned to the place that passed for home. I lived then in a one-bedroom apartment on the second floor of a twelve-unit teardown a half mile from the Venice Beach boardwalk. The landlord accepted all species of living creatures, from ex-cons with big dogs to illegal immigrants packed ten to a room, though cockroaches formed the largest population by far. Not many landlords are willing to rent to ex-cons, and those who are compensate for the risk by doubling the price.

In my line of business the phone often rings at two in the morning with a rumored sighting of one A-list actor or another snorting cocaine off the back of a naked model or some other routine paparazzi photo op. Cassie slept in the bedroom because I didn't want my work to wake her. I pulled the futon from the IKEA sofa and laid it flat on the floor, thinking I might try to sleep, but the images from the video still flickered through my mind and I got no closer to bed than kicking off my shoes. I pulled a bottle of Jack Daniel's from the kitchen cabinet, poured three fingers into a tumbler, and sat at the kitchen table to explore the digital camera I'd purchased a few months before at the insistence of *Scandal Times*. The tabloids are catching up to technology, Frank said. From now on the paper would be looking for photographic content in digital form. Get used to it. I still took my most important shots on film but when the subject and conditions allowed I used the digital camera, a Canon SLR as complicated to navigate as a computer, something else I needed to learn to use.

Just past midnight the cell-phone display lit with a call from an unfamiliar number in the 818 area code, originating from the San Fernando Valley. My network of tipsters, finks, and quislings covers most of the 310 area code—the West Side of Los Angeles—but every now and then a tip comes from the hills on the Valley side of Mulholland Drive. I took the call. A voice asked if Ms. Zero was speaking and it took me a moment to place the voice as Sean's. "The night's turning out slower than I thought," he said. "Any chance you can get her photo to me? I might be able to start work on this right away."

I didn't have anything in the apartment larger than a thumbnail image from a proof sheet. "I know an all-night darkroom in Hollywood," I said, and told him I'd meet him there in an hour.

I collected the negatives I'd need from the hall closet, thought about changing from the dress to a more utilitarian pair of jeans, but decided I didn't want to risk waking Cassie by hunting down clothes in the bedroom closet. The Rott was slow to understand that his job was to stay behind and play guard dog, but after I whispered Cassie's name a dozen times, pointing his nose toward the room in which she slept, he curled up at her door, sighed, and watched me go. I didn't want her to wake and feel abandoned.

Sean was waiting for me when I pulled into the mini-mall parking lot, sipping a cup of take-out coffee as he leaned against a pole sign advertising discount dry cleaning, a Korean nail parlor, video rental, an optician, a Thai restaurant, a postal store, a photo and camera shop, and the all-night donut shop that sold him the coffee. Many people in Los Angeles hated the garish ubiquity of mini-malls—there seemed to be at least one at every commercial intersection, and often two on dueling corners—but where else were you going to get a frozen yoghurt to go while you mailed a package and picked up the dry cleaning? In a city increasingly blenderized by corporate franchises, mini-malls were thriving shrines to the small businessman and the best places to find exotic but cheap cuisine, from Argentinean to

Vietnamese and most every nationality in between. I slid the Metro between the chalk in front of the photo store and shouldered my camera bag.

A confused look must have clouded my eyes when the door snapped open without my touching the handle; it had been so long since a man had opened the door for me I momentarily thought it somehow opened itself. Getting out of the car in a short, tight dress presented another problem, particularly in such close proximity to a man, but I think I managed it with little flash and some grace.

"Did you get a chance to talk to any of Christine's friends?" Sean asked. "Anybody tell you anything that can help us find her?"

I'd asked Nephthys and a few other models, I told him, but nobody had seen her in the past twenty-four hours. He hadn't wanted me to mention the video to anyone, not yet.

"Any idea where she works?"

"Some call service center," I said. "The graveyard shift, I think."

"Did she report for work yesterday?"

"I'll check with another friend," I said, thinking of Nephthys. "I don't know where she works, not exactly. Actresses don't usually go public about their day jobs, even the ones they hold at night."

"Anything else she does every day?" he asked. "The thing about work, it can help us establish when she went missing, if that's what happened."

I told him I'd ask around. I knew she had a roommate, though I'd never met her. Christine came from a small central California town she couldn't get away from fast enough, but I didn't remember which one. When it came to facts, I knew little more than her address and telephone number. A hipster-technician with curly hair and a patch of scrub on his chin appeared behind the photo-shop glass, flipped the security locks, and swung open the door to let us in.

We followed the technician to the darkrooms down a back hallway. Like most darkrooms this one had the square footage of a closet, and when the door shut behind us the environment felt a little too intimate. I asked Sean how long he'd been interested in photography. He stood no more than a foot behind me while I unpacked negatives, proof sheets, and photographic paper from my camera bag, so close I could feel his breath on the back of my neck. I knew it was a stock question. I didn't care what we talked about. He could have been reciting the names of horses running at the track that day and I would have been content, because silence in that small room would have been too powerful.

"I've always liked it," he said. "You ever take photos in color, or just black and white?"

"I took color photos in a studio for a while." I flipped through the proof sheets of the photographs I'd taken of Christine, looking for an image that caught her in an unguarded look, and found a shot in which she sat before a dressing-table mirror, staring at some un-fixed point beyond the glass. "A long time ago I worked in a baby-portrait studio called Hansel & Gretel's, like the fairy tale. All the employees, we had to dress like characters from the fairy tale."

"The wicked witch, too?"

"No, she was considered too scary for little kids."

"It's a scary story. You remember how it goes? A starving wood-cutter and his wife—the wicked stepmother—abandon their children in the forest."

"I don't remember that part." I shuffled through the negatives and found the one that matched the image on the proof sheet. "I only remember the breadcrumb trail, the candy house, and killing the witch at the end."

"That's what everybody remembers."

I loaded the negative into the enlarger and switched off the lights. The safety light cast so faint a red glow that Sean's black leather jacket disappeared and his face hovered in the darkness like the face of a ghost.

"If you go back to the original," he said, "it's a story about felony child abandonment and a serial child killer that ends in justifiable homicide."

"Gretel burns the witch to death, right?"

"She shoves her in the oven and slams the door."

"My kind of girl," I said. I flicked on the enlarger light and fo-cused it onto an eight-by-ten photo, then clicked it off. "Two years of taking photos of screaming babies convinced me that birth control is not a bad thing."

I liked the warm sound of his laughter in the dark. He slid around the room to watch over my shoulder. I flicked on the enlarger light and counted to three, burning the image into the photographic paper, then slipped the paper into the developing tray. Immersed in liquid developer, Christine's image surfaced, the shadows surrounding her like dark clouds to frame the blank purity of her face. Sean leaned over my shoulder to watch the image develop, his face so close I smelled the coffee on him, fused with the light scent of his sweat and the oils in his black hair. When the shadows ripened to a dense black, I tonged the photograph into the stop bath to halt the changes in the image and eased it into the fixer to seal the results.

"You know what I love about this?" Sean asked. "It's like an investigation. You start with a blank and you end up with an image of what happened." He gracefully slipped aside as I turned to the sink to wash the print beneath running water, the final step before drying. "Homicide investigation, it's black and white, too. I'm not talking about moral issues here, I'm talking about how it feels. Things happen in my work that don't happen in the real world, the world of color. Sometimes I think I live and work in a shadow world."

I turned to him, my interest sharply focused because I'd thought the very same thing about my work in the tabloids, that I lived and worked in a world that shadowed the real world but really wasn't the real world at all, in the same way that most people who work graveyard shifts and long nights feel distanced from the daylight world of sun and color. Space in the darkroom was cramped and Sean had been hovering over my shoulder to watch me work, and so when I looked up at his face glowing beneath the safety light, our lips no more than a breath apart, what happened was my fault as much as his; I kissed him as much as he kissed me. Even though I considered it a little odd that a homicide investigator was so willing to talk to me about abstract feelings for the work he did, I hadn't even been conscious of our flirting, in the same way that I wasn't conscious of the terrible and wonderful consequences of kissing him. Yielding to the impulse to kiss him was like the first step toward falling together downhill, all tumbling-forward momentum, our limbs entwined as though the swift exhilaration of our coupling required an even tighter embrace to hold us together, his tongue in my mouth tasting as rich and fertile as earth, and when he penetrated me I launched into free fall, clutching his leather shoulders, my legs wrapped around his waist and my teeth dug into his neck.

He made a sound like weeping when he came, as though he released his pain with his seed. I stroked the back of his head and kissed his brows and it wasn't until I thought about his pain that I thought about anything except pleasure. Wild sex had been far from my thoughts when I entered the darkroom. It had been over a year since I'd made love to a man. Sean and I had coupled with such spontaneous passion that I'd neglected some unpleasant but essential realities. I hadn't asked him to wear a condom and he hadn't volunteered. I had to trust that he'd been surprised by the encounter no less than I, that his sexual history was clean enough that he hadn't infected me with anything, and that I was late enough in my cycle not to get pregnant. That was a lot of trust to place in fate and someone I'd just met. I broke away from him and pulled down the hem of my dress.

He wiped his face with both hands and stared at me above his fingertips. "Have you ever been walking fast," he said, "your mind on something that takes all your attention, so you're not really looking where you're going, and then, bam, you run straight into somebody, and you both go sprawling, wondering what hit you?" He glanced down and saw that he'd kicked himself free of only one pant leg, the other clinging to his ankle. "That's how I feel right now."

Water still streamed over the print in the sink. I closed the faucet and loaded the wet print into the air dryer, turning my back to give him a moment to pull up his pants in dignity. How much did he know about me? Had Frank told him that I was an ex-con paparazza on parole? I packed the negatives, proof sheets, and photographic paper back into my camera bag, wishing I could sort and pack my feelings as efficiently. I'm accustomed to getting screwed by the cops, but this was a first. I gave him the print, said, "This is quick and dirty, not really up to gallery standards, but it should serve your purpose."

I opened the door, letting our eyes adjust gradually to the light spilling in from the hallway. Sean swung the photograph toward the light to examine it. "It may be quick and dirty, but it's beautiful, too." He sounded as though he spoke about our sex as much as the photograph. "I'll make photocopies and return this to you,"

"You can keep it," I said.

"Would it offend you if I asked you to sign it?"

I flipped the print image-side down to sign my name on the back, then slipped the photograph into an oversized envelope to protect it.

Outside, in the mini-mall parking lot, he looked at me strangely but said nothing when I gave him my hand to shake rather than a kiss goodbye.

Among the loneliest places in the world is any street in Los Angeles at 3 AM, where the stray headlights of automobiles skitter past each other like the wary survivors of an apocalypse and every few miles the swift descent of flashing police lights on one car or another demonstrates that no one roving about at such an hour can be up to much good. Los Angeles defines itself by day, a city of sunlight glinting sharply from the glass, metal, and chrome of rushing automobiles. Past midnight, the city extinguishes itself in the absence of the very things that define it, and roaming its streets is like roaming a wasteland. Until that night I hadn't thought myself lonely. I had my dog, my work, and a few close friends, and even though I sometimes missed the comfort and pleasure of another body next to mine, I didn't really see the point. The cool, smog-tainted emptinesses of the city by night harmonized with my spirit far more than the glare and bustle of daily life, as though I felt more at ease with the negative image of things than with the things themselves.

To attach any significance to what happened in the darkroom that night would be a mistake, and given Sean's profession, an error that could only lead to grief. What had he said? That he felt like he'd been looking in the wrong direction while rounding a corner and knocked into somebody. What do you do when you run into somebody without looking? You apologize and move on. Sure, I felt more passionate in those few brief moments than I had in years, probably because I'd been caught so completely unaware, but a moment of spontaneous passion was nothing to build a relationship on, except one of the most casual kind. The problem was, I didn't believe I wanted a serious relationship either. If I disallowed myself casual flings and serious relationships, that left me with the sole possibility of sleeping with like-minded friends I found sexually attractive, a phenomenon so rare I may as well have converted to Catholicism and taken vows.

I keyed the top deadbolt to the door of my apartment and when I didn't hear the thumping gait of the Rott coming to greet me, I dismissed my foreboding with the thought that he liked his sleep too much to get up. Careful not to wake Cassie, I pushed quietly into the apartment and shut the door behind me, listening for the sound of the Rott's limbs stretching on the carpet, his regular prelude to rising from sleep. The door to my bedroom, where Cassie slept, yawned open. I crept to the door frame and peeked inside. The covers to the bed lay flung aside, the bottom sheet indented where my niece had slept not so long ago. I called her name and turned to the bathroom, hoping to see a sliver of light or hear the toilet clatter and flush. I called her name again, louder, and leapt to flick on the lights, fearing what I might find but fearing more the dark and silence.

A sheet of paper, anchored in place on the kitchen counter by an empty glass, caught my eye. I recognized at a distance the unruly scrawl of printed letters as my niece's handwriting. "Baby and I gotta go somewhere to do something," she wrote. "I'll call tomorrow. Don't worry." I crumpled the note and flung it across the room. Don't worry. Right. Might as well shoot me in the gut, tell me, don't bleed.

3

THE VENICE BEACH boardwalk gleams like a carnival during daylight hours, tarot and palm readers competing with merchants and political cranks for the tourists crowding the boardwalk, but after the sun sets the merchants and mystics pack up and the crowds dissipate, leaving the trash behind. Violent crime escalates, and though most of it is perpetrated by drunks and druggies on other drunks and druggies, I did not always feel safe walking the neighborhood after midnight, even when accompanied by the Rott, and this intensified my worries about Cassie. I searched the beach and boardwalk until dawn, asking the drunks, drug addicts, skate punks, and homeless if they'd seen a teenage girl walking a Rottweiler that night. I called the dog as I searched, certain he'd come if he heard my voice, but the only replies sprang from those so deep into one mind-fogging substance or another that any claimed sighting of my niece or dog would be hallucinated.

Cassie had proved capable of taking care of herself on the streets, and that helped me pass the night a little easier. She'd been running wild the year we met, one of a gang of runaways sleeping rough in an abandoned Nike missile base. I hadn't even known she existed until a couple of homicide detectives from the Hollywood station picked me up late one night to identify the body of her mother—my older sister. She had been an even stranger child then, harmless enough to look at but wild and unpredictable, like a feral kitten. She could take care of herself well enough. What I didn't know was how well she took care of others. She and the dog got along, I knew that. Cassie shied from contact with me but didn't hesitate to hug or pet the Rott. I knew the Rott would be fiercely protective of Cassie, but I didn't know how fiercely protective Cassie would be of the Rott.

The cry of the cell phone woke me a couple hours past sunrise, curled in the cramped front seat of the Metro, parked on a residential side street in Los Feliz. I glanced at the call display, hoping to see the unfamiliar number of a public phone box where Cassie might be waiting to be picked up. The display registered a name instead, Nephthys, returning my call from late the night before. After abandoning my search of the beach, I'd driven across town to park and wait for her to wake.

"She didn't say anything to me about it," Nephthys said when I told her about Cassie. "You know what it's like at that age. It's hard to find anything good to say about the people trying to take care of you, but she seemed happy to me, excited to be staying with you. But she's not your average fifteen-year-old. She does what she wants and damns the consequences."

While we were talking I locked up the car, crossed the sidewalk to a 1920s bungalow complex, followed the concrete path toward a rear unit set behind a screen of palm fronds and birds-of-paradise, and knocked on the door. "Wait a minute, someone's at the door," Nephthys said, and a moment later her eye blackened the peephole on the opposite side. "Holy crap! It's you!"

When she snapped open the door I half expected to see hieroglyphics painted on the walls of her apartment to match the tattoos on her body, but Nephthys's fetish for things Egyptian pretty much ended at her skin. She invited me into a tiny, cluttered kitchen, the sunlight streaming onto bright yellow walls. "Don't worry about Cassie, that girl is fifteen going on thirty-five," she said, pouring me a cup of coffee. "She was smart to take the dog with her. The dog will protect her."

"Sure, but who's going to protect my dog from Cassie?"

Nephthys took my comment as gallows humor. "They're both going to be okay, don't worry." She put her hand on my shoulder and looked up at me—she didn't stand taller than five foot two—her Egyptian-lined eyes crinkled with concern.

I was crying again.

"No, it's not that, it's something else, it's Christine." I wiped the sleeve of my jacket across my eyes and told her that someone had sent me a video depicting Christine in an S&M scene that featured strangulation, that it probably wasn't anything serious but I had to find her as quickly as possible. "She told me she worked as a call service representative," I said. "Do you know the name of the company, how to get in touch with her boss?"

"Call service representative? That's what she told you?" The corner of her mouth curved in a wise-girl smile. "That's not exactly accurate."

"You mean she didn't have a job?"

"She had a job, but I think 'call service representative' might be a euphemism." She touched my elbow as though sharing a secret. "She works at one of those 1-900 places."

I must have looked confused.

"Phone sex," she explained.

No wonder Christine hadn't told me the strict truth.

"Do you know which one?"

"Sweet Lasses, I think it's called, but that kind of work, you never leave the house, the calls are patched to your phone line. I have the number stored on the computer." She edged past me, careful of our cups of coffee, into a dimly lit living room furnished with a thrift-shop aesthetic, mix-and-match furniture from different eras and styles existing in happy harmony, brightened by colored fabrics from India and South America draped across the chair backs and hung from the ceiling, flag style. "Christine is another girl who can take care of herself; believe me, she's not as innocent as she looks. But if you're worried, we can take a look at her journal, see if she wrote anything that might explain what's going on."

"Do you have the keys to her apartment?" I asked.

"No," she said.

"Then how do we get her journal?"

"It's online." She plucked a red batik covering from an egg-shaped iMac. "Christine is a Suicide Girl."

"I can't believe Christine wanted to kill herself," I said.

"Suicide Girls isn't about killing yourself." She poked the computer's start button and the thing chimed to life. "It's an online community where Goths, punks, and alts show off their tats and body mods."

"Alts?"

"You know, people into alternative culture." She cracked her knuckles over the keyboard. "For example, I'm a post-post-feminist Egyptologist and body performance artist who reads science fiction and listens to old bossa nova records, and that's just to start. It's easier to say 'alt' and move on." Her fingers clattered over the keys and a website loaded onto the screen, thumbnail jpegs of pierced and tattooed young women on the left, some kind of Internet message board on the right, interviews and weird news stories down the center. The women weren't entirely naked but they didn't wear a lot of clothes either. A logo in the top right corner depicted the letters *SG* and an illustrated woman posed before a background of stars. On closer inspection, a shirt I thought a woman wore turned out to be a tattoo.

The screen flashed purple as the page shifted and Christine's face appeared in the upper left corner, above her personal profile, which listed her age (*21*), body mods (*tongue, nipple, ear, tattoo*), favorite bands (*Bowie, Yeah Yeah Yeahs, The Cure, Sonic Youth, Pixies, Portishead*), favorite films (*Amélie, Chocolat, Boogie Nights, Edward Scissorhands*), favorite books (*Harry Potter*), and the five things she couldn't live without (*chocolate, Veuve-Clicquot, pain, laughter, latex*). To the right of her profile, sentences from her online journal staggered across the page:

my hair crisis is finally solved and I'm closer to my dream of looking like a 1950's movie star for that show I've been writing about.

i wanted to go platinum, like marilyn monroe.

so i went to the all nite drug store to get the die and started fooling around with a pair of scizzors and i woke the next morning my hair like a haystack, just dry and all over the place ugly.

i thought i'd have to wear a bag over my head but boyfiend the bastard treated me to a day at the stylist and now i look bootifull.

tonite i see the guy says he's johnny depp's producer. probably just another cum on.

hey, any of u going to the show nite after tomorrow? if u do the bootifull christine will kiss ur face.

The journal entry was dated the day we'd hung the show, not quite seventy-two hours earlier. She'd dropped by the gallery to model her dress in the afternoon, returned home to type her journal entry, then later that night, if her journal was credible, she'd met the man who claimed to be Johnny Depp's producer. "This so-called producer, how do you think she met him?" I asked.

Nephthys said she remembered Christine had written about him before and tapped at the keyboard again. The previous day's journal entry popped onto the screen:

> i don't know if this is just more elay bullshit but some guy claims to be a producer on one of johnny depp's films (from hell, not his best) wants to see
> ME!!!!???!!!
> this is his line—he said he needed people who could be cool around johnny, said i sounded like somebody might be good to hang with, maybe cast in the picture but no, he wasn't going to lead me on, make promises.
> this means he just wants to screw me, right? whatever. if that's all he wants, no effing way, but i'm not gonna tell the boyfiend . . .
> tg he won't read this, he thinks sg is crap!
> don't don't don't forget two nights from now the show.

I asked when she'd last seen Christine.

"I didn't. I mean, we communicated here on the site but I haven't actually seen her this week." She scrolled down the page to a series of comments made in response to Christine's journal entry that day. A few of the comments were marginally pervy, but most were touchingly supportive messages. *Ur soooo Hawt!!!* One comment read. *I can't believe ur not gonna be a ****. And then, further down the page, I saw a thumbnail close-up of Nephthys next to her name and the exhortation, *U Rock Grrrl!*

"You wrote this?" I asked.

"We all post messages to each other's journals." She darted the cursor to her thumbnail image and clicked. "I can't tell you how excited I was when the first photoset of my tats went online. That's how I met Christine and a bunch of my friends. Here, let me show you . . ."

I dug my address book from my camera bag while she loaded a page that contained her thumbnail photo, personal profile, and journal. She clicked another jpeg at the top of the page and a photograph surfaced onto the screen, Nephthys standing at a brick wall, legs pressed tightly together but arms stretched wide, her hieroglyphic-tattooed body like a canvas framed in red. I took my eyes from the screen long enough to show her the address I listed for Christine and she confirmed it was the same as the one in her book. "I keep calling her cell but I don't get an answer," I said. "Do you know her roommate?"

"Tammy."

"Another Suicide Girl?"

"No, she's an aspiring actress." Nephthys's mouth crinkled as though wrapped around something sour. "Tammy's a real girly-girl. She's on location right now, somewhere in Canada I think, shooting some made-for-dreck movie."

"What about the boyfriend?" I asked.

"I don't want to betray any confidences, but the video you mentioned?" She turned in her chair and looked up at me, her face small and compact as a child's but the look in her eyes not childlike at all. "It doesn't surprise me. They were into some really twisted shit."

Christine's supposed boyfriend, the self-help author Dr. James Rakaan, practiced past-life regression therapy on a dead-end street in the hills above Sunset Boulevard, just east of the Beverly Hills border. I remained a little fuzzy on the underlying theory, but as I understood it past-life regression therapists uncovered a patient's memories of past lives through hypnosis, sometimes because it was just a cool thing to do but most often because some memories were so terrible that they influenced the patient's present life. One case history I read on the Internet described a man with chronic phantom back pain who discovered he'd taken a Roman spear to the liver in the second century while trying to save his family from slaughter. Once he remembered and dealt with the trauma, the pain disappeared. According to the promotional information on his website, www.RakaanHeals.com, Dr. Rakaan was not only one of the most revered practitioners of the exciting new science of past-life regression therapy, but also the author of *New York Times* best-sellers such as *Healing the Past-Life Child Within* and *Soul Mates: One Love Through a Hundred Lifetimes,* plus one title that stayed twelve straight weeks on the self-help bestseller list, *You're Not Crazy, You Really Are Napoleon: How to Unleash the Power of Your Past Lives.*

In his private practice, Dr. Rakaan charged hundreds of dollars an hour to a star-studded list of studio executives and celebrity clients, but almost anybody could afford the price of a book, the website quoted him as saying, and he was happy to make his techniques available for the benefit of the general public. Most impressive of all, Dr. Rakaan not only elicited past-life experiences from his patients—any second-rate past-life regressionist with half his credentials could pull that off—but with certain talented subjects he could invoke future lives as well, telling patients what shapes their reincarnations would take up to six lifetimes from now, something he called future-life progression, or FULP.™

While I drove toward Beverly Hills I called the phone number Sean had left with me, and when his voice mail picked up I left a detailed message about Christine's journal and the name of her employer. When I finished giving him this information I nearly said something sappy about our encounter the night before but restrained myself, instead suggesting he could call to let me know he'd received the message. I figured he wouldn't mind my talking to Rakaan. I tracked people for a living, if celebrities can be called people and photographing them a living.

I parked the Metro in a free slot across the street from Rakaan's office and walked down a winding flagstone path to a garden complex housing an herbal tea shop, an acupuncturist, a practitioner of holistic medicine, and a carved wooden signboard announcing the offices of Dr. James Rakaan, C.H.T. The heady scent of sandalwood greeted me when I stepped across the threshold into the reception area, a junglish room decorated in palm fronds and rattan furniture. The receptionist, a young woman with opaque gray eyes and a nebula of auburn curls framing her pale skin, serenely tilted her chin toward the ceiling and asked if I had an appointment when I said I wanted to talk to Dr. Rakaan.

"Tell him that I'm worried about Christine," I said.

The receptionist advised me that Dr. Rakaan was with a patient at the moment but if I would please have a seat, in a few minutes she'd be able to take a message to him. While I waited, I glanced through a brochure touting a Caribbean cruise to the Panama Canal and spiritual enlightenment, in that order, cohosted by Dr. Rakaan and Thomas Van Voorhees, a renowned medium who claimed he could convey detailed messages from deceased family members in the spirit world. I had barely talked to my family members when they were alive, didn't see what good it would do to chat with them dead, but I figured I was probably in the minority there. The door behind the receptionist's desk eased open and a woman in dark sunglasses, white dress, and floppy hat emerged, looking like an aging movie star who didn't want to be recognized. She succeeded. The receptionist slipped into the gap and a few minutes later Dr. Rakaan himself emerged.

You might think that someone hailed as a revered figure in an exciting new science, even one so unexacting as past-life regression therapy, would be a nerdish gentleman of a certain age, balding at the top and dumpling at the middle, a man given to stay-pressed slacks and half-tucked shirts, his abstract but kind gaze obscured behind thick eyeglasses he likes to clean with the bottom end of his mismatched tie. Not Dr. Rakaan. Not even the photograph on his website prepared me for the striking image of the man himself striding into the reception area, long black hair as sleek as a flag waving to his shoulders, the stout bridge of his nose like the stem of a Y connecting the flying wedge of his massive brow, his glance as piercing as phaser fire set to stun. I didn't doubt he treated a star-studded list of celebrity clients. He looked like a movie star himself.

I asked if he'd seen Christine lately.

"Are you talking about one of my patients . . ." He made a show of trying to pluck the name from memory. "Christine Myers?"

"I'm talking about your girlfriend. That Christine."

Dr. Rakaan stepped aside, the tips of his fingers brushing toward the open door to his office, a gesture I took as an invitation to enter. His office looked like something Dr. Freud might have imagined if he took Prozac instead of cocaine and lived in Beverly Hills instead of Vienna. I avoided the rattan couch and selected a club chair set casually beside a weathered teak desk.

"I'm sorry, but I don't have a girlfriend named Christine," he said. He settled into the swivel chair behind the desk and clasped his hands below his chin, his wide shoulders framed by a window overlooking the back garden.

"I don't care how you characterize your relationship. I just want to know if you've seen her in the past three days or know where she is right now."

His eyebrows puzzled together, narrowing his eyes to slits, an expression no doubt meant to convey his confusion but instead gave his face a cagey look. "And you are . . . ?"

I gave him my name.

"You're the photographer." He nodded as though watching things fall into place. "She was very excited about that, the exhibition I mean, on the verge of euphoria, really. It gave her a tremendous boost of self-esteem, something she needs very much."

"Why would Christine say you're her boyfriend if you're not?"

"Therapy can be an emotionally intimate experience, even more intimate than sex." His face angled into the soft light from the garden window and a smug smile creased his lips, a smile he thought better to contain a moment later. He was not a man unaware of his own handsomeness. "It's one of the hazards—of any kind of therapy actually, not just past-life regression. Even relatively well-adjusted patients form a strong bond with the therapist and sometimes that bond is misinterpreted by the patient to be a romantic one. When a patient is deeply troubled, with a past-life history of abuse . . ." He raised his hands and held them palms up, a gesture of disarming helplessness. "She can fantasize a romantic relationship when none in fact exists."

"Is that what happened to Christine?"

"I can't really tell you without violating the confidentiality between therapist and patient. But what's this about Christine being missing?"

"She didn't show for the exhibition last night. I've asked around and nobody has seen her for three days, not since she was supposed to go on a date with some guy she thought was Johnny Depp's producer."

"A date?" His voice cracked in the middle, as though torn between surprise and skepticism. "She mentioned nothing to me about it. But she missed her appointment two days ago, I can tell you that much. And her karma is so unpredictable this isn't the first time I've worried about her."

"What's wrong with her karma?"

"She was murdered in her most recent past life and in the life before that as well." He spoke as though these events had taken place just days or weeks ago and winced as though he regretted having to divulge a confidence. "Christine loves pain. That's what her sessions are about. Her love of pain. So naturally I worry about the kind of company she attracts. But really, the most likely thing is that she and this producer hit it off and they're somewhere in Vegas, Hawaii, or Mexico together. From what I understand that kind of behavior isn't unusual with her."

He stood and apologized that he had another appointment scheduled and couldn't spare more time. I allowed myself to be goaded into standing but instead of moving politely toward the door, I thought about the jealousy in his voice when he spoke and said, "I don't doubt she's your patient, but you're having sex with her, aren't you?"

Dr. Rakaan pushed past me and opened the door.

"Sure," I said. "She's young, blonde, beautiful, and like you said, liable to have romantic feelings toward her therapist. You may as well sit a man down to a gourmet meal and ask him not to eat. Of course you're having sex with her."

"I'm not sleeping with Christine," he said.

"I'm sure Christine is nothing special to you. I'm sure she's not the only patient you're having sex with. And I didn't say you were sleeping with Christine. I said you were having sex with her."

His fingertips darted to his temples as though his head was about to explode and he said, "You have incredibly filthy karma, I can't believe I didn't see it when you first walked in. Is it possible that you're . . . ?" His face slackened in stunned awe, then he shook his head, revolted. "I'm sometimes hit with moments of clairvoyance. In some cases, I don't have to take someone through past-life regression to discover who they once were. I already know. Do you have any idea who you were in your past life?"

"I hope you're not going to tell me I was Napoleon."

"You were Lizzie Borden," he said. "Now, please, get out of my office."

4

I SHOULD HAVE laughed when Dr. Rakaan claimed I was the re-incarnation of Lizzie Borden, the young Massachusetts woman ac-cused of hacking her father and stepmother to death with an axe in the late nineteenth century. Nothing like being called a reincarnated axe murderer to make you feel good about yourself. Particularly if the call might be accurate. While I coasted down the hill toward Sun-set Boulevard my cell phone chirped, flashing a familiar-looking number that took me several seconds to place. I'd grown up with that number. I hadn't received a call from my parents' house since my mom died. Pop and I hadn't talked for six years, and it would have been just the same to me if we didn't talk for another sixty. I couldn't imagine why he'd be calling now, and because I couldn't imagine a single compelling reason, I took the call.

"Hi," Cassie said. "I'm kinda stuck. Can you come pick me up?"

"Sure," I said, shocked to hear her voice coming from that number.

"I'm at Gramps's house."

"Gramps?"

"You know, your pop. I'm at his place. In Canyon Country."

"Since when do you call him Gramps?"

"He's my grandfather, isn't he?"

"Your mother hated him."

"He's not so bad." Her voice sounded almost cheerful. Her voice never sounded cheerful. "He came out to visit me. In Phoenix. And we've been talking on the phone. So I thought I should go see him."

"Pop drove to Phoenix to see you?"

"A couple of times."

A car turned into traffic in front of me as I neared the bottom of the hill. I hit the horn, hard, but resisted the temptation to flip off the driver when he glanced in the rearview mirror. That didn't, however, stop him from flipping me off.

"Why didn't you tell me?" I asked.

"Because I knew you wouldn't like it."

"Is the Rott with you?"

"He's right next to me." She turned her face from the phone and pitched her voice singsong high to tell the dog she was talking to me. "That's why I need you to come get me. People aren't so fast to pick up somebody hitchhiking with a big dog."

"You hitchhiked to Canyon Country last night?"

A distance of thirty miles.

"Of course not. Somebody I know, he gave me a ride."

"At midnight."

"He could only go at night, because he had to work the next day."

"Without saying a word to me."

"I was gonna tell you but you were gone. I left a note."

Helpless and innocent are not two words I would use to describe my niece. Her stepfather was currently serving a ten-year sentence in Oregon for bank robbery. Her mother had been a con artist at the time of her death and worse things before that. The kid knew how to look out for herself.

"So are you gonna come get me or not?"

"I'm not going inside that house," I said. "I'll honk outside, three times."

For once in my life I obeyed the speed limit as I drove the Golden State Freeway north toward Canyon Country, in no hurry to get where I was going. My feelings toward my pop had mellowed considerably over the years. Used to be I wanted to kill him. Then for a long time I would have settled for a painful, crippling injury. Whenever he hit my mom I went back to wanting to kill him. After her death, when I watched him collapse from something like grief at her funeral, I stopped wishing him violent physical harm. Since then I merely wished never to see him again.

He hadn't been the worst father, despite the beatings he dispensed to one family member or the other with near sacramental regularity.

He despised physical weakness and considered it his duty to demonstrate by example how to defend ourselves from everyone except himself. Had he not decided to instruct us during moments of capricious rage, tindered by alcohol and sparked by unpredictable reactions to words or gestures that struck him as disrespectful, beating the hell out of us one moment and declaring how good it was for us the next, I could have accepted—eventually—the slaps, punches, and kicks as educational.

I don't want to disparage his accomplishments. He taught me many things, more things of true value in life than anyone else. His beatings taught me discipline, how to walk quietly and be silent, how to tune into the moods of your opponent and hit him before he hits you or to run before he strikes. Above all, he taught me how to watch. I'm a photographer because of him, because of my fear of him. I learned early how dangerous it could be to talk, how the wrong word could summon the beast in him with savage speed. I learned to sit silently and watch, my eye like a camera engaged in distant action. These skills have served my career well. And if nothing else, I owe to him my ability to throw a killer left hook and to take a punch without crumpling in pain or intimidation.

Pop was never one to garden much, preferring to spend his free hours tinkering with his pickup truck, but as I looked at the one-story tract house where I'd been raised, the height of the weeds growing from the lawn startled me. Our lawn had always sprouted equal amounts of dandelions and crab grass, but thistle, foxtail, and ragweed now grew a few inches shy of being declared a fire hazard. I circled the block and parked across the street from the house, tapped the horn three times, noticed the paint looked more weathered than ever and the asphalt-shingle roof needed patching. Pop was letting the place run down, not that it mattered to me. While I waited, I searched for Sean's number on my cell phone and called it. His voice mail picked up. I left a message detailing my conversation with Dr. Rakaan and disconnected. If he wanted to call me, he'd call me. I pocketed the cell as Cassie stepped out the front door, without the Rott. She shrugged and turned her palms up, making the gesture theatrically big so I couldn't fail to notice it, then curled her hand toward her shoulder, motioning me to come to her.

I stuck my head out the window, shouted, "What?"

"Baby! He won't come!"

"Grab his collar and pull him!"

"I can't! He's too big!" She drew out the words when she shouted, emphasizing her relative helplessness against the size of the dog.

I vaulted out the driver's door and strode across the street, my patience finally down to the bone, and even though I didn't like to yell at my niece, preferring instead to discipline her with a minimum of anger—not that she listened—this time I planned to tell her exactly how I felt about getting ditched in the middle of the night and then dragged out to a house I considered hell on earth, but the second my Doc Martens brushed the weeds beside the front walk the sweat burst from my skin in a dozen places and my throat constricted as though wrapped by a snake.

"What's wrong?" Cassie asked, no doubt afraid that her attempts at manipulation had irrevocably pissed me off.

I couldn't allow myself to lose my temper with her, not there, where I'd suffered so much from Pop's anger that I had a panic attack just approaching the door. I asked her where the dog was.

"Under the bed in the back bedroom." She took a step toward the door to encourage me to follow. "He won't come out for me."

I shouted for the Rott, heard his bark in response but not the thumping gallop of his paws racing to greet me. Cassie pulled at my arm, her voice rising an octave in fear or frustration, I couldn't tell which. "I told you, he won't come, he's stuck under the bed. You have to come inside and get him." I allowed her to lead me up the steps and across the threshold into a house that had been both a sanctuary and a place of terror for me. The smell wrapped me as my eyes adjusted to the dark, the stale odors of old man, smoke, and fried food as heavy as cloth. I glanced at the rust-colored couch and brown recliner in the living room, both positioned at angles favorable to watching the television set in the corner, the heavy oak coffee table still chipped in evidence of the things Pop had broken against it, a smooth path worn in the beige carpet leading toward the kitchen, where Pop himself sat framed in the doorway, hunched over a mug at the table, staring at me like an animal from its den. I nodded once, slowly. He nodded back and raised his right forefinger from the top of the mug.

The Rott barked again, his paws scratching against the bedroom door. Cassie scuttled down the hall. "Listen," she said, a false cheer running through her voice. "It sounds like he's come out now." She opened the door before I could get to it, the Rott bulling through the gap as it widened, bumping Cassie aside to get to me. I dropped to my knees and we collided, chest to shoulder. I turned with the blow, landing on my back, the Rott thrilled to find me pinned to the floor, squirming to escape his fat, wet tongue. I rolled onto my stomach, his tongue flicking at my ears from behind, the high-pitched squeals of my niece's laughter resonating in the narrow hallway. I'd never heard her laugh before. I struggled to my knees and glanced into the room where the dog supposedly had been hiding. The bed frame stood about six inches above the carpet, barely high enough to give clearance to a cat.

"The dog is bigger than the bed," I said. "No way he could fit under there. And even if he did get stuck, how was he going to open the door? If you're going to lie, at least try to make it believable."

When I saw her cheeks crimson above a pleased smile I realized she had lured me inside the house for some other reason. I'd shared the room with Cassie's mom, Sharon, until she ran away from home at age sixteen. The sight of my childhood room didn't make me sentimental. Except the bed and dresser, everything of mine had long since been thrown out or given to Goodwill. Maybe Cassie was searching for some kind of context. She'd been placed in foster care after her mother's arrest for bank robbery. Before that, the years they'd been together had been troubled. Maybe my presence helped her visualize how her mother lived as a girl.

I told the Rott to sit and then stood behind him, stroking his head down to his haunches, physical contact that bound us and prepared him to obey. Cassie held his head in her hands at the same time, the Rott in dog heaven between us. Then I commanded him to heel.

"That's a fine dog you got there," Pop called. He stood at the threshold between the kitchen and living room, backlit by sunlight streaming through the kitchen window. "Why don't you sit down a bit, have a cup of coffee with your old man."

I understood then that I'd been tricked into this meeting for reasons mystifying enough to hook me into staying. I suspected it would turn into an ambush, some recounting of his grievances against me.

Not that I feared him. When he turned into the light, heading for the kitchen cabinet where he stored the coffee mugs, I noticed his barrel chest now slumped toward his waist and what remained of his hair grew in sparse gray tufts around the balded crown of his head. He was too old to fear. I was more concerned with what might happen to my heart if I turned him down and walked out the door. He was my father; even though we had thirty years of sometimes violent history behind us, to refuse a simple request to talk would be heartless. I'd listen to what he wanted to say and then I'd leave. I didn't have to talk if I didn't want to.

When I sat at the table, the Rott settling next to me on the floor, I realized it was the same chair I'd been assigned as a child, that I'd unconsciously reverted to my traditional place in the family. I'd always been the appeaser, the only one in the family who, when I sensed it coming, could sometimes calm the beast in my pop. I'd stroke his arm, telling him what a good poppa he was, until he calmed, or didn't. I'd been so terrified of him as a child that I'd changed myself to fit his ideas of how I should act, think, and dress, in hopes that by appeasing him he wouldn't hurt me. I took to styling myself like a girly girl, blonde hair flipped at the shoulder or worn in pigtails, fuzzy sweaters and knee-length skirts, open-toed pumps, toenails buffed like paint on a Corvette. Maybe I even wanted Pop to love me. I still don't have that too clear. Looking back, I think he might have loved me more than his other children—not that he loved any of us much—and so when at last I snapped, rebelling violently against him and the false image of myself we'd created, he'd all but disowned me. While Pop fiddled with the coffee, I thought about taking his chair, his place at the table, but decided it was a spiteful impulse I'd best ignore.

"Cassie and me, we had quite the time, didn't we Cass?" He looked over his shoulder at his granddaughter, who stood in the kitchen doorway, uncertain whether her presence at the table would help or hinder the conversation. "She didn't even tell me she was coming last night until just past eleven. Then she gets here and tells me you didn't know she was going, that she took your dog and wrote you some note." Pop set a cup of coffee onto the Formica tabletop in front of me and sat, facing the entrance to the kitchen. "Time was, a child of mine pulled a stunt like that."

"If you ever hurt Cassie, give her a black eye or a split lip, I'll break your leg with a baseball bat."

It had to be said, and it didn't make much sense to delay saying it.

He stared at me, wrinkled skin hooding the expression from his eyes, and I counted, one-two-three, waiting for the familiar signs of his transformation from man to beast: the baleful glare, the flush of blood and sweat across his brow, the clenched jerking of his muscles signaling the moment before scales broke through the skin covering his face and he flung a mug of scalding coffee at my head.

But it didn't happen. He just shrugged and smiled.

"Still the hard-ass, I see," he said.

I stared at him, waiting.

"Don't get me wrong. I'm proud of you. You want to break my leg, fine, just don't forget who taught you how to swing the bat."

Had he thrown his coffee at me, I would have ducked and flipped the table on him, but I didn't see the compliment coming and it caught me flush in the face. "You did," I said. He'd taught me how to throw and catch too, didn't even seem to notice I was a girl until my T-shirts began to strain against what would develop into an unspectacular set of breasts. He'd been the first to insist I put on a bra and stop acting like a tomboy, then whipped me like a boy when I rebelled.

"I been following your work in the papers." He pulled a copy of *Scandal Times* from the chair next to him. "You gotta be persevering to do the kinda work you do."

I nodded.

"You really stand up for yourself, I'll say that much. Sure, you let things get away from you there for a while, got into a little trouble, but strong character showed you through, and you set yourself right." He sipped at his coffee, eyes cagey above the rim of the mug. "I'm no friend of the law's. Never have been. Somebody hits you, you hit them back. That's what I always taught you to do. Doesn't matter if you get in trouble. You do it because you gotta stand up for yourself. You weren't out there robbing banks like your sister." He looked up at Cassie, standing in the doorway, his expression anxious. "Sorry Cass, don't mean to speak bad about your mom."

"It's okay, Gramps," she said. "I know my mom was a lying, thieving bitch."

"Well now, that's a little harsh," he said, genuinely shocked. "I look at your beautiful face and I see your mom did at least one thing right. And you shouldn't swear like that. It's undignified."

"Okay, Gramps," she said.

Where she found her patience with him I had no idea, just as his seeming blindness to her Goth-girl rebelliousness perplexed me. Had I attempted a style like that as a teenager, he would have thrashed me.

"We all get our heads screwed on backwards every now and then, you, your mom, even your aunt here, that's the chief thing to remember." His face split with a sudden laugh and he said, "Hell, sometimes I get my head screwed up my ass, pardon the French. That's what happened between me and Mary here."

Mary Baker, my birth name.

"You mean Nina," Cassie said. "She likes to be called Nina now."

Pop pulled at his face, the subject of my name change still a source of confusion and irritation to him. "She can call herself any damn thing she wants, no skin off my back. Thing is, before, I was wrong. I took it too personal. Thought she was rebelling against me personally, when she was rebelling against everything in the whole damn world, maybe mostly herself."

"I'm not the one needs to hear this," Cassie said.

When Pop shifted in his chair to face me I knew this was in no way spontaneous, that the two of them had talked about this moment some time before, either on the phone or the night before, in person. "I never shoulda turned my back on you like I did, after you got arrested that first time." He sighed so heavily the table shifted, and the sound of that sigh had more sadness in it than anything he'd ever said to me. "Sure, you did some things no father would be proud of, but I raised enough hell when I was young that I shoulda known you were going to raise your share of it, too. But I didn't see it coming, that's why it shocked me so much. You were always a willful little girl, but I thought you'd settled down, didn't understand you'd just delayed your hell-raising. So when you started to do those things you did, it was like somebody punched me, and so I did what I always do when someone hits me. I lost my temper and I hit back every way I knew how."

"You always were good at losing your temper," I said.

"That was wrong of me." He pulled again at his face. "I don't regret being tough with you, don't get me wrong there, I don't regret giving you a little needed discipline. But those times I got mad at you and went a little too far, I'm sorry about that. My temper, you're right, that's never been one of my best qualities. But I guess you know a little about that yourself. I guess you know what it's like to lose your temper, do things you regret later."

"It's true, I lose my temper," I admitted. "But most of the things I've done needed doing and I don't regret them."

"You think you woulda been able to do those things you say needed doing if I'd coddled you your whole life?"

I flinched when the cell phone went off in my pocket and yanked the thing out by the antenna. Frank's name flashed on the display. I didn't want to answer Pop's question because once I started, it would take me six weeks to finish. Let him think I was rude, that I thought the call more important than our conversation. What did he want me to say? That it was okay? That I forgave him? I didn't. I took the call. Some hiker had found a woman's body in one of the canyons north of Malibu, Frank said, the connection breaking up as he drove in and out of coverage. He was checking it out, wanted photo backup. Could I make it? I told him I could and disconnected the call.

Pop watched me carefully, both curious and, it seemed, a little afraid.

"I don't hate you as much as I used to," I said. "Don't feel the need for it."

Pop smiled like I'd just kissed him.

"Well, I guess that's a start," he said.

5

THE SUN HUNG white-hot in the scalded blue sky as we climbed the coastal canyons toward Malibu, the Metro's hamster-powered engine whining on all four treadmills at each rise in the road. Cassie fiddled with the radio while I drove, the signal for college station KXLU fading to static as we wound deeper into the canyons, her bitten fingernails purple on the dial. We didn't speak for miles, but I knew by her dreamy smile she was pleased with herself, her small hands resting on the Rott's massive neck, lost in her own world. I hadn't wanted to take her with me on this assignment, but she was scheduled to fly back to Phoenix early that evening. She had set me up cleverly, I thought, tricking me into the house to get the Rott. I didn't want to lecture or yell at her, but I didn't want her to think I was unaware of her manipulations. "I understand why you wanted to see your biological grandfather," I said. "I understand everybody wants to know something about the family they come from, but why did you have to take my dog?"

"Because if I took the dog, you'd come and get me," she said.

"I would have come to get you. I love my dog but I love you, too."

She worked a purple fingernail between her teeth while she thought about that. "No way you would have come inside the house. The only way to get you inside was the dog."

We crested the ridge at Mulholland Highway, the first breath of cool ocean air brushing our faces. Cassie didn't seem the type to want to promote peace in the family, but then, she had so little family left, maybe she thought it a good idea to get us together again, not understanding that if I was going to bury the hatchet with Pop, I'd be just as likely to bury it in his head. Past Mulholland the road traced the ridge line, the horizon opening to vistas of the coast loping north toward Point Dume, the white-tufted waves in the distant ocean like chalk marks on a vast, blue board. For a few moments, I felt good about myself, about being alive in the world amid so much natural beauty, but then I spotted the patrol car blocking access to Edison Road and the hiking trail leading into the Santa Monica Mountains National Recreation Area. I braked hard and swept to the side of the road, muscles tensed to confront a familiar tableau, dead body in the mountain brush, a staple of *Scandal Times*'s incisive, hard-hitting news coverage, a story I'd photographed a half dozen times in the past year. Though we rarely got close enough to photograph the body, I always disliked the assignment. What we found this time might not turn out to be the anonymous victim of an act of murderous rage but someone I knew, someone I'd worked and dined with and whose face graced some of the best photographs I'd ever taken. I usually felt detached when called upon to photograph victims but this time I felt angry.

"Why are we stopping here?" Cassie asked.

"I have to do a quick job," I said. "Do me a favor and stay in the car, watch the dog for me."

"What's to shoot out here?" Her purple lips carved a mischievous smile. "You get a report Mark Wahlberg is skinny-dipping? I'd see that."

"You'll stay near the car." I pulled my camera bag from the backseat and took a moment to stroke the Rott's head. "It's a body-in-the-hills story. I need to grab a shot of some eyewitness, shouldn't take me more than thirty minutes. Take Baby for a walk if you like, but don't go far or we'll miss your flight."

As I walked away from the car, it occurred to me that my niece might very well intend to miss her flight. She had already proved herself to be a master of manipulation. She might take the Rott for a walk and lose track of time or deliberately lose herself in the hills, returning too late to make her flight to Phoenix. I glanced back as I strode toward the entrance to Edison Road. She stood beside the loaner car, her hand on the dog's head, watching me go. I rounded the corner, certain she was bolting into the brush the moment I disappeared from view.

"Sorry, area's closed for the afternoon," the sheriff deputy said when I approached the patrol car.

I flashed my press badge.

"It's even more closed to the press." He pointed across the road. "You can get some good hiking that way. I heard there's a trail over there that'll take you all the way to the beach."

Or to hell. It was his polite way to tell me to get lost. I spotted Frank's Honda tucked into the brush up the road. I thanked the deputy for his help and flipped open my cell phone while I walked. When the call connected, Frank told me he was interviewing an eyewitness and directed me to take the footpath beside the car; I could find him in the meadow over the hill. Frank needed to lose about twenty pounds to be considered merely overweight and wasn't capable of running any distance greater than to the bathroom without losing his breath, but he always showed remarkable endurance when pursuing a story. I wasn't surprised to find that the switchback trail carved a steep incline into the hill, leading to the top of a ridge that dropped to a meadow studded with wildflowers and fringed in oak.

Frank stood just beyond the tufted shadow of the nearest tree, the eyewitness's face in the sun. Like a television news reporter, Frank always knew where the camera would be positioned and staged his interviews accordingly. I selected the digital camera from my bag and snapped off a sequence of telephoto shots. The eyewitness looked legit enough through the lens, a late-thirties nature boy whose neatly trimmed black beard, ruddy complexion, and green-on-green hiking attire gave him the appearance of an aspiring park ranger. *Scandal Times* didn't generally run large photographs of noncelebrities; at most, his candid would be boxed in miniature within a larger photograph of the crime scene to establish that we weren't making it all up.

Frank greeted me in mock surprise as I kicked down the hill and turned to ask the eyewitness if he minded having his photograph taken, conveniently failing to mention that I'd snapped a dozen images from the ridge above. I didn't ask Frank what he'd been told. I didn't want to know just then. I wanted to do my job. I directed the eyewitness to stand on the slope and stretch out his arm as though pointing at the body in the brush, a style of shot favored by *Scandal Times* that has grown no less hokey since it began to appear regularly in the tabloids of the 1930s.

I took the shot and bagged the camera.

"Just one question," I said. "The body, did she have any tattoos?"

"Did she ever." He tapped his shoulder. "She had a tattoo of that old cartoon character, Betty Boop, right there. Just what I told your colleague. She must have been a beautiful girl, I'll tell you, the sight of her lying there, it brings you to tears. A helluva shame." He scratched his throat at the beard line, started to ask something, stopped himself, then went ahead and asked anyway. "You mind me asking how you knew about the tattoo? Is this some kind of serial thing?"

A shout from the ridge turned me to the sight of the Rott galloping down the hillside, Cassie carefully stepping down the trail as though she'd never walked off-pavement before. I veered away from the eyewitness and snapped my fingers at the Rott, following with a sharp, pointed gesture at the ground, but the dog was too excited and moving too fast to obey at first, running past me before bringing his bulk under control in a holding pattern, his truncated tail wagging him in circles. I gave him a few strokes along his flanks and told him to sit. He did. Cassie approached slowly, uncertain of her footing on the uneven ground.

"I thought I told you to stay near the car," I said.

"Don't blame me." She pointed at the dog. "I'm just following him. He got away from me when I was trying to put the leash on him." She held up the leash, rolled in her hand, as evidence.

I wanted to ask why I hadn't heard her calling him until the last moment, or point out that it was just as likely that she'd led the Rott over the ridge and then unleashed him, knowing he'd run straight to me with little encouragement, but such concerns seemed petty under the circumstances. Cassie peered around the meadow and focused for a moment on Frank, who asked a few meaningless wrap-up questions to the eyewitness. "Where's the body?" she asked. "Anywhere close?"

"Do you know who the body is?" I asked.

She shook her head, purple-limned eyes gleaming.

"Christine," I said. "This is why she didn't show at the gallery last night. Somebody raped her, strangled her, dumped her like trash."

Cassie blinked, shielded her eyes from the sun, asked, "Christine?"

"Sorry, I gotta go." I strode toward a grove of oaks at the edge of the meadow, heeling the Rott to my side. I'd delivered the news to

Cassie too brutally, but I knew no other way to talk about acts of brutality. Despite my rage I worried about her, how she'd handle the death
of a woman she'd taken as a role model, like Nephthys, cool and sexy
and all screw-the-world attitude. The oak grove spread from the
meadow up the flanks of the ridge, the sweet, woody scent not enough
to soothe me. Not nearly enough. I walked deep into the screen of trees
and picked up a weathered branch as thick as a table leg. The Rott,
sensing my temper, scouted the grove far to my right. I stepped up to
an oak split by lightning, its bark charred black, and slammed the limb
against the stump, the contact jarring me to the bone. And then I lost
myself to my rage, flailing at the tree as though I battled a circle of
demons, my face flushed as I struck again and again, the tears steam-
ing from my eyes as though vented from a superheated core. When I
slipped to my knees, muscles trembling with exhaustion, I realized I
was done, the rage burned clear. I wiped the sweat from my forehead
and the tears from my cheeks, then glanced at my hands, black with
soot, my face now streaked with ash, the ancient mark of someone in
mourning. I was feeling eye-for-an-eye and tooth-for-a-tooth just then.

"Are you okay?"

Cassie stood a dozen yards distant, the Rott clutched to her side,
her expression both serious and afraid. When I nodded she edged
closer, carefully, as though approaching a wounded but still dangerous beast.

"You really lost it," she said.

"No, this isn't losing it." I stood, my thigh quivering with the effort, and tossed the branch aside. "This is just exercise."

"Better a tree than someone's head, I guess." She took another
step closer, the carefully drawn line around her eyes unbroken by
grief, her arms wrapped around her thin chest and her mouth held
tight in a thin, straight line.

"You're crying again," she said.

"Of course I'm crying. Normal people cry when someone they
like dies."

"Normal people," she said and paused, thinking it over, "don't go
around beating the crap out of dead trees."

The Rott crept close enough to touch, head low and tail wagging
cautiously, and when I reached to stroke him he banged against my
leg. I told her she had a point and hiked toward the ridge, the

strength returning to my legs with each step, my momentary exhaustion emotional as much as physical.

"Who do you think killed her?" Cassie walked closely behind, taking each step as though the ground might drop out from beneath her.

"I have no idea, not yet."

"Are you going to look for her killer?"

"That's the police's job."

I'm sure she noticed my shrug, as though I wasn't sure of my answer.

"You'll follow the story? For the paper?"

"A story like this, a dead-body-in-the-brush story, normally it's one issue and out because, really, who cares? Once the girl is dead, she's dead. We'll only do a follow-up if the police publicly point to a suspect or arrest somebody."

"Who do you think killed her?"

Her morbid curiosity unnerved me.

"How do I know who killed her? This shit happens all the time. Every month somebody finds a body in the mountains or desert around here, every week some kid riding a bike or playing on the lawn gets gunned down by gangbangers, every day somebody beats, stabs, or shoots somebody to death, bodies stuffed in closets, suitcases, the trunks of cars, people shot down in their own bedrooms or stabbed in their kitchens, assaulted on the street by total strangers, beaten, robbed, raped, crumpled up and tossed aside like trash in the gutter, and those are just the fatalities; that doesn't even count the dozens of people who don't die, who survive their wounds to linger on in one pitiful shape or another."

Cassie called for me to wait up, trailing so far behind I doubt she heard much of what I'd said. I paused at the crest of the hill, the canopy of oaks billowing down to the meadow. She stopped a dozen feet below and looked up at me, bone-white forearm shading her eyes from the bright blue sky.

"I was thinking you might know someone more specific," she said.

"That's the whole point. How can I be specific when death is everywhere? Christine was wild but she wasn't stupid, no more than other girls. Do you think she realized the guy who asked her out was going to kill her? That's why you have to be careful. What happened to Christine? That's the price of running wild in the world."

"Some guy asked her out? Who?"

"Somebody who claimed to be a producer."

"So you do know a little more than you're saying," she observed, and stepped up the hill as though she hadn't heard anything more than what she wanted to hear.

Frank was gnawing on a foot-long sub, scribbling notes on a legal-sized pad propped on the hood of his Honda, when I hiked around the curve. Cassie dawdled far behind, lost in her own Gothic, death-obsessed world. "I'm sorry it was Christine," he said as I heeled the Rott. "I didn't know her, of course, but I'm sorry for you."

"You want the flash card?" I asked, referring to the removable memory chip that stored the digital camera's photographs. "Or would it be okay if I stopped in tomorrow to transfer the images?"

"Tomorrow will be fine." He turned his back to the car, leaned against the front fender, said, "We could hear you banging on that tree a hundred yards away. You scared the shit out of our eyewitness, thought you were a crazy woman."

"That was nothing," I said. "That was just my normal homicidal PMS rage. You should be glad you don't have to deal with hormones that make you temporarily insane."

"I count my blessings every day."

I thought about whether or not I should ask about Sean, whether it would clue Frank something was going on between us, then decided I should just go ahead and act as though nothing had happened.

"You mean Detective Tyler?" Frank jutted his chin toward the access road. "He's up there. "

"His case?"

"Jurisdictional issues. This is LASD turf." He narrowed his eyes at me. "Since when did you get to be on first-name basis with a cop?"

"Why does LASD get it?" The Los Angeles Sheriffs Department patrolled the coastline between Pacific Palisades and the Ventura County border. "The video wasn't shot out here. I mean, where she was killed, that's who gets jurisdiction, right?"

"But where was she killed? The video doesn't show one way or another. It's just a room." His eyes tracked over my shoulder. "A case like this, cross-jurisdictional conflicts, possession of the body is nine-tenths of the law."

Cassie collapsed against the Honda's passenger door as though worn out by the hike and stared up at Frank. "Nina says you're going to drop the story. Why would you want to do that? It's a great story. Beautiful dead girl, bloodsucking killer rapist, I'd think readers would eat that up."

Frank stared her down, asked, "What do you care, you little ghoul?"

Cassie beamed as though she'd just been called the most beautiful young woman in paradise. "I care a lot, you fat fuck," she replied. "Christine was my friend."

"First of all, 'fat fuck' is cheap alliteration. You should be writing headlines for *Scandal Times*." Frank crossed his arms over his chest and leaned forward, scowling. "Second, I never said I was going to drop the story."

"Don't encourage my niece to swear," I said. "She doesn't need it."

"You were swearing yourself just a minute ago," Cassie said.

"No, I wasn't. I never swear."

She looked at me like I'd lost my mind or lied, or maybe both.

"I don't think Christine was this guy's first," Frank said.

"You think it's a serial killing?" Cassie asked. "What makes you think that? Is he collecting trophies?"

"I didn't say serial killing," Frank said, wagging a corrective finger. "I said he probably wasn't her first. A couple of weeks ago a girl with bruises on her throat was found wandering naked in the desert near Palmdale, with no idea how she got there."

"How does that connect?" I asked, not getting it.

"The cops suspect ruffies."

"Rohypnol, that stuff is nasty," Cassie said with too much authority.

"How do you know?" I asked.

"You think I'm not supposed to know stuff like that? That I'm too *little*?" She crossed her arms over her chest, offended. "I started seeing that stuff in the seventh grade, all the date-rape drugs, particularly Vitamin K."

"Vitamin K?"

"Slang for Ketamine," she said. "Kids use it to get high."

"So maybe she took it recreationally, or one of her so-called friends gave it to her," I said. "Isn't that more likely?"

"You're right, probably doesn't mean anything." Frank smiled, suddenly cheerful. "But it's almost summer, readers are going to want a story they can take with them to the beach, and when you can cross genres like this, movie starlets and murder, it makes great beach reading."

6

FRANK'S INTENTION TO continue following the story animated
Cassie during the ride south to the airport, the loaner car rolling with
the curves along Pacific Coast Highway as she calculated the possibility that Christine had been victimized by a serial rapist and the
certainty that Frank wouldn't let her killer get away with it, declaim-
ing in a thin, high voice that the press coverage would pressure the
police to catch the bastard if she didn't find him first, as though she
planned to join the *Scandal Times* staff as a combination research assistant and amateur sleuth. Her reaction worried me. Frank could be
a crack investigative journalist when the desire moved him, but I
didn't think his interest was all that genuine. He wanted a hot story
to sell newspapers, not the truth. Cassie gave far more credence to
his interest than experience and common sense warranted. If the
story didn't develop over the next day or two, he'd drop it. That
would disappoint her, but life is full of disappointments. I didn't
worry about her disappointment. Her emotional detachment and
morbid curiosity, that worried me.

"I don't get it," I said. "The way you reacted when I told you
Christine was dead, I never would have guessed you knew her."

"What do you mean?"

"You didn't cry, you didn't even look shocked. You went from
hearing she was killed to wanting to find out who killed her without
any of the emotional steps in between."

"Like what steps?"

She was curious. She really didn't know.

"Like grief. I'm not sure you really care. Don't you feel sad?"

"I'm not like you." She leaned back hard against the passenger seat, offended. "I don't beat the crap out of dead trees and think it solves anything."

"Maybe it didn't solve anything, but I feel better."

"Maybe this makes me feel better." She bit at the edges of her purple thumbnail. "Are you going to look for the guy who did this to Christine?"

I shrugged.

"It's like you get angry and then you forget about it. What's the good in that? And you tell me I don't care? At least I care enough to want to do something."

"I'm a tabloid photographer, not a detective."

"You think the cops should handle this? Is that what you think?" She made a face to let me know what she thought of that idea. "You used to be hard core."

"What happened to Christine is terrible," I said.

"She was your friend!" Cassie shouted. "She modeled for your photographs and took care of your niece! We have to avenge her death."

"You have to go back to school," I said.

She made a sound in the back of her throat, sounded like a growl.

"Do I want to find whoever did this?" I nodded, once. "Frank wants to follow the story. That's a good start. We'll follow the story."

We rode a while in silence, the sun firing bright orange as it arced toward the sea. The Rott, made uncomfortable by the tension between us, stirred at Cassie's feet and attempted to clamber onto her lap. She pushed him back onto the floorboard, then remembered to give him a scratch as consolation. "Do you remember when we first met?" she asked.

"Sure," I said. I'd tracked her to an abandoned missile base north of Los Angeles, hoping to convince her to leave, and when she refused, I hit her with a right hook and dragged her out.

"You were really hard core then," she said. "You really kicked ass."

"I'm trying to mature a little."

"If you mature any more, I'll think you're dead."

I glared at her.

She gave me a big, smart-ass show of teeth. "If I find the asshole who killed Christine?" She mimed a pistol with her right hand and pulled the trigger. "Bang!"

I tried to remember how I'd felt about death at her age, hoping it might help me understand her reactions, but I was far more innocent at fifteen than my niece—or her mother. My sister had run away from home at sixteen, uncertain of what awaited her on the road but knowing she couldn't live with the old man's violence anymore. She'd hoped for a little excitement, I guess, and got it quickly enough, landing in the Las Vegas hooking scene, where her youth made her a prime commodity until her eighteenth birthday turned her legal but far less exotic. She stayed in the trade for several more years, moving on whenever the cops busted her for soliciting, from Vegas to Phoenix to Houston to Dallas, until she hooked up with a con artist who saddled her with Cassie and introduced her to a drug dealer who married her, convinced Cassie was his kid. A couple of years later, the dealer decapitated two of his slow-pay accounts with a ceremonial samurai sword and left enough evidence at the scene to make his arrest, conviction, and execution a simple legal formality. My sister had acquired a taste for the con by then, mostly small-scale sleight-of-wallet jobs involving drunken men, and she drifted up and down the coast, Cassie in tow, until one night in Portland she met Hank Bogle, a man accustomed to taking what he liked and he liked her. They lived in larcenous bliss for a little more than three years before a bungled bank job sentenced her to three to five years in Coffee Creek Correctional Facility and strapped Hank Bogle to a ten-year ride in the Oregon State Penitentiary.

Cassie entered the terminal at LAX oddly cheerful, but as we wound our way through the long lines to the Southwest ticket counter her chatter ceased and she fidgeted with her hair, sweeping it back or twisting it in knots, checked and rechecked her ticket and student identification, and rifled through her overnight bag for one thing or another, a constant flutter of seemingly meaningless activity. I figured she suffered from anxiety, her jitteriness no more than a case of pre-flight nerves, but after she collected her boarding pass from the ticket counter she said, "I'm moving in with Gramps."

"Nice fantasy," I said, not taking her seriously.

"I've almost got it worked out with my caseworker." She nodded emphatically. "Gramps is filing for custody here, too. Says he'll adopt me if that's what it takes. Says the courts will grant him custody because he's a blood relative."

"You can't move in with him," I said. "Your mother ran away from him because he beat her. Wait until your caseworker hears that."

"He's changed. He's not like that anymore."

"He'll always be like that," I said.

"You won't adopt me, so you got no say."

She clutched her boarding pass like a badge and scurried into the line snaking toward the baggage x-ray machines, aware that no one without a boarding pass was allowed past that point and our argument would end.

"You know I can't adopt you." I said.

"Why not?"

I couldn't figure why she asked. She knew the answer.

"Because I'm on parole," I said.

The man before us in line glanced back over his shoulder.

"You mean you're a criminal," she said, stating a fact. "Like my mother."

I glowered at the man in front of us, told him to mind his own business. His head snapped forward like it was attached to a string.

"You know all the shit you accuse me of?" she asked.

"Don't swear," I said.

"Like swearing, that, too." Her voice scratched higher, like nails on chalkboard. "You lecture me about running wild in the world, getting myself into some dangerous shit, but you did the same things yourself. So you got no right to criticize me!"

I didn't know whether I was dealing with typical teen rebellion or something deeper, her reaction to Christine's death connected to the death of her mother and feelings of abandonment. "I'm not criticizing you," I said.

"You were just telling me I couldn't go live with Gramps!"

"I warned you about him. Nothing more."

"And you criticize my language!"

"Have I ever told you I was perfect? Of course I criticize your language. Swearing is ugly. Sorry if that offends you. It's not like I'm saying you're a bad person."

"You fucked up your life so you think you can tell me how to run mine?"

"That's kind of the point of being your aunt, isn't it?" What she said hurt me but I kept my voice low and level, refusing to play to her emotions in that public place. "I'm older. I've made lots of mistakes. And so I want to protect you from making the same mistakes I made. I'm not trying to criticize you so much as warn you what's likely to happen. Swearing makes you look cheap and vulgar. Running wild in the world can hurt or kill you. You're fifteen years old. The things I did that got me into so much trouble? They happened when I was over twenty. I didn't have anybody advising me what could happen. I'd like things to turn out a little better for you."

"But I don't want to run wild anymore!" She grabbed my arm, panicked now because only one passenger remained between her and the x-ray machines. "I'm tired of running away from foster homes. That's why I want to live with Gramps."

The security officer directed her to set her bag on the conveyor belt, place any metal objects on her person into the plastic tray, and step through the metal detector. "I'm going back to Phoenix just long enough to collect my things," she said, as she dropped her pack onto the conveyor belt. "Then I'll come back and spend the summer with Gramps."

The metal detector bleeped when she passed beneath the arch. A matron stepped forward to wand her down one side and up the other, the detector emitting a high-pitched whine when it passed Cassie's stomach. The matron scowled in puzzlement and placed her hand flat on my niece's black velvet blouse near the abdomen.

"I've got a pierced belly button." Cassie lifted the tail of her blouse to show it. "Sorry, I should have guessed it was gonna set the thing off."

The matron nodded and pointed her toward the back of the conveyor belt. My niece grabbed her pack and ran, turning once on her way to the gate to wave goodbye.

7

I BAILED MY Cadillac out of the garage the next morning, engine tuned, lubricants and filters changed, rear bumper replaced, right rear fender mended, and a new money-green paint job shining from hood to trunk. A twenty-something punk in a BMW Z3 had rear-ended me two weeks before as I braked for a yellow traffic signal outside Beverly Hills. The driver wore a cell-phone headset as good as surgically implanted into his ear when he stepped out of the car, and as he strode to inspect the damage he complained to the head-set—presumably he was talking to someone—that a stupid bitch had slammed on the brakes in front of him and now he was going to be late to his meeting. The Caddy was a vintage '70s Eldorado, five thousand pounds of rusting steel and pitted chrome, and the Z3 had crumpled like a bird against bulletproof glass. When he saw the damage up close, he jabbed the stubby antenna of his cell toward my chest and screamed, "It was a fucking yellow light! Nobody in L.A. brakes on yellow!"

At the garage I bid farewell to the four hamsters powering the Chevy Metro, bent to kiss the Caddy's laurel-wreath hood insignia, happy to have a real car again, and drove to the converted sewage-works warehouse that served as the corporate offices of *Scandal Times*. While I joined Frank in his office the Rott stayed outside to play a little ball with the security guard, something they both liked to do. I plugged the digital camera into the back of Frank's computer and watched the downloaded images in a silence broken by his loud sighs of disappointment. He didn't blame me for the unimaginative framing and ho-hum staging, he said, certainly aware that such a statement was a backhanded way of blaming me. He knew I'd been shocked by the death of my model. But the results spoke for themselves, and they spoke badly. The images might work for mid-paper, continuation-of-story visuals but didn't have enough zing for the first three pages, and if they dared put one of them on the cover, the entire *Scandal Times* readership would fall asleep in the supermarket checkout line from sheer boredom.

"We'll run a vidcap for the front-page visual," he said. "Blow up just the image of her face, play the angle that the killer sent you the video. That ties the murder directly into *Scandal Times,* makes us look like a central player in the investigation, even if the cops are ignoring my calls at present."

I unplugged the camera and packed my gear. The thought of running an image from the video sickened me, but Frank was right; the photographs I took in Malibu weren't dramatic enough to sell the story. Every issue hit the stands with a photograph of a celebrity or some type of mayhem, and preferably both. If the story didn't get to the front page, someone who had seen Christine in the company of her murderer would be less likely to notice. Front-page publicity was essential to collecting casual eyewitness evidence like that. And I was going to be part of the story whether I liked it or not.

"Why did he send the disk to me?" I zipped the camera bag and thought about it. "Why not send it to the *Times?*"

"Publicity. The *Times* wouldn't put it on the front page."

"How does that matter to him?"

"I'm a tabloid journalist, not a psychologist."

"So make something up."

"I'm good at that, right?" He groped toward a box of donuts, looking for a sugar rush to help him think. "Let's say Christine isn't his first, let's say he assaulted that girl out in Palmdale. You know the details of that?"

"None."

"A hiker found her near a popular trail, half naked and her neck bruised. She couldn't remember how she got there. Loss of memory, that's one of the effects of Rohypnol. Her larynx was crushed. She couldn't even speak. Whoever assaulted her came within a few seconds of killing her but stopped."

"Do the police think it's the same guy?"

"Too early to tell. But let's speculate."

"He's not the spontaneous type," I offered.

"You're right there," Frank said, nodding. "He doesn't pick up some girl hitchhiking, strangle her on a whim and dump her in the desert, not this guy. If Christine is typical, he mounts a production. He scouts a location and sets up his bondage and video equipment like a director or film producer."

"Maybe he even pretends to be one," I said, and told Frank about Christine's plan to meet someone who claimed to be Johnny Depp's assistant.

"Depp's assistant? What a headline! And she believed it?"

"Actresses are desperate, you know that."

"Maybe he comes on like somebody important to gain just enough of her trust to slip a ruffie into her drink, or even better, maybe he is somebody important, though certainly not Depp's assistant." He yanked open a desk drawer organized like a garbage dump and rifled it. "You saw the video. Do you think he could be a pro?"

"No idea."

"Would it help to see it again?"

"I thought you gave the disk to Sean."

"I burned a copy first—that's how we'll grab the vidcap." He pulled a plastic CD sleeve from the back of the drawer, shook loose a disk, and fed it into his computer. "Imagine going to all that effort. Location, lights, camera, stirring performances, and nobody notices. The girl in Palmdale, she's just another victim to the cops, a sad and tragic story but nothing they don't deal with fifty times a year. Her story makes the front page of the *Antelope Valley Press*—a box in the lower right corner, no headline—but the *L.A. Times* and *Daily News* bury it in the journalistic equivalent of where the sun don't shine. It's like he released a film into an empty theater. Nobody even noticed. So he decides to do it again, and this time, send a copy to the press. No way he's going to be ignored a second time."

I drifted behind Frank to stand and watch the parts of the video that I could stomach, too uneasy to pull up a chair. A small, black box popped onto the screen of Frank's computer. He pressed a few keys and the video zoomed full screen, Christine already chained to the wall, sheathed in latex, a black ball strapped into her mouth. From the angle and steadiness of image, the camera looked to be mounted on a tripod in the corner of the room. The lens framed her in long shot, no sound, the frame wide enough to show a section of cream-colored wall and a wide swath of ceramic-tiled floor, the white of each tile enclosing a gold, Walk of Fame–style star. Her arms hung slack against the chains, hips thrust back as she stooped slightly forward. She glanced over her shoulder toward the camera as though she watched someone behind the lens, even though the man who assaulted her entered the frame from the opposite side of the room.

I mentioned the discrepancy in her eye line.

"Someone on ruffies, they don't know up from down," Frank said. "She may be looking but I don't think she's seeing much of anything."

The man approached Christine with a strutting confidence, a black latex suit stretched taut over a tall, athletic frame that matched Rakaan's and a hundred thousand others. His lips protruded like obscene fruit from a slit cut at the mouth of his hood, and twists of latex cowled his eyes in a nightmare image of man as Minotaur. I couldn't distinguish man from beast behind the mask. She flinched when he first touched her from behind, perhaps not expecting someone to come from the opposite side. She bucked away, once, as he mounted her, but he was big if not particularly strong, and Christine was a small girl, drugged and bound to the wall. She didn't have much of a chance to resist. He outweighed her by more than fifty pounds. But still, she seemed resigned to the act, and if I hadn't seen the violent end, I could have mistaken it for a harmless game of bondage captured on home video.

"Whoever shot this left the sound off," Frank said, fiddling with the sound control at the base of the player. "Or maybe he purposely exported the video file without sound before burning the disk."

As I watched the scenario play out I tried to remove any thoughts of Christine from my mind, and above all from my heart. I didn't need another excuse to break down in tears. I needed to watch the video for evidence of the identity of the killer, and so I told myself that this wasn't Christine being violated, this wasn't how she spent her final moments, gagged and raped on camera, drugged so far out of her mind that she may not have been all that aware of what was happening to her, but when the killer looped the strap around her throat and jerked her head back so sharply it could have broken her neck I couldn't keep my eyes on her approaching death and glanced away the moment a ghosted image flitted across the corner of the screen.

"Stop, go back." I grabbed Frank's arm so fiercely he nearly jumped out of his chair in fright.

"What is it?" He lurched forward to pause the video.

"Can you play it back in slow motion?"

He hadn't seen it, his eyes focused like Sean's two nights before on the act of strangulation, not on the periphery. The action reversed looked not much different from the action in forward motion, just a little more hellish.

"Where's the light source?" I asked, and when Frank guessed it came from somewhere in the ceiling, out of frame, I traced the way the shadows from the chains binding Christine slanted right to left on the wall. "Light from directly overhead, the shadows would hang straight down, and you'd get subtle hot spots on the black latex here." I pointed to a small, glinting reflection of light on her right shoulder, then traced a closely observed line to the upper right corner of the screen. "From the angle of the shadow and the positioning of hot spots on the latex you can track the source of the light, probably a portable film light on a stand, mounted maybe eight feet high. Look, see the way the wall is brighter on the right side of the screen than the left?"

"Okay, I'm convinced," Frank said. "But so what?"

"So watch the lower right corner of the screen, the floor there."

The action moved forward again, the killer unbuckling a strap that circled his chest and looping it around Christine's neck, and when he jerked the strap taut, crossing his wrists behind her neck to increase the killing power of his hold, a shadow crossed the floor in the lower right corner of the frame. "See it?" I said, gripping his arm again. "Go back and freeze the image if you can."

Frank inched the action backward and stopped. The shadow hovered from right to left on the floor, a gray ghost on the white and gold tiles, squat head and shoulders clearly defined on a curiously compressed torso—the type of shadow cast by a strong light placed above and behind a man.

"They aren't alone in the room," I said.

8

WE DROVE THE Antelope Valley Freeway out of Los Angeles late that morning, top down on the Cadillac, the Rott banished to the back to make room for Frank, who huddled with the cell phone in the passenger seat, his forefinger plugging the opposite ear to block the wind noise while he made one call after another, tracking down leads to the Palmdale assault. The Caddy's air conditioner had expired long before I bought her, and as we approached the 25,000-square-mile hot plate of the Mojave Desert, the dry, hot air whipping over the windshield did no more than wick away the sweat like a combination fan and blast furnace. As I drove, I thought about why the killer had sent the video to me care of *Scandal Times*. Frank had said he wanted publicity. That raised a question that made me even more uncomfortable than the heat: Why Christine? Enough people had died around me that I sometimes felt like a modern Typhoid Mary, an unwitting carrier of death to those I touched. I didn't want to think about it anymore. I noticed Frank checking his notes between calls and asked, "How do you know Sean?"

He said something I couldn't hear above the noise of the road, something about a club. At speeds above forty-five miles per hour, holding a conversation in the Cadillac was like shouting into gale-force winds.

"I met him in a strip club," he repeated, this time shouting.

"What was he doing there?"

He looked at me like I'd just asked a particularly stupid question.

"Okay," I said. "What were you doing there?"

"Same thing Sean was," he said and laughed. "He used to work undercover. This was before you started shooting freelance for us, before he got promoted to Homicide."

"What station?"

"North Hollywood now. Van Nuys before that."

"He was working undercover when you met him?"

Frank put his cell phone away and pulled down the bill of his baseball cap. "I thought he was just another sleazeball in a strip club, like me, even if I was working on a piece at the time."

"A piece of what?" I asked.

"Journalism, wiseass. We were doing a series on amazing identical twins, you know, one case study a week, each written up by a different reporter, and I drew stripper siblings from Scandinavia, Fawn and Dawn Svedenson."

"Their real names?"

"Hardly. Try Cristina and Krisztina Szegedi from Budapest." He smiled as though remembering something pleasant. "They didn't quite have the Swedish accent down but I think I was the only one in the joint who noticed, besides Sean."

"So he was working undercover," I said.

"What do you care?"

He stared at me with a little too much curiosity.

"Because I'm trying to figure out how you knew he was a cop."

"I interviewed him after he got his transfer to North Hollywood, remembered drooling next to him at the strip-club bar. We're both from the north side of Chicago, originally." He pointed to the Cubs logo on his baseball cap. "When we were at the bar he asked me why I wore the cap and I told him because I was a rabid Cubs fan suffering from premature male-pattern baldness. We talked baseball—this was the year Sammy Sosa and Mark McGwire were breaking Maris's record—and when I mentioned I worked for a newspaper he vanished like a vampire. I thought he was a drug dealer at the time, because, you know, what do drug dealers do for entertainment except go to strip clubs? And he looked like one."

I thought I should just drop it there, knowing any more questions would tip Frank something was going on, but I couldn't help it, I had to know. "Did you tell him anything about me? That night, I mean, when he came to the show."

"Why? Did he make a move on you? And more important, did you knock his teeth out?"

"Did you tell him anything about my history?"

He settled into the wedge between the seat and door to watch me while I drove, looking for signs of embarrassment or dissimulation. I adjusted my sunglasses and draped my wrist over the wheel to conceal the fluttering in my stomach.

"That was fast," he said.

I glanced down at the speedometer, said, "I'm barely doing seventy."

"You just met and already you're banging each other?"

"Just answer the question."

"No, I didn't tell him you're an ex-con on parole." He pursed his lips and whistled a high note. "When he finds out it's gonna be like a dog discovering he's sniffing the tail of a cat in doggie drag."

We met Charlotte McGregor near the student cafeteria at Antelope Valley College, a flat desert campus of concrete buildings huddled low to the ground against the heat, students picking their way from shade tree to shade tree along the concrete paths. Charlotte waved to us from the trunk of a poplar tree a few steps from the cafeteria entrance, wearing a champagne-colored cotton jacquard dress that fell just above the knee and a gold silk scarf tied loosely around her neck. Even at a distance her beauty was striking, her hair the color of weathered brick and her pale skin an act of defiance against the desert sun, but like a trick of perspective she didn't get much bigger as we approached, her height about eight inches short of fashion-model regulation, reminding me of a young Holly Hunter. She studied acting in the Theater Arts Department, Frank told me, and hoped to be admitted into UCLA for the coming fall semester. Charlotte extended a shy hand, and when she spoke her voice rustled and creaked like the broken reed of a clarinet.

"I'm sorry," she whispered, high cheekbones flushing a vibrant pink against her pale skin. "My voice hasn't recovered yet. Maybe we should get started? I'll fill you in while we drive out to where I met him."

Charlotte began communicating with the man who claimed to be Brad Pitt's assistant through Hotornot.com, a dating website devoted to the game of rating sexual attractiveness on a scale of one to ten. He'd been one of hundreds to respond to her photograph and bio— she'd scored a 9.8, she said—and they e-mailed back and forth for a week before agreeing to meet. She'd thought posting on the website would be a good way to hook up with people in L.A. She wanted to become an actress and spoke of the same kind of discovered-in-a-drugstore dream most young actresses have—a small but significant role in an independent film or television show that would launch her career. Los Angeles can be cruel to aspiring actresses.

The Starbucks where they initially met was separated from campus by a few barren miles of landscape notable for the lack of anything in particular to look at, the broad streets laid out on a grid and named after numbers or famous letters in the alphabet, as though something a little more distinctive might ruin the minimalist effect of the place. Outside, the Starbucks offered a drive-through service window for those who had been permanently grafted to the seats of their vehicles. Inside, it looked like just about every other outlet and the coffee tasted the same, which is what most people accept as the charm of the place, if such a thing can be said to exist. I leashed the Rott to a handicapped parking sign near the shaded entrance and followed Charlotte and Frank up to the service counter. The coffee shop's air conditioner had been set to stun, the effect of walking in from the hot desert like jumping from a sauna into a cold pool.

"What made you believe he was Brad Pitt's assistant?" Frank asked.

"He sent me a snapshot of him and Brad hanging out together at some event, a film premiere maybe." She paused at the baked goods counter, staring at her reflection in the glass. "I mean, why wouldn't I think he was legit? Sure, maybe he could be exaggerating about the assistant thing, maybe he'd show up and say he'd worked as an assistant on a film that starred Brad Pitt, sorry for the misunderstanding. But you have to understand, where I am now?" She turned her head from the glass to give us a look both grim and self-disparaging. "Even a gofer seems glamorous. Anybody connected to the film business is a step up from Palmdale. Of course it turned out the picture was a fake." She stepped up to the counter to order a cup of Nepalese tea from the *barista*.

"What did he say his name was?" Frank asked.

"Tyler Durden."

"Tyler Durden? *Fight Club*, right?"

"The movie? Wasn't it incredible?" She smiled and for a moment she seemed transported, one memory connecting to another, until the smile abruptly dropped from her lips. "He played Tyler Durden. Brad Pitt. In the movie. That was his character name." She brushed a strand of hair from her face, hand trembling. "He used Brad Pitt's character name as his own and I didn't even recognize it. I'm too stupid to live."

She picked up her tea and walked toward a window table lacquered in sunlight, hung her purse by its strap on the chair back, and sat down facing the front. I liked the look of the sun slanting across her face, tinting her skin gold and lighting the tips of her long, red eyelashes, but I didn't want to pull out my camera, not yet. A photograph of the teary-eyed victim might sell to the readers of *Scandal Times*, but I didn't want to traumatize her. I didn't normally care so much about these things. Maybe her lack of size inspired the kind of compassion I felt for children. Maybe I felt that through her, the one who lived, I could soothe Christine's ghost. I again observed how small she was, her wrists the size of a champagne flute. Christine in heels didn't reach five foot seven, and she'd weighed less than 110 pounds. Maybe Christine and Charlotte had been stalked and seized not just for their beauty but for their size; small girls are easier to physically control and dominate.

"You told the cops the name, of course." Frank took a chair at the two-seater next to her table. I wasn't surprised he'd caught the reference to *Fight Club;* trivia like that stuck to his mind like pasta to a wall.

"They didn't say anything about it one way or another," she said.

"That doesn't mean they didn't get the reference. I'm a big fan of the police. Most of the time they do a great job, given the resources at their disposal, particularly homicide detectives. But they aren't exactly open about sharing information." He popped the top of his medium-sized coffee to let it cool. "What time were you scheduled to meet Mr. Durden?"

"Four. But then he didn't show and I started to feel incredibly anxious, you know? Like wondering if he'd set me up as some kind of joke, this hick girl from Palmdale." She glanced out the window, her fingers cupped around the tea like a prop, though she showed no intention of drinking it. "Sometimes I get myself so emotionally wound up about things I make myself sick, you know? I mean, like, literally. I thought it was that, at first."

"You started to feel, what . . . sick . . . drugged?"

"I didn't know what I felt like, to tell the truth. I don't do drugs, not really, just a joint every now and then." She stared at the ceiling and bit her lower lip. "Don't print that, okay? About the joint."

Frank shrugged, said, "I think I can forget I heard that without losing my journalistic integrity. But you knew something was wrong."

She nodded and rotated the cup in her hands a half circle, the bottom rim scratching softly on the table top. "When it kept getting worse I thought I was having an allergic reaction to the tea. But a few minutes later, I really didn't care. I didn't feel anxious anymore. I felt really good, kind of heavy and super relaxed, like I didn't want to move but that was all right, I could just sit there and watch the sun set and it was all good."

"Do you remember leaving the café? Or did you black out?"

"Wait a minute, let's back up here." I drew a flicking, annoyed glance from Frank, who didn't like to be interrupted when interviewing a subject. "Did you notice anyone in line behind you? Someone who might have reached across the counter while you were picking up your tea?"

The shake of her head was quick and tight, as though she'd already been asked this question. "The store was pretty empty. I mean, I wasn't the only one in here but there wasn't a line. But I think I know why you're asking. The cops wanted to know the same thing, after they gave up on the idea that I'd taken the drug 'recreationally,' as they put it."

"They said that?"

"They were real assholes when they first picked me up. Thought I'd been out raving the night before, got so stoned I passed out, implied the whole thing was my fault. But the doctor who examined me, she was good, she knew I'd been strangled, and . . ." She compressed her lips tightly and took a deep breath. ". . . that other thing, the rape, she saw that, too. When I told her how I couldn't remember what happened, she asked me to pee in a cup, and the whatchacallit, the urinalysis, showed positive for Rohypnol."

"Can you remember anything that happened between the time you ordered the tea and when you started to feel different?" I asked. "Did anyone approach or talk to you?"

She touched the scarf at her throat, a quick gesture to check its position, and nodded. "Less than five minutes after I sat down, this guy? He came toward the window, and it was like he wasn't watching where he was going, he bumped into me." She lifted her tea and wobbled the table. "You can see, the tables aren't so stable, so he reached down, like immediately, to hold it, and of course some of the tea spilled, so he got a napkin to wipe it up."

I didn't notice a dispenser on any of the tables.

"Where did he get the napkin?"

She pulled her head back an inch, surprised by the question, and it took her a moment to remember. "He had it with him. Had to. He was mopping up where the tea spilled a second after he bumped the table." She pushed her tea forward and folded her hands carefully in front of her, the pressure of her grip reddening the tips of her fingers. "Do you think he was the one who drugged me? You think he put something in my tea?"

"No way the *barista* does it," Frank said, glancing toward the service counter. "Unless he leaves the country the next day. The guy who bumped the table, what did he look like? Can you describe him?"

"I can try." She closed her eyes and tilted her head toward the ceiling. "He wasn't big or small, kind of average in height. About my age. I can't describe his face in detail because he wore sunglasses and one of those floppy hats guys like to wear. You know what they look like?"

"Bucket hats," Frank said. "Like a fisherman's hat."

"Exactly. This one was sky blue, with a red band. What else?" She tapped her index finger against her knuckle and nodded. "Right. A faded red sweatshirt turned inside out, his jeans fashionably baggy, but not hip-hop baggy, more surfer baggy. I got the idea he was posh."

"Why posh?" Frank asked. "A lot of young guys dress that way."

"But only someone who comes from money, serious money, knows how to put it all together so perfectly. It's like they all go to some fashion school for rich kids, learn how to get the perfect slumming look." An expression of pure class awareness lodged in her eyes, as though she so keenly felt the differences in class that she'd become expert in spotting them, something I'd noticed in those with money and in the less advantaged driven to achieve financial and social success. "It was in his voice too the way he talked. He had that lazy, laid-back kind of voice, like he didn't have to bother with things like money or achievement because he'd been born with his, you know what I mean? He wasn't from around here, that's for sure."

"Did he stick around?" Frank asked.

She shook her head. "He went into the bathroom, I guess to wash his hands or something, and then he took off."

"How long before you started to feel funny?"

"About twenty minutes, I think. Long enough to drink my tea, and worry that the guy I was supposed to meet wasn't going to show. After that, I don't remember things so clearly."

"Do you remember how you got out of the café?"

She shook her head and said, "Vaguely. I remember somebody came up, said he was Tyler Durden. I remember hearing his voice, hearing him say his name, but I can't remember what he looked like. Wait a minute!" She nodded, remembering. "He was standing behind me. That's why I couldn't see him. He was standing behind me, asking if I was okay, and then he helped me up, out of the café, and into a car."

"Do you remember what kind of car?"

She cupped her hands to her face, hiding a grimace. "It gets really blurry after that. I see shapes, colors, light, but it's all like a ghost world. The car?" She shook her head. "Black. We took a drive, then I remember a room somewhere. I think he must have kept drugging me because I blank out completely after that. I can't even remember him, you know, doing things to me. Not really. All I remember after that is coming out of it, sitting in the desert, half my clothes flung around me, the other half just gone."

Charlotte tugged at the loose knot tying the scarf around her neck, her lips drawn into a tight, defiant line. The scarf slipped away to reveal a faint bruise the width of a purse strap circling her throat and two thumb-sized blotches of purple on opposite sides of her larynx. "The doctor can't tell me when I'll be able to regain my voice." She nodded as though coming to some decision with herself and swiftly unclasped the hook at the back of her dress, pulled down the zipper, and turned in her chair to show us the cross-hatching of faded red welts between her shoulder blades. "I asked the doctor about these. She said it looked like somebody whipped me."

She zipped up the back of her dress but couldn't locate the clasp.

When I reached over to help her she thanked me, her voice cracking right down the middle, and she bit her lip, hard, to keep from crying. "How can I be an actress with a voice like this?" she croaked. "How can I play to the back of the theater if the audience can't hear me in the front row?"

9

THEY BURIED CHRISTINE about a hundred feet from U.S. Highway 99 in Cherokee Memorial Park just outside of Lodi, the pastor's portable sound system dueling with the diesel roar of produce trucks plying the lettuce route between Stockton and Sacramento. I stood outside the immediate ring of mourners, more interested in witnessing the service through the lens of my Canon than aligning myself with Christine's old friends from high school, her new friends from Los Angeles, or the members of her family. I didn't know her as well as the others who gathered for the funeral and I hadn't driven three hundred miles just to mourn her passing. My motives were more complicated.

The pastor eulogized Christine with platitudes that sounded to my ear more predictable of a small-town girl than accurate of a big-city one. I knew little about her life except that it had been short, and remarkable mostly in the brutality of her death. She had been born in Lodi twenty-one years before they buried her, the third child of five. Her mother served in the local Methodist church as a secretary and her father worked as the manager of a chain supermarket. She hadn't excelled in school except for the theater arts classes she took in her junior and senior years. Even though she'd been dragged to church every Sunday, she never had been particularly devout. At the age of sixteen she had—to the dismay of her parents—simply refused to go anymore, except for Easter and Christmas services. On her eighteenth birthday she took a Greyhound bus to Los Angeles.

I wasn't the only one who felt more comfortable standing away from the cluster of family and friends. Dr. James Rakaan stood several steps beyond the fringe of the crowd, eyes cloaked behind Dolce

& Gabbana wraparound sunglasses, his long black hair waving dramatically to the shoulders of a black suit. The suit tapered to his waist in a way that only the finest tailoring can provide and a single white lily dangled by its stem from his clasped hands. If *GQ* ever decided to come out with a special funeral style issue, he was ready to model for it. Though I hesitated to take photographs while the pastor spoke, a man sitting in the passenger seat of a sedan parked on the fringe of a nearby service road wasn't so timid, taping the crowd with a video camera. I traced the line of his lens. He thought Dr. Rakaan looked as photogenic as I did. I wondered if the cameraman worked for the local police department or had driven north from Los Angeles.

A flutter of white in the cemetery beyond Rakaan caught my eye and I shifted a step to get a clearer view. The tissue wrapping a bouquet of flowers flapped in the breeze, lightly held by a man in a sport coat who squatted over a distant headstone as though he'd come to pay his respects to a dead relative. I caught my smile before it surfaced and forced it back down. Sean. He noticed when I raised my camera to look at him and blew me a kiss. Very funny.

A good documentary photographer sees not only through the lens but also to the side of the frame, a difficult trick to master but critical in catching a more arresting image to photograph or a rock hurled at her head. While I watched Sean through the viewfinder my opposite eye caught a glimpse of a young man at the back of the crowd looking away, as though trying to keep his face out of the shot. Like Rakaan, he wore a black suit and black sunglasses, and though his hair was blond he too wore it long, in the style of young Kurt Cobain, a combination surfer-grunge look. He stood so far to the side of the frame the movement wouldn't have diverted my attention for more than a moment had he not looked out of place. None of Christine's friends from L.A. dressed like him; most wore oddly matched clothing of various colors, including red and yellow, as though they wanted to celebrate her life more than her death. Her local friends dressed more traditionally, the young men in sport coats and slacks but nothing so obviously Italian. He looked like he'd stumbled across the wrong funeral, as though he hadn't known Christine well enough to have met her friends or family.

He might be her secret lover, I speculated, or just a casual one who'd fallen for her more than she cared for him, someone who still carried a bright enough torch to see his way to her funeral. And he was rich, I thought. Like Charlotte, I had an eye for the telling differences between the rich and the rest of us, particularly those born into money. I saw it in his clothes and the way he stood, and I'm sure if I'd been able to get close enough I would have seen it in his hands.

I lowered the camera and strolled clockwise around the back of the crowd, looking for a better shooting angle like a wolf looks to cull a herd, and when he glanced back to see where I'd moved, what I was doing, I took his photograph. He looked young, no more than nineteen or twenty, the wisps of hair on his chin as thin as cigarette smoke. I lowered my head when the pastor spoke in prayer and I added my own to go along with the official one, nothing poetic, just rest in peace and all that, and when he said amen the crowd broke apart.

Nephthys stood arm in arm with two young women, one with long, blonde dreadlocks and the other with home-chopped hair dyed red and black. As I walked toward her someone touched my elbow from behind, as though trying to catch me, and I turned to a petite young blonde in a long-sleeved black blouse and iron-gray skirt, her makeup tracked by dried tears.

"I'm Tamara, Christine's roommate; we haven't met yet." She hooked her hair behind her ears and stared at me with granite-gray eyes both curious and a little afraid, her immaculately pinked lips twitching as though smiling came so naturally to her she needed consciously to repress it. "You're Nina Zero, right? The photographer? I just got back from location yesterday, I can't believe what's happened, I'm just in like total shock. Total."

"Like everybody," I said. "You were where, Canada?"

"Toronto. That's where we were shooting. It's cheaper up there— at least, that's what they tell me."

"It must have been hard on you."

She looked confused.

"Not to be here, when your roommate was murdered," I said.

"Oh yeah, totally." She shrugged, a gesture she meant to convey helplessness. "We talked on the phone, like, every couple of days, so it's not like I felt out of touch. Christine was so happy she was going to be in your show. She was struggling, you know? Going to auditions, doing a small part here or there, the typical struggling actress life, but nothing that made her feel good about herself, and when she saw I was starting to get work, it was like really hard for her. I know what it's like to struggle, believe me. 'You're going to be next,' I'd say, you know, trying to get her to believe in herself." Her smile finally broke through, unrepressed, a bright and shiny show of teeth and lips. "But the photos? She thought they were way cool. Believe me, I was sad I couldn't break away from shooting to fly down, attend the premiere." The recognition of something horrible flew across her face like a shadow. "Of course, she was already dead by then, at least, that's what I've been told."

"Can we talk about this later?" I asked. "Not here, not at the funeral."

"Of course." She stepped quickly back, thinking she'd offended me.

"We'll meet in L.A.?" I reached out and touched her arm. "I want to talk to you, not like this, but really sit down and talk."

"Christine was into some wicked dark stuff," she whispered. "But she had a great heart." She crossed her arms over her chest and moved toward the chapel, her steps long and careful around headstones set flush in the ground. She knew I worked for a tabloid. Her comment about Christine hadn't been malicious, but she was letting me know she had a story to tell and assumed I'd already heard enough to understand the reference to dark stuff. She looked back, once, to mime a phone with her thumb and little finger and mouth the words, "call me."

Further on, Nephthys walked toward the chapel with a group of L.A. friends. Between the growls of trucks on Highway 99 I heard the sweet sound of their singing, "If I Ever Leave This World Alive," a song I recognized from an Irish band, Flogging Molly. Nobody like the Irish to celebrate the dead. I knew I'd start crying if I listened to more than a verse and struck out across the cemetery, spotting the distant figure of the young man in the black suit. He strode casually beside a group of locals who headed for their cars as quickly as they could without breaking into a sprint.

I veered across a short stretch of verdant lawn, rounded the back corner of a massive concrete mausoleum, and ran, out of sight of the others, for the length of the building, intent on reaching the parking lot in time to see if the kind of car he drove matched my expectations. At the far end of the mausoleum a circular fountain sprayed water in long, pulsing arcs, and beyond that stretched the parking lot, studded with cars. I skidded to a stroll. The young man in the black suit hurried across the asphalt and stopped improbably to key the door of a vanilla Hyundai Sonata, a car so plain even suburban dads thought it too conservative. I crouched behind the fountain and maxed out the lens to full telephoto, framing the rear bumper as the Hyundai lurched away.

At the sound of footsteps behind me I glanced over my shoulder. Sean jogged toward the fountain, his hands swinging free. He'd left the flowers behind. A dozen yards distant he stopped and caught his breath. "If you don't want to talk, just say so. You don't have to run away from me."

"What are you talking about?"

"You didn't hear me?"

I raised the camera and took a quick candid, his hand on his hip, doubt in his eyes.

"Not since I gave you Christine's photograph."

"I was just calling your name, back there," he said, ignoring the dig.

"Didn't hear you."

I kept the camera to my eye, aware that it distanced him, and snapped the shutter on his wry smile. He stepped forward, forcing me to lower the lens when his face blurred the lens, too close to focus.

"You see something interesting?"

"Did a second ago." I turned away from him, toward the parking lot. "Young guy in a black suit, expensive cut, didn't look like he knew anybody here. You notice him, too?"

"I was looking at other things, mostly," he said, looking at me. "You already got the pictures you need? You mind if we take a walk?"

I capped the lens and slung the Canon over my shoulder, stomach jittery in a way that I'd never before experienced in my many and varied experiences with the law. I always felt uneasy around cops, particularly when they wanted to talk to me. The act of passion we'd committed earlier that week only made it worse and as we stepped away from the fountain the fluttering in my stomach turned to nausea, the result of combining my fear of the I-don't-think-we-should-see-each-other-again speech with my dread of the I'm-going-to-have-to-arrest-you lecture. "Did you get my messages about Christine's diary and her so-called therapist, Dr. Rakaan?" I asked, seeking distraction.

"Yeah. I passed it on," he said.

"Passed it on? To who?"

"To Parker Center," he said, referring to the administrative center of the Los Angeles Police Department. "They probably shared it with LASD but it's their case now. Nobody's contacted you yet?"

"You're not working on it?"

"It's not like the news business, it's not like I get the exclusive because a source handed me some evidence." He pointed us toward an older section of the cemetery, behind the mausoleum, where the funereal style changed from mower-friendly headstones set flush in the grass to the granite rectangles, arcs, and spires of traditional memorials. "Every department works from a certain geographical region. Christine lived in Los Feliz, that's in the Northeast Station. I work out of North Hollywood. And her remains were recovered by LASD—an entirely different jurisdiction. Right now it's been kicked over to the big dogs working Robbery Homicide out of Parker Center. You know those guys?"

"Not personally," I said.

"Good thing," he said, as though he hinted at something else. "Anything that crosses jurisdictional lines, it's their bone. And when I say big dogs, I mean they growl and I back off. Right now RHD and the Sheriff's Department are, quote, cooperating, unquote, with each other. I'm just as happy to stay clear of it."

"RHD, they also take on high-profile cases, serial killings too, right?"

He looked at me as though he suspected I knew more than he

thought I did. "O. J., Blake, Spector, RHD gets all the big ones. Some guy stabs his wife because she burnt the toast, I get the call."

"So what are you doing up here?"

"It's a personal thing." He stared down at his feet as we stepped onto the grass of the old section. "Whenever there's a funeral in a case that involves me, I go."

I knew investigators attended funerals to observe and often videotape the results—hence the guy with the camera in the parked car—but Sean didn't talk about it like police procedure, like just another part of the job. "The flowers," I said, momentarily touched by his compassion. "They were for Christine."

He paused at a waist-high white marble tombstone set on a pedestal, braced himself against its arched top, and watched me as though carefully preparing what he wished to say.

"Why didn't you tell me you were on parole?"

"When did I get a chance to talk to you about anything?" I walked to a granite headstone with a pitched roof, like a little house, and stood behind it, braced like Sean for an argument. "You have my phone number. You want to know anything about me, all you gotta do is call the number."

"I'm not the most by-the-book cop in the world," he said. "I thought I could deal with the tabloid stuff. Sure, somebody might get their boxers in a twist, warn me about compromising an investigation by talking to you about one case or another, but cops and reporters have dated before, and you're a photographer, not a writer, so you'd be even less of a threat. And North Hollywood, it's not exactly jam-packed with the kinds of stories *Scandal Times* likes to print. So what was anybody going to say, in the end? I can deal with rumor and innuendo, done it my whole career. If we don't talk about cases, nobody could say anything." His hand shot to the Windsor knotting his tie and pulled it loose so fast and hard he nearly popped the top button. "I hate ties," he said, angry now, at the tie, at the situation, at me. "I always feel like I'm going to strangle when I wear one. I think I must have been hanged in a past life."

When he pulled the tie from his collar I noticed a dark bruise on his throat, and while I was wondering if he'd worn the tie to conceal the bruise I realized that was where my lip had fastened to him the night we'd lost ourselves; I'd marked him.

"You said something about dating," I said. "I don't remember being asked out on a date."

"A euphemism." He stuffed the rolled tie into the side pocket of his sport coat. "Do you know what happens to me if we're caught dating, or whatever it is you want to call it? It's against regulations for a cop to be romantically involved with a parolee. Maybe they won't take my badge for it but they'd punch my ticket to someplace like the Pawn Shop Unit, where I'd spend the rest of my career checking swap meets for stolen watches. They'd slaughter me."

"Who said anything about romantic involvement? You don't even return my phone calls. You think I'm going to let myself get involved with someone doesn't even have the common decency to call me back? Why are we even talking about this?" I turned and walked away, got as far as the next headstone before I stopped, circled back around to face him. Why didn't he simply pretend nothing had happened? That would have been the easy way out. To argue about our relationship as though we had one was ridiculous. We'd never appeared together in public. No one saw what happened in the darkroom. To my knowledge, then, no evidence existed of our lovemaking. If all he wanted was to protect his career, he'd stonewall me. Why make himself even more vulnerable by admitting to me the risk he faced? Did he suspect I'd hidden a camera somewhere in the darkroom and filmed our encounter? "Do you think I'm going to blackmail you? Is that what you think?"

He looked up at me from beneath his brows, eyes screened by the angle, then back down to his hands. "No," he said. "I don't think that."

"Because as far as I'm concerned, nothing happened."

"I'm glad forgetting is so easy for you."

"Easy?" I wanted to knock him onto his smug behind. "I did not plan what happened in that darkroom. I didn't set you up. I didn't even come on to you. The last thing I expected was to be overwhelmed by passion while printing a photograph for a homicide detective. When did I have the chance to say anything to you? It was over before I even knew what hit me. I'm supposed to tell you my entire life history the moment we shake hands hello? Maybe you should have made your intentions clear at the start. Maybe you should have told me the photograph was just a pretext for something else on your late-night agenda."

"I didn't know what was going to happen that night," he said. "Not consciously."

"You're an ex–undercover vice detective. You've lived half your life with your left hand not knowing what your right hand is doing."

He drew his head back like a hammer and a surprised laugh shot from him. "Your aim is lethal, you know that?" He spread the lapels to his sport coat, as though baring his heart to a firing squad. "You want to shoot me dead, here I am."

"I don't want to shoot you. I want to know your intentions."

"I don't know what my intentions are." The sport coat draped shut and he leaned one hand against the tombstone, the other cocked on his hip. "I know how I felt the night I met you. I know that much. And I know how I felt when I learned you were on parole."

"What do you want me to say, that I'm sorry I am who I am, that I've done what I've done?" I stepped away from the headstone, let him look at me head to toe. "I'm not. You can't pick one part of me, throw away the other. And the fact that you even want to try means you don't know me."

"And you? Do you know anything about me?"

I walked toward him, the pained and wary expression on his face like the look of an animal with a trap-caught paw. Then I reached out and pushed him, just hard enough to move him off his spot. He laughed, surprised, but he didn't push me back. "This thing blindsided both of us," I said. "Maybe we should look at it like just another L.A. moment, nothing more than a late-night traffic accident, a fender-bender, no one seriously hurt, nothing more significant than an exchange of phone numbers and a few minutes lost by the side of the road."

The muscles at the hinge of his jaw flexed like something alive beneath the surface of his skin and he nodded, once, obviously unhappy and just as obviously relieved. I resisted the temptation to raise my camera and capture that look on film, instead glanced down at the shoebox-sized marker at my feet. A cursive script carved into granite the name of the person buried below, followed by the dates *October 30, 1932–October 31, 1932.*

The poor child had lived a day and died.

An appropriate epitaph for my relationship with Sean.

10

MY PAROLE OFFICER decided Monday morning at seven o'clock was as good a time as any for an unannounced search of my apartment, her stentorian knock startling the Rott into a fit of barking that didn't stop until I crawled out of bed and creaked open the door. When I complained about the hour she tartly suggested I look at the parole agreement I signed upon release from prison, and then she proceeded to cite the relevant section in the event I'd forgotten. "You, your residence, and property can be searched any time of the day or night—" She glanced over the shoulder of her gray blazer as she attacked my kitchen cabinet, emphasizing the word "any" as though I should be thankful she hadn't come knocking a couple hours earlier, before continuing, "—with or without a search warrant and with or without cause. While on parole, you must obey the conditions of parole. If you do not obey, you can be—"

"I know, arrested and returned to prison," I said. "You mind if I make a cup of coffee while you tear apart my kitchen?"

"Help yourself." She turned to face the living room, separated from the kitchen by a waist-high counter. "I see you've done your usual crack-up job of interior decorating." She showed her teeth, midway between a smile and a snarl. She was being funny. Most of what I owned tumbled in and out of fruit crates I'd rescued from the back of the local supermarket, with the exception of a fold-out futon that served as a couch, and tacked to the wall, a museum poster of a Diane Arbus photograph depicting a strange-looking child holding a toy hand grenade. Graves lifted the corner of the futon with the black toe of her stub-heel pump. "I guess I don't have to waste a lot of time searching in here." She moved into the bedroom. "I'm sorry about your model, what happened to her," she called. "What was her name?"

"Christine," I called back. I didn't want to witness her going through my things. I stayed in the kitchen, watched the coffee stream black into the pot. I didn't have much to search. She banged around in the bathroom cabinet for a few minutes, then walked back into the kitchen and leaned against the counter, arms folded over the size .38 bulge under her left shoulder, her pistol six points bigger than her bra size. I offered to pour her a cup of coffee. She shook her head, and watching my reaction closely, asked, "Did you have any involvement in what happened to her?"

She had to ask the question. I'd been convicted on charges of manslaughter and I was on parole. It was her job to ask me the question. When I told her that yes, I thought I did have something to do with it, she stilled like a dog on point. "Tell me exactly how you're involved."

"Someone sent me a video of her murder, care of *Scandal Times*."

She nodded, once, her glance charged with authoritative focus.

"The reporter I work with, he thinks whoever killed her wanted publicity. Why else send a recording to a tabloid? He knew we'd give it front-page treatment."

"So would the *L.A. Times*."

"No way. The front page is for national and political news unless a celebrity is involved. And the *Times* doesn't offer national coverage. *Scandal Times* does."

"So he sent the video to you." She shook her head, her lips taut. "That doesn't mean anything. You said yourself, it made sense to send it to *Scandal Times*."

"But why Christine, except for me?"

"I see what you're saying. You don't think she was a random victim."

"What if he chose her because she modeled for me?"

"You don't know that, so maybe you should just calm down a little bit." Graves brushed past me to open the refrigerator door. "When you said you were involved, that's what you meant?"

"What else?"

"In my job, it could be a lot else, trust me."

She stooped in front of the refrigerator and rearranged the cartons of milk, juice, and eggs, then dug open the meat and cheese drawers.

"What are you looking for?" I asked.

"Drugs. A lot of parolees, they store them in the fridge."

"I've just told you one of my models maybe was murdered because of me and now you're accusing me of using drugs? You know I don't use drugs."

She glanced over her shoulder, steel-gray eyes annoyed.

"A stick of dynamite, then." She rattled the drawers shut and stood to peer inside the freezer compartment. "From what I've heard, nothing that's happened so far is your fault. I'm not saying you're not capable of doing something stupid, but what happened to your model was just bad luck. You can't hold yourself responsible for it, do you understand? You had nothing to do with the crime, no more than any other victim."

"I feel like I victimized Christine just by knowing her."

"That's nonsense. Everybody dies in the end, whether you know them or not." She pulled a carton of Häagen-Dazs ice cream from the freezer and stared at the label. "I knew I'd find something if I looked hard enough. Chocolate Chocolate Chip. Do you know how addictive this stuff is?"

I opened the flatware drawer and offered a spoon.

"Absolutely right. How do I know it's the real thing unless I give it a taste test." She set the carton onto the counter and pried off the top. "A homicide detective from North Hollywood called me a couple of days ago, told me a little bit about what happened."

"Sean Tyler," I said.

"Detective Sean Tyler to you," she corrected. "The investigation got kicked automatically to Parker Center, so I was wondering why he was bothering to call me, particularly when he asked about your marriage history."

"What did you tell him?"

"The truth. That you once had a green-card husband."

"He was more than that and you know it."

"You still have a perverse attachment to the idea that you were in love with him, that's what I know." She dug a spoonful of ice cream from the carton and held it up for inspection. "You knew him for a couple of days, he treated you badly, and then he died. Move on with your life. Anything I should know about your relationship with Detective Tyler?"

"He liked my photographs," I said. "But considering my legal problems, that's about all he likes."

"Smart career move." She slid the spoon into her mouth, held it there for a moment, and when she pulled it free the thing was so clean it could have been pulled from a dishwasher. "This stuff is deadly. Maybe I should confiscate it for your own good." She grinned, pleased at her joke, and tossed the spoon into the sink. "How much longer she on parole?"

"Six months, I think."

"I know that." She returned the ice cream into the freezer. "I was repeating what he asked me. Detective Tyler. He wanted to know how much longer you were going to be under direct supervision of the California Department of Corrections." She strolled to the front door, where she stopped long enough to scratch behind the Rott's ear. He sat absolutely still beneath her hand, even more intimidated than I was. "Do me a favor. Don't do anything stupid the next six months, okay? I've put a lot of work into keeping you straight, and I'd hate to lose it because you did something dumb."

She showed her teeth again, waited for my submissive nod, and left.

When I walked the Rott to the Cadillac later that morning I wasn't particularly surprised to see someone had slashed my ragtop. Angry and depressed, but not surprised. My apartment bordered gang turf held by the Venice Shoreline Crips of Oakwood. Someone had tagged the right rear fender months before, a compressed black scribble left by the same moron with a spray-paint canister who tagged every neighborhood surface in reach. For a brief moment I was thankful the Caddy's money-green paint job hadn't been tagged. It would be easy enough to mend the ragtop with a sail needle and some canvas thread, then reinforce it with duct tape. I reached for the door, peering through the driver's-side window as I pressed the thumb-latch. A copy of the current issue of *Scandal Times* lay on the driver's seat, front page facing up. I didn't remember leaving it there. The Rott sprang forward as the door swung open, intent on leaping over the frame and onto the shotgun seat. I lurched to grab his collar and kneed his shoulder to keep him out. He barked and strained forward, trying to sniff beneath the newspaper. I gave him a sharply

voiced command to sit and he obeyed, a single bark of protest to signal his reluctance.

I pulled the door open until the hinge caught and then kneeled on
the pavement beside the door frame. The video image of Christine in
a bondage hood ran on the front page of that issue, in the lower
right-hand corner, prime real estate by tabloid standards because it
encourages the reader to turn the page to read the story, or, if that's
above their particular skill level, to look at more pictures. The issue
didn't lay flat or follow the contours of the seat. Instead, it mounded
upward. I glanced at the Rott, who licked his snout, something he
did when excited about something, usually food. I turned back to the
driver's seat and carefully lifted the corner of the paper to reveal a
long, black tail, then the gray, short-haired hindquarters of a rat.

I lost my temper and shouted. The Rott broke out of his command to sit and stuttered back on all four paws. I told him to sit
again and leaned into the passenger compartment. A yellow packet
lay on the passenger floorboard, bearing the illustrated image of a
rat and the skull and crossbones. Rat poison. I broke out my cell
phone to call the police, then Frank, and last of all Christine's roommate, Tamara, to postpone our breakfast date. I didn't figure a
neighbor was expressing his displeasure over the loudness of my
stereo. I didn't have a stereo. The rat had to connect to our story
about Christine's murder. Whoever left it thought the rat and poison
would serve as a warning. But a warning against what? If the killer
sent me the video, why would he drop a dead rat in my car after the
story ran?

I locked the Rott in the apartment and shot a series of digital images of the slash in the convertible top and the objects left on the
front seat, fudging the position of the rat for greater dramatic im-
pact. When I got the shots I needed, I sat on the curb and found myself wishing someone would invent a fast-forward drug, something
I could take in the morning to get the bad days over with fast, because this was showing all the symptoms of being a real tit-trampler
of a day.

An LAPD squad car rolled up to the Cadillac's rear bumper a little
more than a half hour after I called, the two black-uniformed officers
inside taking last sips of take-out coffee before cranking out another
call response. The dispatcher had probably reported a code 594, van-

dalism of a motor vehicle. The officers—a baby-faced Latino and a husky white woman with curly blonde hair—expected to verify the damage and tell me to contact my insurance company. When I told them someone had left a dead rat on the seat of my car, the Latino looked at the female officer as though either I was nuts or this was going to be one of those days. He wedged his hands into a pair of latex gloves, lifted the corner of the newspaper, and verified that it was indeed going to be one of those days. I explained that my name was mentioned on the front page of the paper draping the dead rat and suspected it had been left as a threat. They absorbed the information slowly, then the Latino poked around the interior of the car looking for other items of evidence while the curly-haired blonde spent her time in the squad car, working the computer.

Frank pulled his Honda to the curb some minutes later and emerged from behind the wheel proffering a business card between two sausage-sized fingers. He made a joke about the dead rat that the Latino officer did not find particularly funny, and it took a minute of careful explanation to convince him that Frank belonged on the scene because he'd written the article that featured my name. The offense was no longer considered an act of vandalism but a death threat, the officer said, and they needed to secure the crime scene. In a few minutes someone from the detective bureau would be out to interview me. When Frank tried to interrupt him, he said, "Why don't you wait over by your car until someone asks to talk to you?" He was polite but firm. Like most cops, he was accustomed to dealing with assholes.

"I called the investigator assigned to Christine's death," Frank said as we walked to his car. "A detective out of Robbery-Homicide named Robert Logan. He's coming over from Parker Center, though I can't say he sounded very happy about it. You get photos of the rat?"

"While I was waiting. Couldn't get him to smile, though." I lifted my camera bag onto the hood of Frank's car and slid an eight-by-ten from an envelope containing photographs I'd taken at Christine's funeral, printed from a flash card hooked directly into a printer. The image of the Hyundai Sonata's back bumper was awkwardly framed but clear enough to make out the plate numbers. I asked him if he knew someone who could trace the owner.

"It costs money to trace a plate. Who's paying?"

I pulled a photo of the young man in the black suit from the envelope, told Frank that he'd attended Christine's funeral looking like he didn't know anybody, then gave it a little extra spin by mentioning the police seemed as interested in him as I was.

Frank turned the print toward the sun, said, "He's the right age group, isn't he? We should show this to the woman up in Palmdale, see if she recognizes him. He doesn't look like the guy from the video, though. Too short."

"Three people were in that room, plus Christine," I said.

"Three?" Frank puffed his cheeks, thinking about it. "Where did you learn to count, the school for the mathematically impaired?"

"The latex suit, the shadow that passes through the frame—"

"That's two," he said, flashing two fingers.

"—and the person behind the video camera," I said, rolling right over him.

"You don't know that." He looked at me like I was cheating.

"Maybe not, but I've spent most of my life behind a camera so I know how the world looks through the lens. The guy in the latex suit did not set up that camera. From the way he glanced at the lens it looked to me like he was taking directions. And not from the shadow, because when you shoot anything, you stand behind the camera, not way off to the side of the frame."

A beige Crown Victoria slid behind the squad car. I sheathed the photos in the envelope. Frank turned, cued by my glance, and waved to the figure stepping out of the Crown Vic, a mid-forties man with side-parted hair and a dark mustache that gave him a retro, 1970s look. The detective buttoned his dark blue blazer and strode toward the officer taking prints off the glass of the Cadillac's side window. Frank gave a friendly shout of his name and ambled forward, hoping to get a quote, until the detective leveled his finger like a sidearm and ordered him to return to his vehicle.

"Hard-ass?" I asked.

"That's the one place he doesn't need body armor, that's for sure." Frank took the envelope, tossed it onto the passenger seat, and lit a cigarette, making the most out of the wait. "They could take a skin graft off Logan's ass and use it to grow Kevlar vests."

The detective spoke with the uniformed officers at length, then broke huddle to strap on a pair of gloves and stoop beside the driver's seat. He examined the evidence with quick, efficient gestures and craned his neck to an awkward angle to read the text of the front page of the paper blanketing the rat. The way he shook his head, I don't think he liked the article. He stripped off the gloves and walked toward me.

"Your car?"

I contemplated a half dozen smart-ass replies to such an obvious question but kept my mouth shut and nodded. He slipped the gloves into his jacket pocket and leaned one hand against the roof of Frank's Honda, subtly trapping me against the side panel. "I gotta tell you, if this is some kind of publicity stunt, I'm gonna be really ticked off."

"My name's Nina Zero." I extended my hand. "Nice to meet you."

He looked at my hand, then at my face, and cracked his mouth in a smile that looked like he'd trapped a piece of beef jerky in his back molars. "Bob Logan, Robbery-Homicide Division." He grazed my hand so briefly I suspected he wished he'd kept on the gloves. "I don't mean to be rude, but that rat isn't the only thing that smells here, so if either of you planted the damn thing you'd better tell me now before you face criminal charges. How many years are you looking at if you violate parole? I know I saw it in the file but I forgot."

"Oh please, if you're not going to take this seriously, bag the rat and let me get on with my day."

"Bag the rat! I like that." He bared his teeth to a sharp exhalation of breath that might have been a laugh and shifted his shoulders toward Frank. "You didn't get an idea to play a funny prank on your photographer pal here? Except she doesn't get the prank, instead she gets hysterical and calls the cops. Is that what happened?"

Frank shook a cigarette out of his pack and stuck it into the corner of his mouth, trying to figure out where Logan was going with this. "Don't forget I called you, suggested you come down and take a look at this. I don't know what your criminal profiling textbooks tell you but that doesn't sound like a prankster to me."

"Sure it does. If you get me to fall for your prank, it becomes news, just the kind of so-called news you like to print."

"Why don't you give us a little respect here?"

"Because your paper isn't fit to wipe my ass."

"What exactly don't you like about our coverage?" Frank thumbed open his silver Zippo but didn't strike the flint. "We played by the rules. We handed over the disk the same day we got it. We didn't print anything you told us we couldn't print. Hell, I even tithe my income to official LAPD charities. I don't see why we have a problem here."

Logan stared at Frank, no less angry than when he first approached us but curious about something. "Were you aware Charlotte McGregor was arrested at a rave in the desert this spring, five tabs of ecstasy in her purse?"

"Why should I be?" Frank asked. It was a legitimate question but it sounded too glib, even to my partisan ears.

"Because you just printed a story suggesting McGregor and Christine Myers were assaulted by the same party." Logan leaned in so close to Frank's face he could have bitten his cheek. "Have you met Ms. McGregor's sometime boyfriend?"

"Don't believe I've had the pleasure," Frank said.

"A twenty-six-year-old repeat offender convicted four years ago on charges of assault and battery. Guess the sex of the victim."

"Female?"

"That was easy, wasn't it? Care to guess the nature of the assault?"

Frank clicked his Zippo, said, "No idea."

"He throttled her. And if we get enough evidence to arrest him, your article is going to be presented as the Holy Bible in court, because he has an alibi for Myers. Investigative reporter, my ass. If you were a cop, I'd bust you down to meter maid." He pulled a black leather notepad from the inside pocket of his blazer and leaned forward to get in my face like he had Frank's. "I'll take your statement now, if you still care to give it."

11

CHRISTINE'S ROOMMATE, TAMARA, sat hunched over our sidewalk table at the Fig Tree Café, her long blonde hair tenting the mug of green tea she cupped in both hands as she stared at the sea. The fog had burned off early that morning, leaving bright sunshine and the smell of salt water in the air. A beautiful late spring day brings out the crowds no matter what day of the week, and a parade of bicyclists, Rollerbladers, power walkers, and joggers plied the bike path just beyond our table. With a fresh cup of coffee and the prospect of good food, the bad start to my day had started to burn off with the fog until Tamara looked at me for a brief moment and said, "I don't know if this is such a good idea, talking to you."

I resisted the impulse to remind her that she'd suggested we meet. If she really didn't want to talk, she wouldn't, but I suspected she just needed a little gentle prodding. "So don't say anything. We'll have a nice brunch together, maybe take a walk on the beach." I caught the attention of a passing waitress, a young retro-hippie in a flowing skirt who held her notepad six inches from her face while she took down our order.

After the waitress hustled to the kitchen, Tamara said, "The police interviewed me, you know, when I got back from the funeral." She wore sunglasses to shield her eyes from the glare of the late-morning sun, the color of the frames matching the blue of her cling-wrap jeans. "Talking to the police about the death of a friend, that's a scene I never thought I'd have to play."

"Did they tell you not to talk to me?"

She shrugged, said, "I don't think they like tabloid reporters."

"Some do, some don't. Depends on the cop. No different than

some actresses. You, for example, when I met you at the funeral, I thought you were the type to want a little free press."

She turned to me as though I'd just kicked her under the table. "I'm not going to profit from Christine's death, okay? What happened to her was horrible. I don't want my name mentioned in the paper. I want to see the person responsible suffer."

Actors are ciphers by profession, and the sunglasses made her even more difficult to read. I slipped my napkin from beneath the flatware and worried it between my fingers, trying to balance Tamara's reluctance to talk with the idea that she had approached me. "Then why do you want to talk to me if you don't want to talk to me?"

"I do want to talk to you, that's the point. But I don't want to talk to the tabloid photographer. I want to talk to the person who knew Christine and cares about what might have happened to her."

"If you want to talk off the record, that's fine with me. But you have to understand I'll probably use whatever you tell me. I'm not going to hold your hand and tell you how terrible it is, because I'm past that point."

"So it's just a story to you," she said.

I couldn't tell if she was disappointed or relieved.

"More like a quest."

She cocked her head to the side. It wasn't the answer she expected. "What kind of quest?"

"It's the way I approach things. If all I wanted was to take pictures of movie stars, I'd get myself certified to work the red carpet at events like the Oscars. That doesn't interest me. I think truth has a private face. And the only way to capture that private face on film is to wait long enough for the subject to give it to you, to catch it by accident, or to hunt it down and take it. The photographs I took of Christine were consensual. She trusted me enough to give a little bit of her true self, in the disguise of the role she played. To see the true face of whoever killed her, that's something I have to hunt down and take."

"Is that what you're going to do? Try to find out who killed her?"

"I'm not a cop," I said. "I can't arrest anybody. But whoever killed Christine has already involved me."

"It involves me, too. It involves everyone who knew her."

"It's more than that." I looked down at my hands, saw that I'd torn my napkin to shreds. "What happened would be bad enough if her murder was some random event. But what burns me is that somebody sent me a video they'd shot of her, moments before her death, and ever since, I haven't been able to figure out why. Were they playing me for the publicity? Or was it a taunt?" I sat back in my chair, thinking I talked too much.

"What kind of video?" Tamara asked.

"You didn't see the paper?"

"You mean the one you work for?" She shook her head. "I'm sorry, I haven't gone grocery shopping yet."

"It involved Christine chained to a rack."

I shut up when the hippie waitress arrived. She set a salad and more hot water in front of Tamara and slid a three-egg omelet and whole-wheat toast onto my half of the table.

"How can you eat that and not get fat?" she asked, like I'd just gotten away with robbing a bank.

"Easy," I said. "I'll just go into the bathroom twenty minutes from now and throw up." When she looked ill I assured her I was kidding and we talked about dieting for a while, or rather, she talked about dieting and I talked about running and weight lifting. She asked me to show her my muscles so I did, pulling my arm from my jacket to flex a biceps that wasn't bad for a girl. She thought that was impressive and funny at the same time and asked if I was gay. I told her I preferred men but most of the time I wasn't anything.

She looked at me for several seconds, sucking on her lower lip as though she wanted a more definitive answer, but when she spoke again, it was about something else. "It was a bondage video, wasn't it?"

"Something like that."

"Who else was in it?"

"Hard to tell," I said.

She picked at her salad, head down, and shrugged. She thought I knew and wasn't willing to say. I thought she knew and wasn't willing to say either.

"They wore latex suits and hoods," I said. "I didn't even know it was Christine until the back of the suit got unzipped and I saw her tattoo."

"Betty Boop?"

I nodded.

"She loved that tattoo." Tamara held her napkin to the bottom rim of her sunglasses and seemed ready to break into tears but sighed instead and blew her nose. "We went down to Hollywood one night three months ago, drank tequila shots at the Viper Room to screw up our courage and got work done at Tattoo Mania on Sunset. Want to see mine?" She stood from the table and bent to roll the cuff of her jeans to reveal a multicolored hummingbird etched into the skin just above her ankle. "It hurt like hell. The skin's really sensitive there. But I'm glad I got it done. Do you have any work done?"

"Nothing so beautiful," I said. "Who do you think was in the video?"

Tamara rolled the cuff down again, sat, and pulled her hair away from her face. "Do you know where she worked?"

I shrugged, maybe yes, maybe no. I wanted her to tell me.

"She did phone sex, you know, one of those 1-900 numbers."

"Sweet Lasses," I said.

"Not Lasses." She shook her head. "Lashes. Sweet Lashes."

"You mean whips, that kind of lashes?"

"She worked for a service that specialized in S&M; you know, I've been a bad boy, whip me while I kiss your feet." She scrunched shut her eyes and stuck out her tongue as though spitting out something bitter. "It was really gross. She said it was making her a better actress, you know, a role-playing exercise. I listened to her do it a couple of times and sure, it's acting, kind of, but so is pornography. I mean, it's not as bad as that because she's not, like, doing anybody but still, just to be pretending while the guy on the other end is, you know, I don't even want to say it, I mean, yuck, it's just disgusting."

I plowed into the eggs while Tamara talked, thinking how a single shifting consonant not only changed "Sweet Lasses" to "Sweet Lashes" but made what seemed an embarrassing and sleazy job into something far more sinister. "At the funeral, when you said Christine was into some dark stuff, that was what you meant?"

Her hair fell back to her shoulders when she released it and she nodded as though coming to a difficult decision, the kind of nod someone might make before deciding to take a running jump over a chasm. "I was thinking, what if she met someone that way? I mean, on the phone. It was a bondage video, right? What if someone offered to meet her in the flesh and she said yes?"

"Did she?"

"That's what I'm asking you."

I shook my head, confused. "Sure, it's possible."

"Will you check it out?"

"Do you have any reason to think that's what happened?"

"You mean, like, evidence?"

"You lived with her. Did she meet anyone else that way?"

"There was so much she didn't tell me." Tamara pushed her salad away, more pecked at than eaten. "I know for a fact she was having at least one secret affair, maybe more."

"Did she ever talk to you about Dr. Rakaan?"

"Her therapist?"

"I heard they were more than doctor and patient."

"Who told you that?"

I shrugged, not wanting to betray a source.

"Were they?" I asked.

"It's possible." She made a face as though she smelled something spoiled and tapped the table three times with the lacquered nail of her right forefinger. "I loved Christine but sometimes it was hard to keep up with her, because she wasn't exactly chaste, you know? The work she was doing with Dr. Rakaan involved how she felt about sex, I know that much, I know it dealt with her past-life relationships, and let's face it, she was pretty hot. Any guy not dead below the waist is gonna respond if she comes on to him and Rakaan is not dead below the waist." Tamara's hand shot to her mouth and she stood so abruptly I thought she was going to be sick. "Christine was a slut. Maybe something did happen between them. But that's the thing about sluts—it usually doesn't mean anything." She excused herself and clipped the table with her hip as she darted toward the bathroom, an odd reaction to our conversation that made me feel guilty I'd joked about bulimia.

12

THE SAN FERNANDO Valley is to the pornography business what Hollywood is to the feature film industry: a dark star whose sheer mass of production draws actors, producers, and technicians from around the world. When I suggested to Frank that we locate and interview the owner and manager of Sweet Lashes—this was one assignment I did not have the courage to attempt alone—he obliged with an enthusiasm and promptness I'd rarely seen in him before, producing the name of the holding company and its address within the hour. Sweet Lashes was only one of several 1-900 numbers the company operated spanning the gamut of human sexual tastes—and tastelessness. By the time we pulled up to the address, attached to a courtyard building that looked like it might have housed medical professionals in more reputable days, Frank had managed to set up an interview with the owner, who was surprisingly willing to talk.

I expected to meet a slovenly man with untucked shirttails and crumbs in his beard, whose busty, big-haired secretary polished her nails over a dusty keyboard, hired more for her oral than typing skills. I expected to open the door to the musty smell of unidentifiable stains on old carpets and cigarette smoke tarring the walls, scents I associated with losers who couldn't get a real girl and so resorted to varying forms of fantasy ones. My expectations were not fulfilled. Frank opened the door to a small but tidy lobby decorated in fresh flowers, one bouquet on a coffee table set before a blue couch and another spraying blooms above the desk of the receptionist, a blonde-haired man in his early twenties with lacquered nails and a sweet, nervous smile. My gaydar is not the most sensitive instrument, but he pinned the needle. He notified the owner we'd arrived and waved us through, asking if we wanted coffee or mineral water as we passed by.

The owner of Sweet Lashes was hovering over the open drawer to a filing cabinet when Frank and I entered the office, a pencil clenched between her teeth and a manila file folder in her hands. "Christine's employment records," she said, then remembered the pencil in her mouth and tossed it onto a desk cluttered with papers, cups, pens, and computer gear. "My name's Anabelle Lash."

"I'm a big fan, Ms. Lash," Frank said, the skin at his scalp line tingeing pink in an unexpected blush. "I wasn't sure it was you when I saw the name on the corporate records but I'm delighted to see it is. I'm Frank Adams, feature writer for *Scandal Times*."

The woman shook his hand briskly, her black hair falling in waves around a face all the more striking for not being classically beautiful, her prominently ridged nose curving above lips so full I suspected collagen injections to match the silicone implants ballooning her breasts. She wore just enough makeup to cover time's weathering marks on her skin but not so much that it reduced her face to a mask. I guessed her age at mid-forties. I introduced myself as the cameraperson and asked if she minded my taking a few photographs while Frank interviewed her.

"Not at all," she said, her voice surprisingly husky. "One of the first things I learned in the adult film business was to make love to the camera, if not the camera operator." She wagged her finger playfully. "The only thing you can do wrong with a camera is to make me look ugly."

"Impossible," Frank pronounced.

I slipped the digital camera from my bag while Frank chatted her up, gleaning from the conversation that Anabelle Lash had been one of the most celebrated adult film actresses of her time, which surprised me because it never occurred to me that something like that would be celebrated. She'd won not one but multiple AVN Awards, pornography's equivalent of the Oscar, for her performances in films whose titles could not be printed in a family newspaper, even a family newspaper as dysfunctional as *Scandal Times*. I surveyed the lighting conditions as she talked, and fiddled with the curtains to use the light coming from the window as a key light and the lamp on her desk as fill light.

"Christine came to work for us six months ago," Lash said, following every adjustment of the lights without changing the angle of her face. "I have to tell you she was a natural. It wasn't my idea to cast her with Sweet Lashes. I originally wanted her to work the Wet and Wild number, which is our soft-core surfer-girl fantasy line, but she insisted on Sweet Lashes, said it would be more fun for her." She smiled, polished teeth gleaming, as sincere as any sales manager. "That's really important to us. Our people, they have to enjoy the work. If you don't like what you do, do something else, that's what I tell people. And Christine? She enjoyed the work. You remember what she looked like? The girl next door, right?"

Frank nodded, seemingly so enthralled his eyes bugged out. He always fawned around film people, complimenting their most recent projects and hailing their older ones as classics of whatever genre fit, but his personal servility never encroached upon the articles he wrote, a Dr. Jekyll in the art of the interview and a Mr. Hyde behind the pen.

"We called her the Mistress of Kink. She could work both sides of the aisle, so to speak, but she excelled as a dominatrix. I mean, nothing was too wild for her." She shook her head as though such a thing was to be both pitied and admired. "She could have been a star in the adult film business if she wanted. Christine was really special."

That struck me as odd because from what I knew, Christine had played the submissive role in her relationship with Rakaan. Frank decided to go in a different direction with the interview, asking instead about Christine's experience in adult films.

"Christine was all talk," she said. "I know for a fact she never worked in adult films. It's a small world and news gets around. I don't think she even modeled topless. But the girl had a mouth on her that could boil dirt."

Frank sat up and looked over his shoulder. "The calls, are they routed through here?"

"This is just the business office. We'll screen applicants, meet employees when necessary, but the calls are processed through a call center off the premises, a service we contract out. And the employees, of course, all work at home, where the calls are forwarded."

"Do you ever monitor the calls?"

"That would be an invasion of privacy." She placed her hand flat on her desk and arched her back, a theatrical gesture meant to convey indignation. "I don't know about you, but most people would not want someone uninvited listening to their private fantasies of licking the boot of a dominatrix—unless of course that was part of their fantasy."

"Nice reply," Frank said, smiling, charmed by her performance. "But it doesn't answer the question."

"I can monitor any call I want, but do I want?" Lash glanced at the ceiling, shrugged, and then fixed a darkly blunt look on Frank. "Do I really want to hear another freak shout 'beat me baby, eight to the bar?' I mean, excuse me, this is what I do and I'm not ashamed of it—the career choices of adult film stars of a certain age are shall we say limited—but it's like I'm a fertilizer salesperson, maybe I sell bullshit but I don't need to take a bath in it. I listen only when training someone, and taking live calls is the last step in the training process, so I listen just long enough to make sure she's got it."

"So if a girl, say, wanted to meet someone who called her through the service, you might not know about it?"

"Stop right there," she said, flashing her palm. "This is not a front for prostitution. No way, no how. If one of my girls or boys tries to set up a date with one of our clients outside the service, they're gone. They can't have so much as a cup of coffee, and if they do, they're fired." Lash flipped open the cover of the file on the desk and brandished a document several pages long, stapled at the top left corner and signed on the last page. "It's all in the standard contract everybody signs, including Christine."

"I take it this means your answer is no," Frank said.

"No, what?"

"No, you wouldn't know about it."

He met her glare with a calm smile.

"The front-for-prostitution angle, I don't really care about that." He shifted in his chair and leaned forward, his shoulders slumped and baseball cap tipped high. "I'm a tabloid writer, not a cop. But Christine met someone dressed in latex who chained her to a rack and then strangled her to death. Given that she worked an S&M hotline, I have to think it's possible she met the killer through a call routed from your service. This can't be a surprise to you. I'm sure the cops already talked to you about it."

"Talked?" She flung her hands in the air. "I feel like a grilled cheese sandwich. My business is one hundred percent legal. The cops don't like it, I don't give a flying fuck." Her head dropped into her hands and she looked out the window through the grate of fingers splayed over her eyes. The way the light spilled over her, she looked lost.

I took the shot.

"They threatened to subpoena our records yesterday," she said. "We'll fight it, of course. I can just imagine the cops calling every one of our customers, asking why they called Christine and what they talked about."

"Don't you think it would be worth it," I asked, "if one of your customers is Christine's killer?"

"Christine wasn't a whore," she said. "If the police investigate her murder like she was, then it cheapens her memory, ruins my business, and wastes everyone's time." She stood, nodded toward Frank, and stared at me. "And speaking of time, yours is up."

Los Angeles and the San Fernando Valley are twinned economically and politically, part of the same metropolitan area and ruled by the same mayor, but the two regions are divided by more than the high hills that obstruct the view of Hollywood from Burbank. The dozen communities that comprise the San Fernando Valley burst from the razed orange groves in less than twenty years, asphalt, concrete, and steel fertilized by the economic miracle of water piped over the mountains. They rolled the cityscape across the valley like a rug, the streets straight and flat and the blocks largely distinguishable from each other by street numbers more than landmarks. Though not particularly scenic, the San Fernando Valley is a driver's paradise compared to the jammed streets of Los Angeles, surface traffic flowing steadily along the wide avenues even during rush hour. We lowered the Caddy's ragtop and reveled in the late-afternoon warmth, Frank jotting notes of our meeting onto his pad while I drove.

"How's your love life?" I called across the seat.

"The only thing worse than my love life is my sex life." He pocketed his notepad, lowered his Cubs cap over his eyes, and leaned against the passenger door. "If I called Anabelle Lash, do you think she'd go out with me?"

"That's a little like asking if you went up to the counter at McDonald's, would they take your order," I said, trying not to sound catty. "The woman all but had a sign sprouting from the top of her head reading 'Billions Served.'"

"Lucky for me I like McDonald's," Frank said.

I hadn't laughed in a week and that gave me a good one.

"You knew Christine better than I did," Frank said. "Maybe she wasn't a full-time pro but did you ever get the feeling she wouldn't turn down a little money for sex on the side?"

"That wasn't Christine's style. She was more into fun than money. I can see her maybe trying it once just to see what it was like, but to turn it into a regular gig?" I shook my head. "No way. She had too much going for her."

"What if it wasn't a paid gig?"

"You mean, what if she was doing it for fun?"

"I don't know what I mean, I'm just throwing it out there."

I felt something warm and wet on the back of my neck—the Rott's nose. He'd clambered onto the seat back to rest his head on my shoulder. He normally rode shotgun. Just because he was a good sport about giving up his seat didn't mean he didn't need a little attention.

"I guess that depends on the dynamics of the conversation," I said, stroking the Rott's muzzle with my free hand. "If she liked someone enough to want to meet him for one reason or another, the threat of losing her job wouldn't stop her."

"What if the caller said he was Depp's assistant?"

"She'd meet him, no hesitation at all, if she believed him."

The Rott lifted his head from my shoulder and shifted toward Frank. He's a sociable dog and isn't happy until everyone in the immediate vicinity pays him some attention, as though he considers himself the glue that holds our little pack together. Frank pushed him away. The Rott considered that a good game and bulled forward again and again until Frank relented and stroked his head.

"Unless we can come up with a better angle," he said, "we'll play up the Sweet Lashes connection as the most likely way she met the killer."

"I'd like to talk to Nephthys first."

"You mean the tattooed babe?"

As good a way as any to describe her. I nodded.

"Does she have a boyfriend?"

I took my eyes off traffic and stared at him.

"She's hot," he said. "And it's not just the freak-show appeal of the tattoos, either."

"I don't know whether she's got a boyfriend—or a girlfriend."

"Girlfriends are fine as long as she shares."

"You dream," I said.

"Dreams are all I have, so I may as well enjoy them."

He rubbed his knuckles on the Rott's head, giving him a noogie. The Rott rewarded Frank with a wet one to his stubbled cheek.

"Just wanted to warn you," I said, "if you go with the Sweet Lashes connection, it's going to ruin your chances of getting Anabelle Lash to date you."

"I hate it when professional ethics get in the way of opportunities for cheap and meaningless sex, particularly when I have so much of one and so few of the other." He pushed the Rott away and lifted the cell phone from his shirt pocket. "I'd better ask for that date now, before we run the article."

13

NEPHTHYS CURLED HER small body onto a plush red lounge chair in the back room of the Chinese-themed Good Luck Bar, gold silk pajamas flowing from her limbs and bead-embroidered black slippers adorning her feet. Surrounded by her friends, she looked like the habitué of an opium den, a blue drink served in a bowl-shaped glass instead of a pipe balanced on her knee. She called the Good Luck her local bar, and with a postmodern decor of Chinese lanterns, latticework, and lacquered screens mixed with thrift-shop furniture, it was the kind of bar only someone from a Bohemian neighborhood like Los Feliz could call local. Her friends did not dress so extravagantly—two in jeans and bare-midriff blouses and the third in bicycle shorts, calf-high lace-up boots, and boy-beater T-shirt—but judging from the pierced eyebrows, tongues, ears, and noses, they all shared a similar aesthetic of the scarified body beautiful. Everyone had been inked, either along their arms or stomachs or legs, the designs sometimes playfully macabre and other times fantastic; a green dragon flew up one girl's arm, background clouds billowing from her skin like waves.

Nephthys lifted her drink so I could better appreciate the deep blue color and asked in a stage-loud voice, "You want one of these?"

"What is it?" I asked.

"A Yee Mee Loo."

"What does that mean?"

"Blue drink."

Everyone laughed in the spirit of an old gag pulled on someone new. Their faces looked familiar, and after a few minutes of conversation, I realized they had come as a group on the night my photographs were first exhibited. They knew each other from an art school over the hill in Pasadena and were trying to make the transition from studying the arts to the more difficult task of making a career. I pulled up a chair next to Nephthys and ordered a Jack Daniel's neat from a passing waitress. They talked so fluently about the Los Angeles arts scene that I felt like a fraud, not an unusual feeling when I'm around other people in the arts.

I picked up the digital camera to tune out the conversation and found myself the sudden center of attention. The girls were not camera shy; they made faces, kissed each other, and showed off their tattoos, mugging playfully—and sometimes shamelessly—for the camera. The digital revolution has put the world onstage, making us all actors in the theatrical performance of our lives. We're all on camera all the time and more vain than ever. This can be a disaster for a photographer seeking the quiet truth of an unguarded moment. When I want to be ignored, I pull out a film camera. Film takes too long to be developed for anyone to care what you shoot. After I bagged the digital camera the conversation drifted to job opportunities, a topic that didn't interest Nephthys so much. She worked as a set decorator for mostly independent films, work that she liked and paid her well. I told her about my talk with Christine's roommate, Tammy. Nephthys had identified Dr. Rakaan as Christine's boyfriend, something Tammy disputed. "I get the feeling you two don't see everything the same way," I said.

"Just because I think she's a two-faced, lying bitch?" Her lips, painted the color of dried blood, spread in a happy smile. "Nothing wrong with her that a total personality transplant wouldn't cure."

"What does she lie about?"

"She lies about herself to herself. Like she thinks she's going to be this big movie or television star but the roles she's cast in? Bimbo of the week." Nephthys growled like an angry cat and laughed. "Tammy's okay, I'm sure, she's just not my kind of girl."

"Christine must have liked her."

"Christine was a complex girl, more complex than she looked." She raised the drink to her lips, blue against red, and sipped. "Part of her was this conventional, small-town girl, superficial and boring, not much different than Tammy. That's why they got along so well."

"And the other part?"

"Unpredictable. She could light you on fire with her smile but sometimes when you looked deep inside her, the darkness you saw could freeze you. She was wild, incredibly sexy, and . . . what?" She sipped at her drink and nodded, as though alcohol fueled her thinking. "Not immoral. She had a conscience. She never willingly harmed anyone that I know about. But she liked to be a daredevil, to try things other people might find shocking."

"You told me she was into some twisted stuff, with Rakaan."

Nephthys chewed at her lower lip and when she opened her mouth to sip at her drink, she revealed that lipstick had stained the tips of her front teeth red. She shook her head, not to contradict what I'd said but to signal her reluctance to talk about it.

"When I met Rakaan, at his office, it seemed clear to me that you were right, he was sleeping with Christine." I put my heels on the edge of the chair, curled my arms around my knees and stared at her, hoping she might respond to the intimacy of eye contact. "He denied it, pretty strongly, in fact so strongly it was like an alarm going off, you know, *liar, liar, liar.*"

"It wasn't that they just slept together," she said, making it sound like sleeping together meant nothing at all. "And it wasn't that they were lovers either. Christine had more than one lover."

"Were you one of them?" The question popped from me unconsidered. I lifted my hands in apology. "Sorry, none of my business."

Nephthys smiled a small, sad smile and shrugged. "You'd have to put chains on Christine to tie her down and that's what Rakaan did to her, but she slipped loose every now and then."

"You talking metaphorical chains or real ones?"

"Both." Her lips tightened and she leaned forward, coming to some decision, her forehead less than the span of a hand from mine. "Christine told me that she was working out her past-life karma with Rakaan, that her sessions with him began with hypnosis and deep, probing conversations but quickly evolved into bondage scenarios."

"You mean, they'd talk about it."

"No. I mean they'd do it. Not in his office but later, at his house."

I pulled my head back and tried to read her face for signs that she was kidding or trying to deceive me and saw none.

"He'd tie her up?" I asked.

"That was just one of the things he did, with her permission. They'd take turns doing things to each other—whipping, slapping, spitting, hot candle wax, you name it."

"Strangling?"

She bit her lip and nodded. "Choking is supposed to be a big turn-on. That's why, what happened, it wasn't such a big surprise for me. But the way she talked about it, she wasn't doing it just for kicks. The bondage scenarios were an important part of her therapy."

"Her past-life regression therapy?" After a moment of sheer incredulity, I realized my mouth hung open. "Just so we're absolutely clear on this, he would tie her up and do stuff to her, whip her, have sex—whatever—and he did this to her because . . ." I tried to think of a good reason but my imagination failed me. "Why?"

"She said it helped her work out some emotional issues she had about sex and it didn't hurt that the sex was incredible. Rakaan said she got off because she was connecting with her past lives."

I remembered my brief interview with Rakaan, how he'd said their sessions were about Christine's love of pain. "He told me she'd been murdered in her past life," I said. "He made it sound like it happened not just once but a couple of times."

"She told me the same thing, that it was like this thing she had, this violent history with men from one lifetime to the next." She gripped my arm with her free hand. "She gave me one very specific example. In the nineteenth century she was a young widow working in London, as a milliner's assistant she said. She had some health problems and the doctor who treated her fell in love with her. The doctor, he liked rough sex and one day he went too far and killed her. Do you know who the doctor was?"

I shook my head, expecting Jack the Ripper.

"Dr. Rakaan," she whispered. "They were lovers in at least one past life, you see? Christine said when he strangled her to death back in England it was an accident, he didn't mean to kill her. The therapy aspect is, they have to relive in this life what ruined their lives in the past."

"Meaning he ties her up and strangles her," I said.

"Except this time, he was supposed to bring her back, he wasn't supposed to seriously hurt her. That was how it became therapeutical. They were supposed to see how her death in the past lifetime had been an accident and learn how to trust again."

"Except he screwed up again and killed her," I said, feeling sick to my stomach. "What's he going to tell her in the next lifetime, *Oops?*"

Nephthys released my arm and settled back into the lounge chair, the plush fabric haloing her in red. "I don't take this reincarnation stuff so seriously. I mean, it's fun to think about but I don't really believe it. I can't even tell you for sure whether Christine believed it either but it unlocked some serious demons inside her. She really got off on the things they did together."

"Have you talked to the police about any of this?"

She hid behind her blue drink, then slowly lowered it to peer above the rim of the glass, regarding me as though she felt guilty about something, then shook her head.

"Why not?"

"It's not so simple." She released a little tension with a sigh. "If Rakaan killed her, it was an accident. Should he spend the rest of his productive life in jail because he went too far?"

I nodded, said, "Sure, if he killed Christine."

"Look, you can cross an ethical line and get away with it—people do it all the time—but when you cross the line habitually you sometimes forget where the line is, and one day you don't just cross it, you break it, you shatter it to pieces. I think maybe that's what happened to Christine. They just kept crossing the line, venturing further out each time, and they just went too far." A tear spilled from her eye and tracked a black line down her cheek. "I'm trying to figure out what Christine would want. If she and Rakaan finally broke a line they crossed every time they were together, would she want to see him punished?" She wiped her face and saw the mascara on her fingertips. "Crap, I hate it when I cry. Now I gotta spend the next half hour in the bathroom, repairing the damage."

"Why are you telling me this if you don't think he should be punished?"

"You know what I think?" She sat up straight and pressed at her eyes, drawing concerned looks from her friends. "I think he should be hung by his balls, that's what I think. Maybe I didn't go to the police but that doesn't mean I wouldn't be thrilled to see him exposed on the front page of *Scandal Times* for the unethical pervert he is."

"Then the cops will end up knowing anyway," I said.

The next morning, Nephthys told her story to the police.

14

DR. RAKAAN LIVED in a modest million-dollar French chateau in the Hollywood hills—if any French chateau costing a million can be considered modest—on a ridge above Beechwood Canyon. At the top of the ridge the sky cracked open to a vista that on windswept days curved with the earth to the milky-blue band of the Pacific, but on most days terminated in a curtain of smog just past the tar pits at La Brea. Million-dollar views on the ridge were just that; real estate prices began at seven figures and went up from there, depending on the size of the lot and the age of the house. Rakaan's house had been built in the 1920s by one of Los Angeles' many eccentric architects. Back then the area was known as Hollywoodland, the real estate development that gave the world the Hollywoodland sign, later shortened to just Hollywood, which towered above the brush-choked hillside at the dead end of Rakaan's street.

I scoped the weave of hillside streets in the Thomas Guide and decided I wouldn't risk a drive by. Earlier that afternoon I'd tried to stake out Rakaan's office, but the lack of clear sight lines for a telephoto lens and the presence of an unmarked surveillance unit on the street convinced me to try his house instead. At Christine's funeral the surveillance cameraman considered him someone of interest, and Nephthys's testimony probably shot him to number one on the list of suspects. The police would certainly have a unit down the street from his house but I hoped the mixed suburban and wild hillside terrain would provide camouflage. If the evidence and my instincts were accurate, Rakaan would soon be practicing past-life regression therapy out of his cell in the Twin Towers, the city's futuristic jail complex. We had an image from Christine's funeral to run in the event of his arrest but I wanted to take a photograph that clearly implied his guilt, something furtive and hurried and just a little bit sleazy. I let the Cadillac drift to the curb on a side street a half mile down the hill, calmed the Rott with a few strokes to his head, and went to collect my gear in the trunk.

The trunk space of a 1976 Cadillac Eldorado is bigger than some apartments. Mine functioned as a roving closet, office, kitchen, and bathroom cabinet while I drove around town, hunting down one shot or another, sometimes for twenty-four hours a shift and longer. I pulled a running outfit from my change-of-clothing case and loaded a day pack with extra clothing, water, food, and camera gear. The Rott jittered on his front paws and barked to hurry me along while I changed clothes in the front seat. We ran the hill at an optimistic clip, cramped from too much sitting, but the Rott was a sensible dog and when he started to tire he went on patrol. I scanned the street while I waited, running in place to keep my muscles warm, and spotted the surveillance sedan parked across the street and three houses down from Rakaan's. In a neighborhood of fifty-thousand-dollar automobiles and two-thousand-dollar gardening trucks, the sedan—a five-year-old Chevy the color of dirt—didn't qualify as covert surveillance; if Rakaan knew he was being watched, he couldn't miss spotting it.

We took off again when the Rott had left his mark, setting our pace to a seven-minute mile, fast for an uphill run. As we approached the Chevy I reminded the Rott to heel; we wouldn't remain anonymous for long if he decided to mark the cop's tires. Any cop other than Logan would see us as a jogger and her dog, a common sight in the hills. I figured Logan would be out working the case, not warming his butt in a surveillance vehicle. At the end of the street the pavement yielded to a dirt fire road, blocked from traffic by a gate. I glanced at the scrub-brush hills above Rakaan's house as we ran, scouting out a suitable blind. We skirted the gate unchallenged. Fifty paces beyond the gate I knelt to unleash the Rott and studied the hillside, searching for a path through the chaparral and scrub oak. The terrain broke sharply uphill to the left, boulders exposed during the excavation of the road jutting from the brush. Another twenty yards from the road the hill sloped up a cut made by runoff water. I hit the hillside near the cut in full running stride, the brush tearing at the skin of my legs as momentum carried me up the steepest few yards of slope. When I stalled out, I grabbed a stalk of chaparral and pulled myself to a lip of earth that marked a more gradual incline. The Rott followed me part way, then dropped back down to the road and barked. Big dogs aren't great climbers, particularly Rottweilers, and he clearly thought I was crazy. I slapped my side to encourage him and he came bounding up. When he slowed near the lip, I grabbed his collar and helped him over.

We cut diagonally up the hill until the terrain curved to a view of Rakaan's house, well within telephoto range on the street below. I didn't expect to run into any police surveillance in the hills and didn't. I grew up hiking hills like the one above Rakaan's house, felt as much at home there as anywhere. I chose a scrub oak as our photo blind and settled into the hillside for a long wait. The Rott wasted little time in nosing around the day pack. I zipped it open, pulled out a small aluminum bowl, and filled it with water. While he lapped it up I snuck out a pound of hamburger wrapped in butcher paper, his expression turning mournful when I pretended I was going to eat it all. I couldn't torment the poor creature for long, broke it into his bowl and watched him gum it down.

The blind I'd chosen angled down the hillside to a three-quarters profile of Rakaan's house. I planted a telescoping aluminum tripod into the dirt, mounted a 500-millimeter telephoto lens to the Nikon, and screwed the tripod into the camera's base plate. The Nikon came loaded with high-speed Tri-X black-and-white film, and in the event clouds veiled the moon I'd brought along a roll of infrared film, capable of exposing the face of Benjamin Franklin on a hundred-dollar bill in the darkness of a locked safe. Then I leaned back against the scrub oak and waited, reading from a book I'd bought the day before, *Transcending Anger: How to Harness the Power of Rage for Positive Change*. After the first few passages I decided the book wasn't going to help me much, but reading it was as good a way as any to pass the time.

I heard Rakaan's vehicle before I saw it, a new Porsche Cayenne SUV, eight turbo-charged cylinders in full throaty roar as he powered up the incline. It was a beautiful car and he drove it like he might never get another chance behind the wheel, whipping into the chateau's circular drive and stopping with such quick precision that I nailed only one shot before the driver's door flashed open. I reframed the telephoto, left hand gently cupping the lens and my right shoulder pressed like a sharpshooter's against the tripod mount, and when Rakaan's head emerged from the cabin I pinned the shutter release. The Nikon's auto-advance motor hummed in rapid fire, 2.5 frames per second as I followed Rakaan to the front door, where he fumbled his key into the lock and glanced over his shoulder as though he feared something might be gaining on him.

I double-checked my shutter speed and F-stop for accuracy of exposure, noted that I'd burned over twenty frames of film, and decided to reload. I threaded a new roll of Tri-X into the camera and snapped closed the back, satisfied that I'd lensed at least one usable image of Rakaan looking furtive. Arrows of light flashed from the glass facades of the city's midrises as the sun arced toward the sea. I returned to reading my book about anger management. A blood-red mist settled over the city, smog reflecting the last rays of the sun. When the light faded to darkness and the air cooled I slipped into sweatpants and rested my eyes, the Rott snuggled against my side. Like film work, gotcha photography requires moments of intense activity spaced between hours of waiting, and in my experience, the best gotchas almost always occur at night.

The Rott woke me when he stirred, his ears twitching forward like birds on a limb. I traced by sight the line of his hearing to the back of Rakaan's house, where a wall-mounted lantern threw a half-circle of light onto the descending hillside. I tucked the Nikon and tripod under my arm and crept through the brush toward a clearer angle. Like most houses on the ridge, Rakaan's had been partially built into the descending hillside, the structural supports invisible from the street. A figure cloaked in black clipped down a set of stairs at the side, a bag slung over its back. At the base of the stairs the figure paused, facing the abrupt slope below the house. The bag reflected light—probably a plastic garbage bag. I jammed the tripod into the earth, opened the aperture wide, slowed the shutter to a thirtieth of a second, and put my eye to a telephoto image of Dr. Rakaan's flowing black hair. He stepped cautiously off the landing, the slope steep and slick with gravel over packed earth. No more than thirty feet from the back of the house, the hill dropped sharply to rock and canyon. Rakaan stooped over the bag, as though making certain the contents were securely bound, then swung it over his head. He let it go like a rock from a slingshot, and after four seconds of silent free fall it crashed into the deep brush near the bottom of the canyon.

The Nikon's motor hummed in auto-rewind as Rakaan climbed the stairs back to his house—I'd shot out the roll. I didn't think I'd just witnessed the nightly ritual of taking out the trash. The cops had clearly spooked Rakaan. The contents of the bag made me curious but not curious enough to goad me into doing something stupid, like prowling through the canyon brush at night to retrieve something that would be tainted evidence in a murder case if I touched it. I planted the tripod in front of the scrub oak, dug out another roll of Tri-X, and while I reloaded called Detective Tyler. When he picked up the call I said, "A source tells me Dr. Rakaan just threw a stuffed trash bag into the brush behind his house."

"Who's your source?" His voice sounded distracted, as though I'd just pulled him from a task that required concentration.

I yipped and softly howled into the mouthpiece.

He laughed, his voice brightening.

"Your source is a coyote?"

"My source is anonymous and hoping to stay that way."

"And what about you? Are you on record for this if I pass it on?"

"Logan already hates me. He hears my name with this, he'll want to stick me in a cage."

"So the tip I'm supposed to give him is, an anonymous source of an anonymous source says Rakaan is illegally disposing trash behind his house."

"Maybe you can simplify it, say an anonymous source."

"You being the anonymous source who saw the bag in question."

"I can see why you made detective. You're sharp."

He told me to hold for a second and I heard voices in the background, muffled by the palm of his hand. He came back on line, his cadence more hurried. "I haven't heard anybody say Rakaan's the one yet, but remember it's not my investigation."

"What are you working on now?"

"Twelve-year-old kid. Gunned down in a drive-by."

I told him I was sorry.

"Nothing to be sorry about, it's what I do for a living." His voice slowed and softened. "Maybe when you've completed your parole agreement we could meet for a cup of coffee, take up where we left off that night in the darkroom."

I broke down my camera gear and packed it in the bag, wondering how someone could so effortlessly make meeting for a cup of coffee sound like a euphemism for sex. I'd spent enough fruitless nights camped out on hillsides or slumped in the Cadillac, waiting for a shot, not to take Sean's hint that a bust wasn't planned for the night. I liked hanging out in the hills but that didn't mean I wanted to sleep rough. The surveillance cop didn't give me a second glance when I ran back down the hill, the Rott heeled beside me.

Most of the night remained ahead of the clock. I sponged the sweat from my skin in the front seat of the Cadillac, changed into my street clothes, and drove down the hill into Los Feliz to meet Nephthys for a drink at the Good Luck Bar, thinking I might as well drop by while I was in the neighborhood. Maybe I wanted to celebrate getting a photograph that implicated Rakaan and maybe I wanted to feel more like a normal human being. Normal people meet friends for drinks after work. Nephthys and her friends didn't fit anyone's definition of normal, but at least they celebrated their nonconformity together. I missed that in my life. I missed friendship, particularly with other women.

Then again, maybe I just wanted a drink.

Past 10 PM a young arts crowd packed most of the chairs and tables in the Good Luck Bar, the clash of shouted conversations nearly overpowering the chill-out music blasting through the sound system. The Los Angeles club and bar scene divides mostly along the lines of sexual orientation but the vibe at the Good Luck Bar wasn't gay or straight; even though the clientele seemed as sex-obsessed as any other group of twenty- and thirty-year-olds clustered together, sexual orientation wasn't the draw. The girls around Nephthys welcomed me like a friend, and the one who liked to wear boy-beater T-shirts bought me a drink. She'd been interviewed that morning by an abstract painter who needed an assistant, one of the few jobs available to young artists in their actual field of study. Whether or not she got the job wasn't the point to her; she was happy enough just to get the interview. Some time later she and the girl with the green dragon tattoo spotted a couple of wild-haired boys they knew at the bar and drifted over to talk. I told Nephthys about Rakaan tossing a bag into the brush behind his house. She listened from behind the rim of a margarita, the green contrasting nicely with her red silk blouse and black slacks. I was beginning to think she chose her drinks by color rather than taste or alcohol content.

"What do you think was in it?" she asked.

"His dirty laundry."

"You photographed him?"

"It was pretty dark out but yes, I think I got him."

"Maybe I'm not a regular reader of *Scandal Times* but I'll buy that issue, I promise. I only met him once—twice now counting the funeral—but I'll be happy never to meet him again." She flashed a happy, acid smile. "And if he's in jail, I won't have to meet him again."

"You met him just once?"

I'd assumed they'd been well acquainted, if not friends.

"He didn't like being seen in public with her."

"Why not?"

"Because the public considers sleeping with a patient unethical."

"Some people are so narrow-minded."

She smiled at the joke and sipped at her drink, remembering.

"They were eating at this sushi place on Olympic. She asked me to drop by, pretend it was a coincidence. Rakaan wasn't happy to meet me. In fact, he buried his face in the menu like he'd been caught cheating on his wife."

"Why did they continue to hide?" I asked. "Sure, I understand he could get into trouble if it gets around he's boning his patient, but once they formed the connection why didn't they just drop the patient-doctor relationship and come out as lovers?"

"They liked the deception." She glanced behind her, not wanting to share the conversation with a casual listener, and pressed her mouth closer to my ear. "The bondage was only one manifestation of what was going on between them. The idea of two people tying each other up and having sex isn't so wicked, not anymore it isn't, but the idea that two people are murderous lovers through multiple lifetimes, that they've murdered each other before and might very well do it again, that's wicked. I think they both got off on the idea that their sex could end in death, that one could kill the other."

"I thought Christine was the victim." I shifted my stance, aware that such conversations should not be shouted, and spoke in her ear like she'd spoken in mine. "In her past life, I mean. I thought the whole point of the so-called therapy was to relive the past-life experience that's screwing up the present."

"That's like saying you're healed the moment you admit you have a problem. That's only the first step. After that comes the cure." Nephthys pulled back and faced me, her black, scythelike eyebrows arching high to dramatize the idea she wanted to get across. "The scenario evolved from sexual reenactments of past-life murder to her taking revenge in the present life. You understand what I'm saying? Christine became a dominatrix toward the end of their relationship. Their roles reversed. She tied, whipped, and strangled him."

I remembered what Anabelle Lash had said, that Christine had excelled in playing the dominatrix to her phone-sex clients. That Christine enjoyed deception made sense; Nephthys may have known about her relationship with Rakaan but knew little about her phone-sex work. Tammy, who knew about her job with Sweet Lashes, was ignorant of her twisted sex life with Rakaan. "If Christine liked deception in her sex life, do you think she also liked to deceive her friends?"

"I don't think anybody saw all sides to her," Nephthys said. "I think part of her appeal was that she was a little like a chameleon, able to transform herself to meet the fantasies of the person she was with, no matter what the relationship."

"How well does Tammy know Rakaan, you think?"

"About as well as any patient knows her therapist."

"Rakaan was treating Tammy?"

Nephthys stepped back, surprised that I hadn't known.

"Of course. How do you think Christine met Rakaan?"

Nephthys put her hand on my shoulder and turned to say hello to the two boys from the bar her friends were swinging our way. The conversation splintered into fragments, nobody saying anything of much importance but everyone enjoying the diverse company. Nephthys began to flirt heavily with one of the new arrivals, a tall and pale-skinned boy with a wounded look—maybe it was the pierced eyebrow—who said he played guitar in a band. I'd heard of the band so I supposed he was vaguely famous. I hung around long enough to finish my drink and kissed everyone goodbye, apologizing that work intervened.

Frank would want to see the images of Rakaan the next morning and I was far too curious to wait to see how the exposures worked out. I drove to the all-night darkroom in Hollywood, where I developed the negatives and printed the corresponding proof sheets. Four of the shots looked promising, despite the lack of light. I set up the enlarger and went to work printing eight-by-tens. One of the photographs caught Rakaan's unshadowed face in clear focus the moment before he released the bag. I tried enlarging the sweet spot, eliminating the foreground, and dropped the resulting print into the fixer just as my cell phone rang.

The call was coming from Frank's phone. I checked the time; the only stories that break at 4 AM are big ones. Frank sounded wide awake when I picked up the call. A source monitoring the emergency services scanner reported the police were raiding Rakaan's house. I packed up and drove across town as fast as I could risk, but by the time I reached Beechwood Canyon a police barrier stretched across the road a half mile down from Rakaan's house. Journalists and photographers were not invited.

I'd missed the shot.

15

OLD-TIMERS—DEFINED by local standards as anyone over forty—
have told me that rush-hour traffic once moved in predictable directions, from San Fernando, San Bernadino, and the beach communities
toward the center of Los Angeles in the morning, the flow reversing in
the afternoon, with routine and predictable slowing in local commercial hubs like Long Beach. Traffic now jams in all directions, the roads
resembling long and narrow parking lots for three hours in the morning and four hours in the afternoon, with almost as many people trying to get into the beach communities most mornings—particularly
Santa Monica—as those trying to get out. I did the sensible thing; I
found a quiet, tree-canopied street and a level parking spot off Beechwood Canyon and curled up in the backseat, the Rott slumbering on
the floorboards just below my side.

The heat woke us well before noon, inland temperatures rising toward the mid-80s, a beautiful late-spring day if you like it hot. I fed
the Rott some kibbles softened with water, stretched out the kinks,
and drove the Hollywood Freeway north to the *Scandal Times* building, stopping once along the way. I found Frank reclined in his work-
station, feet up on the desk and his head cocked back against the
headrest of his chair, oblivious to time. Like me, he worked odd
hours and was prone to napping during unguarded moments. I
pulled a sugar donut from the box I'd bought on my way to the office and held it under his nose until he woke enough to lift one eye to
see what was giving him such sweet dreams.

"Too late?" he asked, referring to the bust from the night before.

"Way late," I said, and propped against the computer monitor the
proof sheet of thirty-six images I'd taken of Rakaan throwing the

black bag down the hill behind his house. "But maybe this will work for you."

He grabbed the donut, dropped his feet from the desk, and pressed his nose to the proof sheet, looking at the images while he ate. I handed him a viewing loupe and a cup of take-out coffee and told him how I'd climbed the hill behind Rakaan's house the evening before, intending to get a tabloid-worthy shot. Frank pressed the loupe against his eye and hovered over the proof sheet, scattering crumbs with each bite. "Why did he panic?" He mumbled, mouth full. "I understand why he didn't think anybody could see him, why he thought he could get away with it, but why didn't he just hold on to whatever he had in the bag? Why take the risk of dumping it?"

"Maybe he noticed an increase in police surveillance, figured he was about to be busted."

"That hot tattooed girl, she talked to the police?"

"Yesterday morning."

"What she said must have made an impression." He lifted a grease pencil from the coffee cup that served as his pencil holder and tapped it against the proof sheet. "Last night, you call Logan about these?"

"Not Logan, no. I called someone else, a mutual friend."

"Tyler?"

"He suggested I was wasting my time with Rakaan."

"It didn't take him long to screw you, did it?"

"What do you mean by that?"

"Not literally. Figuratively. He suckered you into leaving the scene."

I didn't know if Sean intended to betray me, but that was the way it turned out. When you don't know the heart of someone, results matter.

"So you missed the bust shot. A bunch of cop cars in front of a house. So what? Bust shots are overrated." He circled an image of Rakaan, feet braced against a clump of brickellbush and arms extended above his head, the moment before he flung the bag into the canyon below. "This is the image I'll pitch to go with the story. How do you think it's gonna print up? Will you see enough of his face to know it's him?"

I dug the print of that same shot I'd enlarged the night before and tossed it onto his desk, Rakaan's face as bright and clear as a mug shot. Frank craned his neck to look at the print and smirked with satisfaction; the print gave him a front-page image to sell the story.

"How are we feeling about the cops these days?" he asked, lifting the print toward the light. "Should we say screw 'em—figuratively speaking only—or should I fax the print to Logan?"

"If they bother to look for the bag, the photograph is evidence."

"And withholding evidence is a crime. That's a parole violation, isn't it?"

"I forget to flush, it's a parole violation. Maybe you can trade the photo for information about what's in the bag."

If nothing else, my gullibility managed to give Frank a good laugh. The police did not like to trade information, particularly not with tabloid reporters. They gave you what they wanted to give you and never anything that could remotely compromise their investigation. While Frank photocopied and faxed the print to Logan, I flipped through the sheaf of photographs I kept in my camera bag until I found the one of the license plate I'd snapped at Christine's funeral.

"You find out about this license plate yet?"

"Why do you care?" He tossed the print onto his desk and rooted around for something in the drawer next to the printer. "We're already running with Rakaan in the next issue. If he's good enough for *Scandal Times,* he should be good enough for you."

"He's only one guy," I said. "The video suggests two more."

"You can't seriously tell me you think Rakaan isn't guilty for this." Frank yanked the drawer to the end of its pull and stuck his head into the gap. "Past-life regression therapy that includes sado-masochistic practices with a patient? What a slimeball! I've never even met the guy and I hate him."

"Did you run the plates or not?"

"They're rental car plates." He pulled his head from the drawer, eyebrows twitching as though something completely confused him. "Registered to Budget out of LAX. Anybody could have driven that car."

"What are you looking for?"

"My Nicorettes!"

"You're trying to quit?" I asked.

"No!" he shouted the denial, as though the idea terrified him. "I work in a smoke-free office. What, I'm gonna light up in here, get fined by OSHA, and then fired by the paper?"

A fresh-air fan is one of the benefits of driving a convertible. I told Frank that I'd let him smoke in the car, all the encouragement he needed to grab his gear and accompany me to the airport. He worked his cell phone while I drove, blowing smoke into the wind and tipping his ashes into an empty can of Diet 7 Up. In addition to the Rakaan story, he was writing against deadline on the Komodo dragon attack of Sharon Stone's husband, new medical evidence linking dieting with depression, and a story provisionally headlined "Why the FBI Murdered Elvis," the tabloid defining murder loosely to mean the FBI knew Elvis was addicted to various drugs but did nothing to help him. "All the news that's shit to print," Frank liked to say, and he was neck deep in it as usual.

I drove into the desolate grid of remote parking and air-freight warehouses east of the airport, following the car rental signs until I spotted the Budget pole-sign floating over a flat-roofed building. Frank wrote something on a sheet of paper and stuffed it into an envelope while I parked in one of the few spaces reserved for the drive-in trade—almost all of their customers took the shuttle from LAX.

I told the Rott to stay in the car and followed Frank inside a one-room customer service area with flanking counters and a switchback rope line near the entrance. We arrived between shuttles, the rope line empty and only one of four sales representatives busy with a customer. Frank skirted the ropes, scanned the faces of the waiting reps, and walked up to a mid-thirties Latino with swept-back hair and a broad face whose brass name tag read "Frank."

"Hi, Frank, what a coincidence, my name's Frank, too." Frank smiled and bobbed his head as though genuinely delighted. "I think coincidences like this bring luck. What do you think?"

The man's brow wrinkled toward his eyes and he smiled, a little confused but wanting to be friendly. "I think we're in luck, then," he said. "Do you have a reservation today?"

"No reservations, no, but we're definitely looking for a car."

"What kind of car are you looking for?"

"Kind of car?" Frank asked, as though he didn't understand.

"Compact, midsized, full-sized . . ." He gave us a dubious look. "Maybe luxury?"

Frank leaned back and looked at me for the answer.

"We want a white Hyundai Sonata," I said.

The rep nodded as though I'd just made a perfectly reasonable request. "That would be a midsized vehicle." He shifted to face his computer screen. "Are you looking for a reservation beginning today?"

"We've written down our full itinerary right here," Frank said, sliding the envelope onto the counter.

The sales rep reached for the envelope without taking his eyes from the screen, confirming the current availability of white Hyundai Sonatas, then glanced down to finger out the folded sheet of paper. A clear look of understanding buzzed his eyes when he spotted the fifty-dollar bill, as though the whole thing made sense to him, good sense. He slid the envelope containing the fifty under his keyboard and unfolded the sheet of paper, which listed the license plate number and the date of Christine's funeral. I'd wanted Frank to accompany me to the agency because he excelled at this type of operation; he'd marked the guy he thought would be most flexible and set him up to expect something a little unusual, so the sight of the money was a pleasant surprise rather than a shock.

"I'm sorry, the car for the dates you've requested are completely booked," the rep said, jotting down information from his reservations screen. "Can I help you with another reservation?"

"I think that's it for today, thanks."

"Don't forget your itinerary," the rep said, and handed the folded sheet of paper back over the counter.

Frank played a little game with the paper while we walked to the car, pretending to offer it to me then snatching it away when I reached for it. "I did all the work here," he said. "I should have the right to first look." He carefully unfolded the sheet of paper, put his nose to it, and then thumped his hand against his chest as though he'd just been hit with a heart attack.

I plucked the note from his hand and read the name, birth date, address, and driver's license number the rep had written beneath the plates. The kid's name was Stewart Starbal and he lived in Beverly Hills. I did the math. He was only nineteen years old. "How did he rent the car?" I asked. "I thought you had to be, what, twenty-something to rent a car."

"Not if your daddy is one of the top power brokers in Hollywood." Frank recovered from his heart attack and lit a cigarette. "Our friend didn't give us the credit card info but I'll bet my last smoke that it's an American Express Platinum in daddy's powerful name."

"You mean the guy who did the space vampire films?" I tried to remember the titles, big-budget action films with more computer-generated imagery than live action. The vampire, a wicked female wired and implanted with biocompatible weaponry, worked as a covert assassin, killing in various imaginative ways a diverse array of intergalactic bad guys, most of whom had drinkable blood.

"Each of those space vampire films grossed more than two hundred million," Frank said, shaking his head at the casual way I'd summed them up. "We're up to number five in the series and Jason Starbal not only produced every one of them, he owns the original copyrights."

I opened the door for the Rott, looked at the name again. "But this says Stewart, not Jason Starbal. What makes you think he's related?"

"Look at the address."

The driver's license listed a number on Trousdale Place.

"North of Sunset," I said.

"Not just north of Sunset. Trousdale Estates."

Originally part of the largest private estate in the history of Beverly Hills, owned by the oil-rich Doheny family, Trousdale Estates wasn't developed for residential use until the 1950s and quickly became the address of choice for Hollywood's celebrity elite, from Marilyn Monroe to the great Elvis himself. Strict building codes limited the height of residences to a single story, and each estate was so completely walled and lushly landscaped many houses weren't even visible from the street. Celebrities value privacy and security almost as much as fame and money, and Trousdale Estates offered both, backed by a 24/7 private security patrol. I'd tried to photograph subjects on those streets before and failed. The neighborhood was a paparazza's nightmare.

I located the Starbal estate easily enough on the map and after dropping Frank at the office parked across from its heavenly-white gates, the Thomas Guide on my lap and my eye on the clock. The gate stood seven feet high, keeping a solid line with the brick security wall, also painted white but embossed with gold stars and partially screened by a row of evenly spaced camellias. To see beyond the wall I'd need to vault it or wait for the gate to open. A stakeout wasn't an option, not there. I commanded the Rott to stay and jumped the door frame, leaving my camera gear behind. Near the security wall I broke into a running start and leapt, grabbing the top ledge to pull myself high enough to see over the top. The drive cut through a loping green lawn and circled a fountain centered by a famous nude man, painted gold—a larger-than-life-sized replica of the Oscar award, symbolizing either Starbal's ambitions or unfulfilled career expectations because the Academy had yet to nominate his films for anything. Behind the arcing jets of water sprawled a white neoclassical mansion with glistening marble colonnades. Two vehicles were parked at the garage end of the drive, a new BMW M3 and a more modest PT Cruiser. I released my grip and dropped back to the ground. Something about the wall bothered me and I glanced back as I walked away, noticing I'd left black scuff marks on the immaculate white surface. Oops.

Ten minutes after I'd parked, a private security sedan rolled to the curb in my rearview mirror. The security guard who sauntered toward the Cadillac sported a mustache like a real L.A. cop but not the talk-back-to-me-you-die attitude. His job was to keep order in the neighborhood, not arrest people. When he neared the driver's door I glanced over my shoulder as though surprised and braced the Thomas Guide against the steering wheel. He glanced from my face to the map and back to my face. I tried to look helpless—hard to do when you have a nose stud and multiple ear piercings above the collar of a leather jacket, not to mention a hundred-pound Rottweiler in the passenger seat—and asked him for directions to a street on the other side of Coldwater Canyon Drive. He was happy to direct me and we parted good friends.

Most of the estates in Beverly Hills lie nestled into the Santa Monica Mountains north of Sunset Boulevard and because the roads are relatively few, residents leaving the enclave must funnel down the canyons to less than a dozen streets crossing Sunset; only a couple streets in Trousdale Estates led to Sunset, and of these two, Loma Vista cut the more direct route. Parking on the street north of Sunset is punishable by immediate deportation by the Beverly Hills Police Department. I cut across Sunset and spun the Cadillac into a two-hour parking spot facing north, toward the hills, where I raised the canvas top and set up camp. Lensing the face of every driver rolling toward Sunset from Trousdale Estates was going to be tedious, but I didn't see any other way to do it.

An hour and over two hundred cars into my wait the distinctive grille of a Crown Victoria slid into the spot behind mine, signature police lights folded toward the windshield. I lowered the Nikon into the camera bag, afraid Logan would emerge from behind the wheel and not much comforted to see Sean instead. I zipped the bag with one hand while I watched him approach in the rearview mirror.

"Do you have a minute to talk to me?" he asked.

I half expected him to tell me to put my hands behind my head and step out of the car, a more typical request when I'm approached by a cop from behind, but that was no more than my usual paranoia. I leashed the Rott, figuring this would be as good a time to take him for a walk as any.

"How did you know where I was?" I asked.

"Your colleague told me." He kneeled to take the Rott's head in both hands, wearing the same black leather jacket as the night I met him despite a late-afternoon temperature approaching the high 70s. He was as hard core about his leather as I was.

"You could have just called," I said.

"I wanted to surprise you." He stood and glanced around the street, the homes large but not palatial, a respectable upper-middle-class neighborhood with views of the obscenely rich on the other side of Sunset. "What are you doing parked here?"

"I heard a rumor Madonna was in the neighborhood."

We both knew it was a lie, just like we both knew the reason he hadn't called wasn't because he wanted to surprise me. When he caught me trying to peer through the dark barrier of his sunglasses he folded them into his breast pocket, revealing a glance as warily curious as a coyote's. He'd missed his shave that morning, maybe two mornings straight, the stubble matching his jacket and the color of his hair. He looked pretty hot to me, I won't deny it, but I wasn't going to burn my lips on that flame, not twice. I gave the Rott the lead and followed him down the street, away from the traffic on Sunset.

Sean walked at my side, matching his stride to the Rott's stop-go rhythms, and asked, almost formally, "Did I say or do anything that led you to believe Rakaan was the chief suspect in the murder of your friend Christine?"

"Are you trying to play me?" I asked.

His head cocked to the side. "What do you mean?"

"I mean you lied to me last night, so are you lying to me again?"

The Rott stopped to sniff the skirts of an azalea bush as though they held some promise. I looked at Sean, trying to figure him out. He kept his head cocked to the side and he remained silent.

"You convinced me Rakaan was nothing special. I believed you when you said nothing was happening the night of the bust. I packed up and missed the shot." The Rott lost interest in the azalea and nearly pulled my arm from its socket when he bulled forward.

"I didn't lie to you about last night," he said when he caught up. "Sure, I may not have been completely forthcoming about Rakaan but I didn't know they were going in for the kill. From what I understand, the decision to move came in a hurry, possibly because someone tipped them that he was trying to dispose of evidence."

"My tip, you mean," I said.

"Officially recorded as an anonymous tip." He gripped my elbow to make sure I listened. "An anonymous tip that suddenly wasn't so anonymous after a certain reporter faxed a photo of Rakaan disposing of evidence."

Sean wasn't going to tell me outright what he really meant; he was going to make me work for it. I tried to read his eyes. Something both worried and irritated him. "You phoned Logan to report a tip from an anonymous source," I started.

He nodded. I was headed in the right direction.

"The next morning he gets a photo that identifies the source as me. He knows you know who I am. You know what I do. If I called you on the phone, you'd recognize my voice."

"'How the fuck is she an anonymous source, Tyler?'" Sean said in Logan's voice. "'You knew who she was. You lied to me about my own fucking investigation. Maybe it's a two-way leak. Is it?'"

I winced. I never saw it coming. Neither had Frank. I heeled the Rott and stood over his shoulders, holding him in place with my knees. "He thinks you fingered Rakaan for me?"

Sean nodded.

"I talked to Rakaan before Logan did," I said.

"I'm not the one who needs to be convinced."

"Logan is playing a mind game with you," I said, seeing clearly what was going on. "He didn't even consider Rakaan a suspect until I convinced one of my friends to talk about Christine's so-called therapy sessions. He knows people are willing to talk to me and it ticks him off. And Rakaan? A hypnotherapist with a Hollywood A-list clientele? It's like you couldn't invent a more tabloid-ready suspect. He's trying to back you down, that's all."

"Back me down or throw me off."

"We didn't send the video to him, we gave it to you. He's jealous already. Then the tip that leads to Rakaan's arrest comes through you. If he wants to take credit, he has to slap you down."

"That's the way I figured it too but that doesn't make life much easier."

The Rott squirmed between my knees. I told him to heel and walked him back toward the car, trying to figure why Sean needed to tell me this. Maybe he was telling me not to call him again and being far too subtle about it. "What was in the bag, the one Rakaan threw?" I asked.

Sean puffed out his cheeks, stressed by the question. "I don't know if I can tell you that."

"I told you it was there. The least you can do is tell me what was in it."

"I can't tell you that, not on the record."

"Then off the record."

He stared at me while we walked, and I thought he wasn't going to answer, but as usual I was misreading him, or maybe just reading him half right. "The bag contained bondage gear."

That didn't surprise me.

"His DNA showed on her body, didn't it?"

"Not just his," he said, and followed that stunner with silence.

"Rakaan isn't the only one involved."

"Hard to say what it means."

I spotted the high, sloping profile of a PT Cruiser speeding down Loma Vista—the same car I'd seen in Starbal's drive. I judged the distance to my car as I watched it veer left onto Sunset, headed toward the Strip. I'd need a helicopter to catch him. I turned back to Sean, who watched me with the same anxious interest I'd taken in the PT Cruiser. I forgot about Stewart Starbal for a moment and asked, "Who sent me the video? Not Rakaan."

"The maid," he said. "Nobody can find her. She came in once a week to clean. They think she found out what was going on, mailed you the copy because you were connected to Christine."

"Watch the video. Rakaan wasn't alone in that room. If you look in the corner of the frame while Christine is being strangled, you'll see a shadow cross the floor. I don't think it was the maid."

"I'm not going to watch the video because it's not my case to work. I didn't even keep a copy to look at. It's not my concern. It's Logan's."

I'd figured Sean had bigger eggs than that, and to hear him worry about case protocol disappointed me. I'd thought he was a little bit of an outlaw, like me.

"If you don't care one way or another, why did you come here?"

Sean crossed in front of me and stopped, his look sliding to pure worry. "If Logan is willing to slap me down, I figure someone like you he's willing to take off at the head. So be careful. I know you tabloid types are aggressive by nature—"

"I'm not aggressive," I said. "I'm persistent."

"You want to call it persistence, fine, the end result is the same. If you irritate Logan so much he thinks you're a problem, he's not going to show you any mercy. Trust me, he's capable of setting you up and cutting you down."

"I trust you," I said.

The single line that creased his forehead relaxed and he smiled like a male Mona Lisa. "I came for one other thing," he said, and when I asked him what, he slid into my arms and kissed me with such a fierce tenderness that I nearly felt too stunned to respond. Nearly. But not quite.

When he walked away I wondered if the kiss was off record, too.

16

WHEN I LEFT the apartment with the Rott that evening to run the wet sand at low tide I felt as though someone watched me from a distance, a feeling I imagine I inspired in others who felt no less uncomfortable about it than I did. While I ran, I wondered who would take the trouble and why. I thought about the rat that had been left on the seat of my car the morning before and whether I should consider checking into a motel for the next few days. I quickly decided against it. The Rott and I had faced down scarier situations than a dead rat. I'd installed new security locks the first week I'd moved in and the front windows were protected by quick-release security bars. I'd be easy to find at *Scandal Times* if someone wanted to get me badly enough. At the Santa Monica pier I broke the run to do stomach crunches and push-ups in the sand, then pushed myself a little harder than normal on the run back. Too many thoughts skied through my mind. Pain blotted them out.

Less than an hour after we returned to the apartment, the Rott alerted me with a bark that someone climbed the stairs. He hadn't quite learned the footsteps of everyone in the building—a difficult task considering the transient population—and I figured one of the half dozen illegal immigrants who lived next door had caught his attention, until the doorbell rang. I stuffed down the last bite of a Trader Joe's microwaved enchilada and walked to the door. The bullet shape of my father's skull lurked on the other side of the parabolic peephole lens. I opened the door too shocked to say anything except, "What the hell are you doing here?"

He dropped his head as though it shamed him to appear on his daughter's doorstep, asked, "Is this a bad time?"

"It's never a good time." I lacked the heart to block the door and stepped away to let him in. "Just curious, were you outside earlier this evening?"

He nodded, said, "I was getting ready to come up when you went out for your run, then when I saw you come back I thought I should give you a little time to wash up." He looked me up and down, edging toward the center of the room. "You sure took off like a jack rabbit outta hell. You in fighting shape?"

"Hope I don't need to be, but yeah, I am."

He smiled as though that pleased him and I half expected him to test my reflexes with a punch like he used to do when I was a tomboy, before adolescence turned me into a girl and he only tried to hit me when he was serious about doing damage. I'd never imagined him visiting me where I lived, and the sight of him in my apartment so spooked me I couldn't have aimed a camera without shaking the lens. "I don't keep beer around," I said. He liked beer, one of the reasons I couldn't stand the sight of it. "But I can pour you bourbon if you want."

"That would be good," he said.

"On the rocks, right?" I moved to the kitchen cabinets, where I pulled down two tumblers, put three cubes in his glass, one in mine. I hadn't meant to be polite but I couldn't think of any other way to pour myself a drink without being rude, which I also didn't mean to be. He was looking around the room like he was lost when I turned to hand him the drink.

"I thought you were making money." He glanced pointedly at the stained carpet and then reached to finger the splintered edge of the kitchen counter. "Maybe you could spend a little of it to move someplace decent."

"Tough to find a place willing to take an ex-con with a dog." I didn't tell him I'd been burned out of my last apartment and the landlord would rather shoot himself than provide a reference. I pointed to the dining table, cluttered with proof sheets and camera equipment, told him to have a seat. I wanted to ask him what he thought he was doing there but I kept my mouth shut. He'd tell me soon enough.

"Cassie told you she was coming to live with me?" He reminded me where I get my drinking habits by downing his drink in one pull. "I'm sure you don't think that's such a good idea."

I got the bourbon from the kitchen and refilled his glass, then left the bottle on the table. I didn't answer him one way or the other. Just because he had something to say didn't mean I did. He shook his head when the silence grew long, then stared at me for a clean sweep of the second hand, but he'd come to me for a reason and the days had long passed when he could force me to do anything. I finished my drink and poured another, just enough ice left in the glass to cool the bourbon.

"She needs family and she doesn't have any other choices," he said, watching me as carefully as I watched him. "Her stepfather? He's in prison, the no-good son of a bitch. From what Cassie tells me, he's not the kind of man wants to raise a kid anyway." He pointed his glass to the futon-couch on the floor of the living room and the bareness of the walls. "You'll admit this isn't a good environment for a kid, if you could take her, and the way I understand things, you're a single woman with a criminal record, you can't. Don't take offense now. I'm just tellin' the truth."

"Why do you want her?"

"She's my granddaughter," he said, astonished at the question.

"Her mother was your daughter and you didn't want her. I'm still your daughter and you don't want me either."

"That's not true. I may have been hard but I—"

"You don't like kids," I said, cutting him off. "You liked us well enough when we were too small to rebel. I'd even go so far as to say you weren't a terrible father, except for those moments you lost your temper. It didn't help that you lost your temper at least once every damn day."

He shrugged his shoulders, said, "Mary, I'm not here to—"

I banged the bottom of my glass on the table. Mary was the name I'd been born under, Mary Baker, a name I'd changed long ago. "My name's Nina," I said. "Call me by my name."

As we glared at each other over the table I watched the pupils of his eyes compress to pinpoints of rage, and I began the count to a beating I'd learned in childhood. I planted my feet on the floor and squared to face what had always followed his rage, as inevitable as the gravity behind a falling rock, but instead his eyes dulled and the rage subsided.

"Okay. Nina," he said, without irony.

"Cassie is fifteen years old. When Sharon was fifteen you slapped her around so much she ran away." My hands flew in unfettered gestures, hands that normally lay quiet no matter how great my agitation. "You did the same thing to me; the minute my body started to change you changed, too. Not that you didn't hit us when we were younger. Of course you did. But the way you hit us changed. You hit us like you really meant it. You hit us like you used to hit Mom."

"You think you're the only one who got smacked a little when you were young?" He wiped his eyes. No tears there. Just frustration. "My dad beat hell out of me when I was growing up."

"And that makes it right," I said. No comment. Just said it flat.

"No, damn it, it doesn't make it right, but it makes it what it is. I turn on the damn TV and all I hear is somebody whinin' about how much they suffered because their daddy did this or their momma did that and nobody loved 'em enough when they was growin' up. In the end it doesn't make a damn bit of difference, you play the hand you're dealt with, you just play it out, and sometimes you look back and you don't like the way you've played it, don't like the way you've done some things and it's too damn bad." He stared down at his hands cupped around the glass, machinist's hands cross-hatched with scars blackened by grease that never washed entirely clean.

Cut open his chest, I imagine his heart looked the same way.

"I didn't mean to be hurtful," he said, staring at his hands. "Sharon, I could never figure out how to handle her and so I did what I was trained to do, what I'd been told was the right way to raise kids, the way I'd been raised myself. When she started acting up I beat hell out of her. And you're right, I got harder on you when you turned teenagers, because the consequences in life change when you stop being a child. It's a lot easier to screw up your life at sixteen than nine."

"Sharon, she turned prostitute at sixteen and died a violent death before her fortieth birthday. All that beating, it sure stopped her from screwing up her life, didn't it?"

"I couldn't figure out how to do it any different." He blinked rapidly, as though dirt had been thrown into his eyes. "I thought she was just bad, she woulda turned out the same way no matter what I did. I knew I had a temper. Of course I knew that. I lost my temper and did some things I was sorry for, even then. But then both you and your brother, you grew up pulling in harness and so I thought I was doing things right. Sure, you were headstrong and didn't always mind but damn it you didn't give me one-quarter the trouble Sharon did. You were a good girl, right up until the time you snapped, went crazy on the world."

"What did you do then, Pop?" I asked.

He pulled his head back and shook it, confused.

"What did I do?" he repeated.

"I was a good girl." I stood from the table and backed toward the kitchen counter, taking deep breaths in a vain attempt to calm down. The Rott whined, like he sometimes did when I raged around the apartment. "I couldn't even breathe in the house without worrying you were going to lose your temper and start hitting someone. Of course you thought I was being good. You tie somebody up, stick a gun in their face and tell them to be quiet, you know what? They're going to keep their mouth shut. You keep someone that way their whole life, you think they're gonna have any idea who the hell they are? Of course you thought I was good. You thought I was good because I wasn't even there! The person you were looking at? That wasn't me. That was a hostage, a hostage to your rage and my fear."

"Mary—I mean Nina—I think you should—"

"Shut up!" I shouted, and the Rott barked in response. "You know the worst thing about it? About being held hostage like that? I actually loved you for it. Every day I breathed I knew I was alive because you decided you weren't going to kill me. And I felt grateful. I learned little ways to please you, things to say and do that would calm you enough so that you wouldn't hurt me or somebody else. Sometimes those little things didn't work and you beat somebody, but once you'd hurt us good you'd stop and then I'd be grateful again because I knew it could have been worse, a lot worse. When you gave me a split lip I saw that as you being merciful because you could've broken my neck."

I walked to the bottle and refilled his glass first, then mine. Maybe he was smarter than I gave him credit for. Maybe he knew what I needed to do. Because he didn't move. Not even after I poured his drink. He stared forward and down, at a fixed point on the table just beyond his hands.

"No wonder I went a little loco, eh?" I drank the bourbon I'd poured and made sure to leave the glass on the table when I backed again to the kitchen counter. I knew myself well enough not to leave a weapon like that in my hands. "This gets us back to the original question. What did you do? When I stopped being your good little girl and started to become the person I am. When I lost control of my life, my self, my anger."

He glanced from the fixed spot in front of his hands, looking like he didn't know the answer or was too afraid or ashamed to say. I waited, a step away from flinging open the door and throwing him out.

"Everybody sins and is sinned against in this world." He let go of his drink and turned in his chair to face me head on. "I sinned against you and I'm sorry for that. I ask for your forgiveness."

"I can't give it that fast. I'm sorry, I just can't. One apology doesn't change years of abuse. And one apology doesn't mean you've changed."

"I'm not going to insult you by claiming I've changed. But I've learned some things about myself these past months, since your mother died. Those things I've learned, they don't change who I am, but I don't see myself the way I used to. I've lost my pig-headed certainty about some things. I've changed that, at least. I used to think I was the strong one in the family." He lifted the glass to his mouth and breathed the whiskey before he drank it. "I was a real tough son of a bitch, the toughest guy on the street for thirty years straight, smacking around your mother and anyone else I felt like. What could be tougher than that?"

He looked at the palm of his right hand like he'd never seen it before and slapped himself so hard the bourbon splashed from his glass. I stepped quickly back, startled by the speed of the blow, and before I reached the kitchen counter he pulled his right hand into a fist and punched himself in the face, his neck snapping to the side with such force that he spun off his chair, the glass rolling from his hand onto the carpet. "Damn me," he said and hit himself in the face again, a left hook this time, then followed it with a right cross and another left, chanting "Damn me," with each blow, hitting himself the way he'd taught me to hit others, in a timed combination of punches, each one setting up the more devastating blow to follow, cursing himself as he hit his face again and again, the beast in him finally eating itself with the same brutality it had devoured others.

A good daughter would have rushed to stop him.

I let him go.

He stopped beating himself and wept, hiding his red and swelling face in the crook of his elbow. "I'm not so tough after all," he said. Blood streamed from a ring-cut above his right eye. "Your mother, she was the tough one in the family. All those years, she stuck it out. We had ourselves some good times, I'm not saying we didn't, and she knew I loved her. But I wasn't worth the spit in her mouth, the way I treated her. She could have left me but she didn't." He pulled the bloodied sleeve from his face and stared at me. "Why didn't she? Do you know?"

"No, I don't," I said.

I got rubbing alcohol and bandages from the medicine cabinet.

17

alarm rang the next morning I remained in bed, my limbs like sand and blood, so heavy not even the Rott's nudging licks could rouse me. I counted the drinks I'd consumed the night before, thinking I might be suffering from a hangover, but I'd stopped drinking at three shots of bourbon, and even though I knew the world was not a fair place, I'd never suffered the indignity of a hangover without a good drunk preceding it. If what I felt was the effects of a hangover, it was a strange one, my breasts so tender they felt like they'd spent the night at a soccer match, playing the ball. I rolled into a sitting position and told the Rott to leave me alone while I summoned the energy to stand. My breasts always hurt the day before my period. I stumbled into the bathroom to flush my face with cold water.

The events of the day before still echoed through my head and I winced through a series of self-recriminations as I recalled the visit from Pop. Maybe my fatigue came not from an abuse of alcohol but an abuse of emotions, my hangover emotional rather than physical. Pop had left the apartment with neither my blessing nor my condemnation of his plan to bring Cassie to live with him. Most people would not consider a grown man beating the crap out of himself to be a successful demonstration of fitness to care for his granddaughter, but it convinced me of the depth of his pain and the sincerity of his remorse in a way that words never could. Pop was a man of action more than words. I trusted what he did more than what he said. I'd never seen him weak before and though it disturbed me, it didn't frighten me nearly as much as when he abused his strength. Cassie was going to move in with him no matter what I said. She was far tougher than I'd been at her age. I decided I'd roll with it. Maybe after the first few weeks she'd be the one beating Pop.

And what was Sean's kiss about? I dragged through the morning rituals of face, toilet, teeth, and hair wondering what he'd meant by it. He knew involvement with me was career suicide but he put the gun to his head anyway. Sean had worked undercover, Frank said. Most police officers lead dual lives, the often brutal world of law enforcement balanced with the more tender necessities of family life. Undercover officers added another layer of complexity, working and partying with those they intended to arrest. Maybe Sean was working undercover even now and the kiss had been given to inspire false trust. Deception was probably part of his nature. Sure, that's a good trait to have in a boyfriend. Based on my love history, Sean was just my type of guy.

Whoever drove the PT Cruiser I'd seen at the Starbal estate the day before was even slower than I to get started and it wasn't until midmorning that I spotted the car rolling down the hill from Trousdale Estates. I ordered the Rott to the floor and pulled out behind, pitching down onto Sunset Strip two cars back in the flow of traffic. The driver wasn't in much of a hurry. The Whiskey A-Go-Go slipped by on the left, Book Soup drifted past on the right; two blocks later the driver wheeled left and parked in the lot behind Sunset Plaza. I made him as the guy I'd seen at Christine's funeral when he stepped out of his car. I swung around to the back of the lot and parked. He locked the Cruiser and ambled across the lot, dressed in baggy jeans, red sweatshirt, and blue bucket hat.

Sunset Plaza is a favorite haunt of celebrities slumming incognito, a mile-long stretch of high-rent boutiques where the traffic on Sunset gears down to gawk and tables and chairs spill on to the sidewalk from ersatz European cafés with Beverly Hills prices. I played tourist with a telephoto lens and snapped a few shots at a safe distance. The green-and-beige awning of a Coffee Bean and Tea Leaf franchise hung over the sidewalk midblock. When the guy veered beneath it, I bagged the Nikon and followed him in.

I took a sidewalk table near the door and watched him order at the counter, wondering why he'd risked attending Christine's funeral if he'd been complicit in her death. Maybe his father's wealth, fame, and power gave him a natural immunity against fear. His size didn't match that of the assailant captured in the video. He better fit my image of the voyeur, the shadow flitting across the corner of the frame or the eye behind the camera. Or maybe he'd met Christine in a club, enjoyed a brief romance that he'd never fully given up, and now mourned her as his great, unrequited love. Maybe his resemblance to the man Charlotte McGregor had described at Starbucks was coincidence. The only way I'd find out was to ask. When he carried his coffee and a slice of cake to a dark corner table, I strapped my bag to the back of the chair across and asked if he minded sharing the table.

He checked me out, his eyes dilated and his smile tilting so dangerously over his perfectly dentisted teeth I thought it might fall off, an expression made even goofier by the bucket hat. Beneath his lower lip he was trying to grow a soul patch, and his blonde hair drifted toward his shoulder a little too unevenly, as though he'd instructed his hair stylist to give him a cut that made him look like he wasn't getting haircuts. He wasn't a bad-looking kid, just a little vacant, and I thought he'd probably been smoking something that morning that explained his appetite for chocolate cake.

"You're Stewart Starbal, right?"

He nodded, said, "Sure, whatever, sit down."

He reacted to things with the offbeat timing of someone going through life on a two-second time delay. He still didn't have a clue what I was doing there and was just stoned enough not to care.

"You don't recognize me," I said.

He peered at me and grunted as though slapped on the back. "The funeral. You were the one taking pictures."

"That's me, a camera wherever I go. Christine modeled for me. I took some photographs of her for a show hanging right now in the Leonora Price Gallery."

He fumbled off the lid to his coffee to let the liquid cool enough to sip, looking like he wanted to be awake for this. "You're her? The one who works at that tabloid? I remember she was talking about it. The show, I mean."

"You knew her well?"

He shrugged, meaning I could come to my own conclusion.

"I didn't see you at the opening."

"Yeah, whatever; I hope to catch it, maybe this week."

"I don't remember her talking about you. How did you meet?"

"At the house," he said.

"You mean your dad's house."

He shrugged. Whatever.

"What was she doing at your dad's house?"

"This is boring, man."

He closed his eyes like he was sleeping.

"Just think about how bored Christine is right now." I refrained from calling him a little twerp. "She's dead, remember? Strangled to death while drugged out of her mind on ruffies."

His eyebrows furrowed. I'd upset him. The lid to his coffee skittered away from his fingertips, and when he tried to snare it he nudged the cake with the back of his knuckles. "If I didn't care about her, I wouldn't have gone," he said, meaning the funeral. He pressed the lid back onto the cup, noticed the chocolate, and sucked on his knuckles before backing his chair from the table. "Sorry, gotta go. You want the cake, it's yours."

"You want to be famous?" I asked.

He gave his head a little shake and said, "What?"

I slid a fake mock-up of a *Scandal Times* cover story next to his coffee, a card with my numbers paper-clipped to the top right corner. "Starbal Spawn Mourns Strangled Starlet," the headline ran, above a telephoto black-and-white image of Stewart Starbal at Christine's funeral. Frank had composed the story based on the little we knew about his involvement. The text mattered little, Frank said. The Starbal name would sell the story.

"Arts photography doesn't pay the bills so I moonlight as a paparazza." I pointed at the cake. "You sure you don't want that?"

He looked at my finger, then the cake, said a stunned, "Go ahead."

I could have asked for his shirt and gotten the same response. The cake tasted delicious. I shoveled it down, suddenly ravenous. "You ever been to Palmdale?" I asked, my mouth full of cake.

He shook his head. "Not to stay."

"Ever flirt with somebody online from Palmdale?"

"Who knows where anybody's from online?" He continued to stare at the *Scandal Times* mock-up. "Do you mean they're actually going to publish this? In the paper?"

"Do you know a girl, Charlotte McGregor?"

"No. Why?"

I pulled the newsstand issue of *Scandal Times* from my bag, folded to Charlotte's photograph. I'd taken it in the desert after our interview, the late-afternoon sun setting her skin aglow. "She was given ruffies, raped, and strangled, like Christine. But she was lucky. They didn't kill her."

"No, I don't know her." He didn't look happy about being asked. "But I thought the cops, I thought they already arrested a guy? This Dr. Rakaan?"

"Get this." I leaned across the table like I was delivering secret information. "The killers filmed her rape and murder and the video contains evidence that at least two people were involved, not counting Christine, maybe three. Then somebody sent me a copy of the video as a way to brag about it. Can you imagine anything so stupid?"

I'd never seen someone more likely to melt under the table.

"Maybe they didn't want to brag about it," he said. "Maybe they had some other reason."

"Like what?"

"Whatever. I don't really know. I'm just speculating."

"Of course they were bragging," I said. "What else could it be?"

"Maybe they wanted it to stop."

He appeared so diffident that I doubt he convinced himself.

"I'm just curious." I stuffed the last bite of cake into my mouth and polished the fork. "Why did you go to the trouble of renting a car to drive to Christine's funeral? Why didn't you take your own car?"

He thought about that as though considering the question for the first time. "It wouldn't start," he said. "It was the battery or something."

"So you cabbed all the way to the airport to rent a car to drive to the funeral of a woman who . . ." I shook my head, not believing a word of it, but letting him know I was trying to stay open-minded. "I'm sorry, how did you know Christine? Did I forget, or did you not tell me?"

He didn't answer.

"Wait, that's right, at your dad's house. Was it one of those big Hollywood parties I'm always reading about?"

"I didn't say it was my dad's house, I didn't say anything, and if I did say something, I lied. I didn't know Christine, I'm just a vulture likes to go to funerals, okay?" His eyes, already reddened by whatever substance he'd been abusing, looked like they bled when he cried, the tears pouring from him like blood from a wound. He lurched to his feet, knocking aside the chair next to him before regaining his balance. "I gotta go."

"If you go, I can't stop them from printing this."

"You can print anything about me you want. It doesn't matter." He took a step toward the door and bumped into the table, then swung wide around the back of my chair, shoulders hunched as he stumbled out of the café.

18

NOTHING SELLS LIKE fame, the reasons for celebrity far less important than the fact of it. Since Charlotte McGregor's appearance in the pages of *Scandal Times,* two film agents had approached her about representation and casting people from three different productions had called to encourage her to audition. The phone hadn't been ringing off the hook, she said, only because modern phones don't have hooks. She'd driven into the city from Palmdale that morning to interview with one of the agents and to audition for a small part in a low-budget horror flick. She'd be happy to talk to us again, she said, because we'd brought her so much luck. When she emerged from her casting session, held in the office of a tiered, red granite and green glass building near the *Variety* headquarters on Wilshire, she appeared to glide across the paving tiles. A young man with stylishly tousled hair and a rumpled suit, worn without the tie, held the door open for her, grinned winningly when she thanked him, then wandered toward the courtyard fountain as though waiting for her to finish with us.

"Is that your boyfriend?" Frank asked. He butted his cigarette and returned the unsmoked half to the box, a frugal but disgusting habit that made his clothes reek like an ashtray.

Charlotte glanced back at the boy and smiled.

"Just someone I met at the audition."

"Big part?" I asked.

"Two lines and a scream when I get hacked by an axe." Her fingers traced the contours of the scarf around her neck and adjusted it's position. "I couldn't do the scream because of my throat, you know, it's not healed yet, so I'm not sure I'll get the part."

"If your boyfriend sees this guy," Frank said, the forced casualness of his tone a sure sign of something nasty to come, "won't he beat the crap out of him? I mean seeing that he's a violent criminal who's done time for assault. Or are you thinking he might beat the crap out of you instead?"

"You mean Randy?" Her voice cracked a higher octave at the mention of the name, as though she couldn't believe he'd intruded upon her new reality. "I haven't seen him in months."

"Is that why he tried to strangle you?"

"He never did that to me," she said, her hand again rising to her throat.

"Oh, you mean it was just other girls he strangled, not you."

"It wasn't other girls. He got into a fight with his girlfriend when he was, like, under a lot of stress."

"So he only strangles girls he likes, is that what you're saying?"

"Oh my God, you sound just like the cops." She glanced at me as though deciding whether to stay and fight or turn and run.

"He sounds like the cops because they just blindsided him," I said.

"The blindsiding, that was no big deal," Frank said. "It was the threat to throw us in jail that bothered me."

"So, what, it's my fault you didn't ask me about my ex-boyfriend?"

"No, it's my fault for being such a sucker." He didn't have his notebook out, jotting down her replies. He was angry and being a bully about it. "It's my fault because I believed you were being shafted by the cops. Because you looked like someone had victimized you. And because you look so completely innocent and believable I gave you the star treatment in the pages of *Scandal Times*."

"I am innocent," she said, the blush of indignation firing color to her cheeks. "I was victimized."

Frank tapped his thumb and forefinger together, mime for a running mouth. "Everybody's an actor in this town. What about the hits of ecstasy in your purse? You told us you didn't do any drugs."

"They weren't mine," she said.

"I'm sure the cops believed that when you explained it."

She crossed her arms over her chest, her mouth wrinkling to a sour turn. "Of course they didn't believe it. Not even I could believe the little fucker set me up like that."

"You mean your ex-boyfriend, Randy," I said.

"We were at the rave together and when the cops raided he dropped his stash in my bag." She tossed her head back and her auburn hair jumped from her shoulders. "I didn't even know it. He told me later he couldn't risk getting busted, because of his record. Can you believe anybody could be such an asshole? I was like, sure, just drop it on the ground then."

"But he didn't think they'd search you, right? Because you were a girl." I put on a boy voice, said, "'So what's the big deal, babe? I didn't know they were going to look in your bag.'"

"You read my statement? The one I made to the police?"

"No, but I've been around enough low-life characters in my life to know how it works. You wouldn't be the first woman to take a fall for her boyfriend."

"I hate it when you do this," Frank said.

"Do what?"

"Play the gender card." He fingered the half-finished cigarette from the pack in his pocket and flicked his lighter. "Men are shits. Women are abused innocents."

"It's true," I said, laughing.

"That's why I hate when you play it." He exhaled the smoke like a sigh of exasperation. "Show her the photographs, not that I'll believe a word she says."

I lifted a folder from my bag. I'd pulled a sheaf of random eight-by-tens from the trunk and stuffed them into the folder with a single shot of Stewart Starbal, the same way the cops show suspects in a mug book. "Tell us if you recognize anyone," I said.

Charlotte shuffled through the first few, squinting as though near-sighted or just serious about getting it right. "This one," she said, holding up a photograph of a sunglassed man holding a cup of coffee. "Ben Affleck, isn't it?"

Frank rolled his eyes at me, his way of calling me a moron.

I photographed celebrities for a living. No surprise one had slipped in by mistake. I told her to go through the photographs from beginning to end without commenting, then to go back and identify anyone she recognized. I watched her carefully, looking for the light of recognition and dreading it might be sparked by another mis-placed celebrity.

She completed her pass through the sheaf of photographs and said, "Him." She flashed the telephoto image of Stewart Starbal. "This looks like the guy who bumped into my table, the day I was drugged."

"Looks like or is," Frank asked, blowing smoke.

"He's got the same hat, that's for sure, and it looks like the same sweatshirt, except not turned inside out. How can that be a coincidence?" She pulled the photograph closer to her face, then flipped it toward us and pointed to Stewart's soul patch. "He didn't have one of these things below his lip, at least I don't think he did."

"You don't think he did, or he didn't," Frank said. "Those are two different things."

"I spent thirty seconds with the guy," she said, and stuffed the photograph into my hand as though glad to be rid of it. "And after that, I was drugged out of my mind. He looks like him, but with different facial hair. I can't get any more certain than that."

"Easy enough to grow a soul patch," I said to Frank.

"Easier to grow the patch than the soul," he answered. "But I don't feel comfortable going to print with this." He thanked Charlotte for taking the time to talk to us. "I'm sorry if I offended you but I had to see where you're coming from," he said, the closest I'd ever heard him come to an apology.

The art of acting teaches how to lie with the seamless ease of the truth, and the pressures of trying to make a living at it can make its students masters of manipulation. Charlotte was polite enough to thank us before she clipped away, toward the fountain, the boy, and her new life. I believed her performance but didn't so certainly believe she told the strict truth—not that I disbelieved her either. That was my problem with actors. With the good ones—and Charlotte was good—I couldn't always tell when they weren't acting. If she'd told the straight and strict truth, we'd managed to further traumatize a woman who'd been victimized enough.

"If you're not doing anything, I know this convent nearby," I said to Frank. "Maybe we can go, beat up a few nuns."

"Hell no, nuns are tough," he answered, stubbing out his cigarette. "I went to Catholic school. The nuns, they kicked my ass plenty of times."

"What can you tell me about Stewart Starbal?" I asked.

"Second of four kids, born to Jason Starbal and . . ." Frank flipped back in his notebook until he found the relevant entry, ". . . Minnie, maiden name Minnie Mapes; her first marriage, his second. She was an actress when they met, nothing more distinguished than the usual cute girl roles, sacrificed her career to raise a family. She broke her neck in a slip-and-fall accident six years ago."

"Starbal the elder never remarried?"

"Dedicated his life to being a single dad, lots of high-profile dating, low-profile rumors before his wife died of being one of the names in Fleiss's little black book."

"You mean Heidi Fleiss," I said. She'd been arrested in the mid-'90s for running a call-girl ring to the stars. "No big deal there, half of Hollywood was in her book. But that's ancient history."

"So what if he had a wife and four kids at home, right? I'm not commenting on the man's morality here, just pointing out that if he was active as a married man we might speculate that as a long-term widower he's either found God or someone to replace Ms. Fleiss."

"You're so cynical. How old are the other kids?"

"Jagger, the oldest, he's a product of Starbal's first marriage, already has his own film production company called Illusterious Productions, oddly spelled."

"Oddly spelled how?"

"With an *e*, like a cross between *illustrious* and *mysterious*. Stewart is the second child. He's got a younger brother, Redford, who's already entered one of his student films in a festival, and a baby sister, Dalí, who plays piccolo in the youth symphony."

"Dolly?" I asked, not quite hearing it. "As in baby doll?"

"Dalí, as in Salvador," he corrected. "C'mon, I'll walk you to your car." It was an offer of convenience rather than courtesy; he'd parked his Honda on the street, his front bumper nestled against the Cadillac's rear. "You met Stewart. How does he look to you?"

"Stoned, clueless, and guilty. I figure he's the shadow in the video."

"A shadow, that fits. He hasn't made much of an impression so far." He jangled his car keys as he walked. "You do any kind of search for him and you come up with little more than references to his famous dad. Graduated from high school with grades that wouldn't have gotten him into USC, except Starbal senior is one of the school's most famous alums and biggest benefactors. Rumored to like video games and playing guitar, not supposed to be particularly good at either. No arrests, no trophies, no known girlfriends."

"He could always play for a slacker revival band," I suggested.

Frank stopped at the Honda, not quite making good on his promise to walk me to my car. "You're right, he's the perfect shadow. The kid, he casts no light at all."

19

NEPHTHYS ANSWERED THE door to her courtyard bungalow that night wearing a red kimono draped over black silk pajamas, an Oriental motif that complemented her Egyptian pageboy hairstyle and charcoal-lined eyes. She looked so beautiful, framed by the exotic fabrics that hung on the walls of the living room behind her, that I felt an admiring kind of envy, wishing I was the type of woman who felt comfortable lounging around the apartment in a kimono and silk pajamas and thought interior decorating involved more than tacking a poster to the wall. I carried a sack of Thai takeout from Chan Dara in the crook of my arm, the scents of spices and meats pinning the Rott to my side like a magnet.

"Is it okay if the dog comes in?" I asked. "He gets lonely in the car."

"You're both welcome." She tugged me into the kitchen by the sleeve of my leather jacket. Brightly glazed flowerpots stood in the wood-framed windows and in the few days since I'd visited she'd hung an entire community of Mexican Day of the Dead figures from the ceiling, the costumed skeletons dancing overhead like spirits. Halloween was months away; she'd hung them for reasons that had nothing to do with a seasonal celebration.

"Your apartment is so beautiful." I set the food down onto the counter and laughed, too self-conscious. "Listen to me, next I'll be asking where you bought your dishes."

"At thrift shops and flea markets, if you want to know. That's where we set decorators find a lot of our stuff." From the cabinet beside the sink she pulled out a mixed set of Fiestaware plates, bowls, and platters. "When I work on a film, I try to get inside the characters' heads. I think someone's personal environment says a lot about who they are."

"You just stuck a knife in my chest," I said, and turned to unpack the curries, rice, and noodles from the bag.

"Why? What's your apartment like?"

"A minimalist slum."

"I'm sure it's not that bad."

"It is. I don't decorate. I don't own things to decorate with. I used to, when I was, you know, before I went to prison."

"You're like a nun or monk." She hovered over the curry, her mascara-lined eyes widening at the promise of spice. "I noticed that about you right away. You wear your leather jacket like a habit, you know? Maybe I'll start calling you the warrior nun."

"I don't think I'm that moral," I said, a little offended.

"What I'm talking about has nothing to do with morality in any conventional sense of the word." She dished the curry into small bowls and set them onto the table, next to a larger bowl for the rice. "I'm an epicurean. I surround myself with beautiful, exotic things because I like them. They're my weakness. Not the beauty of gold and diamonds. I prefer a more occult beauty, the beauty of strangeness. If I had to choose between truth and beauty, I'd take beauty half the time. A beautiful lie sometimes is more attractive to me than an ugly truth—particularly in love affairs. You're more the Stoic type. You'd never choose beauty over truth."

"I don't think truth can be separated from beauty."

"Then how can you explain Christine? She loved the lie, loved to tell one, loved to live one, and that made her mysterious and oh so beautiful."

And it got her killed, I wanted to say, but didn't. I removed my leather jacket and strung it over the chair back. When she noticed the scars on my arm, she hit me with a questioning look that I quickly deflected. We toasted to the memory of Christine and devoted ourselves to the rich, red Panang curry and the complimentary tang of pad thai, a noodle dish leavened by bean sprouts, lemon, and crushed peanuts, the meal and our conversation lubricated by a supermarket Chardonnay. We talked about our childhoods—Nephthys had been raised in a middle-class neighborhood near Madison, Wisconsin, the daughter of an English professor and a failed performance artist—before we drifted inevitably to the subject of our toast. "It's hard to remember she's dead, sometimes," Nephthys said. "I'll sometimes have this thought, like, call Christine, and I have to check myself."

I didn't have that problem. When the people in my life died, they died. I didn't imagine them alive again, though I sometimes imagined avenging their deaths. "Do you remember, at her funeral, seeing a young guy, about twenty years old, wearing an expensive suit and looking like he didn't know anyone? Wait a minute, I'll show you." I zipped open my camera bag and pulled from the portfolio of photographs the shot I'd taken of Stewart Starbal wearing baggy clothes and a bucket hat at Sunset Plaza. "This is the same guy, probably the way he dresses most of the time."

She tipped the photograph toward the candlelight and nodded. "Sure, I remember seeing him there."

"Do you know him?"

She shook her head and passed the photograph back to me.

"Did she ever mention the name Starbal to you, Stewart Starbal?"

"Not that comes to me right away." She tilted her head and looked to the far corner of the room as she thought back. "Any relation to the movie guy? Those vampire-in-space movies?"

"His son. Any chance she met him through Rakaan?"

"If she did, she wouldn't have told me." She lifted the rim of the glass to her lips, eyes darkly luminous above the golden wine. "A lot of famous people were on his client list. He insisted on confidentiality and she kept it. It may sound weird to you, but they trusted each other."

"If you're strangling each other unconscious for sex play," I said, "I hope you trust each other."

"Why do you want to know about him?"

I told her about the shadow moving across the corner of the frame in the video of Christine's killing. She stood and carried the dishes to the sink, and when I bumped her aside to get to the dish soap she said we'd take care of the dishes later. "Grab your chair," she said. "We'll hunt back through her diary, see if we can find any kind of mention."

Nephthys carried the bottle of Chardonnay and our two glasses into the living room, where a length of red batik draped her computer.

I pulled a chair from the kitchen and placed it next to hers. While the computer powered up I refreshed our glasses with wine and caught her staring at the scars on my right forearm, one of the reasons I'm partial to my leather jacket and long-sleeved shirts. She softly gripped my wrist and examined in the monitor's cathode-ray light the rough-edged holes that crater my skin from forearm to biceps.

"What happened?" she asked, simply and without pity.

"An asshole burned me with a cigarette," I said. I let her take her time. I knew she'd have to ask, eventually, once she'd seen them. "He tied me to a chair. He'd smoke, ask me questions, and when I didn't answer or said something he didn't believe, he'd stub out his cigarette on my skin. Burning me with a cigarette, that was just one of the tortures he had in mind. The other wounds, they pretty much healed, but I'll carry these to my grave, along with the memory."

She kissed my arm once and let it go to navigate her browser to Christine's online diary. "Is that the one you killed? The one you went to prison over?"

"This wasn't the guy, no. This one was already dead when I shot him."

The screen flashed from page to page, Christine's quirky biographical data boxed on the left, her diary entries running on the right, each entry accompanied by snippets from those who read her diary and wrote comments, mostly compliments and expressions of support. Nephthys scrawled the cursor to an entry dated two weeks before her murder.

The bootiful christine got the guided tour of a bev hills manse today—I'm under blood oath not to give out the name but if I whisper in your ear Father of Intergalactic Bloodsuckers you'll know who I mean.

While my friend made a (wink-wink nod-nod) professional visit I got surprised by the bloodsucker spawn and their posse, they weren't even supposed to be there, but it ended up pretty cool cause they gave me the grand tour.

The place was effing HUGE, room after room, two pools, game room, private screening room, it's like, their walk in closets are bigger than my entire apartment. The boyz already have their own production company, maybe they noticed what a great poisonality I have, they'll make me the next great whatever when they get rich and powerful like daddy.

Too bad they were such spoiled brats.

One was kinda sweet. I gave him my phone number. When he called I told him I was already seeing someone but stay in touch. I'm such a slut/tease.

But at least I'm gonna have some fun.

"She didn't use real names in her diaries, so everything is in a sort of code." Nephthys highlighted the first sentence. "I wouldn't have guessed this without your hint where to look, but the Father of Intergalactic Bloodsuckers has to be Jason Starbal."

I reread the text, fitting the details to the little I knew about Starbal. Nearly every big-time producer who didn't have a place in Malibu lived in Beverly Hills, so that meant nothing. Stewart and one or more of his brothers could be the bloodsucker spawn, but then, Starbal wasn't the only producer to have kids. "The friend making the professional visit?" I asked.

"Has to be Rakaan," Nephthys said. "She usually calls him the boyfiend but she's coming really close to violating their confidentiality agreement so maybe she's just being coy."

"Impossible to prove," I said.

"Let's cross-check her screen name with the site's discussion threads to see if she mentioned it anywhere else. The threads are like the diaries, they don't disappear. So what we'll do is check the threads that were active then." She tapped at the keyboard and the screen flashed to a page containing fill-in boxes for keywords and member names. She typed *bloodsucker* in one and *Christine* in the other. A message appeared stating no results for the search. She typed in a different search term and asked, "When you said the guy who burned you was already dead, did you mean literally, figuratively, what?"

"Dead as in dig-a-hole dead. Somebody I knew, he shot him first. He was dead by the time I grabbed the gun, but that didn't stop me from emptying the cylinder into his chest." I refreshed Nephthys's glass and finished off the bottle in mine. "The guy who ordered me tortured, that's the one I killed."

She tried another search term and hit return.

"How'd you do it? You mind me asking?"

"He drove into a gas pump."

"How was that manslaughter?"

"I was on a Harley at the time, chasing him with a handgun."

"Did you shoot him?"

"Never got close enough. The gas pump blew up. He fried to death." I sipped at the wine, wondered whether I'd do things any differently if I could go back in time. "I was a lot angrier then, more desperate, too."

"Maybe this is one of the reasons you won't let Christine go, what happened to you." Another search term failed. She growled at the screen and tried again. "Most people would back away, let the police handle it. But look at you, you're actually trying to chase down whoever did this to Christine, just like you chased down the guy who had you tortured."

"I work for the tabloids," I said, not agreeing with her at all. "This kind of thing, it's my job."

"You choose your job." She whooped and pointed at the screen with the red lacquered nail of her right forefinger, having found something under the search term *brats*. "This is the day after she wrote about visiting the mansion, a thread called the daily rant, where people vent about things that piss them off."

The threads ran the opposite of blog style, oldest entry at the top and newest at the bottom, member names on the left and their comments on the right. Most people ranted about the daily annoyances of urban life, like bad drivers and people who don't clean up after their dogs, the screen names of the ranters more original than the rants. Someone ranted against Republicans for being rich and a poor Republican ranted against being ranted against. Christine's rant appeared near the bottom of the page.

anybody born not just with a silver spoon but a dinner service for twelve in his mouth. I just met some of these a**holes, and it's not just that they carry daddy's credit card, not just that they haven't worked a day in their collective lives, it's the arrogant attitude they have, that sucksess is their birthright. look in the mirror, a**holes, see the < l.a. bratS > written on your foreheads.

The passage revealed what Christine thought of the people she'd met—assuming they were the same ones she'd mentioned in her diary—but it didn't tell me who they were, not definitively. Nephthys gave me a little dig with her elbow.

"You don't see it, do you? Look again."

"What am I looking for?"

"Look in the mirror, that's the clue."

I knew the asterisks were used to write a swear word without actually writing it, but it wasn't until I considered the way another set of punctuation marks bracketed "l.a. bratS" that I saw it.

Write "la brats" on someone's forehead, stick him in front of a mirror.

It spells Starbal.

20

I DRAGGED THROUGH a beach run late the next morning, my pace on the hard, wet line of sand above the receding tide as slow as a jog on dry beach, the Rott racing far ahead, then charging back to urge me forward. I wasn't surprised at feeling tired. Nephthys was a champion nonstop talker, not someone who dominated conversation as much as pushed, prodded, and goaded it into movement whenever the words slowed; I hadn't navigated the roving traffic cops back to Venice until well past midnight. After the run I lay in the sand to stretch and do stomach crunches but fell into a light doze instead, luxuriating in the heaviness of my flesh on the warm sand. Losing a few hours of sleep didn't usually bother me, but my energy levels had been so low that week I was beginning to believe fatigue was my normal state. When the Rott stirred beside me I woke and sat up with the distinct feeling of being watched. The Rott felt it too, his attention divided between the gulls he thought it his genetic duty to chase and a man who had settled into the sand ten yards behind me.

On late May weekdays the beach at the end of my street attracts a scattering of sunbathers, mostly serious sun junkies and out-of-towners who don't have the two weeks to wait for full summer temperatures, and the beach offers wide stretches of open sand between bodies. The man behind me sat fully clothed, but that wasn't remarkable. People came in all styles of dress to sit or walk the sand. He did not look all that different from most of the denizens of Venice Beach, a mid-thirties man dressed in worn jeans and an old T-shirt. I might have figured he was on his lunch break had he been eating something, had he not selected a spot ten yards away from me when he could have settled another twenty yards distant and still remained thirty yards from the nearest person, and most of all, had he not been staring at me with all the obviousness of a hungry man a piece of meat.

I thought about staring back, one of the power plays allowed to women with big, ferocious dogs, decided I didn't need the trouble. I hugged the Rott and stood, but made the mistake of turning toward instead of away from him.

"That's a nice dog you have," he called, in that aggressive way some men have of making a comment about the weather a challenge.

I looked at him long enough to be polite, nodded, and walked toward the boardwalk. He had the dry, furrowed look and stringy hair of a long-term meth abuser, someone thirty-five going on sixty. Maybe he thought complimenting my dog was a good pickup line.

"I'd take extra good care of that dog, if I were you," he said.

The line and its implicit threat stopped me in the sand and I looked at him again, noticed the lightning bolts home-tattooed into the webbing between his thumb and forefinger. He'd done time, the tattoo said, and he'd done violence while doing time. I'd been an angry person when first released from prison, and had he said something like that to me in those first months I would have taken serious offense. He wasn't me. He needed to mind his own business. I'd matured since then. I thanked him for his concern and ran instead, calling the Rott to heel in a forceful tone he obeyed without hesitation. The guy didn't look in good enough cardiovascular shape to chase me more than a hundred yards, but tired or not, I took the long route back to my apartment, doubling back to make sure I wasn't followed, proud of my newfound maturity and self-restraint but not so mature I didn't fantasize kicking what remained of his teeth down his throat.

After I showered and dressed I worked on a shrine to Christine I'd begun after her funeral, tacking photos to the wall, one by one, as the mood struck me. Earlier that week I'd stopped in a church and bought a half dozen devotional candles in the style popular with Mexican Catholics, the ones in glass holders bearing the appliqué images of saints and the sacred heart of Jesus. I'd arranged the candles on a few upended fruit crates propped against the wall below the photographs. I planned to light them one night and say a prayer for Christine and all the others I've lost. I've always respected the atmosphere of belief if not the text preached from the pulpit. I guess that makes me half pagan.

When my cell phone rang I answered in a meditative mood, staring at a candid shot of Christine laying across Nephthys's lap. I didn't recognize the calling number or the caller, who, without giving his name, asked, "Where do the lost people go when they slip through the hole in the center of everything?" The voice reminded me of some of the drunk or stoned boys who used to call me when I was in my teens and early twenties, so slurred by one intoxicant or another that I struggled to separate the words from the ellipses.

"If they're Catholic, they burn in hell for eternity," I said.

Laughter keeled over the line.

"That's funny. I'm not Catholic."

"But you're lost."

"So lost I don't know the way home."

The silence at the end of the sentence made me think he'd severed the connection.

"What's going on, Stewart?" I pushed a tack in the wall, securing the top two edges of an image of Christine applying a sheath of red lipstick to her lower lip. "I know you didn't mean to hurt Christine. Where are you now? If you want to talk to me about it, maybe I can help."

"You don't know anything," he said, pain spiking through whatever substance numbed him. "The cops, they don't know anything, you don't know anything, everybody's wrong about what happened to her and so it's like, kick the shit out of Stewart time, you know? And who do I think maybe might understand what I'm trying to do? My family, everybody in my family hates me. My friends, they want to soak me in gasoline and burn me alive. And you, Christine's friend, the one person I thought might understand, even you want to beat the shit out of me. I didn't mean to hurt her? You know what I say to that? Fuck my family! Fuck my friends! And fuck you!"

The line closed like a stone door with me on the wrong side, staring at the cell phone in my hand and wondering if the call had been a hallucination inspired by Christine's shrine. From the sound of Stewart's voice he'd taken the kinds of drugs that dulled the emotions rather than excited them, but still he'd lashed out, unable to control his anguish and anger. Why did he think I'd understand? I'd done nothing to help him. Instead, I'd threatened to brand his name into the headlines of a tabloid newspaper. I looked at the return number left on the cell's call display—another cell phone by the look of the digits. In my experience hallucinations didn't leave evidence. I pressed call, let it ring a half dozen times, hung up, then called again after a two-minute wait.

The line connected to the sound of a sigh.

"Tell me where I'm wrong," I said. "You're right, I don't know anything, but I can't help you if I don't know what's going on."

He didn't answer.

"Where are you? I'll come over, see if I can help you out."

"It's too late," he said, his voice no more than a whisper.

"Too late for what? For Christine? Hell yeah, it's too late for her."

"Are you going to publish that story, the one you showed me?"

"It's negotiable," I said. "You need to give me something that points the story in the right direction if you want me to keep your name out of it."

He said nothing, the sound of his breath progressively slower and deeper with each inhalation, as though he was calming down or drugging out.

"Did you ever check out Christine's online diary?" I asked.

A sigh rustled through the line.

"She wrote in code about visiting your house, meeting some people there, maybe you and your brothers."

This time I didn't even get a sigh.

"She wrote you have a film production company. What kind of films are you interested in making?"

The high-pitched strangling sound he made might have been a laugh but it just as easily could have been a cry. "It's not my production company. It's my brother's, his friends'. I have nothing to do with it."

"Christine gave you her phone number, right? Said to call her when she broke up with her boyfriend. She didn't mention your name online, but I think that was you she was writing about."

"She was playing with me."

"No, she wrote you were pretty hot; I mean, why else give you her phone number? Where are you now? We should talk. I can help you. The police may be slow but they're not stupid. They'll figure it out sooner or later, however you're involved."

"See if you can find me . . ." he said, fading away, then snapping back, "I'm in the Marmont, third floor back."

"You're there now?"

"Mickey Mouse stamps," he said. "Remember those?" He made the strangling sound again. "Just wanted you to know my intentions were good."

The line banged and crackled as though he'd dropped the phone. I jumped into my boots, shouldered my camera bag, and nudged aside the Rott, who guessed the moment I picked up the bag we were rolling and bolted for the door. Chateau Marmont lay at the foot of the Hollywood Hills, a thirty-five-minute drive from Venice Beach in light traffic. Over a dozen Mickey Mouse stamps had paid the postage on the DVD depicting Christine's murder. Stewart may have lied to me about other things but he wasn't lying to me about the stamps. He'd either seen the envelope the disk had been mailed in or had mailed it himself. I called Frank and told him about the conversation while I drove toward Hollywood.

"Maybe he heard about Rakaan," Frank said.

"What about him?"

"They just arraigned him on charges of murder two."

"How is it second-degree murder? Accidental death during sex-play strangulation, that sounds more like involuntary manslaughter to me."

"Maybe they're hoping to start high and plead him down," Frank said. "How savvy is this kid, you think?"

"I'd say more clueless than savvy."

"Then he probably licked the stamps."

"And stuck them on with his thumb," I added.

"You want company at the Marmont?"

"I think you'd spook him."

"I could hang out in the bar."

"A tabloid writer in a celebrity bar?"

"I'd be as popular as spit in a sauna, wouldn't I?"

We agreed that he'd drive in from the Valley and wait in the lobby while I talked with Stewart. I couldn't imagine why a Starbal would be willing to go on record, but the story was worth the possible waste of Frank's time. The crime scene technicians would have dusted the envelope for prints and checked the stamps for traces of saliva that contained the licker's DNA, but these techniques wouldn't help the police track down a suspect unless his prints and DNA sample were in the database from a previous arrest. DNA alone wouldn't lead the police to Stewart.

Ahead of me, Chateau Marmont rose above Sunset Boulevard, a 1920s Hollywood imitation of the French Chateau style, it's faux-stone walls and black-tile mansard roofs scaling the steep hillside in multiple tiers. Other hotels in town offered more luxurious digs at comparable prices but none approached the debauched gentility of the place, like a shabby aristocrat with a nasty vice up his frayed silk sleeves, and you'd have to check into one of the meth-and-hooker motels branching off Hollywood Boulevard to find a more partying clientele. The Marmont had the rarest quality of all in a city as devoted to amnesia as Los Angeles: a sense of its own history, the legends of those who frequented the place not so much the supernovas of the present but those whose fame shot across the sky decades ago, from Greta Garbo through James Dean to Johnny Depp. I cruised past the hotel entrance—garage parking was for guests only—and found a two-hour parking spot on the street up the hill. I told the Rott the hotel didn't allow dogs, news he accepted with his usual resignation, settling down in the backseat with one of my old running shoes as companion and chew toy, to await my return.

I'd stayed in the Chateau once before, a splurge that lasted one night because of the narrow difference between the room rate and my life savings at the time. I molded a pair of sunglasses to my face, swept past the registration desk, and climbed the stairs like I belonged there. On the second-floor landing a tall and broad-shouldered guy tried to avert his face behind a curtain of flowing black hair as he clipped past, heading downstairs in a hurry, and at first I thought he might be a nouveau rock star who didn't yet realize nobody played incognito at the Chateau. I watched him round the staircase turn, and then climbed on toward the third floor.

Stewart hadn't specified the room number. Hotel management might not appreciate my visit if I knocked at every door, said, oops, wrong room. I slipped the cell phone from my jacket pocket, hit redial for Stewart's number, and listened at the nearest door while the line connected. Nothing. I moved my ear from door to door until I heard the chirp of an answering phone from a distant room at the very end of the hall, a half-inch crack of light between the edge of the door and the frame. The door had been left ajar. Nobody leaves their door ajar in a hotel. The doors close automatically. I glanced behind me, suddenly cautious of witnesses, and crept forward, the fight-or-flight injection of adrenaline already coursing through my body. A face towel lay wedged beneath the corner of the door, near the frame, as though it had gotten tangled beneath the door as it shut. I gently pressed my elbow against the wood and nudged into the room.

Stewart Starbal lay on the bed, propped up by a mountain of pillows at the headboard, the television across the room playing a syndicated episode of *Cheers* with the sound off. A bruise spread beneath his left eye like a storm cloud, and his upper lip swelled around the cut that split it. His cell phone lay chirping on the floor beside the nightstand. I severed the connection on mine and called out Stewart's name. He didn't move. The plunger of a syringe poked from beneath the corner of a hotel towel draped across the bed—his works. I hadn't figured him for a junkie. A dull blot of blood on the skin at the crook of his elbow marked the spot of the fix. I called his name again and leaned across the bed to touch cool skin at his throat. While I felt for his pulse I thumbed 911 into my cell phone. The bruises on his face looked less than twenty-four hours old, the blood pooled beneath the skin purple and not dried black, but he'd certainly been beaten before he talked to me. His pulse eluded me. I didn't think he was dead. The pulse on an overdose victim is often too faint to detect.

I remembered the young man I'd passed in the hall as I was climbing the stairs. The overdose didn't have to be accidental. Maybe Stewart had been dumb enough to mention that he'd been talking to someone who worked for the tabloids. I sprang out of the room and sprinted toward the stairs, telling the 911 operator a young man lay dying of an overdose in the Chateau Marmont. She could hear me running and told me to stay on the scene. They knew my identity the moment they picked up the call but I didn't care. I hung up and shouted to the lobby desk receptionist that they had a medical emergency in Stewart Starbal's room. His voice chased me down the stairs and out the door that led to valet parking. I dodged a couple waiting for their car and dashed toward the street in time to see a black

Corvette speed from a distant curb, far too fast to catch sight of the plates.

As I watched it go the phone rang in my hand. I checked the number. Frank's. He was driving in from the Valley, probably approaching the hotel at that very moment. I connected and didn't wait to hear his voice, shouting, "Quick, a black Corvette is leaving Chateau Marmont, can you see it?"

He didn't speak for a second, then cleared his throat.

"I'm waiting in the lobby," he said. "You ran right past me."

21

FRANK WAS SAVVY enough to distance himself the moment the staff descended. Luxury hotels may not appreciate guests inconsiderate enough to die in their beds but they've become accustomed enough to the ritual that most have protocols for handling it, and because part of the historical richness that made the Chateau Marmont a destination hotel involved the overdose of one celebrity or another, the staff had more experience than most. Suicide is one of the dirty realities of the hotel trade. Given that price is no object to those who plan to check out permanently, few with a valid credit card will choose Motel 6 over the Ritz. Once the staff ascertained that I was not a close relative of the victim, they shuttled me off to a spare room next to the office. The room served as a catch-all storage space, containing a bed, stacks of spare linens, extra file cabinets, and one reluctant eyewitness to an overdose. They were good enough to bring me a room-service carafe of coffee but refused my request to let me get my dog to keep me company.

Frank called a half hour into my vigil to report that the emergency medical technicians had packed up and left without a stretcher. When a homicide investigator named Mike Dougan from the LAPD's Hollywood station poked his head through the door, nobody had to tell me Stewart was dead.

"I was afraid it might be you." He flashed a name written on his notepad—mine. "Not too many people out there named Nina Zero."

"Nice to see you again, too," I said.

"Still got that toothless Rottweiler?" he asked, in a not unkind voice. I'd met Dougan the year before, during the investigation of my

sister's death. The circumstances of that meeting hadn't been con-
ducive to building any kind of friendship, but he treated me as fairly
as his job allowed. With his push-broom mustache and a chest and
belly so massive it made him look like he was always falling forward,
he reminded me of a human walrus. I was even remotely happy to
see him. I'd been dreading a conversation with RHD Detective
Logan. Logan didn't yet know how Stewart connected to Christine.
The Chateau was Hollywood's turf, so it made sense that Dougan
answered the call.

"The kid, is he dead?" I asked.

Dougan mimed giving himself a shot in his forearm.

"Overdose. Nothing the EMTs could do for him."

"How long?"

"How long what?"

"Has he been dead."

Dougan stared at me, trying to read why I wanted to know.

"He called me an hour before I found him." I clicked open my
cell phone and navigated to the number Stewart had called from—
his cell phone—and the time he'd called.

Dougan crooked his neck to read the display, flipped back in his
notebook to a number he'd scrawled on the page, and asked if it was
mine. It was. He'd found my number on the call list of Stewart's
phone. I wondered if Stewart called anyone after me but didn't have
the courage—or audacity—to ask.

"I didn't see more than the one track mark on his arm," I said. "I
figured him for a pothead, not a junkie. Maybe it was his first time."

"Shooting junk is like Russian roulette," he replied. "Sometimes
once is all you need. And if the dose is hot enough, you're pulling the
trigger on a fully loaded gun."

That implied suicide—or murder.

"Did he leave a note?"

"Junkies don't write notes, not even when they intend to overdose. Most of them, they start to commit suicide with the first fix,
and it just takes them a long time to die."

"I didn't see other track marks," I repeated. "Just the one."

"If you know what a track mark looks like, then you should also
know junkies can inject into the legs or hands."

"Did you check?"

His stare turned aggressive. None of my business.

I decided to impress him with my domestic virtues and poured him a cup of coffee. "I'm only asking because I was thinking he didn't administer the hot shot," I said. "Or if he did, somebody prepared it for him."

Dougan's mustache twitched and he pulled down on his face with the palm of his hand, exasperated. "I'd forgotten how much trouble you were. Maybe you should tell me how you met . . ." He glanced down at his notes for the name and his mouth drooped open. "Oh shit, it's not *that* Starbal, is it? The movie guy?"

"His son," I said. "I first saw him at the funeral of Christine Myers, a girl who modeled for me. After the funeral I tracked him down. I wanted to know why he'd gone, because nobody else there seemed to know him."

He absently accepted the cup when I pressed it forward.

"You recognized him?"

"We tracked him by his license plate."

"Why go to so much trouble to find a stranger at a funeral?"

"Because Christine Myers was murdered."

Dougan looked like a man standing upright in a landslide, nothing he could do about the earth sliding beneath his feet except try to ride it out and hope it didn't get worse. "This is the girl they found near Malibu, isn't it?"

I said it was.

"I should have known."

"A lot of murders in L.A.," I said. "You can't keep track of them all."

"I don't expect to. But seeing you is like seeing a buzzard circling overhead; you figure something's dead close by." Beneath his mustache his lips twitched in a failed smile, as though he half regretted the remark, then he dropped his head to sip at the coffee. He knew the comment wounded me and was decent enough to feel guilty about it. "He called you before you called him, right? Did he say why?"

"He wanted to know what happens to the people who slip through the hole in the center of everything," I said.

"What did he mean by that, you think?"

"That he was lost. At least that's what he said."

"How did he sound? His emotional state."

"Depressed and very stoned."

"Did he say anything or indicate in any way he wished to take his life?"

"He kept saying it was too late for things," I said, remembering the conversation. "But I'm not sure I buy this as suicide."

"Why not?"

"As I was coming up the stairs, I saw someone maybe come out of his room."

"You saw . . . somebody . . . maybe . . ." He drew out the words to emphasize the uncertainty of my statement. "Did you see someone come out of the room or not?"

"I can't be sure, but you saw Starbal's face, the bruises. Looks pretty obvious to me somebody beat him up last night."

"And decided that wasn't enough punishment?" His voice spiked with disbelief. "So he comes a second time to kill him?"

"I'm not saying that's what happened, just that it could have."

"Can you give me a description?"

"About six feet, broad shoulders, long and wavy black hair, mid-twenties. He turned his head away from me when he was coming down the stairs, so I didn't get a good look at his face."

"You know what I can do with this?" Dougan flashed his notepad to show he'd doodled a fat *0*. "Zero, like your name."

I decided not to tell him about the black Corvette. He'd ridiculed me enough. A guy leaves the hotel and drives away. So what? Even if he'd been in Stewart's room, that didn't mean he'd murdered him. Dougan was right, it looked more like a suicide than a murder, but the probability that Stewart had killed himself unsettled me far more than the idea that he'd been murdered.

"Here's what I don't get." Dougan flipped back in his notebook. "A guy you barely know, he's getting ready to give himself a hot shot, and out of all the people he can call to share his final moments with, it's you. I'm not hearing why."

The true answer to that was more complicated than I wanted to admit, at least to a homicide detective, no matter how much he was willing to tolerate me. "He knew I worked for a newspaper. I'm pretty sure he knew something about Christine's murder and wanted to tell me about it."

"Why you?"

"Because I knew Christine."

"But inconveniently someone murders him just before he can talk to you, doggone it." He wagged his head again, his smile tight and unbelieving. "I believe you're sincere. It's not your fault you have a hyperactive imagination. But from what I see so far, I also think you're wrong. Of course, if a strange thumbprint shows on the plunger of the syringe, I'll call you a genius." He flapped his note-book closed and tapped me on the shoulder with his fist, just lightly enough to be friendly. "Stick around while I check a few things out, will you? Shouldn't be too long."

Dougan lumbered out the door, slapping his notebook against his thigh. I watched him go with some reluctance. He'd left me alone with my thoughts, and my thoughts weren't good company just then. Whatever Stewart had wanted from me, I'd failed him. I'd been so emotionally focused on Christine that it never occurred to me to care what happened to him. Did someone set him up with a hot shot or had he shot up intending suicide? Judging by the timing of his call, a lethal dose flooded through his veins while we spoke. Maybe he'd expected to be found in time to be revived, the dose a way of tempt-ing death rather than an irrevocable leap into it. Why else mention that he was staying at the Chateau Marmont? Then again, he might have figured he'd be dead by the time I arrived, the call less a cry for help than a final, damning comment on my lack of humanity.

Maybe I stuck to the idea that he'd been murdered because if he'd killed himself, I was complicit in his death. I'd threatened to publish his name in connection with Christine's murder, a final shove to someone already falling down. Maybe by calling me during his last moments he intended to let me know I'd driven him to suicide. I backed toward the bed and sat, feeling pretty rotten about myself. Certain things he'd said during our conversations jutted out at me. Even when I first met him, in the coffee shop on Sunset, no more than a mile away from the Chateau Marmont, he'd said it didn't matter what I printed. Maybe he knew even then that he was going to kill himself. Maybe he'd been going back and forth about it, try-ing to work up the courage, and I'd showed up with my smart little threat to expose his connection to Christine, hoping to pressure in-formation from him, and I'd pressured him right over the edge. What else had he said during that first meeting? That whoever sent the disk of Christine's killing hadn't been bragging about it. He'd wanted it to stop. But if he knew who did it and wanted them to stop, wouldn't they kill him?

Dougan swung the door open and stared down at me with what looked like suspicion and pity, as though he'd overheard me talking to myself, a bad habit I'd picked up in prison.

"The bad news is I've been ordered to accompany you to Parker Center."

Parker Center. The administrative center of the LAPD.

"What's the good news, you'll loan me a quarter to call my lawyer?"

"You're not under arrest, that's the good news," he said. "Can you get your partner to come out from behind his potted palm in the hotel lobby, take care of your dog for you? We'll go in my car."

22

DURING MY LONG and varied career as baggage in the Los Angeles legal system I'd never been treated to an escorted tour of the Parker Center, the stone-and-steel administrative heart of the Los Angeles Police Department, eight stories of concentrated law enforcement rising from the eastern border of the Los Angeles Civic Center. Dougan led me up the elevator and through corridors to an interview room where all the chairs had seats and the table wasn't scarred by thirty-year-old cigarette burns. Most LAPD station houses are dives, not only unfit for the recently arrested, but overcrowded and decrepit places for the beat cops and detectives who work there, crammed into facilities designed for fewer than half their number. Though tarnished by the sun and smog, Parker Center was an aging beauty with good bones, built in the 1950s by the same architect who designed the Capitol Records building in Hollywood. Dougan asked me if I wanted coffee. I was experienced enough with cop coffee to say no. I expected the subtle humiliation of being made to wait and looked forward to the opportunity to lay my head on the table and nap, but before I could drift off Robert Logan broke through the door, a file under his right arm and a cup of coffee from Starbucks in hand. Dougan stepped in behind and waited for Logan to choose a seat before taking a chair on the opposite side, where he lifted the lid of his cup to let the coffee cool.

"If I knew Starbucks had a franchise in the detective's squad room," I said, "I would have asked for a cup."

"You had your chance," Dougan said, his smile so tight it looked braced by rubber bands. Under the circumstances, he didn't want to make the mistake of being too friendly. "Could you state your name and address for the record?"

Logan opened the file and glanced through his notes while I answered those and other basic questions, his left hand fidgeting with his tie, tugging at the lapel of his blazer, then brushing back and forth along the bottom fringe of his mustache until it finally anchored itself to the coffee cup.

"You have the right to remain silent and refuse to answer questions," Dougan said. "Do you understand?"

I recognized the phrase like the opening line to a familiar movie. "Wait a minute, why are you giving me the Miranda treatment?"

Dougan glanced up at Logan, who merely nodded.

"Simple precaution," Dougan said. "In consideration of your record and your current parole status."

"You told me I wasn't under arrest."

"You're not."

"Not yet," Logan interjected, and turned a page in his file.

"So I'm free to get up and leave," I said.

"I wouldn't advise it," Dougan said. "Anything you say or do can be used against you in a court of law. Do you understand?"

I glanced around, spotted the video camera not-so-covertly hidden in the upper right corner of the ceiling, realized they'd be taping this in the event I confessed or said something incriminating. "Of course I understand, but I haven't done anything."

"You have the right to consult an attorney before speaking to the police and the right to have an attorney present," Dougan said. "If you cannot afford an attorney, one will be appointed for you. Do you understand?"

"What's the phrase? No good deed goes unpunished? I can't believe you're reading my rights. I've cooperated with you from the start."

"Do you understand?" he repeated.

"Yes I understand, and I also understand that if I decide to answer questions now, I can change my mind and talk to an attorney anytime I want, and the way this interview is starting out that's going to be pretty darn soon."

Dougan double-clutched, realizing at the last moment that I'd already answered the next question on his pro-forma list, and asked,

"Knowing and understanding your rights as I have explained them to you, are you willing to answer our questions without an attorney present?"

I rolled my eyes. "I'm willing because you made it pretty clear it would be in the best interests of my continued freedom."

Dougan shook his head. He didn't like the answer but he could live with it. "I take that as a yes," he said.

Logan cleared his throat and looked up to catch my attention, his glance as friendly as a slab of concrete. A surveillance photograph of Stewart Starbal taken at Christine's funeral lay face up in the file spread open before him. "I've asked around and from what people tell me you're not a total scumbag, so I'm going to make the effort here to work with you on this. Don't screw up the chance. If you screw up, I'll make sure your parole is revoked. Is that clear?"

"I haven't done anything wrong and that's twice you've threatened me. I'm beginning to think you'll have my parole revoked no matter what I do." I winced, hearing myself speak. Just another self-pitying ex-con who can't get a break in the world.

"Do you know how to operate a video camera?" Logan asked.

"No," I said.

"I find that hard to believe, you being a hotshot photographer and all."

"What you find easy or hard to believe is none of my business," I said. "I can only tell you the truth and let you work it out for your-self."

He snorted at my mention of truth and decided to try again.

"Have you ever operated a video camera?"

"No."

"Have you ever met Dr. James Rakaan?"

"Once."

"Can you tell me about that?"

"I went to his office the day after I got the video of Christine's murder in the mail." As I detailed my encounter with Rakaan I tried to guess where Logan's line of questioning headed. He wasn't asking random questions. He'd arrested Rakaan and presumably was trying to build a case against him.

"You never met him before that?"

"Never," I said.

"If you're lying, I'll find that out."

"I'm not lying."

"Of course you're lying. The only question is where and how. Did Christine Myers ever mention Dr. Rakaan to you?"

"Never."

"I understand why you don't want to talk about it."

"Talk about what?"

"You're a photographer, she's a model, she and her boyfriend like to have sex together on camera . . ." He settled back in his chair and let his glance roam about the ceiling, as though imagining a scenario. "Sure, I can see how that would happen. The two of you get together, have a couple of drinks, she suggests you shoot some video of the two of them having sex together. Isn't that what happened?" He dropped his voice and leaned across the table. "It's not your fault Rakaan went too far. How were you supposed to know he'd kill her? It was supposed to be a harmless little game, dress up in sexy costumes and screw each other, something you could videotape for them—maybe you were even invited to participate when things got really hot. Only they didn't get hot, she got dead. Again, that's not your fault. You couldn't know that was going to happen."

"That's not only insulting, it's stupid," I said. "Obviously you've tripped to the fact that Rakaan and Christine weren't alone in the room, if indeed it's Rakaan underneath the rubber suit."

"How would you know they weren't alone if you weren't there?"

"It's obvious to anyone with a little camera experience, though it might have taken you some time to notice it," I said, letting him sort out the insult implied in that.

"Didn't you just say you never operated a video camera?"

He cocked his head to an ironic angle.

"A frame is a frame," I said. "Video or photography, same difference."

"So you could use a video camera, if you found one in your hands."

"Just like you could use your eyes, if you opened them."

To my right, Dougan sucked in his breath. I didn't worry about going too far. If Logan had any cause to arrest me, he'd do it no matter what I said.

"Toward the end of the video a shadow falls across the corner of the frame. Look closely enough, you'll see the shadow corresponds to someone moving in front of a light set for taping the action." I pointed to the photograph of Stewart Starbal so aggressively Logan leaned sharply back. "And I'm guessing the person who cast that shadow is staring up at you right this moment."

"Meaning you," Logan said.

"Meaning Stewart Starbal."

Logan picked the photograph from the file, glanced at it, and shook his head, his lips a terse blue line beneath his moustache, blue from repressed anger. "What did you say to Mr. Starbal that drove him to suicide?"

"I didn't call him. He called me."

"Did you threaten to publish his name in the paper?"

If he was looking for the hook to hang me on, that might be it.

"He called to tell me that he sent me the video," I said. "The video of Christine's murder."

"Sure he did."

"The dose that killed him was already in his veins when he called me," I said. "Check the time of the call."

"Looks to me like he called you and . . ." The snap of his fingers sounded loud as a firecracker. "Bang, he kills himself. No test will prove different. The timing is too tight. Were you trying to blackmail him? Said you'd splash his name across the headlines if he didn't give you what you wanted?"

"He called to tell me the cops didn't know anything," I said. "He told me nobody knows the truth about what happened to Christine, and then to prove it he identified the stamps on the envelope the video was sent in, Mickey Mouse stamps, something only the sender would know."

"And something he told only you, conveniently, before he died." He shook his head as though he regretted having to say it. "I'm sorry, but you're just not a credible witness."

"Did you find any DNA evidence on the envelope?" I asked.

"The envelope passed through the U.S. mail system. Of course we found DNA evidence. Some of it yours." He gave me a shrewd look, like he was setting me up for a right hook. "Your fingerprints were on the DVD, on the envelope, too. Did you see or touch that disk before it was mailed?"

"How could I possibly see it before I got it?" I asked. "You think I mailed the video to myself?"

"Interesting idea." He snapped his fingers at my chest. "Did you?"

"Of course not."

"Then why volunteer the idea, if you didn't do it?" He tilted his head toward Dougan, who sipped his coffee, watching the interrogation play out. "Did you hear me suggest that Miss Baker mailed the envelope to herself?"

"No, I didn't," he said, playing the straight man.

I stared at Logan, stunned. I'd walked right into it. But it wasn't a right hook. It was more like a head butt or rabbit punch, a reminder that he could play with the rules however he wanted, because for now he was both opponent and referee. "I think this is the point where I suspect you're trying to set me up and decide to ask for a lawyer to be present," I said. "I've cooperated from the start and you've rewarded me with nothing but outrageous allegations. Just do your job. Check Stewart Starbal's DNA against the samples found on the envelope. He's a twenty-year-old kid, not a criminal mastermind. He probably licked the stamps, and if he didn't lick the stamps, he left a strand of hair inside the envelope."

"He was a twenty-year-old kid," Logan corrected. "Now he's just a dead kid. And I gotta think part of the reason he's dead is because of you. And I'd love to just *do my job,* as you suggested, but everywhere I turn you're there, pissing all over everything. Reporters, they're bad enough as a breed, but tabloid reporters, they're scum, and yes, I do mean to include the paparazzos in that comment." He hunched over the table and motioned me forward, his tone changing from outright hostile to gruffly paternal. "So we're going to make a little deal, you and me, something that will probably keep you from punching the return ticket on your parole agreement. I say probably because I don't know what the current investigation is going to turn up. If you've lied to me, I'll find out, so you'd better tell me now."

I kept my mouth shut and my eyes open.

"Good," he said, accepting that as complicit agreement. He stared pointedly at Dougan for a moment. "A few people have spoken up for you and that's the only reason I'm willing to go this far. You're going to stay out of my way from now on. I don't want to hear your name in connection with another incident, not one. I don't want you talking to witnesses—or victims—and I don't want you taking their photographs, and if you do, I'll charge you with obstruction of justice. Do you understand?"

"Where's the mug book you want me to go through?"

He blinked, looked down at his file, shuffled some papers. "You mean the guy you think might have come out of Starbal's room, the one you supposedly saw on the stairs?" He looked up at me, almost couldn't hold back a smile. "We'll get back to you later if we come up with anything."

"I'm not talking about that," I said. "I'm talking about the other mug book."

"What mug book?"

"You know," I said. "The mug book of those you suspect cut the canvas roof of my car and dropped rat poison and a dead rat onto the front seat. I know you didn't ask me in here to threaten to violate the First Amendment rights of the newspaper I work with, the right to a free press, and my own personal First Amendment rights to free speech." I glanced directly into the video camera in the upper right corner of the ceiling. "And I know you wouldn't be stupid enough to threaten my First Amendment rights with videotape rolling. Because the newspaper I work with is very aggressive about protecting the rights of its journalists. I know, I'm only a paparazza scum, but the newspaper's lawyers insist I'm paparazza scum with constitutional rights, and believe me, you get sued by Elizabeth Taylor enough times, you become very good at protecting those rights. So I have to think you were just kidding around, we're all going to have a big laugh any second now when you explain it's all a joke, you really invited me here to inform me about the progress you've made in identifying the person who threatened my life."

Logan squared his collection of notes, forms, and photographs and closed the file. Some time ago, had a cop bullied me around like that, I might have hidden under the bed for a week. He backed away from the table and stood.

"If you're talking about the code 594 misdemeanor vandalism of your car, that's not being investigated by this division. I suggest you direct your questions to the front desk at the Pacific police station. Maybe they'll be able to help you." He turned for the door, remembered his coffee, and reached back for it. "Oh, and Detective Dougan here will escort you back to your vehicle."

I looked at Dougan, who stared straight ahead until the door closed with Logan on the other side of it. He shook his head, took a last sip of his coffee, and glanced at me over the rim. "Really? Someone stuck a dead rat in your car?"

"A dead rat, a box of rat poison, and a copy of *Scandal Times*," I said. "The rat was left under the story about Christine Myers, to make sure I got the message."

"I'll make a call to the squad room at Pacific, see if I can find out for you the status of the investigation." He stood and tossed his coffee cup into a trash can in the corner. "Come on, I'll call while I take you to your car."

Once out of the room, Dougan took a deep breath and winked at me, a gesture he wouldn't have dared while in sight of Logan or the video camera. "You're really a pistol, you know that?" He led me down the corridor toward the elevators that would take us down to the parking garage. "I thought Logan really had you on the run until you started firing back there at the end."

"I should feel lucky he didn't beat me with a rubber hose," I said.

Dougan laughed and stabbed a finger at the elevator call button, as pleased as I'd ever seen him. "Don't think that won't happen if you continue to get in his way. You're a helluva lot of trouble, but personally I think you're good people. You've always played things straight with me and I like your dog. I'm one of the last guys who wants to violate your First Amendment rights." He laughed again and shook his head. The elevator door whooshed open and he ushered me inside. "So please don't treat me to a speech on the Constitution when I suggest that if you have any vacation time coming up, now's a good time to take it."

23

ON THE MORNING Stewart Starbal died, Dr. James Rakaan was arraigned in Los Angeles Superior Court and formally charged with second-degree murder in the death of Christine Myers. Though precious little information is divulged by either side during an arraignment hearing, Frank heard from sources in the coroner's office that the severity of damage done to the victim's trachea, combined with the graphic video evidence, convinced prosecutors that a charge higher than manslaughter was both justified and winnable. The judge sided with the prosecution during the arraignment, and citing the defendant's financial resources, set bail at one million dollars, off the top end of the scale for second-degree murder. It could have gone far worse for Rakaan. The district attorney could have filed charges of first-degree murder, presenting the video as evidence that he'd tortured his victim before her death. Torture is murder with special circumstance, a crime that eliminates the possibility of bail and qualifies a defendant for the death penalty.

Hollywood relishes the fall of the rich, famous, or powerful—if only because it makes for more room on the ladder—but after a decent interval has passed they're more than likely to welcome the offender's return, because even more than a fall-from-grace drama, the town loves a good comeback story. You can be disgraced and loathed, but infamy is still fame, and once you're famous you're famous. Like death, fame allows no regress.

Rakaan could have called any number of former friends, clients, and supporters upon posting bail. A few even might have answered his call. But his voice was the last one I expected to hear when I answered the cell phone as I walked toward my car, parked on the hill behind Chateau Marmont.

"We need to meet, off the record," he said.

"Why would I want to meet you if it's off the record?"

"Because I didn't kill Christine."

"Right," I said, meaning *wrong*.

"I need to know more about the video," he said. "You're the only one who's seen it. I need to know why they think I killed her."

"Maybe it's because you were tying, strangling, and screwing her for fun and profit."

"Please," he said, his voice cracking. "I need help."

"Try consulting another past-life regressionist," I suggested. "Maybe you got away with murder in a previous life and it's catching up to you now." I severed the connection with a sense of satisfaction that soon deflated to regret. I didn't need his photograph for *Scandal Times* and I sincerely doubted he'd tell me anything that would lead to a major story, not when he insisted that our conversation be off the record, but he might let slip something that I could throw to the cops or into the paper. I definitely wanted to question him about his relationship to Stewart Starbal. Maybe Rakaan already knew Stewart had talked to me and the meeting was no more than an elaborate ruse intended to trick out what he'd revealed to me before his death.

I wouldn't learn anything by avoiding him.

When the phone rang again I answered it.

"I didn't kill Christine," he said, no beg in his voice this time.

"Next thing, you're going to tell me you really loved her."

"No, I won't tell you that. I was obsessed with her, yes, and in a not completely healthy way. She was my personal demon. And my relationship with her has not only very nearly destroyed everything I hold dear but soon will put me on trial for my personal and professional life."

"Don't be so dramatic," I said, getting angry at him again. "Christine is dead. You're not. Count your blessings. At the worst, you can plea bargain down to voluntary manslaughter, do your time, and get your freedom back in five years."

"Easy for you to say."

"As a matter of fact, it is." Ahead of me, something pink fluttered against the windshield of my Cadillac. "Okay, we'll do the meet. But if I hear any more of this self-pitying bullshit, we won't talk for long."

He listed a Los Feliz address, not far from where Nephthys lived. I supposed that he hoped to dodge the news cameras by avoiding his Hollywood Hills home. I glanced up as I pocketed the phone and identified the fluttering pink on my windshield as a parking ticket, my punishment for being taken to Parker Center for questioning and exceeding the two-hour limit. As anyone who lives in Los Angeles knows, parking tickets have been added to death and taxes as the only certainties in life. I stuffed it into the glove box and drove down the hill.

The address Rakaan listed connected to the top floor of a duplex built in Spanish Colonial style, the red tile roof and beige plaster walls shadowed by the gracefully splayed fronds of fifty-foot palm trees, and closer to the ground, the red-and-yellow beaks of birds-of-paradise poked from their green sheaths as though watching me climb the stairs to the front door. Rakaan answered my knock so quickly that I suspected he'd been hovering at the peephole. Lack of sleep bruised his eyes to swollen slits, and he stood with less than the square-shouldered certainty I'd seen on first meeting him. Jail does that to people. He wore the suit he'd been arraigned in, a slick gray model with a creased, slept-in look, top shirt button undone and the tie gone. He stepped back from the door as though aware he carried the stain of murder and that I might want to keep my distance from him. I carried my camera bag slung over my right shoulder, the top conveniently unzipped to allow easy access to the crowbar I'd stashed inside. As a rule, I try not to let my curiosity make me too stupid, and meeting a man accused of murder, alone, was a risk that approached stupidity, if it didn't embrace it.

Rakaan walked toward the couch in the living room. The late-afternoon sun filtered through gauzy white drapes, casting a soft light onto the hardwood floors and beige leather furniture, a spray of yellow roses reflecting from the glass-topped coffee table. I followed him into the room, and when I first spotted the framed candids of Christine on the fireplace mantel I guessed the apartment might have been their love pad, until I noticed that photographs of Tammy held equal pride of place. I realized then that I stood in Christine's apartment. I asked him what he was doing there.

"You didn't recognize the address?" He settled so heavily into the couch it looked like he was falling backward into water. "I thought you'd know it when I gave it to you."

"She's never been here," a voice called from the kitchen.

I backed toward the fireplace, surprised in a not particularly pleasant way. Tamara carried a lacquered tray loaded with pastries into the room and set it on the coffee table.

"At least, Christine never told me you visited, but still, I thought you'd know the address or recognize the number when Jim called you."

It took me a moment to realize she was referring to Rakaan by his first name. She excused herself and slipped back into the kitchen to attend to a whistling tea kettle. I thought back to my brunch with Tammy, earlier that week, and remembered how she'd fled the table when I'd mentioned details of Christine's relationship with Rakaan.

"Now I understand why you claimed you never loved Christine." I moved to a leather chair backed toward the window. "Was Tammy in the room when you called me?"

"I suppose I should expect a tabloid reporter to be cynical." His tar-dark eyes were no less opaque for being sheened in soft, draped light. He watched me carefully as I sat, his glance seeking out mine with a fixed willfulness that soothed as it sought to overpower, like a shot of cognac—or heroin. "Tamara was the one who convinced me to call you. She tells me that you're more interested in the truth than in making sensational headlines, not that I believe it."

"If Tammy is interested in the truth, what is she doing with a huckster like you? She didn't even know about your involvement with Christine. And I think you're far less interested in the truth than in worming your way out of a murder conviction."

He found it difficult to catch and hold my gaze in the shadows the light from the window cast across my face and he sighed, frustrated. "Yes, I acted unethically, but I didn't hurt her, not ever, and I certainly didn't . . ." He shuddered so convincingly I couldn't tell whether it was a trick of theater or came naturally. "I didn't strangle her to death."

"You slept with her," I said, just to get him to admit to facts.

"Yes," he said.

"And you engaged in, what would you call it, acts of sado-masochism?"

"We didn't whip each other, no, but we did explore the, ahh, boundaries of sexuality and cruelty." He wiped at his mouth with the palm of his hand while his gaze sank inward. "Christine and I were too attracted to each other's dark places. You know how, in the early stages of a relationship, two lovers circle each other, looking for advantage? Ours quickly became a spiral and it sucked the both of us down. What started out as therapy became madness, a mutually assured destruction of the self. At first I thought I could help her. But I didn't realize that our dark places were so powerful, not until we'd already fallen in, and by then, I didn't care." He leaned forward and shoved one of the pastries around the tray. "Our roles quickly reversed. She began dominating me as part of her regression therapy, the idea being that she needed to work out her fear and anger at having been murdered in her past life. Some of the things we were doing, she could have killed me, and I wouldn't have objected—in fact, I placed myself completely in her hands. She always seemed to know just how far she could take me out before bringing me back. I'll tell you this, though. Whoever killed her either did it intentionally or knew nothing about erotic strangulation."

Tammy carried another tray from the kitchen, balancing a Chinese teapot and three delicate, bowl-shaped teacups. Herbal tea, she announced, a special blend compounded to promote flows of soothing energy and enhance feelings of harmony.

"And the worst thing is . . ." Rakaan scooted aside and placed his palm on the couch, inviting Tammy to sit next to him. "I hid my relationship with Christine from the one I really do love, the one who is proving to me what love is really about by standing with me now."

Tammy blushed over the teapot as she poured the golden-colored liquid into each cup. It seemed to me she was a girl easily fooled by love, but then, so many of us are. I felt a sudden impulse to dump a pot of scalding tea on Rakaan's private parts. I resisted. "Why do you say the person either meant to murder her or didn't know what he was doing?" I asked.

"My lawyer told me that a ligature was used." He coughed once, uncomfortable, and calmed himself with a sip of tea. "That enough force was applied to damage her larynx and trachea. Ligatures really have no place in erotic strangulation because they can damage cartilage, and they hurt. The idea isn't to cut off someone's air, it's to reduce the flow of blood to the brain." He pressed the fingers of one hand against the side of his throat, just below the jaw line. "You do that by pressing here, against the carotid artery, not full force, not to close it off completely, but to slow the blood, just enough to get high on the lack of oxygen and make the sex more intense."

"Don't try it on me, please," Tammy said.

"If somebody was using a ligature, they weren't trying to make the sex better for her, I can guarantee you that." He dropped his hand gently on Tammy's thigh. "He wanted to enhance his own feelings of domination and control and he didn't care if he had to hurt her to do it. Tell me, what did the video show?"

Never in my young life had I imagined I might one day hold a conversation about erotic strangulation over herbal tea with a past-life regression therapist. As a paparazza working for the tabloids, I suppose I should have been inured or at least accustomed to such things. I wasn't.

"The video showed she was strangled with a strap, from behind," I said, giving him a fraction of the information he wanted. "How did you first meet Stewart Starbal?"

"Who?"

I couldn't tell whether his ignorance was genuine or faked. I repeated the name. He said he'd never met him, never even heard of him.

"Jason Starbal, then," I said.

Rakaan glanced at Tammy and asked, "Isn't he the producer of those intergalactic vampire films, the ones that star Milla Jovavich now?" He received a confirming nod and turned a shrug toward me. "I've heard of him, and certainly I've seen a few of his films, but we've never met."

"Then what were you doing at his house in Trousdale Estates?"

"What house?"

"The one with the statue of Oscar in a fountain in the front yard." He laughed, relieved, and grabbed Tammy's hand.

"I think I'd remember that," he said. "I was never there."

"Christine's diary says you were."

"You mean the thing she kept on that semipornographic website?"

"She wrote that she accompanied you to Starbal's estate, where you had a session with Jason Starbal while she met his kids."

His face shot through with blood, and he tossed Tammy's hand aside to sweep his palm across his long, black hair. "That bitch was not supposed to use my name on that site. That was our agreement."

"She didn't use your name. She wrote in code."

"She lied," he said.

Maybe blood and sweat rushed to his skin because he was having an allergic reaction to the tea, or maybe he realized how deeply her diary incriminated him, or maybe he just lied badly. I didn't care enough to stay and get the definitive answer, not if it required hearing Christine slandered. I thought I already knew. I had enough problems controlling my temper. If I stayed, I'd be tempted to straighten his teeth with a crowbar brace. I thanked Tammy for the tea and walked out the door, Rakaan's protests chasing me down the steps. I planned to call her later to describe the video's brutal contents, let her know what to expect by trying to show Rakaan what true love was really about.

24

I SPOTTED HIM when the Rott and I left the apartment that evening for a run on the beach, a man reading a newspaper in the passenger seat of a dingy white Toyota Tercel, parked on the side street opposite my apartment building. The way he held the paper to his face, he could have been studying the results of the previous day's running at Santa Anita, looking no more suspicious than any of the other idlers who frequented the neighborhood. I tried to enjoy the run, the Rott racing after seagulls as though he thought he had a real chance of catching one this time. One thing I'd learned from the Rott, the familiar amusements are often the best. He never tired of chasing after seagulls, no matter how often they eluded him, just as I continued to pursue life, liberty, and happiness, no matter how often they eluded me. In the distance, a violet haze shimmered above the curved blue line of the Pacific, the last remnants of a day that had extinguished itself an hour earlier. Then I realized why the man reading the newspaper had bothered me. It was too dark to read a newspaper.

I'm accustomed to watching others, not to being watched myself, and the feeling creeped me out more than frightened me. We ran the back streets home, the Rott leashed at my side, and approached the Tercel from behind. A tattooed hand dangled out the passenger window, smoke wafting from a cigarette clipped between two fingers. Twin lightning bolts arced across the webbing of his thumb. I jogged up the steps and opened the door to the apartment without glancing back.

While I laid out my camera gear on the kitchen table, I considered the probability that the man lingering outside my apartment had chosen a spot next to me on the beach that morning for reasons other than chance. I threaded Tri-X film into the Nikon's spools and sealed the back, then picked up the 500-millimeter lens. The lightning-bolt tattoo was a variation of the Nazi SS symbol, used by white power groups in prison to signify the carrier has done violence to a minority. I'd crossed the color line while serving time, making friends with like-minded women whose skin tones shaded darker than mine, but I didn't think he'd come to exact revenge for betraying my so-called race. I left on the kitchen light and moved the camera and tripod to the draped window in the darkened living room, knowing from experience that the eye is naturally drawn to light. I loosened the telescoping legs on the tripod and raised the camera to window height, then nudged the lens past the corner of the drapes.

The world in extreme telephoto is a disorienting place, and staring through a 500-millimeter lens is like seeing one piece to a jigsaw puzzle. I made out a roofline and part of a wall, then tilted the lens until the sidewalk across the street came into view, close enough to read the number written on the curb. I nudged the camera up and to the side until the Toyota appeared, the ex-con still in the passenger seat, his eyes tracing a line to the kitchen window while smoke drifted from the lit cigarette dangling from the corner of his lips. I ran off a couple of shots to capture the Tercel's license plate, aware that his face, barely discernable through the lens, would be lost in shadow no matter how fast the film. I dragged a stool from the kitchen counter into the living room and sat with my eye near enough to the viewfinder to see when he moved, and then I waited.

Ten minutes after he'd stabbed out his previous smoke the inevitable collision between time and nicotine happened again, the flick of a lighter illuminating his face while he lit another cigarette. I pressed the shutter and held it down. The camera went into overdrive, clicking off three images a second for two seconds. The flick of the lighter probably wouldn't make for a flattering portrait, but it would illuminate the face of the smoker enough to identify him. I made sure the security chain was engaged and braced the stool beneath the door handle as an extra precaution, then stripped down to shower off the run.

The fact that someone watched my apartment made the shower a short one. Even with the stool jammed beneath the handle I felt vulnerable and jumped back into my street clothes before the water dried on my skin. I knew the police could put my apartment under surveillance—Logan's way to convince me to mind my own business—but didn't think the watcher had ever worked for the police except as a jailhouse snitch. Maybe he was the guy who'd dropped the rat in my car. That made sense but didn't reveal what he had against me or why.

The door chime caught me beneath the hair dryer. I wrapped my right hand around the baseball bat I kept in the bedroom closet—the closest thing to a weapon I'm allowed under the terms of my parole agreement—and moved toward the door. When the Rott sat a few feet from the threshold, his expression rapt, I knew I wasn't in immediate danger. I checked the parabolic peephole just to be sure, saw Sean Tyler's face bending away from the lens. I opened the door.

"Getting ready to hit my fastball?" he asked when he saw the bat.

"Somebody's staking out my apartment," I said.

The flicker in his eyes read as fear and guilt.

"I'm pretty sure it's not the department," I added, conscious not to turn my head toward the watcher. "White Toyota Tercel parked across the street. I've got a camera set on telephoto by the window."

He nodded as though thinking it over.

"Aren't you going to ask me in?"

Maybe I'd been wrong about the flicker. I stepped away from the door. Sean paused just long enough to give the Rott a quick scratch and slid over to stick his eye to the viewfinder.

"I don't see anything," he said.

I nudged him aside and bent to look. Shadow and pavement showed through the lens, an empty parking space where the Toyota had been. "I just got out of the shower." I ruffled my hair to demonstrate it hadn't yet fully dried. "He must have moved while I was away."

He nodded as though he almost believed me.

I thought about the coincidence of Sean's knock and the Tercel's disappearance, decided it wasn't a coincidence at all. "What kind of wheels are you driving tonight?"

"Same crappy car last time I saw you."

"Crown Victoria?"

"I drive what the motor pool gives me."

I showed him the webbing between my thumb and forefinger.

"The guy in the car? He has twin lightning bolts tattooed right here."

He took that as an excuse to grab my hand, as though he needed to inspect my skin to tell me what I already knew. "You figure he's a con?"

"He knew the car," I said. "That's why he took off."

"You mean the Crown Vic?" He dropped my hand, leaned over to peek around the edge of the drape. "Sure, if he's a pro, that's possible. You write down the plate?"

The scent of him went to my head like a cocktail, the mix of leather, cologne, and body oils a fragrance as uniquely Sean's as his face. I told him I got the plates on film, and backed toward the open kitchen because I knew what would happen if I remained within kissing distance of him. "I was thinking he was maybe the guy who left the dead rat in my car," I said.

"What dead rat?"

I lifted a bottle of Jack Daniel's and two tumblers from the kitchen cabinet. "Somebody cut a hole in the Caddy's ragtop, dropped a packet of rat poison and a dead rat onto the front seat."

"Why didn't you tell me?"

"I reported it to Logan." I showed him the ice-cube tray, pulled from the freezer. "I didn't think you'd want to get involved."

He raised his forefinger to signal one cube and said, "Somebody threatens you, I want to know about it."

"Really?"

He nodded.

"Somebody threatened me just this afternoon. Right in the middle of Parker Center." I slid the tumbler across the Formica countertop and told him about my interrogation. Sean sipped at his bourbon and shifted away from me while I spoke, a sign, I thought, of personal conflict. He couldn't help me without damaging his career and I didn't think either of us wanted that. It would be simpler just to end it, no matter how I felt about him.

Strong emotions can ruin lives.

I told him that Dougan recommended I go on vacation for a while.

"You might take that suggestion a little more seriously," he said.

"I don't get vacation time, not paid anyway."

"Maybe just a few days, then." He leaned against the kitchen cabinet, staring at me. "Up the coast, somewhere like Morro Bay, or maybe inland, to Death Valley. This time of year, it's just hot enough to drive away the tourists, but not so hot to keep us from hiking the desert."

I took down the bourbon in one pull and poured another, dropping an ice cube into the tumbler to slow my drinking. That he asked shocked me. Whenever I'm surprised my curiosity engages, just before my natural suspicion. I didn't know who Sean was, any more than he knew me. "You worked undercover, how many years?" I asked.

"Seven," he said, continuing to stare at me. "Not straight. I was working organized crime, vice mostly. I'd go under, then come back out, wait for another operation, go under again." He smiled. "I was good at it, but the burn rate for that kind of work, it's astronomical."

"You develop a taste for hiding things while you worked undercover, or were you always that way?"

The question puzzled him at first, but then he considered it, and the implications disturbed him. "A little bit of both, probably." He wandered from the kitchen into the darkness of the main room and spoke with his back to me. "My father is a religious man. A deeply religious man. I'm not. Never was, not even as a child. I grew up pretending I was something I wasn't. Went to choir practice, Bible study, I was even going to study for the ministry until I crapped out for lack of vocation, discovered I couldn't fake faith anymore. I'm not saying I'm a Godless atheist . . ." His laugh was short-lived and bitter. "But I don't have the special relationship my father has. In fact, I probably get along better with the devil." The kitchen light glittered in his eyes when he glanced back at me. "Present company excluded."

"I'm not the devil you think I am," I said. "But I am poison to you. Makes me wonder why you're here."

"The good things in life are always a little poisonous." He sipped at his drink and stared at me so intently I felt myself falling into his eyes. "You like whiskey?"

I nodded.

"So do I." He shook his head at how much he liked it. "Too much will kill you. Alcohol poisoning. You chug a fifth of ninety proof in an hour, you'll die. But just the right amount, your heart beats a little faster, your skin flushes, you feel warm all over."

"The trick is knowing when to stop." I walked toward him, the kitchen light throwing my face into shadow, forcing him to peer to read my expression. "Two drinks, three or four, you feel fine, but then a little time passes and you start to fall faster than you climb, and you don't want to let it go away, that high, that wonderful high, so down go five, six, seven, and then it's not so much fun anymore, it all feels sour no matter how much you drink, and if you drink eight, nine, ten, you'll suffer like you're gunshot."

Then I kissed him, because he'd been truthful, yes, and because if he knew I was poison, it was his responsibility and not mine to know how much would be fatal, and most of all I kissed him because he smelled so incredibly delicious. As good as he smelled, he tasted better. I took him down like that second drink, the good one that's sipped and savored and not bolted like the first, the one that brings the flush of joy to your skin and makes you just the right amount of high so that when it's done you immediately want more, even if more is too much. I backed him into the bedroom. We had time and privacy this time, and savored each other in long, slow kisses and teasing caresses, praising with lips and fingertips the skin we found beneath the leather and cotton we unwrapped from our limbs. We had been barely conscious of making love the first time, too rushed to be fully aware of what we were doing until it was done. We wanted to make up for it the second time, allowing the sexual tension between us to build one kiss, one caress, one dispensed article of clothing at a time, pleasure washing over us in sustained moments of ecstasy as mind-altering as any drug. In the depths of my pleasure I heard the phones ring, first the land line and then the cell, but I was somewhere else by then, floating and darting through a sexual landscape I had always sensed existed but never fully experienced before, a landscape so thrilling but terrifying that I bit him in fear and anger and he bit me, pain fueling passion to streak us into bliss.

The door buzzer jarred me from the postcoital languor of Sean's arms and the excited bark of the Rott yanked me out of bed. When I told Sean I'd check out who rang I was speaking to a moving target, his clothes already bundled against his chest as he slid toward the bathroom door. Maybe that was one of the lessons working under-cover taught him, to move fast when uncertainty threatened.

The Rott was stutter dancing by the front door when I emerged from the bedroom, behavior that meant he was excited to see whoever stood on the porch. The bell rang again, the sustained burst of someone leaning on the button in frustration. I tucked a T-shirt into my jeans and put my eye to the peephole. Cassie stood on the opposite end of the parabolic lens, a backpack bigger than her torso towering over her shoulders. I snapped open the door, shocked to see her.

"I was waiting at the bus station for you," she said, her voice so high and stressed that the Rott matched it with a whine of his own. "Why didn't you come pick me up?" She tilted forward to keep from tipping back down the steps under the weight of the backpack.

I pulled her over the threshold and lifted the pack from her shoulders. "I didn't even know you were coming in today."

She wilted once released from the pack, her knees buckling and her shoulders curving into her chest. "I wrote you two postcards!"

I lay the backpack against the wall and winced, not from the weight of the pack but from guilt. I hadn't checked my mailbox. "I'm sorry, but I haven't been around the past couple of days and when I got in tonight I forgot to get my mail."

Cassie glanced at the closed door to the bedroom, her shoulders still huddled toward her chest, and she lifted her chin, sniffing at the air. "I'll bet you forgot." She made an angry but insincere grab at her backpack. "I'll be going now. I don't want to get in your way. I can take care of myself."

I wrapped my arms around her and before she could run or protest I hugged her, hard, telling her that she was staying, and that was final.

"I even called," she said, letting me hug her. "Didn't you hear my voice on the answering machine? Why didn't you pick up?"

"I keep the sound turned down. My parole officer has a habit of dropping in unannounced and I don't want her to monitor my calls."

I released her when the door to the bedroom opened and Sean emerged.

"Thanks for letting me use your bathroom," he said, wiping water from his hands. "The grease from the carburetor was impossible to get off. I hope I didn't leave too much of a mess in there." He grinned at Cassie, the white of his teeth against the black stubble on his jaw making him look like a friendly wolf, and reached out to shake her hand. "You must be Cassie. Great to meet you. Your aunt is incredible, know that?"

"This is Sean, a friend of mine," I said.

"A friend, sure," she said, but she took his hand.

"Don't think too badly of me, but I gotta go. Maybe we'll get a chance to talk later, after you've settled in." He winked at me. "Walk me downstairs?"

I nodded, glanced into the bedroom through the open door, noticed the bed had been freshly made, the bedspread stretched taut to conceal that we'd been twisting the sheets into knots for the past hour. An affair with a cop who once worked undercover had some advantages. I told Cassie she could move her backpack into the bedroom and followed Sean down the stairs. "That was pretty fast thinking," I said at the bottom.

"I didn't want to embarrass you." He turned to give me a lingering kiss goodbye. "I'm going to light a fire under the detectives in Pacific, see if I can get them to assign a patrol to your house, keep an eye on you."

"Sure," I said, not believing that would do any good.

"If this creep shows up again, give me a call, I'll cruise by to check him out. And if you need help with the plates, let me know and I'll see what I can do."

One of the few things I've learned in life about men is that the ones who want more than a midnight fling intrude upon a woman's life in ways that attempt to be helpful, offering to fix things that may or may not be broken, or to buy things that may or may not be needed. It was sweet of him to offer and I thanked him for it as I waved him into his Crown Vic, but I didn't intend to allow that, not yet. I could take good enough care of myself. I didn't want to set him up with false expectations of my dependence or his indispensability, figured that would work better for both of us in the long run.

When his taillights turned the corner I detoured around the staircase to key the box that held my mail, stuffed beyond bursting with neighborhood circulars and other species of junk mail. Cassie's postcards lay at the bottom of the box, one a photograph of Sid Vicious and the other of a saguaro cactus in full bloom, a hurried scrawl announcing the arrival date and time of her Greyhound bus on the backs of both. An oversized envelope stood pressed against the rear of the box, the blank back facing outward. I pulled it free, crumpled the circulars into a ball, and it wasn't until I started to climb the steps that I noticed the Mickey Mouse stamps affixed to the upper right corner of the envelope.

"He's a thief, isn't he?" Cassie asked when I keyed through the door.

"Sean? He's a cop."

I tossed the mail onto the kitchen counter.

Her mouth gaped. "You're kidding. He's too sexy to be a cop."

She followed me into the bedroom, where I opened the door to my closet and pulled a pair of cotton gloves, normally used for handling negatives, from a roll-out bin of photo supplies.

"What are you doing hooking up with a cop?" she asked. "Aren't you afraid he's gonna, like, bust you? Or is it like he's already got something on you, some incriminating evidence, and so he's extorting you for sex?"

I shook my head as I walked back to the mail on the kitchen counter, astonished that she'd asked the question.

"Mom said that kinda stuff happens all the time."

Her mother had worked as a call girl for nearly ten years, before getting into the confidence game. She'd spoken from experience, I was sure, but I didn't want Cassie to think all cops worked like that. "Sean is a friend." I glanced down to slit the lip of the envelope with a kitchen knife. "I hope a good one, but I don't know that yet, and the questions you're asking aren't helping me to figure that out."

"Sorry," she said, as though she didn't mean it.

I turned the envelope upside down and shook out a photograph of a dark-haired man in his thirties, his well-fed face and elegant suit failing to conceal an ice-pick coldness in his eyes and lips sculpted to a permanent sneer.

"My God, it's Andrew Luster," Cassie said.

Heir to the Max Factor fortune, Luster had been arrested the year before on eighty-seven charges of poisoning and date rape. It didn't surprise me that Cassie recognized the man by his photograph; my niece knew criminals like other teenage girls knew boy bands. When the police raided his beachfront home in Mussel Shoals, eighty miles north of Los Angeles, they found scores of videotapes of Luster having sex with unconscious and seemingly drugged women, most of whom had yet to be identified. The search warrant had been issued after a woman accused him of spiking her drink with GHB and raping her. Neither Frank nor I had been assigned to that story but its sleazy blend of spoiled wealth and drug-forced sex had proven irresistible to *Scandal Times,* which gave it extensive coverage. It had been rumored, in the pages of *Scandal Times* and elsewhere, that Luster was part of an international ring of playboy millionaires who traded date-rape tips and video clips over the Internet. I flipped the photo by the edge face down onto the counter. A message of some kind had been scrawled onto the back of the photo in a spidery hand that matched the lettering on the envelope: J, O, K, E (*no S*).

"Who's it from?" Cassie asked, craning her neck to read the message.

"The guy who mailed me the video, the one showing Christine, you know, what happened to her."

"You mean Stewart Starbal?"

I thought about it for a second. We hadn't yet printed Starbal's name in *Scandal Times* and I hadn't mentioned his name to her. I hadn't even met him until she'd already flown back to Phoenix. "How did you know that?" I asked.

"You're not the only one knows about Christine's diary," she said. "I've gone through all her posts a dozen times. I caught the trick with the mirror, 'LA Brats' spelling 'Starbal,' just like Nephthys did."

"You talked to her?"

"Sure, all the time. We're like, girlfriends."

"Suicide Girls, it's an adult website. How did you get in?"

She gave me a scornful look, said, "Please, I've been doing illegal stuff since the day I was born."

"You talked to Nephthys about this?"

"Her roommate Tammy, too," she said, nodding. "I've probably talked with them more than you have. When I heard Stewart Starbal's name on the radio tonight I figured it had to be him that sent you the video, then suicided himself from guilt. You think he helped kill Christine?"

"I don't know, but I think he knew who did." I stared at the letters on the back of the photo, trying to figure out what they meant, then glanced again at the envelope. He'd mailed it two days before.

Maybe if I'd checked my mail, I would have asked the right questions when Stewart called and he'd still be alive.

"'It's a joke, no shit,'" Cassie said, pointing a ragged purple fingernail at the *S* in parentheses. "Maybe it's like a tribute band, you know, Luster is some kind of role model."

I flipped the photo face up and stared into Luster's face.

"If it's a joke, I don't get the humor in it," I said.

25

DETECTIVE ROBERT LOGAN knocked on the door to my apartment at nine o'clock the next morning, responding to a call I'd made to report that I'd received evidence in the mail pertaining to the murder of Christine Myers. I stood in the kitchen, backed against the sink with Cassie beside me, and watched a lawyer in a navy-blue suit that cost more than my entire wardrobe open the door to let him in. The night before, when I'd called Frank about the envelope, he'd insisted I have a *Scandal Times* lawyer present when Logan came calling. He wasn't being sentimental, he said; they'd take away my camera if they arrested me and without my camera I was useless to the paper. The lawyer resembled the jack of spades, hair slicked back over a Botox-smooth face and a cold, knifey look in his eyes. He'd appeared at my door a quarter of a billable hour before Logan, and we'd spent the time discussing the various strategies I might use to keep my mouth shut.

The lawyer introduced himself as legal counsel representing the weekly newspaper, *Scandal Times*, and its work-for-hire employee, meaning me, then backed away from the door to let Logan inside the apartment, gesturing with the manicured nail of his forefinger toward the envelope, lying on the dinette. Logan watched the man's hand until it tired and dropped, a subtle power play to demonstrate he wasn't going to be ordered around by a libel lawyer, then moved toward the envelope, which I'd sealed in a zip-lock bag. "You opened it?" he asked, glancing up at me.

"Ms. Zero opened it as she would any piece of mail addressed to her," the lawyer said, "and when she determined that it contained material that could be evidence in a criminal investigation, she placed the envelope in a secure container and notified the authorities at the earliest possible opportunity."

Logan stared at the lawyer, annoyed, and lifted the baggie by the corner. "What makes you think this is evidence?" he asked, peering at me over the tips of his fingers.

I opened my mouth to speak, remembered I wasn't supposed to say anything until the lawyer approved, and when he nodded, once, an expression of caution focusing his eyes, I said, "The Mickey Mouse stamps on the envelope, for one; those are the same stamps on the video of Christine's killing somebody mailed me."

"If you knew it was evidence by the stamps," he said, letting the plastic bag swing one way and then the other, pinched between his fingertips, "why did you tamper with that evidence by opening the envelope?"

"Ms. Zero didn't notice the stamps until she'd already opened the envelope and looked at the contents," the lawyer explained. "Only after she opened the envelope and noticed it contained a photograph of Andrew Luster did she think to check who may have sent it."

"Who?" Logan asked, as though not hearing right.

"Andrew Luster," I said. "Accused of date rape up in Ventura County."

The baggie swung to a stop and he dropped his hand to his side.

"I'll advise the lab that biological material containing Ms. Zero's DNA may be present in the contents," he said to the lawyer. "The Los Angeles Police Department requests that the publication of any of the material in this envelope be formally cleared with us beforehand."

"That's not the way it works," the lawyer said. "The editors at *Scandal Times* will notify you of what and when they plan to publish, but they're within their rights to publish with or without permission."

Logan made a point of looking at me long and hard, then turned his head to the lawyer. "Remind the editors that cooperation is essential in this case. If they publish this without clearing it with us first, the consequences will be severe."

The lawyer interpreted that to be the threat it clearly was and asked, "Exactly what consequences are you referring to?"

"Consequences to the criminal investigation, of course," Logan said, gracing the lie with an easy smile. "Did the girl come within a foot of the envelope, either before or after it was opened?"

Cassie shook her head, purple-limned eyes enthralled with fascination or fear or a combination of both.

"I suppose if the techs find a purple hair, we can figure it's hers." He laughed as though demonstrating he wasn't such a bad guy after all, then turned and darted away, his shoes clipping down the concrete steps.

Later, when we loaded her backpack and the Rott into the Cadillac, Cassie asked why Logan hated me so much.

"You picked up on that?"

"It's only, like, obvious."

"Obvious how?"

"Just a vibe I had," she said, "that if nobody else was around, he'd beat the shit out of you. I got the same feeling sometimes before, you know, when the cops would come visit my mom and one of the stepdads."

We drove the freeways toward Pop's house with the top down, the radio blasting hip-hop above the roar of wind. Cassie's observation about Logan reminded me that her youth was deceptive when it came to understanding all things criminal. She'd been a passive participant in her mother's cons while still in diapers; when money had been short, Sharon had painted red dots on her daughter's forehead and begged cash from sympathetic men, claiming she needed to take her baby to the hospital. Most of those born into the criminal life continue the family trade well before reaching maturity, often with the self-awareness of a falling brick, and though Cassie might just as easily return to the short cons of her youth, she had an intuitive grasp of the way criminals think that might allow her to build a better life for herself. She was naturally wary of cops too seeming to know how they regarded the people around them, particularly those they suspected of criminal behavior, and unlike her aunt, she understood that it was far healthier to avoid rather than confront the law.

I hoped she might take advantage of her natural gifts by studying law, maybe become a lawyer, and promised myself I'd support and encourage her if she tried, but that may have been more my fantasy than her reality. The night before, she'd stripped down to a boy-beater T-shirt to model her new tattoo, a suggestively winking blonde Betty Boop inked above a banner etched with Christine's name. I hadn't seen too many tattooed, purple-haired lawyers in my travels through the legal system.

I'd hoped to drop off Cassie and her backpack that morning without having to engage Pop in conversation more involved than a wave goodbye, but he stood waiting by the open hood of his Dodge Ram pickup truck and ambled over to meet us before I could take my foot off the brake. He carried a Styrofoam container of hamburger in a grease-stained hand and gave the Rott a good whiff of it before he helped Cassie lift her backpack from the rear seat.

"Brought that toothless dog of yours a little something to eat," he said. "Why don't you come inside, I'll put it in a bowl and he can chow down."

The Rott was all for accepting the invite. I had to grab on to his collar to keep him in the car. "Busy day," I said.

"Sure, I understand, just long enough to feed him the grub."

He gave the meat a little wave to further excite the dog, then he lifted the pack with one hand onto his shoulder and ambled up the walk toward the front door. The thing weighed over fifty pounds, yet he'd picked it up like a sack of groceries. He may have been nearing retirement age but he was still strong, and because he'd figured out a surefire way to get me out of the car, he was craftier than I'd given him credit for. When I let go of his collar, the Rott bounded out of the car and caught up to Pop's heels before whirling around to let out a single bark to encourage me to follow.

Pop had cut the waist-high weeds since my last visit and scattered a seed mix that sprouted small, green blades amid the stubble. The front of the house had been scraped of peeling paint, blotches of white primer soaking into patches where the surface had been stripped down to the wood. Next to the front door he'd painted three strips in varying shades of brown, and he turned to point them out as he crossed the threshold. "You got a good eye for color, let me know if you like one of these," he said, then merged into the interior shadows of the house, the Rott bouncing in behind him.

I stepped into the living room and held my breath as though the air Pop lived and breathed might contaminate me. He continued through to the kitchen, a shadow moving in the open archway, where he clattered a metal bowl to the floor and knelt to feed the dog. Cassie emerged from behind the refrigerator door with a can of off-brand cola, popping the top and swigging away while drifting toward the kitchen table. It shouldn't have felt so sinister to me, that house. My mother had lived there most of her life. I'd loved my mother, even if we didn't talk all that often or well. I let myself breathe in the odors of an aging man living alone, the greasy smell of fried foods mingling with dust, mold, and sweat.

"Hey, what's this?" Cassie asked, hovering over the kitchen table.

"Just an old photo album. I uncovered it the other day while cleaning out some stuff." Pop boosted himself up with a helping hand on the dog's back. "It's got some pictures of your mom in it, back when she was younger than you are now, thought maybe you'd want to see them."

She flipped the album to the first page and squealed, delighted. I edged into the kitchen, watched her bend over a color snapshot of her mother as a baby. My parents owned an early '60s Kodak Instamatic back then, the 126-cartridge film so simple to load that it made photography push-button easy. It wasn't much of a baby shot, angled straight down to Sharon swaddled in her crib, her fat, baby face mottled a sickly blue and purple, the film's chemistry not stable enough to hold the colors true.

"God, she was ugly!" Cassie said.

"All babies are ugly," I said, speaking from the experience of having photographed thousands of them.

"Except your own." Pop leaned his knuckles onto the table and craned his neck to look. "At least, that's what your mom said, that you were all beautiful babies, though to tell the truth I tended to think none of you were much to look at until you got to two or three years old."

I inched toward the kitchen table and looked over Cassie's shoulder while she flipped the page to a montage of baby Sharon photographed in the living room or the front yard, the wheels of Pop's 1959 Chevy Apache pickup truck the most common background. I'd been born ten years later, the image of my sister as an infant as strange to me as it was to Cassie. The beauty of my mother at age twenty-four in a one-piece bathing suit, two years after giving birth for the first time, shocked me. In all my memories she was old, face prematurely lined by worry and abuse, her body settling down and spreading out to a lumpy shape by the time she'd reached forty. She'd been young and beautiful until the years of children and marriage wore her down, my brother, Ray, coming when Sharon graduated to polka-dot dresses, and then, six years later, when she thought she'd finished with pregnancies, I'd come along, unplanned.

Cassie turned the page to a portrait of the family, dressed in our Sunday best circa 1976, though it was more likely our Saturday best because we rarely went to church. "Probably a wedding," Pop said. He'd worn his hair longer then, and the suit he'd donned for the occasion sported the grotesquely wide lapels and bell-bottoms of the times, the fabric a shiny purple that would have served better as someone's bedspread. Mom stood next to him, about a foot to the side and a little behind, her bubble-head hairstyle already ten years out of fashion. Ray huddled on the other side of Mom, shoulders slumping inward, his head raw from the crew cut Pop regularly enforced on him. Sharon stood with her hands on her hips as though annoyed with whoever was taking the photo, about fifteen years old then, her strawberry-blonde hair hanging straight as a plumb line due to the ten minutes she spent every couple of days at the ironing board, ironing it straight. I stood in front of everyone, smiling like a little geek, maybe five years old, my knees scraped red beneath the hem of my lime-green skirt. Something about the photo disturbed me, and it wasn't until I stayed Cassie's hand that I noticed that none of us were even close to touching each other.

That realization saddened me, setting me up for the photo on the flip side of the page. We're all suckers for early photos of ourselves, maybe because they remind us of a time when we still believed in things, when we still had some hope our lives would turn out for the better. In the photograph I'm five years old, sitting on Pop's shoulders, still in the lime-green dress, my legs wrapped around his neck and my hands holding on to his ears like the reins of a horse, my eyes half-closed and face shining with smiling bliss, while he stares at the camera with a look of supreme paternal tolerance, the kind of look men get when their daughters are pulling their hair or ears or trying to see what daddy looks like with his nose pressed flat against his face. The photograph broke my internal ice faster and more irrevocably than any apology, the sorrow for all the trouble that had come between us welling up so suddenly I threw my hand to my mouth to catch the sob spilling out. I turned to latch on to Pop in a fierce, angry hug and I told him that I must have really loved him then. He stood for a moment with his hands to his side, shocked by the sudden gesture of affection, but when I felt his shoulders shift to return the hug I backed sharply away and slapped the side of my leg to command the Rott's attention.

"Sorry, like I said, busy day, gotta run," I said.

I bolted out the front door, leaving Pop stunned speechless, and drove over the pass and down into the San Fernando Valley wondering if I'd unfairly demonized him all these years. Maybe he hadn't been the bad father I'd remembered him to be. We all behave badly at times. We all have our demons.

Maybe I'd allowed his many moments of violent behavior to blot out memories of the times he'd been patient and caring, and as shocking as it sounded to me then, even loving. His violent rages had victimized everyone in the family, but he'd been more than just an angry father. Maybe I'd surrendered to the pity-me ethos of our times, the cult of victimization in which suffering equals personal merit and becomes a source of social status, encouraging us to feel sorry for ourselves rather than to heal and get on with our lives. The photograph implied that within Pop's violent core burned a little family love, and for his young, tomboyish daughter he once possessed genuine paternal caring. This did not excuse his angry sulks and violent behavior. He'd beaten his wife and bullied his children, even if he'd loved us in his own remote and abusive way. I had every right to hate him for that, but any feelings of victimization that lingered from my childhood were my responsibility now far more than his. I couldn't continue to deal with Pop burdened by the pains and resentments of my childhood. Even if he hadn't changed, I was no longer a little girl helpless before him. I was the stronger one now, I thought, and no, he wasn't the same man I'd known as a child. Grief had taught him something about remorse and age had gentled him. I had to learn to deal with who he was now, not what he'd been then.

Under those conditions we might be able to coexist.

26

I RETURNED TO Venice intending to catch a little of the sleep that had slipped from me the previous night but the sight of the white Tercel, parked this time in the grocery store lot down the street from my apartment, made sleep a more distant priority. The slot he'd chosen offered a clear sight line to the apartment steps and the front door to my second-floor unit. I parked in my assigned spot in front of the building, opened the door for the Rott, and led him up the stairs, careful not to tip the guy with a backward glance that I was aware he watched. Sean had asked me to call him if the watcher appeared again, but I didn't intend to play the role of the helpless female. The trip to Pop's left me with a feeling of restlessness. I needed a little action. I called Frank.

"Whoever owns those plates is working some powerful juju," he said, the volume of music blaring in the background signaling I'd caught him in his car, moving from one story to another. Warren Devon, it sounded like. "My guy, he's still searching but the plates don't show in the registry, like somebody's blocked them out. He tells me it's going to take another day at least, and no promises."

"How could somebody block the plates?" I asked.

"A computer hack," he answered. "Or an old-fashioned bribe."

"So we're talking about somebody with a little juice, maybe."

"Or a high school kid with a computer and time on his hands. Give my guy a little more time, he might come up with something."

I'd allowed the ex-con to sit watch on me for days and done nothing about it. I asked Frank if he had time to do me a favor. I didn't even know if the ex-con worked for somebody or was a solitary nut with an inappropriate fixation on me and my dog. A lot of aimless crazy people live in Venice and I couldn't discount that as one of the possibilities. After I hung up the call I pulled open the window in the bedroom and gauged the drop, thinking I might tie a couple of bed sheets together until I realized I only owned two and couldn't anchor them to anything except the doorknob. The two sheets tied together would barely reach the window. The drop measured no more than fifteen feet, but the asphalt below looked hard enough to make my ankles throb just from the thought of landing. Then I remembered the futon in the living room. I stripped away the throw pillows and dragged it through the bedroom door, the Rott watching with the worried excitement dogs sometimes get when humans move things from their familiar places. I propped the futon against the wall and sat on the floor to give the Rott a little quality face time, seeking to reassure him that I was sane no matter how it might look to him.

When Frank's Honda slid into the alley I lowered the futon out the window, held it flat against the side of the building, and let it drop, momentum and gravity tipping the padding flat onto the asphalt no more than a foot from the base of the wall. The Rott barked, once, confused, when I slid my legs out the window. I told him to stay calm and gripped the windowsill with both hands to lower myself. I didn't want to dangle out the window, a coward to let go, and so the moment my body steadied I kicked gently out and released, hoping for the best. I hit the center of the futon with the accuracy of a stuntwoman and tucked into a ball, letting my momentum carry me into a backward somersault, the perfection of my landing marred only by a bump on the head as I rolled back.

Above, the Rott jumped his paws onto the windowsill and barked. I shushed him, pulled the futon behind the trash dumpster, and slid into the Honda's passenger seat, sinking my head below the level of the windowsill as Frank accelerated toward the mouth of the alley. "Is the Rott following?" That was my biggest worry, that the dog would panic and decide to jump down after me.

"Don't worry, he's fine," he said, barely glancing in the rearview. "Nice landing, by the way. You practicing for your next jailbreak?"

I dug into my jacket pocket and handed him a spare set of keys to my apartment and car. "You'll go get him once I'm in place?"

"Somehow, I always imagined it would be a little different when you finally gave me the keys to your apartment." He let a lonely sigh fall from his chest and followed it with a smirk. "Relax, I'll take good care of your dog. You can have him back when we meet Mrs. Starbal the First. You mind coming with me on that? After you take me to lunch, of course."

"What are we meeting her for?"

"She'll talk to us, for one. Not too many people are willing to talk to me about Starbal senior. Certainly nobody who ever wishes to do lunch in this town again."

"What's the angle?"

"Nothing special," he hummed, meaning he wasn't saying yet, and changed the subject. "You know Logan called to twist my arm about the photograph he picked up from your apartment. He does not want to see any mention of Luster published."

"Why's that, you think?"

"I can't figure it out. It's like the connection blindsided him."

"Stewart told me the cops didn't know anything."

"If you look at it from Logan's perspective, he has to treat the whole thing like a gag, right? But what if it's not? He's screwed. If we print it, he'll be forced to deny the connection, and if it turns out Luster is connected in some way? After he's denied it?" Frank grinned and shaped a mushroom cloud with his free hand. "Ka-boom to the old career."

"You mean he thinks somebody mailed the photo as a joke?"

"Isn't that what it said on the back?"

"What it said on the back was *J, O, K, E*, then, in parentheses, *no S*."

Frank turned his face away from traffic to show me a smart-ass smirk. "I know you didn't have the chance to finish college, but that spells joke, singular, as in, *no s*."

"Why not *J* for James Rakaan? Or even Jason Starbal?"

"Why not *J-O-K-E* for joke? People about to kill themselves, isn't that what they think life is all about, a cruel joke?" He swerved into the driveway of a Budget Rental Car franchise and parked next to a blue Ford Focus. He pointed his chin toward the rental car and dropped open the Honda's glove compartment to show me the keys.

I started the Focus and drove slowly back to Venice, figuring Frank was working on something he didn't want to tell me about, not just yet. We were often competitive, trying to outscoop one another, not with the intention of sucking up to the publisher but to goad each other on. If Frank was interested in talking to Starbal's first wife, then maybe he figured Jason Starbal was involved. That made some sense. Jason Starbal was a filmmaker with ready access to video equipment, and Christine's diary implied that she'd accompanied Rakaan to his house. Maybe Jason Starbal and James Rakaan shared the same sick erotic thrill of strangling drugged young women, video-recording the acts either to enjoy later or to share with other perverts over the Internet. That would certainly freak out Stewart enough to want to kill himself.

Frank veered at Rose and circled the block while I pulled into the grocery-store parking lot across from my apartment, parking two rows behind the white Tercel. I pulled from my jacket pocket a point-and-shoot camera with a 4.5X zoom lens, decent enough for a pocket cam but not nearly as powerful as the telephoto on my Nikon. Seen through the lens, Frank carried something in his left hand as he lumbered up the steps to the second floor of my building. The ex-con lifted a pair of binoculars, the cheap kind that can be bought for under twenty bucks in any drugstore. Frank keyed the door and slipped into the apartment. The ex-con shifted his shoulders and leaned over the passenger seat, the door frame concealing the action of his hands from view. It looked to me like he was writing something down—probably a log of my movements and visitors.

Frank emerged from the apartment less than two minutes after he'd gone in, leading the Rott out the door by his leash and dangling the object he'd carried up the stairs—a donut, the zoom revealed. Frank didn't relate to animals any more gracefully than he did to people, but he and the Rott shared a common passion for junk food, and that formed the surprisingly solid basis of their friendship. He led the Rott down the stairs bite by bite, then tossed the stub onto the floor of the Honda, shutting the passenger door after the dog leapt after it.

The ex-con pulled himself out of the Tercel to watch as Frank sped away, then dropped back into the car to light a cigarette and think about what he'd just seen. A few minutes after he extinguished his smoke, he stepped from the car and approached a raggedy man who pushed a shopping cart crammed with clothing, blankets, old books, and brightly colored plastic toys. He shook his head as the ex-con spoke to him and tried to continue his trek toward the sea but paused when a single bill of money waved in front of him. He snatched the bill as quick as a frog catching a fly and swerved across the street, leaving the cart safely parked just inside the sidewalk while he climbed the steps and rang the buzzer to my apartment. He backed away from the door and hung his head, then rang the buzzer again. Then he just stayed there, swaying from side to side, like somebody had put him into neutral.

The ex-con lit another cigarette, thought about what he was seeing, then lifted a cell phone to his ear. He talked to somebody for a minute or two, finishing the call and the smoke at the same time. He stepped into the car and reached to the right of the steering wheel. The Tercel quaked, exhaust trickling from the pipe. I started the rental and let him jet from the lot before I pulled out of my slot. He drove east on Rose before cutting toward the crown jewels of L.A.'s Westside: Century City and Beverly Hills. Mid-afternoon traffic congealed just enough to slow the Tercel, making it that much easier to follow. I fell a few cars back, speeding forward whenever I sensed a changing signal might separate us. He led me east through Beverly Hills, then north through West Hollywood onto Sunset Boulevard, just east of the Strip. After we hit the 6000 block the glitz of the Westside faded into the grime of east Hollywood. He passed Amoeba Records, signaled left, and swung across traffic into a parking lot beneath a black glass and silver steel midrise, pausing just long enough at a parking arm to insert a card into the code slot. I swept past and pulled a U-turn at the next light, coming at the public entrance to the underground lot from the opposite direction.

A ticket flickered from the box beside the parking control barrier. I grabbed it and sped past the rising arm into the first open slot. The clank of a compact door shutting near the far corner revealed where the ex-con had parked his car. I slipped out of the rental and into the nearest stairwell. I took the stairs two at a time, grabbing the handrail to pull me through the turns with greater speed, then skidded to a stop at the top landing to gather my breath before pushing through into the lobby. Across a granite-tiled floor the ex-con stepped alone into an elevator. I waited for the doors to slide shut and stepped across the lobby, watching the lit buttons above the elevator to mark his progress. The elevator behind me chimed. I rode it up to a corridor of offices with the names of minor-league entertainment companies and professional service corporations—mostly accountants and lawyers. I leaned against the wall and listened. Around the corner, a door hissed and clicked as it shut. I veered to the inside wall and peered around the edge. The moment I read the brass letters on the door at the end of the hall, I knew I'd tracked the watcher to his hole: Ray Spectrum Investigations.

"Oh no, not that guy," Frank said, his mouth stuffed with French fries, when I told him that the ex-con keeping watch on me worked for Spectrum. We met at a Fatburger near my apartment after dropping off the rental and picking up the Caddy, a late lunch at a restaurant of his choosing his price for helping me work the tail. I'd accepted without qualm, knowing he wouldn't choose a boutique Westside restaurant that required a bank loan to pay the bill. Frank preferred hamburger to filet, and pizza to almost anything.

"Why not that guy? What about him?" I asked.

Frank slowly unwrapped the paper from the edge of the hamburger and stared as though he'd lost his appetite, a rare phenomenon. "He's a fixer," he said.

"What's a fixer?"

"Somebody who fixes things."

I didn't suffer from the same loss of appetite. When I bit into the hamburger, the sauce spilled over the paper wrapping and dripped onto the table. "What kind of things?" I asked.

"Embarrassing things." He shook his head, flummoxed. "Let's say you have a celebrity actor who gets his kicks from snorting cocaine suspended by his heels from the ceiling, nude, while a hooker whips him with a wet weasel tail."

"Are you making this up or did it really happen?"

"Stranger things have happened, but I'm making up this one." He looked at his burger as though about to take a bite but held off. "Let's say the guy who deals the coke and the hooker are partners working a blackmail grift. They tell the celeb pay up or the photographs are going to start appearing on the Internet. What can he do about it? If he pays, he'll be on the hook for the rest of his life, and if he doesn't, not only will he be laughed off the screen in his next picture, the ASPCA will sue him for mistreatment of weasels."

"He could always confess to the public and beg for mercy," I said.

"If he made a living playing the kind of guy who might like getting whipped with weasel tails while suspended nude from the ceiling, sure, he could work it into great publicity, but what if he plays priests or tough guys? Not an option. So he hires a fixer, someone who promises to make the problem disappear, one way or another." He lifted the hamburger to his mouth and bit down, then continued to speak while he chewed. "The fixer approaches the blackmailers and offers a deal that won't blow back on the celeb. Unlike the celeb, who only plays tough guys, the fixer is physically imposing, a real tough guy who looks like he wouldn't hesitate anchoring the blackmailers to the bottom of Santa Monica Bay. Of course he doesn't actually kill anybody if he doesn't have to, because the bodies could surface and that might lead to bad publicity. He prefers to give the blackmailers part of what they want—it's only money, after all—with the threat of lethal retaliation if they break the deal."

"And Spectrum, he's a fixer?"

"There are two top-dog fixers in this town," Frank replied, chewing now with great enthusiasm. "Anthony Pellicano and Ray Spectrum. Pellicano got his start as a skip tracer working deadbeat accounts. Spectrum was a cop, originally."

"Local?"

"LAPD. Internal Affairs reprimanded him over an officer-involved shooting—he was working vice at the time—and he quit to join the dark side. The fact that he shot some people while in uniform only adds to his reputation. You know what he likes to tell clients?"

I shook my head, no clue.

"'I only make people disappear as a last resort.'"

"You think he might include troublesome paparazzi in that remark?"

"No doubt." He finished the hamburger with a polishing lick of his fingers. "If Ray Spectrum has been hired to fix you, your problems with Detective Logan are going to feel like a minor case of sniffles before a truck hits you."

"Who do you think hired him?" I asked.

"Starbal, who else?" He suppressed a burp with the back of his hand and fingered out the pack of cigarettes in the front pocket of his T-shirt. "Either direct, or through his lawyer."

"You mean Stewart?"

"I mean his father. Spectrum built his business on guys like Jason Starbal. He wouldn't hesitate to drop a dead rat in your car if he thought it would scare you off the story."

"He'll have to try something worse than a dead rat." I swallowed the last bite of Fatburger and grabbed a sack of takeout for the Rott.

"How about a car bomb?" Frank asked. "You want to have to check the undercarriage of your car with a mirror every morning before starting it up?" He led the way out the door, lighting a cigarette the moment he moved from a violation of the California labor code —smoking in a place of employment—to mere public nuisance. "Let's figure Starbal knows his son is involved," he said, fuming smoke from his nostrils. "He sees we're making a major play on the story and he panics, runs to Spectrum, tells him we have to be stopped. Spectrum hires the ex-con, who drops the dead rat on your seat, figuring it will scare you off."

The Rott jumped his paws to the Cadillac's passenger window when he spotted me, his muzzle pressed against the glass, and tumbled onto the asphalt when I opened the door, too dumb to back away or just too eager to get out to where the food was. I let him sniff the bag before I reached in to tear off a strip of hamburger. "Have you considered the possibility that Jason Starbal is more directly involved?"

Frank peered at me over the smoke curling from his cigarette, his expression as cagey as a card player just asked if he was bluffing. "You mean, have I already considered the possibility that Jason Starbal's oeuvre might include more than vampire flicks? Interesting idea. You think we should ask Mrs. Starbal the First a few pointed questions?"

"There's one thing I don't get about this," I said, feeding the Rott the hamburger patty, bite by bite. "Why is Starbal trying to scare me off? I'm not the one writing the story. Why not drop a rat on the seat of your car?"

"Have you seen the interior? I've got so much junk in there a dead rat would just get lost." He glanced inside his car to remind himself of the mess and smiled. "Besides, why should I be scared of a dead member of my own species?"

27

I IMAGINED SOMETHING a bit grander for the first wife of one of Hollywood's most successful producers than a counter position at Bloomingdale's, even if she worked the more exclusive terrain of men's and women's luxury watches, but Meme Richardson had suffered the great misfortune of divorcing Jason Starbal before he made his Beverly Hills mansion money. According to court records she'd willingly sacrificed her alimony payments from Starbal to marry again less than a year after they divorced, her second marriage lasting a spectacularly brief three months. After that, she seemed to have given up on men—on marrying them, at least. She lived in a modest apartment in Westwood and worked in the solidly upscale Century City Mall, less than a mile from Rodeo Drive, never gravitating far from the center of wealth but continually denied access.

Meme—pronounced *Mimi*—had agreed to talk to Frank off the record about Jason Starbal, ground rules we readily agreed to because so few people seemed willing to talk about Starbal, particularly after the death of his son. She didn't want to be seen talking to tabloid reporters, so to please her taste for the clandestine we waited outside Bloomingdale's for her shift to end and followed her at safe distance to Gelson's, a boutique supermarket where she commonly shopped for groceries. Tall and thin, and stylishly dressed in an embroidered linen skirt and off-the-shoulder stretch silk sweater, she looked like she belonged to the class she sold her products to, a mid-forties woman with taste in quality things as high as her cheekbones. The diet-enforced angularity of her face may have imitated an aristocratic ideal of gracefully aging beauty, but it also gave her a sharp and bitter look. She bought a cup of coffee from the in-store bakery and took it to a table in the informal seating area, browsing through the circular of specials and pretending surprise when we asked if we could join her.

Frank began with a nonthreatening question intended to elicit an easy reply, asking, "How long were you married to Jason Starbal?"

"Five years," she said, then tightened her lips as though remembering how unpleasant those years had been. "I've been waiting for over twenty years to hang Jason by his balls—that's why I've agreed to talk to you—but I have to insist that what I tell you stays off the record. It may not look to you like I have much to lose, but what little I have is mine and I don't want to be sucked dry by frivolous lawsuits."

"Why do you think that might happen?"

"Because that's what rich people do, they throw lawyers at problems to make them go away. If you don't have the money to retaliate—*pffft!*" She flicked her fingers into the air in imitation of a small explosion. "They vaporize you in court."

"Has he done that to you before?"

"What hasn't he done to me?" She brushed her hand over her hair, pulled sharply back into a ponytail. "You'd think he might not be so damned hostile to the mother of his first son, but every time I get within a hundred yards of asking him for a little something he sics his lawyers on me."

"Your son, Jagger, right?"

"My beautiful lost boy." She brought the paper cup of coffee to her lips but pulled it away without taking a sip. "He has his own production company now. He'll take care of his mother when the time is right."

"Do you see much of Jagger?"

"Jason doesn't approve of me so no, I don't." She straightened her back and stared aggressively forward. "As you may have guessed, Jason got custody."

Frank hunched his shoulders and leaned over the table, trying to make himself seem as inoffensive and harmless as possible, a visual cue to the initiated that he was about to open a potentially embarrassing line of questioning. "I thought it was normal, in divorce cases, for the woman to be given custody of the children."

"I was a drunk," she said. "I used a lot of drugs then, too."

"And Jason Starbal didn't?"

A high-pitched chime sounded from her rattan-top purse. She unsnapped the catch and withdrew the offending cell phone, a sleek Nokia with a brushed platinum surface. "He drank and snorted coke almost as much as I did, but he held it a hell of a lot better than I could." Her brow wrinkled as she read the caller's number and she dropped the phone back into her purse, letting voice mail pick up. "It didn't help that over the next three months I was arrested for drunken driving, drunk and disorderly conduct, and then, as the coup de grâce to my hopes of motherhood, felony cocaine possession. It wasn't a lot of cocaine, but possessing any amount of cocaine in those days was a felony."

"Still is," Frank said. "But if everybody who did cocaine in Hollywood was caught, they'd have to hold the Oscars from county jail."

She smiled bitterly, happy to find a cynical shoulder to gnash her teeth on. "I spiraled down after we separated and then Jason's career took off. He could afford a good custody lawyer. All my money was tied up in drug lawyers. So the judge awarded him custody, and since then the more successful he's become, the more difficult he's made it for me to even see Jagger." She hurriedly lifted a tissue from her bag to catch a tear sprung from anger more than sorrow. "But my personal faults and abuses aren't going to help you sell newspapers, are they? I'm sure you're more interested in hearing the dirt about Jason."

"Why did your marriage break up, you think?"

"Whores," she said, stuffing the tissue into her purse. "Jason couldn't stay away from them. And I'm not talking about street whores, the kind that give you the clap if they don't turn out to be a vice cop in drag."

"I heard it rumored that he was in Heidi Fleiss's black book."

"I'm sure he's been in every black book penned in the last twenty years. Before Heidi Fleiss it was Alexis Adams. She ran a call-girl service out of a house on Doheny Drive."

"What drove him to visit whores?" Frank blushed, or at least pretended to, and scribbled a note in his pad. "I'm sorry, that sounds naive, I know, but bear with me."

She flashed her hand across the table to cut him off. "I know exactly what you're getting at. Jason liked rough sex. For a while I was perfect for him because, you know what? I was too drunk or stoned to care. But it wasn't enough for him to dominate his wife. He needed new girls to conquer." Her cell phone chimed again and she sighed, exasperated. "I should just turn the damn thing off."

"Does your definition of rough sex include bondage?"

"Are you kidding? I've still got the strap marks." She held up a single finger to pause the conversation while she lifted the phone from her purse. "Give me a second to get rid of this caller."

She pressed the phone to her ear and answered with her name. Her expression shifted from annoyance to shock, and she glanced the supermarket across as though searching for someone. "What, were you going to chase me all the way to the frozen foods section?" Her voice rang in high indignation. "I just sat down for a cup of coffee and these two characters started asking me questions." She dropped her head and listened. "No, I don't respond to threats. Threats don't work for me. What are you going to do, use your pull to force Bloomie's to transfer me to the luggage section?" She tapped a burgundy, talonlike fingernail onto the countertop and nodded once. "That's better. Okay, we have an understanding. You have all my particulars, right?" She disconnected, dropped the phone into her purse, and then held absolutely still, thinking through the ramifications of what she'd just agreed to.

"Was that Jason?" Frank asked.

"One of his minions. Sorry, but I've got to go." She clutched her purse to her abdomen and glanced at her coffee as though deciding whether to bring it along or abandon it with the conversation.

"Wait a minute, help us out here, we've just gotten started," Frank said, rising to his feet as she backed away from the table and stood. "I'm happy that you've managed to use us to cut yourself a better deal, really I am, but I'm having sudden memory failure here. Our conversation was on the record, right? How would you like me to identify your quotes: as the venomously bitter former Mrs. Jason Starbal or as Meme Richardson, recovering drug addict?"

"You're a bastard," she said, as though she expected nothing less.

"Just doing my job," he answered.

"You want to talk to the woman responsible for ruining my marriage?"

"I think I hear the conversation going off record again," Frank said.

"Talk to Anabelle Lash." She snatched her coffee from the table and prepared to flee. "That bitch has been satisfying Jason Starbal's perversions for twenty years."

28

NORMAL BUSINESS HOURS had long since ended by the time we crossed into the San Fernando Valley, but we drove with some prospect of reaching Anabelle Lash in her office that night. Neither of us was particularly knowledgeable about the phone-sex business—at least, Frank claimed not to be, despite his otherwise encyclopedic range of knowledge—but it seemed reasonable that call frequency would pick up in the evening hours, when the clientele returned from work to pursue their lonely fantasies of subjugation and domination. Frank began dialing Lash's numbers—both office and cell—the moment we left Gelson's. She didn't respond to either.

A dozen cars were parked in the lot of the aging courtyard office complex where Lash worked, encouraging hopes we might find her in. We passed along a concrete walk into a courtyard decorated with dying plants, a standing ashtray overflowing with cigarette butts, and a lost-looking garden gnome standing on the end of a wooden bench. The names of some of the building's other tenants suggested a line of business similar to Lash's, which explained the crowded parking lot and the brightly lit windows circling the interior. Frank rang the bell to Lash's office and waited, then rang again. The blue-white of fluorescent bulbs flickered behind the venetian blinds covering the window above the walk. Frank glued his finger to the bell and peered through the slats, seeing little more than a sliver of carpet at the base. When no one answered after two minutes of insistent ringing, he scribbled a brief message on a sheet of notepaper, asking Lash to contact him as soon as possible, and wedged it under the door. Across the courtyard, a pneumatic blonde and Cleopatra-esque brunette, both dressed in low-slung jeans and halter tops, stepped out of a door marked Wildebeast Productions and lit cigarettes for each other.

"You girls seen Anabelle Lash around tonight?" Frank called.

They shook their heads and turned away to discourage further conversation. I wandered over to ask them if they'd ever heard of Jason Starbal. The one on the left shook her head and looked away, but the one on the right noticed my camera and asked what I was doing. When I told her I was a tabloid photographer she introduced herself as Cherry Laurel, "like the poison," she said. "You're talking about the movie guy, right?"

"Cher," her colleague said, the name spoken as a warning.

"What? Anabelle is a bitch."

"So who isn't?"

Cherry pursed her lips around the filter tip of her cigarette and wrapped her arm around the neck of her colleague. "Take our photo?" she asked.

I pulled the lens cap from the digital camera and directed them toward the courtyard, where I could use a security light instead of a flash to illuminate their faces. I told them to have some fun and ran off a series of stills while they vamped for the camera, then displayed the results on the digital's microscreen. They laughed and squealed at the more outrageous shots, the act of being photographed and then viewing the images animating them in a way mere life did not. Then a bearded head poked out the door and advised them that the cigarette break was over, time to get to work. Doing what, I didn't ask.

"Give me your e-mail address, I'll send you copies," I said.

"My name's my address," she said, and listed a popular e-mail service. "And just so you know, I've never seen the guy you mentioned with Anabelle, I certainly didn't see him at her office last week, no way she set me up on a date with him when I was just breaking into the business, and the rumors that he's a complete fetish freak are completely untrue." She gave me a big, cartoonish wink and slipped through the closing office door.

"What have you got that I don't?" Frank asked, walking up to me.

"A camera," I said.

"The pen may be mightier than the sword, but who uses swords anymore?" He sidled up to the camera to view the images I'd just shot and asked, "Didn't you tell me Christine went to Starbal's mansion with a friend making a *professional* visit?"

"And we thought that referred to Rakaan," I said, advancing from shot to shot. "You think she could have been referring to Anabelle Lash instead?"

"She does practice a variant of the world's oldest profession."

The possibility that Christine accompanied Anabelle Lash to Jason Starbal's estate troubled me for several reasons, primarily because it meant Dr. Rakaan might not have been complicit in her killing. I'd wanted him to be guilty because I considered him a user and abuser and I just didn't like him. As I drove back to the beach that night, I played through my mind scenarios of what might have happened that day. Lash was well aware of Christine's aspirations to be an actress and could easily have invited her along when she visited Jason Starbal. Christine would have gone thinking that she'd visit the mansion of a rich Hollywood producer, might get the chance to meet him, and if he met her, who knows, maybe he'd like her enough to cast her in one of his films. Her diary hadn't mentioned that she'd met Jason Starbal, only his kids, but she might have lied about that, or a meeting might have been arranged later.

It all made a perverted kind of sense to me. Christine was a beautiful young woman educated in the techniques of sadomasochism, a rare combination. Of course Starbal would want her. Lash wouldn't hesitate to make the offer if she could convince Christine to participate. Would Christine agree? Maybe she'd been given ruffies to ensure that it wouldn't matter whether she agreed or not. Or maybe she'd gone willingly and drugged herself to take the edge off the humiliation of having sex with a man for purposes of career advancement. The shadow visible in the lower right corner of the video may have been Anabelle Lash's; given her extensive experience in adult film, she'd know how to set lights and operate a video camera. The only detail that didn't fit was Christine's appointment with the supposed producer of one of Johnny Depp's films; Depp had never appeared in one of Starbal's films, and if Lash arranged the meeting, Starbal had no need of the deception. Like a card that doesn't fit the hand I was playing, I discounted it.

I intended to take a run when I returned to the apartment and got as far as laying out my sweats, exciting the Rott with the prospect of late-night exercise, but instead of running I collapsed on the bed, exhausted in a way that felt new to me, dropping like dead weight through semiconsciousness and down into a deep sleep. When the doorbell rang sometime later I felt jerked from the depths into a gasping kind of consciousness. Cassie and Pop had argued, I thought, and she's hitchhiked back to Venice to seek refuge. I glanced at the clock on my way to vertical—an hour before midnight, not late at all.

The Rott stood before the front door, attentive but not excited. I put my eye to the peephole and was neither greatly surprised nor terribly pleased to see Sean's stubbled face in the parabolic lens. I thought about rushing to the bathroom to splash my face with water, freshen my breath, and spike my hair but decided against it. That he hadn't called before deciding to come over annoyed me. I figured he didn't want to call because phone records can be checked, his extracurricular visits to an ex-con documented by the call lists phone companies keep on their customers. I wanted to inch the door open just wide enough to tell him to go away, but within seconds of seeing him I broke into a pheromone sweat as powerful as any drug and instead I opened the door wide.

"I woke you," he said, and tried to back away.

"I can sleep later." I grabbed the lapel to his leather jacket and pulled him inside. He kicked the door shut with his heel while I kissed him, hesitantly at first but then hard and fast, his stubble scraping against my lips like sagebrush. I yanked off his jacket but pushed him away when he came at me, let him get closer before I pushed him away again, then slipped behind to wrap my arms around his chest and bite his neck. A sound escaped his lips, midway between a moan and a roar, and he spun around, catching me from the back so deftly I couldn't have escaped the move had I wanted to. My hands dropped to his belt while he kissed my neck and when he paused, expecting the jolt of skin-on-skin pleasure, I gave him just the smallest bit of pain instead and turned at the moment of surprise to push him back and lift his shirt above his stomach. He raised his arms to help me strip it off, then pulled me toward him, his hands jerking at my blouse in retaliation. If our first session of lovemaking had been spontaneous and the second smoothly deliberate, our third time together pitted strength against strength and weakness against weakness, the act of making love a physical contest not to cause pain—not much, anyway—but to dominate each other through the force of pleasure. We finished an intertwined jumble of limbs, our skin sweat-slick and flushed with blood, agreeing in our pleased exhaustion to call the contest a tie.

"Are you a mountain person, an ocean person, or a desert person?" he asked, cradling me from behind.

I turned just enough to catch him out the corner of my eye with a look that wondered why he was asking. "That's the great thing about L.A., you got all three within walking distance so you don't have to choose."

"I thought we'd try the desert this weekend," he said.

I considered that for a moment, then rolled on top of him.

"Were you going to ask me if I wanted to go, or just abduct me?"

His teeth glowed in the dark like a Cheshire cat's.

"Which would you prefer?"

"I don't abduct easily, so you'd better ask," I said. "And Stewart Starbal's funeral is coming up, so next weekend is better."

"How'd you learn that? I thought it was private."

"Frank heard about it," I said. "He probably bribed the mortician."

Sean kissed my neck and sat up, saying he wished he could stay but he had to check on some things. I suspect we both appreciated spontaneity more than predictability in a relationship, and mystery far more than certainty. The weekend after next was still far away. I didn't worry about it. "I heard Logan came by to see you this morning," he said, hunting in the darkness for where I'd flung his pants. "Everything okay?" He spotted one leg hanging from the top of the bedroom door and shook his head, amused.

I told him about the envelope I'd found in the mailbox. At the mention of Luster he sat down on the edge of the bed and looked at me in a way I couldn't interpret, the streetlight outside my bedroom window glinting across the surface of his eyes.

"Why didn't you call me last night when you found it?" he asked. "I'd left you, what, fifteen minutes before. I could have doubled back, easy."

"And done what?"

"Helped," he said, exasperated. "You have some guy watching your apartment, you get threatening stuff in the mail, maybe I'd like to hear about it." He jumped to his feet and pulled his jeans over his hips, tracked down his shirt, shoes, and socks in the other room. "I'm not trying to set the tone for a relationship here. I'm not implying that you're weak and I'm strong, or that I'm here to protect you, or any other kind of sexist bullshit. But I have a skill set you should be using. I have contacts and resources that can help you. And no, I'm not going to compromise an ongoing investigation by feeding you information you don't already know, but this looks like a particularly dangerous time for you and I can help keep you safe."

"If I call every time a little trouble comes my way, you'll need a twenty-four-hour hotline," I said.

"You got my numbers, call anytime you want."

I threw myself into a robe and went to the kitchen, thinking I'd pour myself a drink, then decided against it. "Do you think Logan is a good investigator?" I asked.

"You don't make RHD without being a good investigator." Sean hopped into a shoe as he followed me toward the kitchen. "The question is whether he's the right investigator for this case."

"Why?" I asked. "Was he beaten as a child with a rolled-up tabloid?"

Sean gave that the laugh it deserved and eyed the bottle of Jack Daniel's I'd set on the kitchen counter. I poured three fingers into a tumbler for him and he limped over, one shoe on, one off, to get it. "Why are you so interested in attending the Starbal funeral? The poor kid's dead, for Christ's sake, let him rest in peace."

"I don't think he's going to rest in peace, ever."

"He sure as hell won't if you tabloids keep hunting him." He sank half the bourbon in one go and bent his leg to slip on the second shoe, looking like an awkward, one-legged bird while he tied the laces. "You know that cops often moonlight in the movie business, right?"

"Everybody who lives in L.A. knows that," I said. You couldn't drive past a location shoot without seeing a half dozen motorcycle patrolmen working traffic control.

"It's a good source of additional income, and not just for uniforms." He dropped his foot and straightened. "About a dozen years ago Jason Starbal produced a police thriller set in L.A. From a cop's perspective, the film got the details right. Guess who served as the technical advisor?"

I stared at him, thought, no way.

"That's right, Robert Logan, working homicide out of North Hollywood then."

"Your station," I said.

"Before my time." He made a face as he sipped the bourbon. "But his legend lives on. One of the reasons we don't get along."

"You and Logan?"

"The bastard thinks he still owns North Hollywood and I don't encourage his delusions." He closed his eyes, sipped again, shook his head. "It's not so bad as that. We're collegial. I wasn't worried about him until you connected Stewart Starbal to the murdered girl."

"You think he has a conflict of interest?"

"I'd be careful mentioning any links to Starbal, let me put it that way."

"You know the package, the one that came in the mail?" I opened the refrigerator door, suddenly ravenous, and finding it depressingly empty, settled for a carton of milk. "I'm pretty sure it came from Stewart Starbal, and the photograph of Luster, it refers to his father, to Jason Starbal."

He stared at me across the countertop.

I glanced at the carton in my hand, thinking it was that.

"So I feel like drinking milk, anything wrong with that?"

"Help yourself," he said and shrugged. "What makes you think the photo has anything to do with Jason Starbal? I don't get the connection."

"The stamps on the envelope were the same ones used to post the video of Christine's killing." I took another swig of milk, not liking the way he looked at me. "Stewart all but told me he'd sent it. I always figured he felt guilty because he was there when the video was made, a passive spectator maybe, but there. That he'd hooked up with Christine when Rakaan brought her over on a visit to his father. But now, I don't think Rakaan had anything to do with it."

A surprised bark gusted from Sean's chest. "Whatever you do, don't tell Logan that. He'll think you're working for Rakaan's defense team, or worse, inventing stories just to make more sensational headlines. They've got all the evidence they need to convict; believe me, it's just a question of time before Rakaan asks to plea."

"To a lesser charge, like manslaughter," I said.

"From what I've heard, that's what everyone from the district attorney on down agrees is what happened here. They had a history of sadomasochistic practices. He just went too far one night and killed her, then panicked and dumped the body."

"And the shadow moving across the frame? In the video?"

"A dog, a cat, a newspaper blowing in the wind, a figment of your imagination." He shook his head and finished his drink, clattering the glass to the kitchen counter in a gesture of frustration and, I thought, anger. "What makes you think the Luster photograph refers to Jason Starbal?"

"Just a guess," I said, not wanting to go into it.

"Glad to see that degree in criminology is finally paying off."

"I think Stewart feared other girls might be killed and wanted it to stop," I said, goaded into responding. "That was why he mailed me the disk and later, the photo. But why not just step up and turn the killers in, unless he couldn't do that either. That's what made me think his father was involved."

"People do all kinds of things because of guilt, you'd be surprised." He lifted his leather jacket from the kitchen table, where I'd thrown it while undressing him. "If he was part of what happened to Christine—let's say he was in the room with Rakaan when she was assaulted and did nothing about it—he'd do small, pretty much meaningless things to chill his guilt."

"Like mail evidence to a tabloid," I said.

"Rather than turn himself in, yes. And when he still didn't feel any better about himself?" He punched his arms through the jacket, glancing around the room to see if he'd forgotten anything. "You get what you found at the Chateau Marmont, a confused kid dead from an overdose, half suicide, half cry for help. But you know what?" He moved to the door, turned, gave me a smart-ass smile. "You don't have proof for any of this, not even that Stewart Starbal sent you the video or the photo. It's all rumor and innuendo. Perfect for *Scandal Times*."

29

THE SUN STRUGGLED to pierce a June haze hanging over the L.A. basin on the morning Stewart Starbal was scheduled to be buried in Forest Lawn Memorial Park, his body marked for a plot near the crest of a green hillock that offered sweeping views of the foothills of Glendale and north Los Angeles. Frank drove like a lost tourist along labyrinthine cemetery roads named Enduring Faith Lane and Precious Love Drive, searching for one that led to high ground. A gardener had tipped him about the time and location of the memorial service, to be held in Wee Kirk O' the Heather, one of the cemetery's three faithful re-creations of Scottish and English churches, and though we didn't plan to crash the service, we did intend to observe the mourners at a respectful distance.

We weren't the only ones at the cemetery not mourning the death of a loved one; along the way we passed a Japanese tour bus parked near the Last Supper Window Memorial Terrace, which boasted Leonardo da Vinci's immortal work re-created in stained glass. Not even the mortuary business is immune to the fairy-tale kitsch culture of Southern California, turning cemeteries into amusement parks of the dead. Casual visitors were welcomed—no, encouraged—by mortuary management to stroll the sumptuous grounds and admire several exact replicas of Michelangelo's greatest works at no charge whatsoever, with souvenirs of their visit available in the mortuary gift shop. I stepped out of the car and gazed down the slope of grass to the pitched roofs and stone spires of Wee Kirk O' the Heather and nearby Little Church of the Flowers. Below the church two late-model Japanese sedans and a black BMW parked at the edge of the road, where it curved around the hill and widened to allow mourner parking.

"There he is," Frank said, pointing toward a cluster of men huddled near the church entrance. "Ray Spectrum, the guy with the black ponytail."

I aimed the camera and caught in the telephoto frame the suntanned face of a man who could have once played professional football, his black and brilliantined hair swept back above a massive brow and tied in place with a black band, the shoulders of his black matte suit so wide he'd need to turn sideways to fit through the average door. At that distance it was difficult to get a good read on him, an oversized pair of Valentino sunglasses covering his face like an eye mask, but from the way he spoke to the two gray-suited bruisers huddled next to him he was accustomed to command, and when he pressed his hand to his ear and glanced up the hill, directly into my telephoto lens, I knew he was wired and we'd been spotted. The way he looked at the lens, I felt he expected to see me there.

I burned a few images into the digital camera to document his presence and then pointed the lens toward the entrance at the base of the hill, where the first in a convoy of black stretch limousines cruised through the cemetery gates, black ribbons flapping from their aerials like diplomatic flags. I zoomed back for an epic shot, the solemn black vehicles moving amid rolling green and misty sky. At the end of the limousine procession drove mourners in private cars, a steady crawl of sports and luxury metal driven by kids who might have been Stewart's rich friends. The black Corvette in the middle of the pack was not particularly remarkable, neither newer nor more expensive than many of the other cars in the procession, except that I'd seen it before. At the curve beneath the church, the limousines parked bumper to bumper and disgorged their cargo of black-suited men and women in elegant mourning dresses and pantsuits. Spectrum personally opened the passenger door to the lead limousine and whispered into the ear of the balding middle-aged man who emerged.

"Jason Starbal," Frank said. "Can you get him?"

A private bodyguard hustled around the hood with something black in hand that blossomed into an umbrella when he approached Starbal, blocking him from view and shielding the next person to emerge from the passenger compartment. I'd caught a few frames of the back of Starbal's head but nothing more; Spectrum had no doubt warned him that we were watching from above. I'd seen umbrellas deployed before—it

was a favorite trick of security teams to shield celebrities from paparazzi cameras. I lowered the camera to locate the position of the
black Corvette and noticed two cemetery security guards in a modified
golf cart sputtering toward our position on the hill.

"Uh-oh, we're busted," Frank said.

The security guards looked to be nice enough guys, their duties at
the cemetery entailing the use of calm authority rather than conflict,
a law enforcement posture emphasized by their near-retirement age
and dumpling-shaped bodies. The lead officer was a gray-haired black
man with crinkled eyes that made him look worried we might cause
more trouble than he could handle. "Sorry folks, no photographing
the memorial services, I have to escort you off the premises."

"You're telling us you don't allow cameras?" Frank's voice spiked
with indignation. "We just passed a busload of Japanese tourists
with cameras. Are you going to throw them out, too?"

"Please, sir, we ask you to respect the rights of the mourners to a
little privacy." He pressed his palms out in a calm-down gesture
while his partner lifted a walkie-talkie to his lips, ready to report a
disturbance on Loving Kindness Lane.

I apologized to the officer and walked to the car, glancing over my
shoulder when I ducked into the passenger seat. On the road below,
a twenty-something with flowing black hair stepped out of the
Corvette to exchange fist-taps with two other men in their early
twenties, then hugged another young man who approached the
group, the last to arrive. I snuck the lens over the doorsill and maxed
the zoom to isolate the four of them. The late arrival looked vaguely
familiar, but at that distance, I couldn't get a clear enough look at his
face to know why.

"You get anything worthwhile?" Frank asked, poking his head
through the driver's window, and when I told him about the group of
four young men gathered by the black Corvette, he pretended to
stretch and checked them out. "The one on the left," he said, referring to the late arrival, "he's Stewart's older brother, Jagger. The
Corvette, think it's the same one you saw at Chateau Marmont?"

The feigned casualness didn't fool Spectrum, who hustled to the
group the moment he caught the direction of Frank's glance and ushered the boys toward the chapel entrance. I pointed the lens out the
side window as we pulled away from the security guards, catching

the Corvette driver as he moved toward the chapel. I hadn't seen his
face clearly when he'd come down the stairs of the Chateau, but the
hairstyle and body type matched closely enough. I suggested we wait
outside the cemetery gates, then tail him to see where he went after
the funeral.

Frank dropped me off at the Cadillac—like true Angelenos we'd
driven out in separate cars—to let the Rott out for a quick patrol
while he backed into a parking spot across from the cemetery, using
a white panel van in the space ahead of him like a blind to conceal
his car. The Rott went about his business efficiently, accustomed to
short bursts of activity between hours of waiting, and hopped into
the rear seat of the Honda without complaint. To pass the time we
talked about Anabelle Lash. Since our visit to her office he'd continued to call and leave messages that Lash had so far ignored. We both
speculated that she'd been warned against talking to us; if Starbal
watched his first wife so closely that she'd been spotted talking to us,
then he'd probably posted armed guards around Lash, who could divulge far more dangerous information than old news about a failed
marriage.

"Something else might be interesting," I said. "You ever hear rumors that Logan worked as a technical advisor on one of Starbal's
films?"

"Who told you that?"

"A source," I said.

He tapped the rearview mirror to an angle that reflected my face
and fingered a lit cigarette outside the window. "How much are you
seeing Sean anyway? Like, every night?"

I stared at him in the reflection, stone-faced.

"I never figured he'd move so fast and then stick around."

"He have a reputation for quick moves and moving on?"

"No more than any other guy twice married and divorced by
thirty-five."

I waited for the smile that signaled a joke, but Frank didn't tip me
that one had been made. He puffed at his cigarette, obliquely watching my reaction as he stared out the windshield. "He didn't tell you,"
he guessed.

"Any kids?"

"None that he claims formally."

This time he smiled.

I shouldn't have been surprised. Sean and I had been together no more than a few times and though I never felt we couldn't talk to each other, our bodies spoke with far greater urgency—and probable honesty. Neither of us had fully or even partially disclosed the shadows trailing our lives. Not having to talk about the past liberated us from incidents that encumbered us, things we might not have regretted but that required too much explaining to justify to someone else. Animal attraction was one thing and true compatibility something else. I didn't know Sean, not really, no more than he knew me, even though I was already more than a little bit in love with him. We were ciphers to each other, attracted to the mystery of who the other might be as much as the reality of who that person really was. Our moments alone took place in a world of our own making, far from the intrusions of the outside world, and when the time came, inevitably, that the world flooded in, the relationship might not survive it.

The Corvette took good advantage of its speed after the memorial service ended, streaking between the exit gates at the head of a like-minded queue of those who didn't want to waste the entire morning at a funeral. Frank was slow to start the engine and extricate the Honda from its blind, and by the time we were rolling, the Corvette had vanished over the horizon line. My shouts to hurry up didn't improve our speed or Frank's driving skill. Neither of us thought to look behind us. Frank was too enthralled by the hunt to worry about traffic cops, and I was too busy hanging on to the restraint strap with one hand and the Rott's collar with the other. We caught our next sight of the Corvette as it crossed the concrete-lined Los Angeles River and swung left to ramp onto the southbound lanes of the Golden State Freeway. Frank settled back into the seat after we merged into the fast lane, several car lengths behind, confident we could keep up. I put my eye to the viewfinder and waited until shifts in the traffic flow created a gap between the Nikon and the Corvette's titanium exhaust pipes. The license plate that slid through the telephoto frame read OZZY13.

"You mean Ozzy like Ozzy Osbourne, the singer?" Frank asked when I read him the plates.

I thought about the kid behind the wheel while Frank called a contact with access to the DMV's database. The kid had met up with

Jagger Starbal and two other boys of similar age at the funeral, the four of them looking like a tight group of friends. What had drawn him to the Chateau Marmont on the day that Stewart had died? Had he been a close friend of Stewart's, his number called either just before or after mine? He might have been responding to a plea for help from a drugged friend. But if he was a friend of Stewart's, why hadn't he phoned the front desk on finding him unconscious? Even if they'd been doing drugs together, he should have summoned help before fleeing—unless he didn't mind seeing Stewart die. I again considered the possibility that Stewart had been given a hot shot, then realized it didn't have to be murder. Ozzy might have gone to the hotel not to talk Stewart out of committing suicide but out of going to the police or confessing to the tabloids. If Ozzy thought Stewart was cracking, about to confess their involvement in Christine's death, then finding him dead or dying of an overdose would be a relief, even if they were so-called friends. He wouldn't call emergency or the front desk. He'd run. He'd let Stewart die.

"All we need now is a Keaton and an Einstein to get the joke," I said.

Frank told his DMV contact to call back with the information as soon as possible and disconnected. "Get what joke?" He asked.

"Jason, Ozzy, Keaton, Einstein."

"*J-O-K-E*, you mean? Like what was written on the back of Luster's photo?"

"Why not *J* for Jason and *O* for Ozzy?" I suggested, voicing the thought out loud to hear how it sounded. It sounded only half right. Ozzy belonged, but not Jason. My head spun from the centrifugal force of reversing suspicions. "No, not Jason. *J* for Jagger."

"Jagger?" Frank shouted the name, incredulous. "First you're so convinced it's Rakaan you almost single-handedly get him arrested, then you decide it's not Rakaan, it's Jason Starbal and Anabelle Lash, and now just to piss everybody off you're saying it's not Jason, it's Jagger?"

"Jason pays women to have sex with him," I said, stroking the Rott's head to help me think. "He's a pervert just like Rakaan but he doesn't need Rohypnol, and even if he decided to try it for kicks, he's too experienced to accidentally strangle someone to death. He's been doing it for years, remember. And where does Charlotte McGregor fit in? She doesn't. And neither does Luster. Stewart sent me the photograph of Luster because he wanted to show what was going on involved more than just Christine. Luster was a serial rapist who used Rohypnol on his victims. That doesn't fit Jason Starbal."

"And Anabelle Lash?" Frank groped the dash for a cigarette, disturbed enough to need a calming hit of nicotine. "Christine connects to Lash and Lash connects to Jason Starbal. Come on, it fits! And it makes a great headline."

"That's how Christine met Stewart," I said. "She went with Lash, not Rakaan. She probably met Jagger there, too. That's how he got in touch with her later. He got her number when she gave it to Stewart and then contacted her, claiming to be Depp's producer."

"And what it said on the photo, *no S?*"

"Not Stewart."

Frank responded with derisive laughter and lit his cigarette.

"He was trying to tell me he was innocent," I said. "That he wasn't part of the group involved in this. It shouldn't be hard to find out who the *K* and *E* refer to. Wait a minute, didn't you tell me that Jagger had a film production company?"

"Right, the one with funny spelling." He swore with the force of sudden realization and fumbled for the notepad in his front T-shirt pocket.

"Illusterious Productions, wasn't it?" I said.

Frank fought the smoke in his eyes while he watched traffic and tried to find the entry he'd made in his notebook. The Corvette headed steadily west, toward the wealthier neighborhoods nestled in the hills or sloping toward the ocean, but instead of turning north toward Beverly Hills it swung south toward Long Beach and Orange County. Frank swore again and tossed the notebook onto my lap, turned to the page of notes he'd made about Jason Starbal's family. "You're right," he said.

I read what he'd written after Jagger's name: Illusterious Productions.

"I don't see any other names here," I said. "Where's his partners?"

"It's a pun on Luster, get it?" Frank stabbed his finger at the page. "Luster is right in the middle of the name of his damn production company. Read it aloud."

"Illusterious," I said, rhyming with *mysterious.*

"No. I'd pronounce it different." Frank grabbed the notebook and peered at the entry. "I'd pronounce it, Ill-Luster-Us."

When the Corvette slid right at the off ramp to Los Angeles International Airport, Ozzy's final destination opened to any number of possibilities. Frank sped around a couple of slow-moving cars in the fast lane, careful to hang close enough to the Corvette to avoid losing the tail at a traffic light. We speculated that he might be leaving the country. It made sense. He needed to show up at the funeral because he would have drawn attention to himself by missing it, but now that he'd deflected suspicion he could take a long, unearned vacation in Mexico, away from worries about the law. We didn't change our minds after the Corvette bypassed the remote lot and entered the terminal itself. Judging by the sticker price on his car, he wouldn't have problems paying the daily rate for short-term parking.

"Time to run and gun," Frank said.

I pulled the film camera from my bag and sped through my pre-shoot routine, guestimating the shooting conditions, loading extra rolls of film into my jacket pockets, and deciding if the lens on the camera was still the best lens for the job. Run and gun meant guerilla-style journalism, Frank shooting shock questions at the subject while I backpedaled ahead, photographing his alarmed, amused, or violently annoyed reactions. I'd need the greater light sensitivity of film in the low-light conditions we'd encounter in the parking structure and decided to swap telephotos to the faster 28–70–millimeter lens.

The Corvette collected a ticket at the parking control arm and rolled up the ramp to the first parking level, hunting, as almost all Angelenos do, for that one elusive parking space nearest his eventual destination, spending three minutes looking for a spot that might save him a sixty-second walk. Frank hovered one lane over, watching from a distance, and when the Corvette braked by an empty space at last, he sped toward several free slots near the back and squeezed on the brakes. I was already reaching for the door when the Honda lurched and my head snapped back to the sound of crushing metal and splintering glass. Frank cursed and the Rott yelped as the car shot forward, out of control, toward the rear fender of a pickup truck to the right. The moment we struck the fender the world turned white and something smacked me full in the face, knocking me back against the seat. When I opened my eyes, too stunned to move, I realized someone had rear-ended us at speed. The passenger-side air bag had deployed when we hit the pickup truck, the air bag now dribbling from its compartment like a spent condom. The collision knocked the Cubs baseball cap from Frank's head and his hair spiked straight up in protest. I asked if he was okay. He nodded without really being conscious of what had just happened. The Rott barked in the backseat, traumatized, but fine. I felt my neck to make sure the tendons were still attached and elbowed open the door.

Behind the wheel of the blue Toyota Camry that struck us, the driver clutched his hand against his jaw in a way that suggested he might be hurt. I took a step forward, shaking off the effects of the crash easily enough, and saw the cell phone in the driver's hand. Had he been conversing with someone, not watching where he was going, when we collided? Or was he just now calling to report the accident? He spotted me walking toward him. His hand flashed and the cell phone vanished. A moment later the driver's door winged open and he emerged, a large white man in a gray suit. I'd seen him before, one of the two bouncers huddling with Spectrum at the funeral.

"You folks okay?" he called out in mock concern, then glanced back to where I'd last seen the Corvette.

I pretended not to recognize him and pointed toward the Honda, shouting like I was completely freaked out, "My friend! He's not breathing! The air bag! I think he's having a heart attack!"

He hurried forward, reaching into the outside flap pocket of his suit coat for his phone, ready to dial in a medical emergency. He'd been sent to stop, not kill us, and a serious injury could have legal ramifications he'd rather avoid. When he moved toward the Honda I slipped behind the pickup truck we'd hit, then sprinted toward the exit leading to the terminal, the same exit I supposed the driver of the Corvette had taken. I heard a shout behind me but it was too late, I was already gone, out from the shadows of the parking structure and into the bright sunlight, the Tom Bradley International Terminal straight ahead across four lanes of busy airport traffic. The guy in the Corvette was already across the roadway, wheeling a hard-shell suitcase from Louis Vuitton behind him. I shouted, "Hey, Ozzy, wait up!"

He turned when he heard the name. I waved like an old friend and raised my camera. He shook his head, panicked, and bolted toward the terminal entrance. I eyed the flow of traffic. I didn't have time to wait for the light to green. I leapt toward a gap between cars, jerked back, and fell on my butt. The bouncer from the funeral loomed over me, his gray suit blotting out the sun. He'd taken me down so effortlessly I stared up at him in astonished admiration.

"You'll be happy to know your friend is gonna be okay." He extended a hand to help me to my feet. "Sorry if I was a little rough, but he's asking for you."

30

WHEN I RUSHED from bed the next morning to vomit in the bathroom sink, I realized I needed to face a little reality rather than turn my back to it and took the Rott for a walk to the drugstore around the corner, where I bought a package of five test strips. I followed the instructions on the box, the Rott watching from the bathroom doorway, his expression alternating between concern and amusement as I peed into a cup, dipped the test strip into the urine, and laid it onto the comparison chart. I've spent a good part of my adult life waiting, either in a prison cell or in a car, serving time or staking out one celebrity or another. I'm good at waiting. The three-minute gap between application and result was the longest three minutes of my life, and when the second line emerged within the strip's results zone, signaling a positive, I felt awed and overwhelmed, my life consumed by natural forces seemingly beyond my control.

The Rott sensed my emotional change and barked once before nudging against my leg, looking for a reassuring pat. I sat on the floor and gave him a good rub. I'll fight for a woman's right to choose as hard as anyone else, but I was thirty years old and wanted to be both strong and mature enough to take responsibility for the gifts and hardships dealt to me. I hadn't particularly wanted a child and felt more dread at the consequences than joy over the possibilities, but I figured that would change once I came to accept the inevitability of pregnancy and birth. My relationship with Sean was probably finished. I knew that would be just one of the costs of my pregnancy. I wasn't even sure I'd tell him the baby was his. If he wanted to figure out the cause-and-effect relationship of my pregnancy, he could do it without a pointed finger. I'd spent almost a year with the Rott, proving myself capable of caring for another creature. How much more difficult could it be taking care of a baby? I laughed at myself for thinking that. The Rott was easy. A baby wouldn't be. But I knew I could do it alone. The baby might miss out on having a father, but she'd have lots of uncles and a big dog with even fewer teeth than she had.

I needed to clear my head. Walks on the edge of a great wilderness are one of the great benefits of life near the ocean. I leashed the Rott, shouldered my camera bag, and jogged down the steps toward the street, so consumed by my thoughts that I didn't spot the white Tercel parked at the curb just beyond the base of the stairs until the rear passenger door squeaked open. Red flashed too high in the cabin to make visual sense until I realized it was the ex-con's polo shirt, exposed as he leaned over the front seat to open the back door. I jerked on the Rott's leash and pulled up as the ex-con shouted a single command of attack. A streak of brown raced from the rear passenger compartment, too compact to alarm me until I saw the muscular shoulders, blunt snout, and bone-shielded eyes of a pit bull mix.

The Rott turned instantly to meet the attack, the power of his lunge ripping the leash from my hand. The two dogs hit head to head, the pit bull's jaws snapping to the side, deflected by the force of the collision. The Rott whirled to catch the pit bull at the base of the neck, using his superior height and size to advantage. In less than a second Baby became an animal beyond my control, acting from a primitive instinct to attack and survive, completely unconscious of his unsuitability for fighting another dog. Without teeth, his jaw couldn't hold and the pit bull rose up, twisted, and snapped, its teeth digging into the flesh above the Rott's shoulder, near the throat. The Rott bucked, shocked by the pain, but the other dog clenched down, hind legs kicking to raise and straighten its stout body.

I shouted and tried to beat the animal off, my kicks like hitting a concrete block with a stick. The Rott stood his ground, bravely enduring the pain, but the pit bull vised his neck in jaws strong enough to snap wood. I backed away and sprinted up the steps to my apartment, fingers trembling to identify the door key amid the jumble of metal, counting each second in the Rott's blood. I screamed in anguish as the key bounced away from the lock on my first try, the adrenaline so charging my nerves it deflected my aim. I jammed the key into the lock on the second try and opened the door just wide enough to reach for the baseball bat inside the jamb. On the pavement below, the pit bull had taken the Rott down to one foreleg, securing its grip closer to the killing zone of the throat. I charged midway down the stairs and leapt.

As a breed, pit bulls suffer a physical weakness that doesn't hinder their deadly effectiveness as head-to-head fighters, one immediately apparent from a glance at their muscular, sloping profile—all jaws, neck, shoulders, and chest—the narrow join between torso and hips safe from attack by another dog but susceptible to a blow of great force. I landed at the base of the stairs and braked. The pit bull mix didn't bother to glance at me, its teeth sunk deep into the Rott's shoulder and neck. I cocked the bat and swung, the blow crashing down upon the animal's hips. Pit bulls have the highest resistance to pain of all breeds, and though the animal shuddered and yelped, its jaws didn't release their grip until a second blow, a few inches higher, brought wood into contact with bone and shattered its spine.

As I cocked the bat again, I tracked the shouts and charging footsteps of the ex-con as he skirted the hood of his car, and when he curved toward me I whirled and swung. He jerked back and flung his arms to deflect the swing, but the barrel of the bat skipped off his forearm and struck a glancing blow to his forehead. His feet shot out from beneath him and he fell back hard, stunned but still conscious. He rolled once and scrambled to get his feet onto the pavement. I didn't see that as an option. I swung the bat again, toward his ribs this time, and caught him hard enough to flip him onto his back. He screamed more in anger than from pain. Blood streamed down the Rott's neck and pooled at his paws. I didn't have time to negotiate. I golfed the head toward the ex-con's ankle, the crack of bat on bone solid as a struck fastball. The ex-con screamed again, this time not in anger, not at all.

I dashed to open the passenger door to the Cadillac, parked in its slot opposite the stairs. The Rott stumbled toward me, the fur at the wound in his throat flapped open, his eyes sheening like glass. He swayed at the door's threshold, unable to make the jump alone. I stepped over his back and gently wrapped my arms around his chest to boost him onto the passenger seat. It wasn't until I gently nudged the door shut that I looked up and spotted a burly man in a ponytail standing across the street, next to a BMW sedan, a video camera pressed against the right lens of his oversized sunglasses—Ray Spectrum, videotaping the entire incident. I bolted toward my camera bag, left on the pavement near where the Rott had been attacked, and threw myself behind the wheel.

I pushed the Cadillac close to flight speed down Lincoln Boulevard, swerving around traffic without regard for law or safety, pressing a towel against the wound in the Rott's neck to stanch the flow of blood. The anger I felt while striking the ex-con with the bat had flashed through me so quickly it didn't stick, and in thinking about Spectrum my anger directed itself too much at myself. Shortly after the Rott had first trotted to my side, a refugee from a brushfire in Malibu, he'd attacked someone who wanted to kill me and took a bullet as the reward for his heroics. He was a juvenile, less than three years old, but it had taken him months to fully recover, and he still limped a bit when he rose in the morning. How could I possibly allow myself to raise a child if the work I did routinely endangered my dog? What trick would Spectrum have pulled had I carried an infant in my arms rather than led a dog on a leash? I couldn't raise a child in peace and security if I couldn't safeguard my dog.

Maybe I was a fool, too willing to annoy people with the means to hurt me and those I loved, but I could drive, I'd say that for myself. I talked to the Rott while I ran yellows and dodged oncoming traffic, telling him he was a good dog, everything was going to be fine, and slalomed up to the veterinary hospital's emergency entrance in less than five minutes. The vet responding to the bell took a quick glance at the Rott and ran back to grab a gurney. I crouched by his head, noted that his eyes had blanked completely, his breath rapid but shallow, the leather seat beneath him a slick pool of blood. I lowered the seat back and when the vet returned, we lifted him onto the gurney's metal surface. He'd gone into shock, she told me, and pushed him through the entrance at running speed.

After the receptionist directed me to the bathroom to wash the dog's blood from my hands, she gave me a clipboard form and a glass of water with instructions to fill out the first and drink the second. The form gave me something to do, the effort of pushing the tip of a pen across paper focusing my thoughts on something other than the Rott's trauma, one of the calming effects of bureaucracy. What right did I have to think I could have a baby and raise it safe from harm? Aside from the extraordinary events of the past few days, a little rough-and-tumble is part of the paparazza's normal life. Could I risk backpedaling from a star's advancing entourage, seeking the elusive celebrity photograph, when slowed by six months of pregnancy? I doubted it. I'd have to beg for red-carpet jobs, the star-sanctioned photo ops at celebrity events like film premieres and awards shows. I didn't know who would hire me for that. Red-carpet and gotcha photography are not the same trade, as different as a domesticated dog and a wild wolf. I signed my name to the form and wrote a check to cover estimated costs, explaining to the receptionist that I didn't carry credit cards.

Spectrum had set me up like a true pro. He'd staked me out, done his research. He knew I was on parole. He knew how I felt about my dog and knew my reputation for angry outbursts. He'd hired the ex-con first to watch and then to provoke me, sure that he'd found my weakness, certain that I'd respond to an attack on my dog as though it was an attack on my own life. He knew the law made an important distinction that I did not. Assault with a deadly weapon was still assault, provoked or not. Spectrum had video-recorded me assaulting a man with a baseball bat, a felony serious enough to warrant immediate revocation of my parole, even if the State declined to prosecute, or if they did prosecute, failed to convict. Sure, I'd been provoked by a life-threatening attack on my dog, and yes, I had genuine cause to fear for my safety when the other dog's owner charged toward me; these might explain the use of a baseball bat to strike the attacking dog and then the first swing at its owner, but not the second blow to his ribs, and certainly not the third shot that shattered his ankle. Given a good lawyer—and I had a good one—I might win if the case ever went to trial, but even though a sympathetic jury might decide in my favor, the parole system would not. Assault with a deadly weapon was a clear violation of the parole agreement, provoked or justified or not. Arrest and return to prison were inevitable, the only question remaining the amount of time before my parole officer came calling with a pair of handcuffs.

I should have been angry, and I waited for my old friend and confidant, rage, to consume and thrust me toward one irresponsible act or another, but where before I'd burned with a liberating intensity, I now felt hollow and ashen. I burst into tears as I paced the hospital waiting room, just broke down and cried like a normal person whose dog lay near death and who now, pregnant for the first time in her life, faced two more years in prison. Rage always moved me to action. These feelings were different. They paralyzed me. For the first time in a long while I didn't know what to do. I felt helpless.

Then I got a call that put events in a different perspective.

"I got a message for you from Cassie," Pop said, so loudly I thought he'd lost his hearing.

"Things are a little crazy right now," I said. I didn't know where to start. Should I say goodbye to him now, or later? I doubted I'd have time to call again before they arrested me.

"She said it was important," he shouted. "She said if she wasn't back by now, I should call you with this message."

"What message?"

"That she's meeting Mick Jagger's assistant. Said he could get her a role in some new movie, what did she call it? *L.A. Cats? Brats?* Something like that. I told her it damn well better not be a rock band. And she said you shouldn't worry, she wasn't gonna drink anything. You got any idea what she's talking about?"

"Where is she? Did she say?"

"She's somewhere down near your part of town, Hollywood."

"Did she leave any way I could get in touch with her?"

"Well sure, I bought her a new phone yesterday, you know, the kind you kids put in your pocket. Why the little meathead didn't want to call you direct, that's what I want to know. You want the number?"

I grabbed the pen from the receptionist's desk and inked the ten digits he recited into the skin of my forearm. I punched the numbers into the cell and paced, listening to the distant rings with increasing anxiety. "Mick Jagger's assistant" could only be Jagger Starbal. How had she tracked him down? I hated feeling helpless. When voice mail picked up, I grabbed a services brochure from the counter and ran out the door. I knew why she hadn't called me direct. The clever little fool had connived a meeting with someone she knew I'd try to stop her from meeting. I left a message instructing her to call me immediately and started the Cadillac. After I hung up, I called again and left a second message repeating the same information just in case she somehow lost the first.

Ray Spectrum had staked me out and set me up, but maybe he

wasn't aware I knew who he was or where he worked. Midmorning traffic toward Hollywood flowed no worse than usual, the stream of cars trickling through knots near Westwood. I cut north to Sunset Boulevard west of the freeway and tracked a Porsche through the hills, just enough distance between bumpers to spot any traffic cops pulling out to stop him for speeding. The sight of the Rott's blood on the passenger seat and floorboard brought me close to tears again, but I shut them down and mopped at the blood with a towel as I drove. I'd have my time for revenge, and soon. Spectrum had been hired to stop me from looking into the Starbal connection, I felt sure of that. He'd started with threats and harassments, and when I'd refused to back off he decided it would be simpler to get rid of me legally, easy enough to do with someone serving out her sentence on parole.

I parked around the corner from Amoeba Records and took the bloody towel, camera bag, and baseball bat to the trunk. A parking sign near the corner advised no parking one day distant. I'd have to make sure I got the car moved before then. A parking ticket, documenting the presence of my car that close to Spectrum's office, wouldn't improve my legal situation, not considering what I planned to do that morning. I removed the camera and lenses from the camera bag and secured them inside an aluminum-padded case I kept in the trunk, decided to slip the point-and-shoot camera into my jacket pocket just in case. I wrapped the handle of the baseball bat in a sweatshirt from my change-of-clothes suitcase and stuffed the barrel into the emptied camera bag, then shut the trunk.

Nobody paid much attention to me when I walked through the lobby of Spectrum's building, the handle of the baseball bat protruding from the camera bag clenched to my side. I stepped into a parking elevator and rode it to the second subterranean level. The cars to the left were parked by assigned space, all owned by tenants and their employees. I backtracked toward the far-corner spot, where a three-car gap in the line revealed where the ex-con had parked his Tercel on the day I'd tracked him. I didn't see Spectrum's black BMW. Lucky me. He wouldn't have left the ex-con on the sidewalk, writhing in agony. If not worker's comp, then common decency required him to drive an injured employee to the hospital—even if a check of his employee records would find no mention of the ex-con's name. Checking someone into a hospital, that took time. I regretted what I'd been forced to do to the pit bull mix. I wondered what they'd done with him. Put him down, I guessed. I added that to my list of sins and slid under the Ford Taurus parked next to the empty space.

What had Cassie been thinking? On the night she appeared at my door, lugging that towering backpack, she'd shown an interest in the details of Christine's murder that I'd attributed to the morbid curiosity of an adolescent. As I lay under the car and waited for Spectrum to show—I guessed the third space was reserved for the Camry that rear-ended us the day before—I plotted out the days since she'd returned. She could have set up the meeting with Mick Jagger's so-called assistant while still in Phoenix, or at least begun the process. How could she have contacted them? Through the Internet? Pop didn't have an Internet connection. She could have used the library, but not enough time had passed to search, connect, and set up a meeting.

The night she appeared at my door, Cassie already knew about the Starbals through the appearance of the code word, *L.A. Brats*, on the Suicide Girls website. She'd talked to Nephthys and Tammy, and unlike me, she probably navigated the Internet with ease. I now assumed she knew everything I knew, if not more. But why was it so important to her? Did Christine's death fuel such outrage that she was willing to risk her own life to expose the killer? Adolescents make warped calculations of the risk of things, admittedly, and perhaps she didn't understand the dangers of her enterprise. But why had she made such an extreme effort rather than content herself with the usual teenage pleasures of chewing gum, cigarettes, bad music, and hormonally induced mood swings?

But no, she knew the risks. Cassie knew the risks of crime from the perspectives of both victim and perpetrator. I'd underestimated her capabilities a couple of times. She may have just turned fifteen, but she had criminal experience beyond her years and a natural ability that, had it been in a more conventional field, would have been considered prodigious.

When I heard the approaching swish of radials on concrete, I breathed deeply to calm any fluttering of nerves and turned my head to watch for tires swerving into the space next to me. Spectrum didn't seem like the kind of guy who'd be easy to sneak up on, and I knew that if I hesitated or allowed adrenaline to deflect my aim, the consequences could be fatal, if not for me, then for Cassie. If he backed in or carried a passenger, I'd be forced to abandon the plan altogether, but he headed straight into the nearest slot and braked with a scorching screech of rubber, the passenger door on my side of the space. I slid out from beneath the Taurus and pulled my feet under me, crouching in wait between the two cars. The motor fluttered to silence and the moment of inaction that followed stretched to uncomfortable seconds. I gripped the bat one-handed, a few inches above the knob, and focused on controlling my breath. The locks popped and the driver's door on the opposite side clicked open, the car shifting with the weight of someone stepping from behind the wheel. I leapt as Spectrum's head rose above the roof and I jabbed the barrel of the bat forward to spear him in the skull, just above the spine. He never saw me or the bat. He fell like a big bird shot from the sky, arms flapping as he dropped. I glanced around the parking structure. No witnesses, not yet.

Spectrum lay face down beneath the open door, briefcase dropped to one side, sunglasses splayed to the side of his face and keys sprawled a few inches from his fingertips. I snapped the keys from the pavement, and watching the body carefully for signs of movement, I opened the trunk. I'd hit him pretty hard in the back of the head and hoped I hadn't killed him. I grabbed his heels and dragged him to the back of the car. Desperation lent me extra strength. I bent at the knees, dug both hands under his belt, and trying not to cry out with the effort, I hoisted his midsection just over the top lip of the bumper, got my knees under his chest, and rolled his torso into the trunk. A quick frisk yielded cell phone and wallet but no videotape. When I shoved his legs inside he grunted, once, and blinked his eyes. I'd done the job right, hadn't killed him. That made me feel better about things. Technically, they called what I was doing kidnapping.

What the hell, in for a dime, in for twenty years to life.

I slammed the trunk.

31

RAY SPECTRUM DROVE a new BMW 540 sedan with leather seats and power everything, the 4.4-liter, 325-horsepower V-8 engine growling like a beautiful beast when I turned the ignition. I backed the thing cautiously out of the slot, careful not to scrape the car next to me or ding the one across the aisle, far less willing to put a dent in the fender of such a fine car than in the owner's head. He kept his parking card within easy reach, in the padded armrest behind the stick shift. I rolled up to the parking control arm, inserted the card, and accelerated onto Sunset, heading toward the Hollywood Freeway north. The car responded with an awesome surge of speed when I pushed the RPMs and it maneuvered with precision at every twitch of the steering wheel. I could outrun Jeff Gordon's Dupont Chevy in such a car, though I resisted the temptation of demonstrating it. Even a far more talented liar than I might have difficulty explaining to a traffic cop why she was driving a car with the registered owner stuffed in the trunk.

Now that I had Spectrum's attention, I needed to find a quiet and secure place to talk to him. I thought about driving into the parking lot at Dodger Stadium, a vast, empty space at that time of day, or perhaps up into Griffith Park, but neither guaranteed privacy from the awkward intrusion of a witness or cop. I could drive the BMW north, against the base of the desert mountains west of Palmdale, but that would take time. I didn't want to involve anyone else, but in the press of time I couldn't think of another way to work it. I called Pop to tell him Cassie was in trouble and I needed his help to get her out of it. Pop lost his temper, stringing together swear words that brought back less-than-pleasant memories from my girlhood. I waited for him to wind down, told him I needed his pickup truck out of the driveway and the garage door unlocked, enough space cleared in the garage to park a big sedan, and after that I'd need plenty of privacy. He asked me what I planned to do and we disconnected after I told him the less he knew, the better. I didn't want to involve him more than I had to. The scene could play out according to plan, Cassie released unharmed and the Rott recovered with no assault charges filed, or the scene could go bad, with unforeseen consequences. If he didn't know why I wanted his help, he couldn't be charged with a felony. Or so I thought.

I tore the vet's services brochure from my jacket pocket and called the number listed while I merged onto the Golden State Freeway toward the San Fernando Pass. The receptionist transferred the call to the vet. The dog had come through in good shape, she said, considering the loss of blood, but they wouldn't know for sure until a little more time passed. She spoke carefully to give me hope but not false expectations. When an animal goes into shock like that, kidney function is always impaired, sometimes fatally. The risk would decline and the prognosis improve with each passing hour. If the Rott made it through the next twenty-four hours, his chances of surviving the attack were good. I thanked her and promised to call again later that afternoon.

My phone beeped when I disconnected, Frank's name flashing across the display. I took the call, said, "This is not a good time to talk."

He picked up the stress in my voice, asked, "Anything wrong?"

"I won't know the answer to that for another hour."

"Anything I can do to help?"

I thought about it, not too proud to refuse, the freeway asphalt a blur beneath the BMW's long, black hood. "Spectrum have any weaknesses that you know of?"

"Why? Is he bothering you again?"

I glanced back toward the trunk.

"Sort of the other way around at the moment."

I couldn't drag Frank into this, not yet. If I told him what was going on, he'd be an accessory to whatever crime I committed.

"Why'd you call?" I asked.

"Because I get the *J-O-K-E*."

"What do you mean?"

"I heard back from my guy at the DMV and did some checking at a production database called Filmtracker-dot-com. Ozzy's real name is Oren Flushberg, son of the producer Gary Flushberg, who won an Emmy for *American Firefighter.* Ozzy is one of four founding partners in Illusterious Productions, with Jagger Starbal, Bryan Kane, and Dustin Edwards. Kane and Edwards both have famous dads in the film business."

"Jagger, Ozzy, Kane, and Edwards," I said. "But not Stewart."

"Like I said, I get the joke, but why didn't he just tell you?"

"And rat out his own brother?"

"Isn't that what he sort of did by sending us the video?"

"Just the opposite," I said. "It was his only alternative. He couldn't go to the police without betraying his friends and family . . ."

"So he went to the tabloids?"

"Exactly. Sending us the video, that was meant to warn his brother off, let him know he couldn't keep getting away with it. When I threatened to publish Stewart's name in *Scandal Times,* it flipped him out. No wonder the poor kid killed himself. He didn't have anywhere to go except down that hole he was talking about."

"Suicide is just another word for spineless," Frank said. "If the kid had any character or guts, he wouldn't have killed himself."

"What was he supposed to do? Talk to his father? His father is such a whoremonger and bondage freak he probably inspired Jagger to follow in his footsteps. Was he supposed to go to the police? When the cop heading the investigation once worked on a film for his father?"

"Wait a minute," he objected. "I can't confirm that. Are you sure Sean said it was Logan who worked with Starbal on that film advisory thing?"

I noticed the cars falling rapidly away on my right and glanced down at the speedometer. The BMW was doing one hundred miles per hour like a knife through water. I downshifted to fourth and moved one lane to the right. "Yeah, that's what he said. Why?"

"The Internet Movie Data Base lists somebody else for that film."

"So maybe it's a mistake," I said. The IMDB listed every cast and crew credit for every film known. They couldn't be 100 percent accurate. Why would Sean tell me something like that unless he knew it for fact? I told Frank to double-check his sources and asked him to ring me back in an hour.

The freeway cleared of traffic near the pass and I risked a little extra speed to get over the hump. The briefcase Spectrum had been carrying lay on the passenger seat, next to a bottle of designer water. I pressed the lever and the locks flipped to reveal a Hi8 video camcorder—an older videotape technology. I understood why Spectrum hadn't yet converted to digital. Digital leaves too many records, the possibility for duplication as infinite as the Internet. How many times had I read that police technicians successfully salvaged from confiscated computer data files that supposedly had been deleted? Spectrum was too smart for that, his business too confidential to risk loss of control over the material. It's easier to control tape-to-tape duplication, and, if necessary, destroy all copies completely. Technically savvy young guys with deep pockets, they'd buy the newest and most expensive technology without fully understanding the consequences. They'd buy and shoot digital. Maybe that was how Stewart acquired the video copy of Christine's killing. Brothers have few secrets from each other. He'd hacked his older brother's computer and burned the digital file onto a disk.

I ejected the videocassette from the camera and stuck it into my pocket. The crime recorded on the tape would be minor compared to the crimes I'd be accused of should events spin beyond my control. As I drove, I contemplated an eye-for-an-eye approach: if the Rott died, I'd maim Spectrum in revenge. I tried to fantasize doing it and failed. He may have deserved severe injury for what he'd done to the Rott, but I wasn't going to take that responsibility on myself. I made no such promises if he refused to cooperate and Cassie was harmed as a result.

Pop was standing on the porch when I wheeled onto his street, the garage door propped open and his pickup parked at the curb in front of the house. He tracked the BMW with a slight lean forward. Cars that expensive were a rare sight on his street. He didn't spot me behind the wheel until the tires turned into the drive. I coasted under the garage door into a space cleared of boxes and tools. Pop's image slid into the rearview mirror and he pulled down the garage door. I turned off the ignition and stepped out of the car.

"You want to tell me what's going on?" he asked.

I was surprised to see him inside the garage. On the phone I'd asked for privacy. "Somebody in the trunk," I said.

He looked like he was about to ask the obvious question—why was somebody in the trunk?—but guessed the reason quickly enough. "He know where Cassie is?"

"That's what I'm going to ask him. You mind waiting outside?"

Pop reached into the shadows beside the garage door and pulled a shotgun from the wall. "My house. I'm staying."

"This isn't what I asked you to do," I said. "I need to talk to him alone."

"Sorry, it's either my way or the highway."

He'd used that expression a lot when I was growing up. I'd hated it no less then than now. I glared at him, trying to will him to back off. The fool was going to implicate himself in a crime. He backed toward the trunk, shotgun dangling casually from the crook of his arm. I reached into the passenger cabin to retrieve my baseball bat and contemplated the wisdom of giving him a little tap on the head, just enough to make him go night-night. Hitting someone over the head with a baseball bat isn't a surgical procedure, and I decided I'd be just as likely to do serious damage. "You do not lose your temper, under any circumstances," I said. "If anyone loses her temper here, it's me, particularly considering that shotgun you're holding." I keyed the lock, hoping I'd be able to swing a deal that would get Cassie back unharmed and keep Pop and me out of jail. Pop raised his shotgun and when I popped the trunk, Ray Spectrum's Southern California tan had gone deathly pale.

"Don't shoot, I'm gonna be—" He didn't finish the sentence before he leaned his head out the lip of the trunk and vomited at our feet.

Pop jumped back to avoid the splatter, the barrel of the shotgun dropping less than an inch, the difference between taking Spectrum's head off at the chin or the throat. "What's the matter, boy," he asked, "you didn't like your lunch?"

Spectrum cursed him and looked ready to vomit again.

He wasn't faking it. I backpedaled to the open driver door, leaned into the cabin, and retrieved the bottle of water. The year before, I'd gotten whacked hard enough on the head to make me sick. I knew how he felt. "Drink some water, wash the taste out of your mouth, you'll feel better," I said.

He eyed the water suspiciously and cursed me too but he took the bottle, washed out his mouth, and spat carefully away from our feet. Then he remembered his manners and thanked me. "You got the tape, I suppose?" he asked.

"You'll be happy to hear my dog is probably going to make it," I said.

He grunted. So what.

"What's this about your dog?" Pop asked.

I told him about the pit bull's attack.

"That's just mean," Pop said.

"It's only going to get worse because you're fucking with the wrong people." Spectrum wiped his mouth and looked at the sleeve of his suit as though the stain distressed him. "We tried more polite ways of convincing you to cease and desist but you weren't willing to listen, and one kid's already dead as a result."

"The way I see it, this is a lose-lose situation," I said.

Then I didn't say anything; I just watched and waited for him to engage. He put the bottle to his lips and drank so deeply the plastic sides caved, then dribbled a few drops into the palm of his hand and splashed his face. "Can I get out of the trunk?" he asked.

"No," I said.

He capped the water and lay back on one elbow, the tan seeping back into his face, and calculation trickling into his eyes. "What do you want?"

"Not to lose everything. Just like you and your client."

"Then you're willing to deal?"

"If I didn't want to deal," I said, very carefully, "you'd be under a foot of desert sand right now."

"Tough bitch, eh?" He spat outside the trunk, making a comment as much as clearing the taste from his mouth. "Tell me what you're thinking."

"The son of your client belongs to a group of young men dedicated to meeting gullible young women, slipping them ruffies, then gang-raping and sometimes killing them."

He stared from the depths of the trunk, his eyes as black as his hair but not as lustrous. It was my first good look at him without his sunglasses. He was a good-looking guy, in a block-headed, pugnacious kind of way. "That's just total bullshit," he said.

"Is that what's happening to Cassie?" The shuffle of Pop's feet on the garage floor signaled his agitation, a bad sign.

I shoved the palm of my hand toward his face to shut him up. "It's not bullshit," I told Spectrum. "That's what we're going to print in the next issue unless we come to an understanding."

"*Scandal Times?* Nobody believes anything they read in that rag."

"Guess that's why you're so interested in shutting me up," I said. "But that's only part of the deal."

"Deal? We don't have a deal. What deal are you talking about?"

"The deal that keeps you alive."

"Oh, that deal," he said, nodding. "What do you want?"

"My niece."

He cocked his head and stared at me, clearly thinking I was crazy.

"She got suckered into meeting Jagger Starbal. I don't know, maybe the others are there too Kane and Edwards at least, the ones who help him drug and rape his victims." I got the shakes while I spoke, images of what could be happening to Cassie blowing through my mind. "The thing you gotta understand is, my niece is fifteen years old."

"So what do you want me to do about it?"

I tapped the barrel end of the bat against the concrete, one-two-three, the nerves twitching my arms and brain, telling me to break the guy's leg to encourage better cooperation. I resisted. "Call Starbal, Jason or Jagger, whoever's paying you your fee. Tell him it's a standoff. If he releases my niece, unharmed, I'll stop going after the story and do my best to keep it from publication. I can't guarantee *Scandal Times* won't print anything because it's not my paper, but they won't get the story from me."

"What guarantee can you give that you won't go to print?" A wry smile gapped his lips, as though he found some humor in his situation. "I mean, what you say is good enough for me, particularly that part about staying alive, but to sell this I gotta have something you can't go back on."

The sweat beading on his forehead belied his cool. I didn't know whether or not I could trust him, but I couldn't think of another way to play it. I pulled the Hi8 videocassette from my jacket pocket and tossed it to him. "That's over a year in prison to me," I said. "Assuming I beat the assault rap."

"What's to guarantee you won't just whack me over the head and take it back?" Again, the wry smile, as though he accepted his predicament but didn't fear it.

"Honor among thieves."

When he stretched out his hand, I returned his cell phone and watched him touch two numbers; whoever he called was on autodial. "We've got a problem here," he began, and heard in response an answer that didn't please him. "I don't give a rat's ass whether you're busy or not. You want to extricate yourself from the mess you're in, you unbusy yourself and listen." He rolled his eyes at the reply and cut off the speaker. "That's exactly the problem I'm talking about, a problem that's now part of the solution. Tell me exactly what the situation is, where you are, and what condition everyone's in." He looked up at me, the phone pressed against his ear, and nodded, encouraged by what he heard.

"Somewhere public," I said. "He can name the place."

"The girl's aunt will be there in thirty-five, forty minutes. If she finds the girl unharmed, then the current problem you have with the tabloids will go away. You understand what I'm telling you?" Spectrum listened for a moment, then dropped his voice and whispered, "She's fifteen years old, you asshole." He pressed disconnect, smiled as though everything was going to be fine, and dropped the phone into his side pocket, as though by habit.

"Has she been drugged?" I asked.

"They're in a Starbucks, the one at Sunset and Gower. She was late getting there, something about getting off the bus. He hasn't even talked to her."

That didn't mean she hadn't been drugged. If she'd been drugged, they could deny kidnapping her without fear of contradiction. Anything could have happened and she wouldn't know about it until results from the rape kit came back. "If she's there as promised, you'll be released, no more questions asked," I said. "If she's been harmed in any way, we'll talk again about the deal."

He nodded like that was fair, his eyes tracking my hand as it moved to the trunk lid. "I'll be good," he said. "You don't have to do that."

"Sorry, but I do. Watch your head."

I shut the trunk and backed to the garage door.

"You'll take me with you," Pop said, the shotgun cradled in the crook of his arm. "If something's happening to Cassie, you'll need me."

I told him to hide the gun and then I put my shoulder to the garage door, the afternoon light stabbing at my eyes. I looked at the BMW, then at Pop's pickup truck, thinking about it. "You're right, I need you," I said, words I never thought I'd hear myself say. "I need you here, with the BMW, and I need you to loan me your pickup. Can you hear the phone if I call the house?"

"I can hear just fine," he said, insulted.

"Then listen for it. After I pick up Cassie I'll call to tell you where to drop the BMW. Be sure you wipe down the interior—steering wheel, dash, door handles—anywhere we've possibly touched. The key, too. Don't forget to wipe the key."

He nodded as though I'd told him the obvious.

'The guy in the trunk?" I let the question hang, trying to think if I'd forgotten something while I waited.

"What about him?"

"Don't let him out until you drop the BMW. Don't let him know who you are or where you live. He's a pro. If you give him any advantage, he'll put *you* in the trunk."

"He won't, you can count on that." He tossed me the keys to his truck. "This Starbal you mentioned, he the same guy from the movies?"

I nodded.

"That rich son of a bitch, as if he doesn't have enough already."

"I'm not going after him," I said. "I'm going after his son."

Pop looked at me in a way I remembered from my childhood, when he was teaching me one sport or another and I'd made solid contact with a ball or chin. "Don't know when I'll get another chance to say this so I'd better say it now. You two girls are everything to me. No matter what happens, remember I'll do anything to protect you."

I flushed with unexpected emotion, a mix of pride and regret, and stepped up to kiss him on the cheek, breaking it off quickly to slap at my pockets to make sure I still had my cell phone. Then it struck me, the thing that had been bothering me since I'd walked from the garage, and I rushed back to the trunk, Pop scrambling behind to grab his shotgun.

Spectrum glanced up at me when the trunk popped open, blinking his eyes from the light, pretending to be surprised to see me again. I pointed to the side pocket of his suit coat.

"Your cell phone," I said.

32

POP'S BIG AND ugly Dodge Ram pickup perched me a good four feet off the ground, the better to see the subcompacts crunching beneath its oversized tires. I fiddled with Spectrum's cell phone while I sped the surface streets toward the freeway. He owned a new Nokia, the controls different from my older Ericsson. I'd left him in the trunk with his phone just long enough to make a call. I couldn't immediately figure out how to get to his call list, not while maneuvering the pickup through traffic. Who could he call? He knew his life depended on the safe return of my niece. He could have called the police, but what could he tell them? That he was stuffed in a trunk somewhere? They wouldn't know where to begin to look. He couldn't tell the cops about me. Even if he was willing to risk exposing Jagger to arrest on charges of kidnapping a minor, he didn't know Pop's truck or license plate. He could have called one of his employees—maybe the bruiser who smashed his car into Frank's Honda at the airport. An employee made the most sense. He'd want someone to monitor my meeting with Jagger and intervene if something went wrong. Either that or he'd called his priest to make sure the warranty hadn't expired on his latest confession. I decided not to worry about it. When the cell phone in my pocket chirped with a call, I tossed Spectrum's phone onto the passenger seat.

"I double-checked the production info on Starbal's films and didn't find Logan mentioned anywhere," Frank said, getting straight to the point of his call. "I also ran Logan through both the Internet Movie Data Base and Filmtracker and didn't get a single hit. If he ever worked for Starbal—or on any film for that matter—he kept his name off the credits."

"Can you think of a reason why he'd do that?"

"Not anything that makes sense. I suppose he could have made sure his contribution went uncredited because they paid him under the table. I found out something interesting about Spectrum, though."

I leaned forward in the cab to check the side mirror as I blasted onto the Golden State Freeway south. Spectrum's interrogation had taken too much time, traffic already beginning to thicken as the day spun toward mid-afternoon, the start of rush hour. I flexed my foot against the accelerator and swept a glance toward the rearview mirror, watching for the Highway Patrol. "I don't think Spectrum's going to be much of a problem now," I said.

"Maybe you're wrong there," Frank said, the smugness of a scoop infiltrating his voice. "Guess where he worked when he was with the LAPD."

I immediately thought, *no way.*

"North Hollywood," he said, beating me to it.

"When?" I asked.

"Fifteen years ago. Guess who else worked there at that time?"

"Logan?"

"You got it. Spectrum worked vice and Logan robbery-homicide. They weren't partners but they knew each other, guaranteed."

"Looks like I'm in more trouble than I thought." I ground my teeth and added another foot pound of pressure to the accelerator. The way I looked at it, I was in so much trouble a little more didn't make any real difference. What's another bullet to a corpse?

"You want to tell me what's going on?"

"Not particularly, but if I don't contact you within two hours, call your sources in law enforcement and find out if I've been arrested."

"You want me to call the *Scandal Times* lawyers?"

"It's way past libel lawyers. You know Belinsky, my criminal lawyer?"

Belinsky had represented me on an illegal weapons charge the year before, a Philadelphia-born lawyer in cowboy boots, bolo tie, and fringed leather jacket who pontificated like a cracker-barrel philosopher, an act juries found irresistible. Frank had been at my arraignment and still had Belinsky's number in his address book.

"One other thing," I said. "I need you to get my car. It's parked around the corner from Amoeba Records."

"I'll leave it in front of your apartment," he said. "I know why you don't want to tell me what's going on and I don't know whether I should be grateful or just plain mad."

"A little bit of both," I said.

He wished me luck and disconnected. I veered off the freeway at Gower, a five-block straightaway from Sunset. That Spectrum and Logan worked together at North Hollywood didn't necessarily mean that they'd stayed in touch and exchanged information on cases of mutual interest. It didn't necessarily follow that Spectrum had approached Logan with a request to pressure me. Logan could have been acting independently when he threatened to revoke my parole if I didn't back away from the Starbal family. The connection could have been a coincidence, but it made me feel no less surrounded. I took solace in the fact that I was, at that moment, less hemmed in than Spectrum. The green-and-white Starbucks logo glistened near the corner of Sunset and Gower. I'd never been so happy to see the franchise in my life. I swung into the parking lot and jumped from the cab, leaving the baseball bat and my camera bag behind.

Cassie sat beside a table along the back wall of the franchise, her hands wrapped around a large plastic cup that frothed whipped cream at the top. Next to her, a cockily handsome young man leaned with his back to the wall, the Abercrombie & Fitch distressed denim baseball hat that tilted over his eyes unable to conceal the intense interest he took in my arrival. Cassie noticed the subtle change in the young man's focus and turned her head toward the entrance. When she saw me moving toward the table, her eyes widened and she shook her head as though panicked. "What are you doing here?" She covertly jerked a look toward the guy next to her as though trying to warn me something was up.

"Are you okay?" I asked.

"Of course I'm okay. Why wouldn't I be?"

Four tables away, backed into the corner of the café, two men in their early twenties sat hunched over their creamed coffee drinks, pretending not to observe my entrance. I recognized their faces from Stewart's funeral—they'd greeted Ozzy when he'd stepped from his Corvette—and figured they were the other two charter members of Illusterious Productions, Bryan Kane and Dustin Edwards. None of the few customers that afternoon were large, athletic men in the slick attire of professional bodyguards; if Spectrum had called an employee, he hadn't yet arrived. I pulled out the chair across the table and sat, examining Cassie for any sign of trouble other than the distress she showed at my arrival. Her Goth look was gone for the moment, replaced by a long-sleeved striped cotton shirt and a pair of preppy chinos, her breasts swelling against the shirt as though she'd gained two cup sizes since I'd last seen her. Or three. I flipped open my cell phone, found Pop's number on the call list, and called it.

"She's my aunt," Cassie said, as though my presence embarrassed her. "I don't even know why she's here."

"Please, be quiet for a moment, something's happening you don't know about." While I listened to the signal ring Pop's distant phone, I observed Jagger. He reclined as though utterly relaxed, one arm slung casually over the back of his chair and his opposite hand loosely clenched into a fist on the table, a week-old scab running like a stain across the knuckles. He looked familiar to me, but then, he dressed so much like he'd stepped out of a casual clothing catalog—cargo pants, Timberland hiking boots, and a down vest from North Face worn over a baseball tee—that he looked familiar in the ubiquitous way of all devotees of name-brand clothing. He had Stewart's broad, sloping cheeks and full lips, and though the eyes clearly belonged to a different, more feral kind of human being, I could see how someone might confuse them, particularly if one of the brothers encouraged it. I pointed to his knuckles, said, "You got those from beating Stewart."

His upper lip, plump and ripe, curled into a smirk.

"The time you picked up that girl out in Palmdale you wore your brother's sweatshirt and bucket hat, didn't you?"

He shrugged, maybe yes, maybe no—who cared?

Pop's phone continued to ring like a rock falling through space. He wasn't picking up. His hearing wasn't that great, but it wasn't that bad, either. Had he been so addled with bravado that he'd opened the trunk? Maybe he'd forgotten to open the door from the garage into the utility room and couldn't hear the phone through the closed door. Or Spectrum had called someone on his cell who managed to track down the BMW. But how? It didn't seem possible, unless he'd equipped his wheels with a GPS tracking system, the receiver signaling the car's location to a remote computer. Too much time was passing. I needed to make it look good if nothing else. "About time," I said to the ringing phone. "She's here and okay. You can let him go." I disconnected the cell and stuffed it into the side pocket of my jacket.

"Did you mean to implicate your brother when you raped her?" I shifted in the chair to face Jagger, both feet planted to move quickly. "I'm confused, because I can't figure why else you'd steal his clothes to wear when you abducted her."

"I didn't steal his clothes," he said. "I borrowed them."

"And now, thanks to you, he's dead."

"The little traitor deserved everything he got."

"You don't sound like you're grieving."

"So the weakest bird in the nest fell to his death. More food for us all." He tapped his fist on the table and opened it to reveal a microcassette recorder. "Goodness, look what I found."

"You get a kick out of recording things," I said. "I already know that."

"The little bitch was carrying this." He flipped his wrist and the recorder clattered onto the table. "I think she wanted to record something incriminating."

Cassie stared at the drink in front of her, the whipped cream substance melting over the top rim, the flare of her nostrils with each deep breath a sign that she worked to control her temper. Then she looked at me, and from the heat of her glance she seemed angry with me as much as at him. She was working on something, the look said, and I was interfering. If she was working on something, tough. It was my turn.

"You ever meet Andrew Luster?' I asked.

He glanced up, surprised to hear the name, and spun the microcassette recorder around the table with his forefinger.

"Your friends at the next table, any of them meet Andrew Luster?"

He smiled and spun the recorder faster and faster, said, "You can't print any of this anyway, so what does it matter?"

"Did you know Stewart had a crush on Christine before you killed her? Or did that make it an even bigger thrill for you?"

He slapped the recorder to stop it from spinning.

"I didn't kill her," he said.

"Who did, then? Ozzy?" I cocked my head toward the table where Kane and Edwards sat. "Bryan, or maybe Dustin?"

Jagger spun the recorder and watched it go with a studied diffidence.

"Stewart didn't betray you," I said. "He knew you were raping and killing girls. He wanted to make you stop. That's why he leaked the video to me. But he never mentioned your name, or the names of the others either."

Jagger lifted a single finger and said, "Just one died."

"Just one? Charlotte McGregor's lucky you didn't kill her, too."

"Charlotte who? Who's that?"

"You don't even remember her name? The woman in Palmdale."

He rolled his eyes, spun the recorder again. "How the fuck am I supposed to know her last name?"

"Maybe because you almost killed her."

He shook his head. I had it wrong.

"I remember that one, just not her name," he said. "She was pretty hot. But this super moral attitude you're copping, it only means you don't understand the scene. These girls are players. They know the score. They get drugged out of their minds all the time. So what if they wake up and can't remember what happened? It's like, what's the big deal? If you ask for it, don't complain when somebody gives it to you."

Cassie said, "Then you admit to drugging her?"

Jagger had the courage to look at my niece that he lacked when speaking to me. "I've got your tape recorder, darling, so go ahead, ask all the incriminating questions you want, or better, just shut the fuck up."

"I first thought your brother had been there, in the room when you raped her." I tapped the table to get his attention. "I figured he felt so guilty about it he sent me the video, but I was wrong about that. He didn't participate, but he knew what was going on. He couldn't go to the police, couldn't tell the cops his own brother was raping girls. The only thing he could do was try to make it stop another way, by involving me."

He spun the tape recorder again.

I lunged forward to stop it with a clenched fist.

"Did your brother beg you to spare Christine? Did you taunt him with an invite to join in the fun of raping and killing her?"

"She wasn't supposed to die." He stared forward, eyes fixed to the table, waiting for me to remove my fist. The physical intrusion on his personal space disturbed him, and he glanced up and away, pretending to be bored with it all. "Ozzy got a little carried away, put too much pressure on the strap, and I didn't notice until it was too late. It was a mistake. Regrettable. But hey, shit happens."

I said, "So it was an accident."

"Totally." He drew out the "o" in that word, sounding like just any another affected Southern California kid. "I mean, half the fun was imagining what happened afterwards, you know, after they came out of their trance." His brows compressed and he leaned forward, animated by the importance of what he wished to say. "You can't take it so fucking seriously. I mean, the girl who died, sure, that was a shame, but the others? It was just a game, a little harmless sport. Most of the girls, they didn't have a clue what happened. They'd wake up the next morning, or whenever, and—I'm imagining this part—they'd go, like, whoa, I'm a little sore, where was I last night?" He laughed, finding that funny. "Only one bitch even got as far as the police. The rest of them? Nothing. Nada. They never knew what happened." He stared at me head on, daring me to understand the logic. "It's a victimless crime, don't you see? Like the tree that falls in the forest. If you don't remember it, did it really happen?"

"If you kill someone, the victim doesn't remember either," I said. "Does that mean you didn't kill her?"

"I didn't think you'd understand," he said.

"She's too old," Cassie said. "She's, like, thirty. She doesn't get the joke."

Jagger slipped his head back to give her a sidelong glance, said, "Well, aren't you the freaky one."

I think he meant it as a compliment.

"Freaky-deaky," she agreed. "How many bitches did you play?"

"Nine. Too bad, you could have been number ten." He shook his head, regretting the loss. "Come back and see me when you make eighteen. I don't want to corrupt the morals of an underage girl."

"I'd cut you up with a knife and stuff the flesh down your throat as you died, starting with your balls," she said. "And then I'd stick your head in a box and mail it to your dad as punishment for bringing your sorry ass into the world."

Jagger inched away from Cassie as though she spooked him.

"You drugged and raped nine girls," I said, stunned by the number.

"And the true shame? You can't do anything about it. Even if you go back on your promise to Ray, I've got other resources you can't even imagine."

"You hired Spectrum?"

He shrugged.

"You've got a rich, powerful daddy."

"The police can be bought. Shocking, isn't it?"

I figured he was referring to Logan.

"Does he know what you're doing" I asked.

"Dad?" The cell phone in one of the multiple pockets of his cargo pants riffed a tune. He ignored it. "Dad taught me everything I know."

"Like father, like son?"

He winked at me, deadpan.

"Look, we're sorry about your friend. We promise not to be bad boys anymore." He glanced at his friends in the corner. "But really, considering the fact that our families practically own this town and your family aspires to the level of white trash, you should be happy that you're not dead or in jail, understand?" The cell phone continued to ring, as though the caller had hung up before the call switched to voice mail and called again. He glanced down to lift the phone from his pocket and gave the calling number a puzzled look. His voice morphed to an agreeable whine when he lifted the phone to his ear. "Hi! What's up?" His smirk straightened and then drooped to open-mouthed surprise. He listened, shoulders slumping as his chest deflated, curling him over the surface of the table. "Yes," he said. "Yes, I will. He can talk to them right now if he wants." He listened again. "Okay. I'm really sorry about this. I'll tell them."

He hung up the phone and dropped it onto the table, still clutching Cassie's microcassette recorder in his opposite hand. "Someone who says he's your father just broke into our house. Can you fucking believe it? He's holding my dad at gunpoint and won't let him go until he knows you're okay."

"Pop?" Cassie backed sharply from the table. "What's he doing there?"

"Give me your house number, I'll call him," I said.

"He won't accept that," Jagger said, calculations of bloodshed flickering in his eyes. "Dad said he demands to see you in person before he'll back off."

"Just give me the listing," I said.

I punched the numbers as he recited them and listened to a distant phone ring unanswered. I wondered then if he'd given me the correct number. I turned to Cassie and told her we had to move—fast.

She stood and thrust her hand palm up toward Jagger.

"Give me my recorder back," she said.

"Fuck off, you skank."

I didn't think about it. My feet shifted and hips rolled with the muscle memory of a right cross, my fist crashing into the smirking point of his full lips. His head snapped over the chair back and he toppled spine first to the floor. I leapt to my feet. He lashed out, his mouth smeared with blood, and tried to stand. I kicked him in the face as he rose, the force and weight of the Doc Marten boot breaking his nose to the side like a branch from a tree.

Kane and Edwards backed from their table in the corner, the sudden violence sucking the testosterone straight from their veins. Across the café, the *barista* bent over the service counter, stunned still while handing a cup of cappuccino to a T-shirted young woman. The recorder clattered to a stop on the floor. Cassie dashed to retrieve it and despite my shouted command to hurry, she stopped to look down at Jagger Starbal writhing on the floor.

"This is just the start," she said and spat on his face.

33

THE RAM'S TIRES played a serenade on asphalt peeling out of the Starbucks parking lot, rubber smoke drifting across my rearview mirror as we sped onto Gower. No one popped from the café to give chase or record our license plate number, and from what I could tell from brief glances in the mirrors as I drove, no one staked us out from a car parked in the lot. I accelerated around a floral delivery van to catch the tail end of a yellow onto Sunset, the pickup truck careening through the turn like a wild beast. We were twenty minutes from Beverly Hills in thickening traffic. I chased the next pack of cars ahead, intent on working to the front and then timing the traffic lights.

"That was awesome!" Cassie shouted, fumbling with the buttons to her blouse. "Will you teach me to hit like that?"

"Ask Pop. He's the one taught me."

"He says my arms are too thin, I got no power."

"If your form is right, you'll have power enough." I sped into the far right lane, cleared of curbed parking at the start of rush hour. "You might not have the strength to lay someone out like that, not unless it's someone your own size, but you can hit hard enough to surprise them, sure."

"We've already been working out together, you know, with the gloves." She plunged her hand into the gap in her shirt and pulled from behind the padding of her bra a microcassette recorder, the twin to the one she still held in her hand.

"You had two recorders? You were recording that?"

"I let him see the first figuring he wouldn't look for the second," she said and pressed the rewind button. "Always give a sucker a little something to let him think he's winning. It's something Mom taught me. And always keep your real stash separate from your giveaway stash—the money or drugs it won't hurt to lose if you're robbed."

"Your mother taught you that?"

"Don't sound so shocked. I did my first cons in diapers." She pressed play long enough to confirm Jagger's voice had been recorded on the tape, muffled, but audible. "Rich daddy or not, I think we got him."

I held out my right hand, palm out, and she slapped it. I'd promised Spectrum that I wouldn't seek to publish photographs or stories about Starbal; I never vowed to keep my niece from taking evidence to the police. Spectrum might expose the videotape in retaliation, a risk I'd be willing to take if it yanked Jagger Starbal and his pals out of the breeding pool. Anger mixed with pride, and I felt compelled to play the role of cautioning auntie. "What you just did was incredibly stupid and dangerous," I said.

"No, what I just did was justice," she replied, her self-certainty unassailable. "You want to see stupid and dangerous, I'll tell you about some stuff I did before I met you."

"They could have seriously hurt or killed you."

"Those punks?" A burst of disdain blew from her lips. "I used to hang with a crew who'd steal the wheels and wallets from punks like that and leave 'em stark naked by the side of the road. Pop get his instructions mixed up?"

"What do you mean?"

"He wasn't supposed to call you for another hour. And then I was late getting here because of the stupid bus. I can't wait until I get my driver's license."

I glanced at her between lane changes. No doubt or remorse troubled her brow. Criticizing her just then wasn't going to help. Later, given time and a quiet place, I might sit her down to explain things. "How'd you set up the meeting?" I asked.

"I called him, said I wanted to hook up, the kinkier the better." She ejected the tape from the recorder and dug into the front pocket of her pants for another cassette. "The first time I called him, it was from Phoenix. I told him I was visiting relatives, I'd contact him when I got back to L.A."

"He didn't think you were a cop?"

She gave me a scornful look, eyebrows furrowed and lips pursed.

"I think I know what cops sound like. Trust me, I didn't sound like a cop. And that shit he was trying to sell you about not knowing my age? He knew. That was part of the turn-on. Besides, how many fifteen-year-old cops do you know?" She stuffed the recorded tape down the front of her pants—another trick her mother probably taught her. "What's going down with Pop? What's he doing at Star-bal's, and why are you driving his truck?"

Cassie cursed violently when I told her what happened to the Rott. The swear words she used and the way she strung those words together shocked me. "I know you're mad," I told her, "but you have to learn different language to express it. Those words you're using, they're just plain ugly."

"Okay, Mom," she said. "Next time I lose my temper, I'll hit somebody."

"You're right, I'm an idiot," I said, and we laughed together, laughed a little of the tension off.

"Did he just lose it, or what?" Cassie asked. "Why didn't he stay home?"

"I suspect he thinks he's got something to prove."

"Like what?"

"That he loves you, for one."

"Not just me." She turned away to stuff the recorder back under her bra. "He talks about you all the time, at the house. It's kinda weird, actually, how much he talks about you."

"I'm sure he taught you a few swear words talking about me."

"No, it's like he admires you." She buttoned her blouse over the recorder, then looked down to make sure her falsies lined up. "Says you were the only person with the guts to stand up to him and it taught him something, only he's sorry it took him so long to learn. Says if he ever loses his temper with me, I should stand up to him like my Aunt Nina." She shifted in the seat to face me, asked, "Does it show? The recorder?"

Not to anyone who didn't know she had yet to grow much in the way of breasts, I thought, but just shook my head. "Do you see a cell phone, maybe between the seat and the door?"

Cassie squirmed and reached behind her, the cell phone emerging with her hand. She'd been sitting on it. "Wondered what that was," she said. "Whose is it?"

"Spectrum, the private investigator I was telling you about. Do me a favor and see if you can figure out the last person he called."

She tucked her feet under her and brought the display close to her face, pressing buttons in rapid trial-and-error style. It took her less than five seconds to find it. The ten-digit number she recited sounded familiar. I asked her to repeat it, then said, "Call it."

I grabbed the phone and pressed it against my ear, listening to the signal buzz and then click over to voice mail. One word into the announcement I recognized the voice and flung the phone against the windshield, the cell bouncing off the dash and out the open window on Cassie's side. The tears came to my eyes unasked and brought little solace.

"At least you didn't swear," Cassie said, "Who was it?"

To stay silent was to admit to weakness.

"Sean," I said.

"That cop? Why would the P.I. call him?"

We swung right onto Hillcrest and into Beverly Hills, sweeping past the manicured lawns, sculpted shrubbery, and ornately turned gates of fairy-tale estates that sheltered princes and dragons in equal number. I tried not to think. I needed to get Pop away from Starbal before the cops were called to arrest him on charges of breaking and entering. Holding a shotgun on someone, what kind of crime was that? False imprisonment? Hostage taking? Making criminal threats? If things turned out badly, he could spend the rest of his life in prison.

But we were on a roll, I thought; everything would work out for us. What was I going to figure out by thinking? Spectrum had called Sean. So what? It didn't have to mean anything. It didn't have to mean the realization of the worst fears given to my imagination. My brain spun inside its case of bone, all my assumptions reversing at high speed. Logan wasn't the only cop who worked the same station that Spectrum had—Sean was currently assigned to North Hollywood. I didn't know if the dates lined up—Spectrum might have resigned before Sean made detective—but Sean was well acquainted with Logan and it made sense he'd also know Spectrum by reputation, if not personally. Given my sudden change in perspective, nothing that happened between us seemed genuine. Little wonder he'd been so eager to get me away for the weekend. He'd known Stewart was to be buried then. He wanted me out of the way. And when we showed up at the funeral Spectrum had spotted us immediately, as if he'd been tipped that we'd be there. Even his seeming hostility toward Logan could have served a different, insidious purpose. Hadn't his warning that Logan once worked on a film with Jason Starbal proved false? He didn't want me talking to Logan. He wasn't trying to protect me. What I knew endangered Spectrum's clients. He wanted to distance me from Logan because information we were uncovering would change the course of the investigation and lead him directly to the Starbals. Seemingly innocuous things, such as the time he'd pulled up behind my car when I was staking out the Starbal estate, did not now seem so innocent.

But Sean had been genuinely passionate when we'd made love, and those times he'd angered me his remorse had seemed sincere. He didn't have to be a two-faced, lying son of a bitch. I couldn't believe that night in the darkroom had been staged. And later, when he'd appeared at my door and we'd nearly assaulted each other with sexual passion, that had been as real as anything I'd ever experienced. Maybe Spectrum knew that Sean and I were sleeping together and called him from the trunk to guarantee his safety. Of course. The ex-con had been staking out my apartment the night that Sean appeared at the door. He'd made Sean's car as a police vehicle. A man with Spectrum's resources could track the plates to the vehicle sign-out sheet or identify him from the ex-con's surveillance photos. He'd call Sean from the trunk to beg for help, reasoning that a cop boyfriend would have the power and smarts to restrain me. It hurt to think. I wanted to run. I imagined the sand beneath my feet as I ran to the rhythm of high surf, breathing the sea air deep into my blood.

The gilded gates to the Starbal estate hung open at the end of a sweeping curve. I swerved into the driveway and stood on the brakes, twisting the steering wheel to the left as the rubber bit into brick. The pickup fishtailed right, the back end spinning out. We rocked to a stop just beyond Spectrum's BMW, the grille facing the gates, ready to throw the car into gear and speed onto the street once we grabbed Pop. Cassie leapt down from the cab before I jerked the transmission into park. I shouted at her to stop but she raced away, up the golden brick drive and around the gold-plated monument to Starbal's failed Oscar aspirations. Past the marble colonnades, the double front doors at the top of the steps stood ajar.

I jumped from the pickup truck and sprinted. Cassie took the steps two at a time, her footwork as awkward as a colt's. She paused at the door, looking back to hurry me on, then whirled and dashed into the house. I gauged my speed and distance and hurdled the steps. The door came up fast and I clipped it with my shoulder, bouncing into a foyer tiled with gold, Hollywood Walk of Fame–style stars.

Cassie ran to the end of the hallway, stopped, and turned into a wide, arching doorway to her left, shouting Pop's name. I'd seen the tiles before, on the floor in the room where Christine had been killed. The air split with a sound like snapping metal—once, twice—then a monstrous roar washed through the hall, the unmistakable sound of a shotgun blast. Cassie screamed Pop's name and rushed forward. I yelled at her to stop. She didn't. I caught sight of her heels as I breached the doorway into a room so vast and empty it might have served as a ballroom. She slid into another archway to the right, her scream shredding the air.

I flew across the tiled floor, the biting smell of cordite thickening near the archway, fragments of a room that looked like a study flashing to my eye—a desk, bookcases, and a balding, bespectacled man hugging the far wall next to a floor-to-ceiling window overlooking the swimming pool. The light from the window spilled across a ponytailed man sprawled guts down on a blue Persian carpet stained with a gush of blood, the revolver just beyond his outflung hand pointed toward my niece, who kneeled, keening in her sudden grief, over the fetus-curled body of my father.

The man huddling against the wall watched me as I dropped to my knees, his angular, mid-fifties face frightened as a child's. He risked a few steps away from the wall, toward Spectrum's corpse. I crawled on my hands and knees to Cassie's side, wrapped my arm around her shoulder, and stared down at the dead face of my father, his eyes staring forward like they'd been welded open, his mouth gaped in shock. Two ragged blotches of blood, shaped like deformed flowers, stained his shirt at the back, the fabric blown out at the center of each to reveal the meaty core of his wounds. In the clenched hand that curled toward his chest he still gripped the shotgun by its stock, down near the trigger guard.

"He broke into the house," the bespectacled man said. "He forced Ray to unlock the gates, he held a shotgun on both of us. This is just terrible, a terrible thing." He edged away from the desk, toward Spectrum's heels. "You're his daughter? The tabloid photographer?"

"We were right here," I said. "Why did they have to shoot?"

"He must have panicked when he heard footsteps in the hall," he said. "Ray tried to stop him. He was going to kill us both. This is just terrible."

The presence of death slows time and dulls the mind, and I didn't think clearly about what I'd heard. "We had a deal. Why did he shoot? Pop knew we were coming. Did Jagger lie to you? Did that murderous son of a bitch say something that got Pop killed?"

"No, really, he just went crazy, that's all."

"Do you even know your son is a killer?"

Starbal pulled his chin back, as though my words offended him.

"That's pure nonsense. Beneath comment."

"Your son was drugging and raping young women," I said.

"Jag wouldn't do anything like that." He edged around Spectrum's legs. "Why, Ray told me you had some wild ideas, and might try to take advantage of our family in our time of grief. I just lost my son Stewart. A terrible loss. And now, both Ray and your father. This is just terrible."

I'd heard three shots, two sharp cracks from a revolver before the answering roar of the shotgun. A moment of clarity strobed my image of what happened in that room, just before the triggers were pulled. Starbal was lying. I'd frisked Spectrum in the trunk. He'd been clean. Yet he'd pulled the trigger first. "The gun," I said. "Where did he get the gun?"

Starbal glanced back toward the open drawer to his desk and then dived over Spectrum's body toward the pistol on the carpet. I spun and rolled to block the lunge with my curled back and scooped the gun to my chest. He punched at my face, frantic to get the weapon from me, afraid, I suppose, that I wished to kill him. I trapped his arm beneath my shoulder and rolled again, against the grain of his elbow joint. He screamed in pain, gold-rimmed glasses twisting from one reddened ear. I spun free and stood. I didn't bother to point the gun at him. I said, "Stand up and step back."

He held up his hands and backed into the edge of his desk.

"I'm not going to shoot you. I should shoot you, but I won't, not unless you give me more cause than you've already given me." When he cautiously lowered his hands I turned to look again at my father. Cassie had crept around his body to cradle his head, her eyes blood red from crying. I looked back at Starbal, said, "You hired Spectrum, didn't you?"

"I've already lost one son. I can't lose another."

"You knew what Jagger was doing."

"He'll stop," he said. "I promise."

"Bullshit!" Cassie shouted. "He won't stop!"

He held his hands out in a gesture of peace.

"I know this is an emotional moment for you," he said. "I mean, this is just terrible. It never should have come to this. But we can work something out, right? Ray said he'd already struck a deal with you. We can sweeten it." He nodded, impressed by the offer in his imagination. "We can sweeten it a helluva lot. My family is precious to me. What just happened, it's a terrible thing, but we can straighten it all out. There's no reason you two should suffer because of what's happened. The compensation, I promise, will, well, I'll compensate you generously for your loss."

As he spoke, his eyes tracked with the movement of something in the room behind me. I glanced over my shoulder. The light from the window reflected from the tiles onto a black-jacketed man advancing through the archway, the silver barrel of the pistol he pointed at my back glinting as his face breached the shadows. I whispered his name, balanced between disbelief and hope, the name of the man whose baby swam the prenatal ocean of my womb, realizing he didn't know that I was pregnant and knowing that even if he did, it wouldn't deflect his aim if he intended to shoot, even if by killing me he killed a part of himself.

"She's got a gun!" Starbal shouted. "Shoot!"

I glanced down to the pistol in my hand and flung it to the right as I dove to the left, my body spinning with the force of a .38-caliber kick to the back of my ribs, the sound of the shot ricocheting from the marble-plated walls. My body hit the rug and rolled onto the tiles, stunned by the bullet into a blunted, stupefied pain.

Sean shuffled across the room, the barrel of his pistol pointed at my chest. I clutched below my ribs where the bullet had blown out, the blood trickling through my fingers, and raised my head to look at him, uncomprehending up to the moment of my death how it could have come to this. I expected a smile or wink of recognition when he peered at me over the top of his gun sight but instead I saw no more than a detached curiosity as he examined the seriousness of my wound. I tried to speak and couldn't. Recognition sparked his eyes back to life, as though he just then realized that he'd shot someone he pretended to love, and he took the Lord's name not in vain, but in despair. The clack of metal on metal turned his head to the right and his lips compressed with the shock of an expected blow just before the shotgun fired and the pellet spread blasted him off his feet.

Across the floor Cassie knelt on the Persian carpet, the shotgun at her hip. She slid her hand along the walnut forestock, her fingers thin and pale against the darker wood, and pumped another round into the chamber. She shouted at Starbal to call 911, and when he blinked instead, failing to comprehend what he'd just witnessed, she stood and pointed the shotgun at his head.

The pain rushed in with suffocating speed and I tried to take a deep breath to push it away but the air bubbled in my lungs and I gasped, drowning in my own blood. Had the light reflecting off the tiles blinded Sean to the identity of his target? Did he not realize he'd shot me until that last moment before the shotgun blast knocked him down? I pulled the soles of my feet flat on the floor and kicked out, leaving a red smear as I slid across the tile toward the sound of moaning. When my shoulders brushed against a leg I rolled onto my side, grabbed the pocket of Sean's leather jacket, and pulled myself up his body. His pistol lay just beyond his feet. I kicked it away and raised my head. The lead shot had ripped through his right arm just below the shoulder, shattered bone jutting through the red-and-black scramble of shredded muscle and leather. He tried to smile when he saw me looking down at him, recognizing me in a primal way that failed him when he'd pulled the trigger. I wanted to hit and kiss him both. I fought to pull the air deep enough into my lungs to ask, "Why?"

His eyes glassed over for a moment, but he blinked and clarity returned. "Something you said about me, once," he whispered.

I pulled myself higher, asked, "What?"

"My left hand, it doesn't know what the right is doing."

I laid my head on his chest and waited for the ambulance.

34

THE TEMPERATURE ROSE into the mid-80s the morning they held Pop's funeral service, the sky above the San Gabriel Mountains bleaching white with early summer heat as they interred the plain brass urn containing his ashes into a concrete niche, next to the blue porcelain urn that held the ashes of my mother. Not many mourners showed for the ceremony, just my brother and his family and a few coworkers from the machine shop where Pop worked. The publicity surrounding his death might have scared away a few who otherwise might have attended, but Pop hadn't made a lot of friends in his lifetime, and I doubt the crowd would have topped a dozen had he died a normal death. As the oldest remaining member of our dwindling family, Ray bore the responsibility of placing his ashes into the niche. Given the opportunity to say a few words about Pop and what he'd meant to us, he declined.

I don't know more about the ceremony than these few basic facts, because the California penal system doesn't allow funeral leave for prisoners. I'm not sure what I would have said had I been there, whether I would have shown the courage to speak the uncomfortable truth about a man most everybody hated and feared until the last few months of his life, or whether I would have mouthed the usual platitudes. If I'd been granted the privilege to attend the funeral, I would have tried to speak truthfully about his end. He'd tried to subdue the demons that drove him, expressed remorse for how he'd lived his life, and shown genuine love for his daughter and granddaughter. He'd scarred our lives with fits of self-serving rage and violence. He'd wanted to turn that rage at the end to the service of others. That his action did far more harm than good to the ones he'd been learning how to love shouldn't be held against him.

The walls and bars of a prison begin to look alike after just a few days. That's one of the things that makes it a prison. Some days I feel as though I never left, my two brief years on the outside a single night's dream. My current cellmate is a recovering meth addict serving a five-year sentence on burglary charges. She suffers from nightmares. She'd been housed with the general prison population until her screams so unnerved everybody they decided to confine her away with me. I don't mind her so much. She talks a fast and meaningless patter, words like raindrops on a tin roof, then she conks out until two in the morning, when the screams start. The other girls used to beat her when she screamed. I've found it works better to drop down from the top bunk and hold her until the nightmares fade to black. She strikes out at me in her terrified sleep, but I'm stronger than she is and generally avoid much more than a scratch or two. Looks like we'll be together for a while, so I try to make the best of it.

One of my deepest regrets is my lack of contact with Cassie, who remains in the custody of the Los Angeles County Juvenile Justice System. I pass letters to her through my lawyer, Charles Belinsky, who represents us both. He assures me that she's doing as well as can be expected for a teenage girl held in custody at Central Juvenile Hall and facing adjudication on charges of aggravated assault and possibly attempted murder of a police officer. The prosecutor tasked with her case would like to try her as an adult and put her in prison for the next fifteen years, minimum, but Belinsky isn't going to let him get away with that and, oddly enough, neither will Logan.

The deputies charged with Cassie's processing into juvenile detention sealed the tape they fished from her pants with the rest of her belongings, not having a clue to the tape's importance. Belinsky claimed possession of the tape, made copies, and passed one to Logan, who didn't care about Jason and Jagger Starbal any more than the cops in Southern California have cared about O. J. Simpson, Phil Spector, or Robert Blake. Logan interviewed Cassie extensively and matched architectural details from the video recording of Christine's killing to the pool room on Starbal's estate. He didn't gloat at seeing me strapped to a bed in the Los Angeles County–USC

Medical Center Jail Ward, even said it was kind of a shame it worked out that way. He needs my testimony—and more importantly, Cassie's—if any case comes to trial, so I'm not convinced the sympathy he expresses is genuine.

Sean hasn't contacted me, not that I expect or want him to come calling. The department conducted no more than a cursory review of his conduct during the shooting and found his actions fully justified by the situation. He'd entered the house after hearing gunfire and saw the suspect holding a pistol. I hadn't given him time to issue a warning, he reported. He didn't see me drop the weapon when I made a sudden movement. He discharged his weapon in full accordance with his training, fearing not only for his own life, but for the lives of the others in the room.

Belinsky's ability to charm the reason out of prosecutors and juries doesn't extend to parole judges. The videocassette retrieved from Spectrum's pocket unambiguously displayed a fight between two attack dogs that resulted in one owner, a paroled felon, assaulting the other owner, an ex-con, with a baseball bat. My parole officer spoke up for me at the hearing, attesting to my good character and history of exemplary behavior while on parole, both untrue but nonetheless appreciated. The judge said he might sympathize with the mitigating circumstances but they didn't blind him to the clear parole violation he'd just witnessed. "I don't think the State has a dog in this fight," he joked, and then denied continuation on parole.

Sometimes, when I lie in bed at night, waiting for sleep to fall over me and wash away the smells and sounds of incarceration, I try to figure out what was going through Pop's mind that day, why he'd taken heroic measures when more ordinary ones would have served us all better. When the forensics team rifled his pockets, just before tucking him into a body bag, they found a handwritten note in the back pocket of his grease-stained jeans, claiming responsibility for kidnapping Spectrum from his office. He knew the salient details because I'd told him, and he used the information to claim the act as his own. Just before sleep pulls me down, his face in the darkness is the last thing I see.

I didn't expect to escape unscathed, not when events began to spin so wildly from my control. It's not going to hurt me to serve out my sentence. I've put a few photographs on the wall to help me pass the time: my mother standing at the kitchen sink, giving herself a home permanent; a candid I took of Cassie mugging at the beach; one of my dog staring at the camera as though it might be food; and the Instamatic snap I claimed from the family album, the one of me riding Pop's shoulders, my face shining while he stares at the camera with a look of supreme paternal tolerance. It's the look I want to remember him by.

California is a three-strikes state; if the D.A. presses charges and the court convicts me on both the assault and kidnapping counts, that's my three strikes, I'm going down for life. But still, I count my blessings. The Rott recovered from the attack and lives with Frank. It helps me to think of them together, two big, sloppy guys with inexhaustible appetites for junk food. The bullet left some scars, but the baby is all right, and that matters more than my discomfort and scarification. Maybe this is the best place for me, at least for the next nine months or so. The women institutionalized here have been convicted on charges ranging from prostitution to first-degree murder. Since they learned of my pregnancy they have been caring sisters; even those who might normally challenge my right to breathe nod to me in careful recognition. In an institution raging with race warfare, I'm a civilian. We joke that the child will be born with one thousand aunties. If it's a boy, he'll be in heaven. If it's a girl, she'll conquer the world.

ACKNOWLEDGMENTS

The novelist's ability to convincingly render the most arcane subjects is often due to the guidance of persons truly knowledgeable about things novelists only pretend to know. The experts whose advice guided me in the preparation of this manuscript include priests, parole agents, lawyers, filmmakers, and photographers. Special thanks go to Kate Buker, a prosecutor working in Madison, Wisconsin; to Allen Plone, who always seems to know the answer to everything I ask; and to Craig Paulenich, whose collection of poems, *Blood Will Tell*, provided inspiration.

This manuscript was edited by Amanda Murray at Simon & Schuster, who again proved an ideal reader.

I owe a debt of hospitality to the inhabitants of the city of Prague and the Catalan village of Sant Pol de Mar, Spain, where this book was written. *Děkuji Vám, přátelé. Gràcies, amics.*

ABOUT THE AUTHOR

A graduate of the University of California at Santa Cruz and UCLA, ROBERT M. EVERSZ pounded the pavements of Hollywood for a decade before fleeing to Europe to write his five novels about Nina Zero and the American obsession with celebrity culture: *Shooting Elvis, Killing Paparazzi, Burning Garbo, Digging James Dean,* and *Zero to the Bone.* One of the leading literary voices in Prague, the setting for his novel *Gypsy Hearts,* he helped found the Prague Summer Writers' Workshop, now the Prague Summer Program, where he currently serves on the faculty. His novels are widely translated and have appeared on critical best-of-year lists from Oslo's *Aftenposten* to *The Washington Post.*